DIANNE OREN

Running to the Rescue

A sweet firefighter romantic comedy

First published by Dianne Oren Books 2025

First edition

ISBN (paperback): 979-8-9920634-5-5
ISBN (hardcover): 979-8-9920634-6-2

This book was professionally typeset on Reedsy.
Find out more at reedsy.com

Dedicated to the brave men and women who are firefighters all over the world...who put their lives on the line to keep the rest of us safe.

If you enjoy this story, please consider donating to the National Fallen Firefighters Foundation at https://www.firehero.org/donate/ or to the firefighter organization of your choice.

Contents

Acknowledgments

There are so many people to thank in the making of this story, but I'm going to start with you. Readers will always have a special place in my heart. Thank you for buying this book and reading my work. I appreciate your support more than you know.

To my family, I love and adore all of you and appreciate your love and support. I get all squeaky just trying to say thank you for having my back. Special shout out to my cousin Nancy, who is more like another sister than a cousin, my cohort when we celebrate my book launches by leaving signed copies of my books around town and then sitting back and watching people find them. (We're total lurkers). I love our travel adventures together, even when you trip and fall onto my butt in front of Buckingham Palace.

To Emma St. Clair and Aven Ellis, two of the most inspiring authors I have ever had the privilege to know. Thank you so much for your guidance and wisdom. I will forever be a dork in your presence, but I am so grateful you show me grace and kindness.

And to my editor, Victoria Straw, you are the slayer of my imposter syndrome so many times. I truly appreciate you.

One of the most special groups of women ever in the universe: my Beta Team. During the creation of this book, they were called the Phoenixes. :-) They voted to change the group name with each book, so by the time you read this they'll be known as...The Horsemen. I don't make the rules. Ladies, thank you so much for reading my work before anyone else gets a glance, giving me feedback, and calling me out for earbud mistakes and icemaker issues. IYKYK.

To my ARC Team...thank you so much! You read my books, you send feedback, you post reviews...you are amazing. I truly appreciate everything you do to support me on this journey.

And to the nicest, kindest city councilwoman ever...Nikkie Hunter, who helped me donate my books to the libraries in my community and is always there for me when I ask ridiculous questions like "Hey, do you know any firemen?"

To all of my friends and colleagues who have supported me and listened to me yammer on about Scarlet and Andrew...thanks for still talking to me.

Special friend shout out to Christine...for your unending cheer and positivity. Thank you so much for being the most awesome book signing buddy to sit at book events with. You are the awesomest.

And finally...a shout out to some of my former colleagues: Diana, Nick, Leonard and Todd.

Diana, you're just the best. Thanks for always being so upbeat and supportive.

Nick, thank you for coming up with Scarlet's nickname in this book... and for your amazing cheerleading skills. Aircraft dispatchers ROCK!

Leonard and Todd...working with you two was the best (also with you, Nick....don't get crazy). I miss your humor...sarcasm...random videos of ghosts on the security cameras...work was a party with you two. :-)

A Note From The Author

Hello, friends,

This is a special story…in that there are certain elements with which some of you will identify with more than others.

Andrew is a firefighter, so the profession is prevalent in this story. There are also a few scenes that take place in a hospital. I've tried my level best to stay true to the basics of the professions mentioned, including research of my own and speaking with professionals in these fields. In the interest of not over complicating the story, I tried my best to keep things *simple*. If I've gotten something wrong, I ask for forgiveness. It isn't intentional.

As always, the romance is the center theme of this story.

Content Warnings

This book is a sweet romantic comedy, which means you're getting a swoony, romantic story with a touch of humor, plenty of swoons, and no spice. Some sensitive topics appear in this story as follows:

Death of a parent (in the past)
Being rescued from a fire (on the page)
Hospital stay and trauma related to surviving a fire (on the page)
Smarmy DJ who uses finger guns

No one gets sick, no one dies. Don't worry…everything's going to be okay. :-)

I hope you enjoy Scarlet and Andrew's love story as much as I enjoyed writing it!

Chapter 1

Scarlet

All men can be sorted into three categories. Dangerous in a good way, dangerous in a bad way, and meh.

Am I being a tad too judgy? Yes.

Do I care? No. Not at all.

I don't have time for boys, men, or anything in between. Two of my closest friends, Marina and Ashley, love to tease me about their similar feelings about men and relationships until they got bit by the love bug. Marina is now married, and Ashley's engaged. They think it'll happen that way for me as well, but nope. Not happening. And the living proof of it just walked in the door.

His name is Black Leather Jacket, and he's been coming to my coffee shop almost every morning for about a month now. Well, it's not *my* coffee shop in the sense that I own it. It's my coffee shop because it's right around the corner from the beat-up old warehouse I'm temporarily living in. This coffee house is my first stop every morning when the sun rises, and it's safe…or safe-ish…to leave the warehouse.

Right now, Black Leather Jacket (or BLJ for short) is ordering his usual green tea latte.

Gross.

As soon as he has it in hand, he will walk purposefully over to the table in the corner against the window. He'll sit there and sip away with a very zen-like look on his face, watching the busy city of San Francisco wake up. He may scroll through his phone occasionally. Pretty boring, if that is it. But it's not. Every once in a while, he looks in my direction…our eyes meet…and the whole world slows to a halt. Not cool.

"Is that him?" my friend Merry whispers excitedly from across the table.

I give her a look that says hush, and she makes a face at me.

"He's way over there," she whispers. "It's not like he can hear me."

I shake my head slowly. "Not sure I agree, Mer. He might have superpowers."

"Nope," she says succinctly, flipping her shoulder-length dark brown hair over her shoulder. "People with superpowers are very rare. We aren't just standing around on every street corner."

I lift my eyebrows. "*We?* So you have superpowers?"

She smirks. "Duh. You too. Hence…the we."

I giggle. "And what is my superpower exactly?"

Merry smiles warmly. "You can take the ugliest warehouse ever and transform it into a fairytale bedroom."

"*And* an elegant, beautiful library," I add with a wink, then I bob my chin at her. "Your superpower is…?"

Her eyes go as round as saucers as she whispers, "Buttercream."

I snicker and shake my head, looking away and right into the warm, brown, I-see-into-the-depths-of-your-soul eyes of Black Leather Jacket. He holds my gaze, as always. He doesn't smile like a hundred other men would, looking for an opening. He doesn't nod. He doesn't do anything but look at me. Not in a creepy way, but in a…hey, I see you, way that completely unsettles me. And I do *not* like to be unsettled. I have an iron grip on settled.

"Wow…" Merry mutters.

When I finally break my gaze away and look at her, she's staring into her coffee. I nudge her foot with mine. She gives me a stern look and nods.

"I see what you mean," she murmurs. "I looked away, so I didn't get caught in the big brown-eyed tractor beam too."

I turn to face Merry fully, so I'm not tempted to look back at BLJ.

"But it's not creepy, right? He doesn't smile or anything, but it's still not creepy."

Merry snorts. "No, it's the opposite of creepy. He's dead sexy. He's got an energy about him."

I nod and take a sip of my coffee. I don't know why this guy gets under my skin like he does. It's been bothering me so much that I dragged Merry here to give me a second opinion. Although perhaps I should have dragged Marina or Ashley. Merry is such a positive, happy little unicorn, and I doubt she'd be creeped out by Jack the Ripper.

"So go talk to him," Merry murmurs as she breaks a piece off her cookie.

"What?" I whisper. "Why on earth would I do that?"

Merry shrugs and pops the piece of cookie in her mouth.

"Do *you* feel creeped out?" she mumbles while crunching her cookie.

"No."

"Harassed? Icky?"

"No."

She leans forward and whispers, eyes big.

"Do you see the hotness?"

I click my tongue. "Could anyone *not* see that hotness?"

I glance back at BLJ for a moment. I think it's possible that even his muscles have muscles. The guy is cut. His hair is perfect. His jaw is always freshly shaved. And those eyes. They make me want to go swimming in their depths.

Merry shrugs again. "So, what's the problem? Other than this violation of baked goods sitting in front of me."

She points to the cookie and shakes her head at it like it slapped her in the face.

"No, I'm not looking for a relationship, you know that," I reply. I say it a lot. "I just…I don't know. I wanted a second opinion because I wasn't freaked out."

Merry frowns at me. "You were worried because you *weren't* freaked out?"

I nod. "With the staring."

"Yes, well, now that I've seen him…he's not really staring, is he? He's just looking. Straight into your soul."

"Yes, but why?"

She shudders. "I could ask the same about this cookie. Why?"

I laugh under my breath. "Still a big no from Nonno on the bakery?"

"Yep. I'm not sure Nonno even knows how to say yes. I'm still not giving up."

"Good," I say with a reassuring wink. "You'll wear Nonno down. I know you will."

Sweet Merry. She works miracles with anything that's baked. She makes beautiful pastries, cakes, and cookies. It's her passion. For years, she's been limited to using an old, unloved spare oven in her grandfather's Italian bistro. He's allowed her to sell grab-and-go desserts from a small bakery case in the restaurant's entry, which he thought she'd grow weary of. Instead, it only inspired her, and she's been begging him to let her re-open her grandmother's little bakery next door for ages. But dear Nonno, as we all call him, can't seem to let anything new grow in the shadow of her Nonna's memory. He'd rather let it sit unused, a partial storage facility for his restaurant.

I love Nonno like my own grandfather. He's a grandfather figure to all four of us. There's something else going on here because he is usually nothing but big pasta sauce smelling hugs and loud kisses on the cheek. He gets positively grumpy when the bakery comes up.

"So, what are you gonna do?" Merry asks, rousing me from my thoughts.

I'm confused for a moment.

"About tall, dark, and sexy-not-creepy over there?" she clarifies.

I risk a glance over my shoulder. BLJ is frowning at his phone, scrolling. Even when frowning, I have to admit the guy is gorgeous. The black leather jacket he's always in isn't a biker-style jacket. It's a coat. A blazer. Today, he's wearing it with blue jeans, black suede boots, and a dark gray t-shirt that looks tailor made to hug his chiseled freaking chest. I force my gaze back to Merry's.

"Nothing at all."

Merry looks disappointed, but not at all surprised.

"Then why are we here?" she mutters. "Let's go shopping or something."

I smirk at her. "You have to have money to shop, Mer. I'm really trying not to spend anything I don't have to."

She leans forward with a smile. "You are going to win this whole thing this year. Everyone else should be petrified of your determination."

I laugh softly. I love that Merry is such a cheerleader for her people, and I'm lucky to be counted as one of them.

"Thanks, Mer."

"So, how long do you have to work on your two rooms?"

"Almost two months," I reply with a tight smile. "It'd be more than enough if I hadn't gone a little crazy with the details. I'm committed now, so there's no going back."

She nods. "Our paint party will help, though?"

"Definitely. I'm not too proud to accept all that help."

Merry, Ashley, Marina, and I were all out to lunch last week when Merry volunteered the whole group to come and paint my two rooms in the warehouse. As if that weren't enough, she volunteered *the men folk* to move the furniture I'm using too. In this case, the men folk also happen to be The Royal Rebels...a world-famous indie rock band. Zach Adams, the lead singer, is married to Marina, and Rick Archer, the lead guitarist, is engaged to Ashley. Sam and Jimmy, the other two band members, were thrown in for good measure by Merry, but cooler heads prevailed.

There are a ton of reasons why The Royal Rebels can't move furniture and perform manual labor for me, mainly to do with the insurance on their very valuable persons. Plus, I can't even imagine the chaos that would erupt if they were identified and fans started showing up.

Zach offered to pay for professional movers to take care of moving everything for me, which was incredibly generous, but that's who he is. It's why we all love Zach. Rick, my favorite Rebel, has volunteered his awesome woodworking abilities for my use and abuse. Last year, he made me a set of gorgeous corbels that I designed and turned into shelves. They got some air time on the Home Network's TV show about the competition, which helped me tremendously. Because of it, I now have a fairly steady stream of interior design customers.

"What kind of details did you get obsessed with on this project?"

I grin. "Embroidery."

Her eyebrows shoot up to her hairline. "What? Where?"

"The library room. I'm putting in mock windows, and I want it to look like it's twilight outside, so I was messing with the lighting for that when the idea hit me. I found these gorgeous sheer curtains on clearance, but they needed a little extra something. So I'm embroidering white flowers and vines onto them and running some little silver threads through it to give it a little sparkle."

"You don't think you have superpowers...but you can pick up embroidery just like that?"

I laugh. I'm resourceful and scrappy. I'll find a way. I always have. It's just what I do.

"How's your mom doing?" Merry asks.

I nod. "Good. *Really* good. First vacation she's taken in ten years. I get a huge dump of pictures every morning when I wake up. It starts my day off with a big, stupid smile."

Merry opens her mouth to ask the question I know is coming next, and I hold my hand up to stop her.

"No, she doesn't know I'm living in the warehouse," I say quietly. "And no, I'm not going to tell her."

She shakes her head. "Momma's not gonna like that..."

I scoff openly. "Our apartment is too far away, and I don't have a car. Taking the bus is not an option," I explain. "It's fine in our bougie neighborhood, but the closer the bus gets to the warehouse, the freaks start boarding. I tried it once. It's not safe."

Merry looks at me incredulously.

"It's not safe to take the bus in this neighborhood, but sleeping in an abandoned warehouse in the same neighborhood is?"

"The warehouse is secure. There's an alarm that I set when everyone leaves. And, while we're talking about it, I might as well tell you that I'm not going to tell Marina or Ashley. This needs to be our secret."

Merry frowns. "Why? We don't keep secrets from each other."

She's right, we don't. Guilt hits me in the gut like a sledgehammer.

"This is going to sound ridiculous, but you have to hear me out."

Merry nods and stays silent.

"If I tell them, they're going to intervene," I explain calmly. "Especially Marina. She won't be able to help herself. She'll insist on having a security guard here to protect me or something, but I'm fine. Really. The warehouse has been empty for ages. Brad's dad says there have been no break-ins for over a year."

"He's the owner?"

I nod. Brad is a friend and one of the other designers on our little team.

"I don't want to be a burden to my friends, and I don't want this to be a big deal," I continue. "But I do take my safety seriously, I promise. I did some research on crime in the neighborhood. Retail theft, carjacking, and muggings are all on the rise here. The warehouses on this block haven't been impacted. The local criminals are more interested in robbing the liquor store than some empty warehouse."

Merry shakes her head at me. "That doesn't make me feel any better about you living there."

"What if we implement a check-in system while I'm staying there?"

She eyes me warily. "Like what?"

"I'll promise not to go out after dark, and I'll text you every night when I lock up," I offer.

"And first thing in the morning when you wake up," she adds.

I nod. "Agreed. And believe me, I want out of the warehouse as soon as possible. It's no fun living there."

She makes a face. "What about showers?"

"Ah," I say, scrunching my nose. "I'm not sure what this warehouse was used for previously, but the bathroom has an open, tiled area with a sprayer attached to a hose hanging from one wall. It's cold, but I can tough it out. It's only a few weeks."

Merry sits back in her chair. "That's a lot of cold showers in the pursuit of fame and glory."

I laugh softly. "Hopefully, that's how this story ends. Fame and glory."

Merry's eyes flick over to the offensive cookie and back to me.

"All right, c'mon," she says, standing and stretching. "Show me this warehouse and get me away from that horrible cookie."

I stand and turn around to grab my bag off the back of the chair. BLJ is gone…and again, I wonder where he went.

***

Andrew

She's back, and this time she has a friend with her. I focus on the menu board in front of me, but she fills my peripheral vision. City Girl, or CG as I call her, is a mystery to me. She doesn't belong in this neighborhood. That much is clear. So what is she doing here?

My favorite barista, Rosa, tells me she comes in every morning. Even weekends. She sits at the same table every time and orders a black coffee.

Gross.

Most of the time, she has a sketch pad on the table with her. I wonder what's in it, way too often. Does she just love to doodle, or is she an artist? Every time she walks in the door, I'm full of questions that are never answered.

"Green tea latte, please," I tell Alfie, another barista here, at the counter when it's my turn.

He smiles and rings me up, then I step to the side and wait.

This place has only been here a few months, but I love it. It's part of a revitalization effort in this part of the city, which I'm grateful for since I spend a good amount of time in this neighborhood as a fireman for Engine 14. We work twenty-four-hour shifts every other day, so having a nice place to grab a latte in the morning is a luxury I enjoy having. I just wish the rest of the neighborhood would hurry up and revitalize as well because some parts of it are pretty sketchy.

Which brings me back to CG. She doesn't look anything like most of the locals here. I noticed her right away, and not just because she's pretty. If I looked up the word *driven* in the dictionary, I'm pretty sure I'd find her picture. Right next to mine. I recognize it in her because that's how I live my life. With purpose. From her determined walk to the fierce glint in her gorgeous blue eyes, this woman's on a mission, and I find myself far too curious about what it is.

"Andrew," Rosa says with a smile as she passes my latte to me over the counter.

I smile my thanks and head to my favorite corner.

I steal a glance over at CG's table, and her friend is looking in my direction with undisguised curiosity that's almost feral. She looks away immediately. They're talking about me. That's confusing because everything about CG screams *go away*. It's why I've never approached her. She's clearly not interested in anything but whatever's in that sketch pad. Someone like that doesn't want some random guy in a coffee house sliding into the seat across from her to talk about the weather. She couldn't care less for cheesy pick-up lines. But what *does* she care about? I really want to know.

My phone vibrates in my pocket, and I pull it out to read the text.

Jake: Hey, kid. You at that fancy coffee house?

I smirk at my phone.

Andrew: Yep. You want your usual?

Jake: Well, if you're offering...

I chuckle under my breath. Captain Scheffler, or Jake as we all call him, is an old family friend. My dad's best friend, actually. They were fire cadets together. Earned their chops as firemen together. Until one day, when an arsonist tried to take out a high-rise office building, and my dad never made it out. I was five years old. A lot of kids who lose a parent early in life barely have any memory of them. Jake made sure that didn't happen for me. He's been a constant in my life ever since, and I owe him a lot. When I first joined the fire department,

I was over the moon excited to be assigned a position under him. Especially at Engine 14, where he and my dad were first assigned as new recruits.

I look over in CG's direction again. Half a second later, she looks my way, and our gazes lock. This happens frequently. Whenever my gaze drifts to her, she looks. It's as if our subconscious minds seek each other out. I can't seem to look away when it happens. I want to smile at her, but I feel like it'll be perceived like I'm hitting on her. She looks away before I have a chance to do anything, and I return my focus to my phone.

Andrew: I'll be back soon. Just needed to stretch my legs.

I return to the article I was reading about an arsonist in Florida. Fire fascinates me in all forms, but it's deadly and must be respected. While my mom loves watching documentaries about serial killers, I'm immediately pulled into anything about arsonists. I guess we all have our hobbies. Either that, or we're the weirdest family ever.

I take another sip of my latte and start scrolling through my social media accounts. I don't spend much time on it, but a local reporter named Kevin Starbuck has been trying to focus the public eye on this neighborhood. He's written some great human interest stories lately, all involving local residents and businesses. Some struggling, some new. I've never met him, but he gets mad respect from me for trying to make a difference.

I look over towards CG and her friend again. Wow. Her friend really doesn't like the cookie she's trying to eat. What a face she's making. I laugh under my breath and gulp down the rest of my latte, then head over to the order counter, where Rosa is already smiling at me.

"Almond croissant again?" she asks with a grin.

I nod, then watch as she bags it up. I tap my credit card and take the bag from her.

"Thanks, Rosa," I say as I pace toward the door.

I turn and push my back against it so I can steal one more glance at CG. She doesn't notice, and I step out onto the sidewalk in the waking city, wondering if I'll ever get her attention.

Chapter 2

Scarlet

Three hours later, I'm standing in the only warehouse in San Francisco that holds the futures of four very hungry, driven interior designers. I have pooled all my savings together with my friends Kayla, Brad, and Sarah to share resources and bounce ideas off each other in a collaborative effort to win the ultimate prize. The Home Network's Decorator Showcase competition. The winner gets $250,000 and a feature on their TV network, not to mention enough notoriety to start their own lucrative home decor business and never have to shop at the dollar store again.

There is only one winner, and a lot of the designers in the competition have unlimited budgets. That's not us. We've all lost this competition multiple times, so we decided to team up and support each other through to the judging phase. So far, our little collab has gone really well.

Kayla has called us all into her portion of the warehouse to get our opinions on the art déco living room she's creating. She's way ahead of the rest of us right now. The room is beautiful, done in hues of powder blue and a lighter sky blue for the accent wall. She's started adding touches of rose gold metallic here and there. The problem? It's her *creative take* on art déco, so she's taking some liberties that may not pay off for her. That's why she's pulled us all in here to stare at the partially furnished space.

Kayla runs a perfectly manicured hand over her closely buzzed hair, a gesture I've come to recognize as one of self-doubt. Worry wrinkles her brow, the only crease visible on her luminous brown skin. Brad frowns behind her, and Sarah looks confused at his side. Kayla gives us all a sideways glance.

"Verdict?"

"Doesn't work," Brad says emphatically.

"Yeah, I agree," Sarah chimes in.

Kayla turns to me.

"To be clear, you're asking about the bean bag chair?" I ask, hopefully with a light tone.

It's a cool chair, but it doesn't work with the otherwise beautifully decorated space. I need time to form the right words.

Kayla nods. "Yeah. I fell in love with it at Swap House, but now that I see it in the space..."

I wrap an arm around her slim shoulders and squeeze.

"It's a great piece," I say gently. "But Brad and Sarah are right. It doesn't work in here."

Kayla nods. "Stupid Swap House. I have no control in that place."

I laugh out loud. No self-respecting interior designer has any control at Swap House. It's a low-budget shopper's dream come true. I never know what I'll find, but I've found so many one-of-a-kind pieces there. It's a gold mine if you have the patience to sift through all the useless stuff.

"You can save it for something else," I say gently.

She snorts. "So much for pushing the boundaries of art déco."

"You're gonna do great," Brad says consolingly. "Just...no bean bags, girl."

I give Kayla a huge hug. "Keep pushing those boundaries. Sometimes it works, and you make magic."

She steps back and nods in the direction of my two rooms in the warehouse.

"How are you doing over there? Doesn't look like much is going on."

"Don't worry about me," I say lightly. "I've spent the last few days embroidering accents onto curtains, but I've got reinforcements coming with paint and furniture tomorrow."

Brad pipes in. "Furniture? Did someone win the lottery?"

I laugh. "No, actually, a lot of it's coming from my bedroom at home."

Sarah pats me on the back. "Smart move. Don't spend money where you don't have to."

"Besides," Kayla adds, "interior designers have the best stuff."

"Right?" I say, giving her a high-five. "And since I'm living here while I work, it'll be nice to have my own bed. I'm already tired of the air mattress, and it's only been a few days."

"And your mom still has no idea you're actually living here?" Sarah asks.

"Why does everyone keep focusing on that?" I ask in an exasperated tone. "My mom is on her first vacation in forever. I'm not going to give her anything to worry about, especially when there is *nothing* to worry about. While we're at it, my friends don't know either. Well, one does, but the rest don't. So when you meet them…don't say a word about it. They'll just worry and drive me nuts."

Kayla nudges me. "This neighborhood is hinky, though."

I nudge back. "I don't go out after dark. I have my little cooler with drinks. I have snacks, a book, jammies, and a toothbrush. All the things I need. I'll even have my own bed after tomorrow. When it gets dark outside, I just set the alarm and stay put until morning."

"What if someone breaks in?" Sarah pushes, her expression full of concern.

"I've got a big lead pipe back there and plenty of feminine rage," I offer. "Now, can we change the subject before you guys really creep me out? It's only for a little while, anyway."

Brad claps his hands together. "Yes, back to business. Scarlet, do you think you'll have any of that charcoal gray paint leftover after tomorrow? I don't even need a gallon."

I raise my chin, challenging him. "Do you have something to trade for it if I do?"

"I saw how you were eyeballing my turquoise throw pillows," he says wryly. "I might be able to let two of them go."

I squeal and extend my hand.

He shakes it.

"Deal," I declare loudly. "Now I'm heading back to work, guys. Carry on!"

***

"Oh, hello, gorgeous," I say to my bed frame as the movers bring it into the freshly painted bedroom space the next afternoon.

One of the movers, whose name is Mike, according to the patch on his shirt, laughs. I walk backwards into the space and point to the location against the wall where I want it.

"The bed goes here, gentlemen."

"Yes, ma'am," Mike replies. "Where do you want the dresser and nightstands?"

I show him quickly, then leave them to it and head into the library space, which is currently full of my friends. My heart swells with gratitude as I walk in and see them all hard at work, supporting me. Marina and Zach are on the north wall, painting the walls and bookshelves with a lux charcoal gray paint. Ashley and Merry are in the final stages of assembling one of the only pieces of furniture I actually bought. A desk from a discount warehouse. It doesn't look like much now, but when I refinish it and add the decorative trim Rick is currently cutting to size for me with his power tools in the corner…it'll be amazing. Rick catches me watching him and grins at me.

"Almost done, boss lady," he jokes.

I laugh softly. "You're doing great. You guys have no idea how much I appreciate this."

Merry holds the drill in the air and revs it up, a crazy smile on her face.

"We got you, girl!"

Ashley laughs. "You're scary with power tools, Mer."

We've been working since early morning. Painting, assembling furniture, cleaning the floors so I can paint the bedroom floor, then bringing in faux flooring and rugs for the library. Rick and Ashley brought breakfast and coffee for the whole crew, and Zach and Marina sent their driver to pick up lunch. We invited Sarah, Brad, and Kayla to eat with us as well, then they showed everyone the work they're doing on their own rooms. It's been a fun but exhausting day.

"Woohoo!" Marina hoots as she brandishes her paint roller. "Coat number two is done!"

"It looks so great," I say breathlessly, stepping back to admire it with eyes that are a little watery.

Marina steps over and wraps an arm around my shoulders.

"I'm so proud of you," she says. "I would never come up with something like this. I wouldn't even think of choosing this color. It's dramatic and elegant."

I grin, taking it all in. My vision for a beautiful, elegant library is taking shape, and it's incredibly exciting.

"Wait 'til you see the wallpaper," I say, stepping over to a box in the corner and pulling out the single roll.

I walk back to Zach and Marina and hand it over. Marina gasps as she runs her fingers over the ornate paper. Covered in a rich floral pattern of deep blues and greens, the background of the paper is black. Gold leaf accents give a shimmer to it. It's the perfect thing to pop out as an accent on these dark gray walls.

"This is why you didn't want the wall in the opening between the bookcases painted?" Zach guesses.

I nod. "Yep. I didn't want the space any bigger than that. This stuff is two hundred dollars a roll."

Marina gasps and pulls her hand away, making me laugh. I'm frugal when I have to be, but I'm also trying to win a huge contest. This is perfect for my library space.

Thanks to Rick's ingenuity, all four walls are lined with bookcases now painted in charcoal gray. Even undecorated, at first glance, it looks like a library that would be in a stately home. He took shortcuts he wouldn't usually take but did it with my full permission. These aren't real bookcases, which would take a lot longer to build. They only have to *look* real. They'll hold the weight of the fake books I'm going to make just fine, but if this were built inside someone's home, it would have been done with a lot more care and attention to craftsmanship.

I had Rick leave a five-foot wide opening between bookcases on one wall, which I'll cover with the wallpaper. I found a large gold wall clock and two lighting sconces that'll look perfect against the paper in that space.

As for books, that's been another challenge. I'm on a really tight budget, so I bought the cheapest hardcover books I could get at the public library sale a few weeks ago. The problem? They're mostly expired books on tax codes and things no one would find in a library like the one in my mind. I'll rip a lot of the pages out to keep the weight load limited, and I plan to use a printer, fancy scrapbook paper, and my cutting machine to create covers for them all.

Rick joins us with a proud look as he pulls me into a bear hug.

"All done, Scarlet."

I look behind him at all the pieces of trim neatly arranged and tagged on the floor. Amazing.

"This is why you're my favorite Rebel, dude," I say with a grateful smile. "No offense, Zach. You wield a mean paint roller."

Zach lets out his trademark throaty laugh.

"No worries, love," he growls in the British accent we've all come to know and love. "The wifey still loves me."

Marina laughs softly. "Are you ever going to get tired of calling me 'wifey'?"

He winks at her. "Not likely, Siren."

I smile to myself as Rick steps away to check on Ashley and Merry. Zach and Marina's story is such a sweet, romantic one. Seeing how cute they are together even hits *me* right in the feels, and I have fierce boundaries about romance right now. Later, sure...I'd love to meet someone who lights up my whole world like Zach and Rick do for Marina and Ashley. Now is just not that time.

After thirty more minutes of Merry brandishing the drill with that crazed expression on her face, the desk is assembled, and the final task on today's list is checked off. We take a few moments to admire both rooms and how great the paint looks, and then hugs are given. I give extra hugs to Merry, who snuck into the bedroom space to find my linens and made the bed for me. I feel like I could sleep for days.

I walk everyone to the door, and Marina looks out into the neighborhood with concern etched on her face. Zach steps outside to greet their driver. They're giving everyone else a ride back to their apartment.

"Hey, I'm fine," I insist. "I know it doesn't look great, but it's not like there are gunshots going off or zombies in the alley."

Marina narrows her gaze. "And you don't leave alone? You guys all lock up together?"

"Don't worry about us," I reply, side-stepping her question. She has no idea my partners in crime tip-toed out of here an hour ago. "We're all fine."

Satisfied, Marina hugs me and steps out into the alley with the others. Merry hangs back for a moment.

"You're going to have to tell your mom before she gets back," Merry says quietly. "She'll be home before you're done. She's going to notice all your furniture missing. She's going to notice *you* missing."

"I'm twenty-eight years old!" I whisper in frustration. "I've got this. I don't need to clear everything with my mommy."

Merry just stares at me as if I have a turnip growing out of my forehead.

I shrug.

"And yes, of course, I'll tell her beforehand so she doesn't get home and freak out. Chill."

More staring.

"Please, Merry. I'm all right."

Finally, I get a hug. I make a lot of promises. To call if I need anything. To be safe. To be careful. I make them willingly, and I mean to keep them. Merry climbs into the waiting SUV. I wave as the driver pulls away, then I shut the door and bolt it. I set the alarm immediately, and I'm in for the night.

I jog back to my two rooms with all the enthusiasm of a kid on Christmas morning. The work we did today was such a huge push forward. Now, I have a canvas on which to create an interior design masterpiece. The library room looks so good. Too dark, of course, without the wallpaper accent and added flair I'm about to bring in. There's a lot more work to be done here, but I can see the end result in my head, and I'm excited. I check my watch. It's after 6 pm already, so I don't want to start any big projects tonight. Instead, I set up my workstation in the library.

I grab my big folding table and drag it into the room, opening it up and positioning it near an electrical outlet. Then I get my laptop and charging cord from the bedroom and pull my cutting machine out of the storage closet near the entrance door to the warehouse. I set it all up on the table, then retrieve my weeding and cutting tools from a tote bag I hung on the back of the bedroom door. Next, I pull the box of craft supplies I brought over. Everything to make up all the faux books is in here from glue to paper to some cool gold leaf stickers I found.

With that all set up, I head to the bedroom to unpack the two suitcases full of clothes I brought with me. I'll have to head home to do laundry once in a while. There's no way around that, but I have enough clothes here to last two weeks before it's necessary. I turn on both bedside lamps to have a look at how the lighting hits the space. We painted the walls a rich peacock blue in here, and I'll lighten it up with some large art pieces I'm getting from Kayla. Turns out she's not just a brilliant interior designer. She also creates mixed media art. She's loaning me a few of her pieces for the bedroom.

I nest one suitcase inside the other and shove them underneath the bed, and my stomach growls so loud it sounds like a wild animal dying. I laugh under my breath and head to the storage closet where I stow my cooler and the large rolling bag I call my mobile pantry. I pull them out and bring them to the library space, where they'll stay until the day before the judges come.

I flip open the cooler and...oh. Two bottles of water and a single bottle of diet soda are floating around in melted ice slush. I meant to stop at the mini mart down the street this morning, but Marina and Zach got here early, and I forgot. I look in the pantry bag. A couple cookies are left. Empty cracker box. Almost empty cereal box. I really did mean to go to the store. Darn it.

I steal a glance at my watch again. It's just after seven. I don't have to look outside the high windows of the warehouse to know it's well and truly dark out there. Officially not safe to go anywhere in this neighborhood. And the only pizza place nearby refuses to deliver here. I learned that last week when the guy grumbled "Pick up only" into the phone and hung up on me.

A tingle of anxiety ripples up my spine as my stomach growls again. I can't sleep with an empty stomach. It'll just get worse. And I need sleep because I have another full day ahead of me tomorrow. All my days are full for the next several weeks. Walking around this neighborhood to go grab something is out of the question. I'd rather stay up all night with an upset stomach.

There's really only one possibility.

I head to the bedroom to grab my mobile phone and swipe open a food delivery app. I enter the warehouse's address and pray for anything to pop up. I'm not picky...I just need one meal, and I'll never let this happen again. I nearly shriek with joy when Kebabs & More pops up. It's the only option and I totally don't care.

I look through the menu and place my order. Delivery time, thirty minutes. Score! I throw in another bottle of diet soda with my order, and I complete it with a sigh of relief. For delivery instructions, I make sure I give clear directions on how to find the warehouse door and tell them to bang on it really loud. Then, I sit at my work table in the library and connect the cutting machine to my laptop while I wait.

Brad's father owns this warehouse, so he left the electricity and water on as a favor to us, but there's no internet or gas. That means

I'm taking cold showers, and I download designs and patterns for the cutting machine when I'm at the coffee house so I can use them here. I position the table a little closer to the wall so I'm not in danger of tripping over cords, then I connect everything and turn it on to test it. I heave a huge sigh of relief when everything works perfectly.

While I wait for my food, I decide to indulge in the new paperback I bought last week. There's nothing like a good romantic comedy to smooth out the rough edges in my brain and quiet my mind a little bit. I flop onto my bed and grab the book off my nightstand, taking out the bookmark and setting it aside. The heroine of the story was just caught in a rainstorm and I'm pretty sure—

A loud thump sounds from across the warehouse, making me jump. It didn't come from the direction of the door, and it's too early for my food delivery to be here. I swipe my thumb across my phone screen to check. A little car icon shows that my delivery driver is at the restaurant but hasn't left. Another thump, this one not as loud, and my heart begins to pound so loud I can hear it pulsing in my ears.

What is that?

I've spent a few nights here already, and I've never heard anything rattle the metal exterior walls like that.

I head back to the bedroom where I've stashed the big metal pipe I keep on hand. I grab it and walk through the warehouse...listening for another thump to happen. Now it's quiet. Eerily so, and my imagination is beginning to come up with all kinds of reasons for those two thumps. My head knows it's ridiculous, but the rest of me isn't so sure.

I quickly walk around the entire warehouse, listening carefully for anything out of order. There's nothing. I turn the lights on as I go. I usually just work at night with the lights on in my two rooms, but tonight, I feel like having all the lights on is a good idea. Brad's ironing board looks like it fell over again, but nothing else is out of place. And if someone was actually successful in breaking in, the alarm would have sounded. I take measured breaths, in and out, until my pulse calms down.

My phone chimes in my pocket, and I pull it out to find the delivery driver has arrived, but he's one warehouse to the east.

Dinner Dash Driver: Where are you? I don't see a door with a white star painted on it.

The star was Sarah's idea so people could find us in the small maze of warehouses in this area.

Scarlet: Looks like you're one warehouse away from me. Come over one to the west. Closer to Larkin Street.

Dinner Dash Driver: No way. You come to me or I take your order back to the store. Five minutes.

My stomach growls again, and I grumble in frustration. Fine. I can do this just once. I saw a news story once where a woman survived during a riot by acting just as crazy as all the rioters around her. I'll just go out there, and if I see anyone that looks like they're going to be trouble…out comes the crazy. Merry doesn't need to know I broke the rules this one time.

Scarlet: I'm on the way. Do not leave or no tip.

Dinner Dash Driver: Four minutes.

"Ugh!" I scream, throwing a dark hoodie over my tank top and slamming my feet into a pair of flip-flops. I hide the big pipe up my right sleeve, turn off the alarm, and head out the door.

The alley is dark, but it's quiet. I walk quickly toward Larkin Street, comforted by the fact that the street lights are on and there are still cars driving around the area. Someone shouts a profanity-laced stream of insults at a passing car. A car horn blares in reply, and I mutter a prayer under my breath as I reach the street, searching for the Dinner Dash driver. A lone car idles across the street, right in front of the mini market. No other cars are around except the broken-down shells of abandoned vehicles covered in graffiti that litter this area.

I grip the end of the pipe through my sleeve and sprint across the street to him, not feeling at all guilty when he squeals in fear as I knock on his window. Karma. He glares at me and rolls his window down, looking at me incredulously.

"You live in this neighborhood?" he says, shoving a bag at me.

It smells like chicken kebab salvation.

I grab it and glare back. "Yep. I'm just that crazy."

The bag feels light, so I pull it open. There's a takeout container inside, but nothing else.

"Where's my diet soda?"

He looks guilty for a moment, eyes darting to his cup holder with a newly opened bottle of diet soda in it.

"I got nervous, and my throat was dry."

I give him a withering look and turn away, watching the traffic for an opening. I dart halfway across the street and stop on the median to wait for more cars to pass.

"Hey, blondie!" a random guy yells out a passing car window. "Let's go!"

I carefully hold my takeout bag in one arm while I pull my hood up to cover my blond bob.

"Hey," the delivery driver yells behind me. "You didn't leave a tip, lady!"

I jog the rest of the way across to my side of the street, then turn to face him.

"You stole my diet soda!" I yell loudly. "There's your tip!"

I step into the alley, walking quickly and fueled by the adrenaline of the whole experience. Probably about thirty yards to go, and I'm home free. The alley is wet because it rained a little today, so I'm avoiding puddles as much as possible. I'm about thirty feet in when I hear footsteps behind me. I quickly peek over my shoulder, hoping for an old bum or a staggering drunk. Nope. Big, strong man. Wearing all black. Coming down the alley behind me.

In less than a second, I decide nope…not today. I race down the alley toward the light that's on over the warehouse entrance. I grab the door and pull, my panicked brain not realizing I need to key in the code to unlock it. Strong hands grab me as I reach for the keypad, and I scream my lungs out, pulling hard to get away from him.

"Hey!" he shouts over my screams, turning me around to face him. "Hey, hey…calm down, ma'am."

My scream dies in my throat at the word ma'am. Attackers don't usually have good manners. His iron grip on my shoulders loosens as we stumble under the big light by the door, and his face is illuminated. I gasp so hard I nearly choke. I'm looking up into the very concerned eyes of Black Leather Jacket.

Chapter 3

"Black Leather Jacket? What are you doing here?" I whisper in shock, clutching my kabobs against my pounding heart.

He maintains his grip on my shoulders, looking me over as if he's not sure whether I'm hurt...or crazy.

"I'm sorry I frightened you," he says lowly.

I don't miss how his eyes dart nervously up and down the alley, looking for threats.

"I saw you yelling at that car and wanted to be sure you were all right. What are you doing out here after dark? Do you actually *live* in this neighborhood?"

His voice is almost soothing. Strong, but full of compassion. Kindness. The naturally cynical side of me that wonders if he has some sort of creepy purpose in this alley immediately fizzles away. I know in my gut he's okay. I shrug out of his hold and look around the alley to make sure no one else is near.

"Temporarily, yes," I whisper. "Do you?"

He nods, pointing over my shoulder. "At the fire station down the street."

My eyebrows shoot up. "Fire station?"

He nods again. A lovely, clean scent…citrus and something else… wafts by. Cologne? Soap? Whatever it is, it's wonderful and so unexpected in the alley. Citrus and spice is way better than anything I usually smell around here.

"Engine 14 is a block away."

A car horn blares, and another phantom voice begins yelling and screaming, making me jump. I shake my head in frustration and glance up at Black Leather Jacket.

"I need to get inside," I mutter under my breath. "I only came out after dark to get my dinner order."

BLJ's nervous gaze flicks to the warehouse behind me.

"You live *here?* In this warehouse?"

I nod. "For the next few weeks. I'm working on a project."

Another shout in the distance, and I'm done. I turn and key the code into the door lock, then step inside and hold the door open for him.

"It's safer in here, come on."

He follows me in, then hovers by the door, watching me with that same look of concern.

"What?" I ask defiantly, lifting my chin.

The corner of his mouth tilts up, and he extends a hand slowly.

"I'm Andrew."

I blink back my surprise, frozen in place.

Oh.

I didn't really think this through. I didn't want to know his name.

The first rule when finding a stray animal: do not name it.

Soon you'll be buying collars and cute little beds, and now you have a new pet. Why did he tell me his name? Not that he's a stray animal, nor would he ever be a pet. It's just so much easier to start liking someone when you know their name. Soon we'll be talking. I immediately regret my decision to let him in here. Sort of. I mutter a curse under my breath and shake his hand.

"Scarlet."

He smiles fully, and I fight hard to suppress the smile that wants to bloom in response. Dimples. He has dimples. My biggest weakness. And they're so beautiful. This is already bad.

Help me.

Something pokes me in the chest, and I realize I'm clutching my dinner so hard I'm literally skewering myself in the boob with a kebob. I pull the bag away, and there's a big grease stain right in the middle of my chest. I snicker and shake my head as Andrew stands there, watching me curiously.

"This is what I get for breaking my own rules and going out there after dark," I mutter. Then, just to make myself look like a bigger idiot, I point to my chest. "*This* is what karma looks like."

Andrew laughs softly, holding his hands up.

"At least you're okay."

I tilt my head. "That's true. And I smell delicious."

I burst into nervous laughter. I'm literally standing here, pointing at my boob and laughing in front of one of the hottest guys I've ever seen. I want it to stop, but getting gut punched by fear in the alley seems to have had some kind of effect on me. It takes me a minute to get myself back under control.

"Sorry," I mutter shakily. "Running out there, combined with the scare in the alley, seems to have shaken me up a little too much. And I'm kind of going through a lot right now."

He nods. "Are you all right?"

I nod back, more on auto-pilot than anything else. I'm fine. I'm always fine. Always all right.

Andrew's eyes start darting around, taking in the whole warehouse. Since I turned on all the lights earlier, he can see bits of decor on some of the walls that are visible from our vantage point. It's a stark contrast to the rest of the space that actually looks like a warehouse is supposed to look. I let his eyes wander for a while, taking the opportunity to let my eyes wander over him. That's when I notice the uniform. The black leather jacket is gone, and he's wearing a very nicely fitted fireman's uniform. It's dark blue. The city of San Francisco Fire Department's insignia is embroidered on a patch on his chest. Right over his heart. I look up to find him watching me, and that familiar pull tugs at me, the same one that hits me every time our eyes meet in the coffee shop.

"It's none of my business," he says gently, "I know that. But why do you live here?"

I consider showing him the door. It's what I should do. I don't want to let this guy in. I've already admitted that he's hot, and now I know his name. I'm both proud and a little sad over the fact that this is the closest I've gotten to a single man in three years. And I may be totally wrong, maybe he's married and has two adorable kids, but there's something about the way he looks at me that tells me he's single. I really don't need any complications right now, but being kind to a person who came running down a creepy dark alley to make sure I was okay doesn't have to mean we're about to get engaged. I think I can be nice for fifteen minutes. There's something about him that makes me want to slow down and actually talk to him. I think I'm beginning to understand how Marina and Ashley's minds changed so much when they met Zach and Rick. Their other halves. Not that that's what Andrew is. Not by a long shot. Still, he's the first guy who's been worthy of my attention in a long time.

"C'mon," I say, pivoting and walking towards my part of the warehouse. "I'll show you why I live here."

He follows me, and we pass the bedroom first. I point at it quickly but lead him towards the library.

"Don't pay much attention to the bedroom," I say. "This space is the best one."

Andrew stops in the doorway and looks around the library, jaw slack in wonder. The bookcase-lined walls with ornate trim, even with the empty shelves and other clutter in the room, are a stark contrast to the high warehouse ceiling above us. It doesn't match when you look all around, but the walls of the rooms are high. The warehouse ceiling is only noticeable if you look straight up, making all the rooms immersive experiences.

Andrew's gaze drifts back down to mine. It's one thing to see him across the expanse of the coffee shop and another to be standing within arm's length of him…close enough to really see his eyes. They're a deep brown. Warm. Inviting. But there's a striking ring of gold feathered through the lightest part of his iris. Like a ring of golden fire. I don't realize I'm staring until he clears his throat. I look away quickly.

"So, is this some kind of a business you're moving into the warehouse? In this neighbor—"

"No," I say, laughing softly. "Have you ever heard of the Home Network?"

He nods. "Sure."

"They have a Decorator's Showcase competition every year," I explain. "It's a pretty big deal. I've entered and lost it four times."

I'm not prepared for the wide, gorgeous grin that slowly lights up his face. He looks around again, taking it all in with an expression that has my heart swelling with pride. He gets it. He looks back at me and shakes his head.

"I don't think you're losing the contest this year," he murmurs as he looks around the library. "This is your year. What could possibly beat this?"

I laugh again. "Lots of things. But I appreciate the vote of confidence."

He stands there. Smiling softly. Watching me with those expressive eyes. Whatever this connection is between us, it stretches taut like a guitar string. It seems to me that this should feel weird…standing here and just looking at each other like this, but it doesn't. Eventually, he breaks the connection.

"And you're living here temporarily…why?"

My stomach growls in protest, and I wince.

"That requires a longer explanation," I reply. "And I'm starving. Do you want a kebob?"

He considers my offer for a moment.

"Do you have a dining room hiding around here somewhere?"

I grin. "Yes, actually, my friend is working on one. But it's just for show. I can offer you a seat on the finest five-gallon paint bucket this side of town."

He chuckles, then nods. "Deal."

I lead him off to a space near the door where Kayla, Sarah, Brad, and I have set up a makeshift table with four large paint buckets for seats. I gingerly open the crushed takeout container to reveal six smashed but still tasty-looking chicken kebobs and slide it between us. He eyes it all carefully.

"Is this all you're having for dinner tonight?" he asks incredulously.

"It's more than enough."

He throws me a skeptical look and takes the smallest one. How very sweet. It's a gesture that, combined with the knowledge of what he does for a living, tells me he's the guy who opens doors for little old ladies at the grocery store and rescues kittens from the street.

"Thank you," he says as he pulls a piece of chicken off the skewer and pops it into his mouth.

I shrug. "It's the least I can do for the attempted rescue."

He smiles at me. "My pleasure. Running to the rescue is my job."

I nod my thanks and devour two chunks of chicken almost

immediately. I'm so hungry I feel like there's a hole chewing its way through my stomach. I'm beyond eating like a lady. I'm famished. Besides, do I really want to make a good impression on the very handsome fireman with a perfectly sculpted body sitting right in front of me? No. No, I don't. Maybe I should snort for good measure. Whatever it takes for him to retreat back to the fire station like a good boy. But dang, he's awfully nice to look at for a while.

"So basically, I live way on the other side of town," I begin, throwing another chunk of chicken in my mouth. "My mom is a successful lawyer, and she's an awesome mom, so I normally live with her. That way, I can throw all my energy into the interior design thing. I have a steady stream of customers for small design jobs, but I'm trying to save as much as I can to start my own business. The grand prize for this contest is two hundred and fifty thousand dollars and a feature on the Home Network Channel."

Andrew's eyes get so big I'm not sure whether he's impressed or choking on a kebob. I fill him in on all the other details, including our little team of budget-minded designers. I chew another piece of chicken, not even bothering to suppress the very satisfied moan that escapes my throat. Fear works up quite an appetite, and even though I'm a little bit edgy over having this gorgeous man's full attention...I'm not quite ready for him to leave. His presence is comforting after such a scare.

"Well, lucky me," he says as he scarfs down the last of his kebab. "I can say I knew you before you were famous."

I smile as I chew and grab another kebob from the container. I offer another to Andrew, but he declines. We just sit together while I eat, and he lets his gaze drift around the warehouse again before settling back on me.

"I see you have a security system here. I don't suppose you checked to see if the sprinkler system is working?"

I laugh softly, and his eyes come back to me.

"Do you always worry this much about total strangers?"

He smirks. "It's not really a weird question for a fireman to ask."

Okay. He's got me there. Maybe it's not that weird.

"Honestly? I didn't check that," I admit, then add when he rolls his eyes, "but I'm sure it's fine! Besides, we don't have a kitchen here. Or a fireplace. Where's the fire coming from?"

He shakes his head, apparently bewildered at my summation.

"You don't need an actual flame to start a fire," he says. "Faulty wiring. Any heat source. Combustible materials. There's a long list of things that can cause a fire, Scarlet."

"Well, lucky me...I just happen to know a fireman who lives right down the street."

He laughs and shakes his head at me.

"So, is this what you're sketching in your book when I see you in the coffee house?" he asks genuinely.

I nod. "I have a singular focus right now. I don't own a car, and the bus isn't safe on this side of town, so I decided to just live here until I've completed my project."

He nods, then quiets again.

"Speaking of the coffee house," I say with a barely suppressed grin, "Why green tea? In a *coffee* house."

A knowing smile spreads across his face, and I instantly regret asking the question.

"How do you know what I drink at the coffee house?"

I don't bother hiding the guilty look on my face as a low chuckle escapes.

"I may have asked Rosa some questions," I say with a casual shrug. "Doesn't mean anything."

The grin on his face tells me it does, and I don't like the fact that his reaction has my pulse picking up. What is wrong with me? I turn to complete goo so fast in front of this guy.

"Of course, it doesn't, Black Coffee Girl."

I laugh out loud, and he chuckles in response.

"Looks like you asked some questions too."

He nods. "I couldn't resist."

An easy silence settles between us for a moment as we both take each other in. Not staring. Just looking. Like we're in the coffee house. Finally, I break the silence.

"Why?"

He purses his lips, thoughtful for a moment.

"Because I see such fierce determination in you, and I admire it," he replies. "The first time I saw you, your walk caught my attention."

My brows knit together. "My walk?"

He nods again. "So determined. Confident, focused. You reminded me of me. I get teased a lot about how determined I can get when I want something. But then you're also gorgeous. And I started wondering…who is this woman? Dressed impeccably, you were wearing a tangerine orange pantsuit of all things the first time I saw you. Much too bougie for this neighborhood. I couldn't help wondering where does she come from? What is she doing here?"

I feel a smile creep up my lips as I listen to him share his first thoughts about me.

"And yet you never tried to talk to me."

Andrew levels his gaze at me.

"Everything about you screams 'go away'," he says. "Am I wrong about that?"

My subtle smile turns into a wide grin, and I laugh out loud.

"Do you deny it?" he presses, those beautiful brown eyes pressing me for the truth.

I shake my head, still grinning. "Nope. Kind of proud of it, actually. I don't have time for relationships."

He tilts his head and smirks.

"Just because a man talks to you doesn't mean you're headed for a relationship."

"True," I admit. "But it's how they all start. And there's no room on my calendar for one right now."

His expression stills.

"You can't schedule everything in your life on a calendar, Scarlet."

I shrug. "It's worked for me so far."

He nods just slightly.

"It did for me once as well."

"And then?"

The corner of his mouth twitches just a bit.

"Life taught me otherwise."

There's a sadness in his tone that makes me want to ask him what happened, but I don't. It feels like an intrusion in a way since I don't know him that well, and also because of my own rules about relationships. I'm intrigued, though, to meet someone who makes me want to throw that rule out altogether. Because, if I'm being honest, I would love to just sit here and talk to him all night long. It's been a long time since I had any male company, and it's...nice.

He shakes his head.

"What if the love of your life walks into that coffee house tomorrow...but you don't have space on your calendar. What then?"

I smirk. "I see what you're trying to do."

He smirks back. "Yeah? What's that?"

I double down and just stare at him with a knowing look on my face until he laughs.

"Fine," he says. "You obviously noticed me at some point if you asked Rosa about me. Other than being grossed out by my green tea...what did you see?"

I'm thoughtful for a moment, my gaze passing over his handsome face as he waits patiently for my reply.

"Definitely the black leather jacket," I say, fighting against the stupid grin that wants to take over my face.

"Is that why you called me 'Black Leather Jacket' in the alley?"

I nod sheepishly. "Guilty. I had to figure out some kind of name for you, so I went for the obvious."

The corner of his mouth tips up.

"Or you could have just come over and asked me what my actual name is."

"Ugh," I mutter, then laugh. "Now I know what my friends put up with."

He raises his eyebrows curiously.

"I'm the real one in my group of girlfriends," I explain. "I have a rep for telling it like it is."

He grins, and those dimples call to me.

"Me too."

I offer him half of a smile and a nod.

"For what it's worth," he begins. "I had a nickname for you too."

I sit straight up and regard him expectantly.

"City Girl."

I roll my eyes. "Oh, please. That's it? How unoriginal."

He laughs out loud, and a little thrill shimmies down my spine. His laugh is deep, throaty, and rich.

"I apologize for letting you down, Scarlet. I'll try harder in the future."

The thrill I get at the sound of my name on his lips sends alarm bells blaring in my brain, and I feel my defenses rising. I have years of experience keeping men at arm's length, and my brain is ready to push him back down the street to Engine 14 where he belongs. I'm supposed to be focusing on my design project. I can already see that I'm enjoying this too much. It's easy to put off men who approach me randomly, but I actually like this one. I've felt a kind of connection with him since that very first day we looked at each other across the coffee house.

"So you live with your mom...she's okay with you living alone in a warehouse? In this neighborhood?"

I cringe inwardly. I hate guilt, but I get a heaping spoonful of it every time I think about keeping the truth from my mom...and most of my friends. I hate having to ask Merry to keep it from the rest of our inner circle too.

"She doesn't know," I say lowly, making a face when he looks shocked. "She's on the first vacation she's taken in ages, and I don't want her worrying about me. I plan to tell her right before she gets back."

"Please tell me there's someone besides me who knows you're living here," he says incredulously.

"My friend Merry knows," I answer quickly. "I check in with her every night before my head hits the pillow and again in the morning when I wake up."

A look of realization spreads over his face.

"Was she in the coffee house with you the other day?" he asks. "Petite brunette. Giving dirty looks to a cookie. Possibly feral?"

I laugh out loud. Wow. I've never heard a better description of my sweet friend. I can't wait to tell her about it.

"Yes!" I exclaim. "Merry is very...extra. I love that you used the word feral to describe her. It fits so well. I can't wait to tell her."

He grins at me, and those dimples tempt me again.

"I love your laugh, Scarlet."

My pulse thrums in response to the compliment, even as I feel my defenses building higher and higher. I clear my throat and look down at my shoes.

"Thanks."

The sound of his soft laughter brings my gaze back up to his.

"Don't panic. We don't have to be in a relationship just because I said I love your laugh."

I nod. "Sorry. I'm just determined to avoid distractions right now."

Here come the dimples again. And those warm, beautiful brown eyes. He really is fun to look at.

I can hear Merry's voice in my head, whispering *Do you see the hotness?*

Yes, I do.

"Do you find me distracting?"

Help me.

I clear my throat again.

"A little bit, yep," I admit. Then, deciding to embrace my knack for being real, I add, "the whole fireman thing is really working for you."

He raises his eyebrows, and I shake my head.

"I'm not going to help you figure that out. I already like you too much."

He smirks. "And we can't have that. It'll be anarchy."

I grin and nod at his sarcasm. I really, really like him. He's funny. And talkative. And oh, so pretty. I hate it so much.

"Will you do me a favor?" he asks quietly.

I watch him curiously.

"Will you let me give you my phone number so you can call for help if this happens again?"

I hesitate, and an awkward pause hangs in the air. My first reaction is elation because this gorgeous man wants me to have his number. And that leads to a silent scream inside my head.

No. Stop. Don't get wrapped up in a guy right now.

And now here we are... Awkward City. His expression goes from hopeful to disappointed to knowing within a few seconds.

"So that's a no. Okay...well," he says knowingly, standing and stretching. "I'm just bothering you now. I should get going."

I instantly feel terrible. And then I feel terrible for feeling terrible, because I have every right not to take someone's number. But I also care about his feelings, even though we've only known each other for about thirty minutes. Another danger sign. Maybe I should just let him assume what he wants and walk away. I bite my lower lip and consider doing just that.

Chapter 4

Scarlet

"Andrew," I say calmly, holding a hand up. "It's probably not what you're thinking."

He takes a step closer to the door and pauses, then turns and offers me a soft smile. I feel that familiar tug again.

"I'm not thinking anything, Scarlet," he says quietly. "I respect your passion and your focus. I'm just disappointed. For myself. That's all."

I nod in understanding. He makes me want to throw all my rules right out the window, but that's exactly why I feel I have to dig in my heels, too.

"I'm not saying no," I clarify gently. "I'm just hesitant because I've been solely focused on this phase of my career for so long...I can't afford distractions. Especially when they come in the form of a gorgeous, muscled-up fireman."

I don't expect the slow, sexy smile that spreads across his face. He steps closer. Not too close, but certainly close enough for me to have to tilt my head up to look into those remarkable gold-ringed brown eyes.

"You see it too," he murmurs as those captivating eyes rove over my face. "You *feel* it. Don't you?"

I realize in this moment that I'm standing before a person who likes to be just as real as I do. Any other man could read this situation and try to use it to his advantage. He might try to charm me until I gave in and took his number, or he might try to play games. Not Andrew. He's going to walk right up to it, shine a light on it, and get real.

Just like I would.

Respect.

I nod but stay silent. His gaze flicks to my lips.

"When we're in the coffee shop and our eyes meet," he says lowly. "You feel that?"

I swallow, even though my mouth is suddenly dry.

"The pull?" I ask hoarsely. "Yes."

He nods, regarding me quietly for a moment.

"And you're not curious?"

I take a deep breath. This really must be what others feel when they're talking to me about something difficult. Things that hit too close. Things they'd rather leave hidden until I come barreling in with a spotlight to look at it all. There's no getting away from it. And I know, because I know what I would do, he won't be distracted by any attempts to throw him off the scent. I wouldn't either.

"I *am* curious," I admit. "But—"

He nods curtly. "Duty first. I get it."

I smile softly. "A fireman's duty is far more noble than an interior designer's. We are not the same."

He tilts his head and studies me for a moment with an appreciative glint in his eyes.

"You have passion, Scarlet," he says in a honeyed tone that makes me want to abandon all my principles immediately. "*Drive*. In that regard, we are the same. I see it in you because it's also in me, and I respect it."

I square my shoulders and don't even try to suppress the proud smile on my face.

"Thanks."

He grins, threatening to disarm me with those dimples.

"I still think you're wrong."

I laugh. "Maybe. My gut's been wrong before."

"And what about your heart?" he asks, taking a tiny step closer. A challenge.

I can't describe the effect it has on me. This man's energy is like a force of nature. He's confident without being cocky. Authoritative without being overbearing. He makes me want to ask a million questions. I want to know more about him. What makes him tick. I want to challenge him as much as he's trying to challenge me.

I shake my head slowly.

"My heart is all heart. No brains. It doesn't get to make decisions."

A wide, knowing grin spreads on his face.

"Fair enough. It's been nice to meet you, Scarlet."

He moves toward the door, and I follow, my head at war with my heart. I key in the code to turn off the alarm, and he puts his hand on the door handle. He moves to open it, then turns back to me.

"For what it's worth," he begins. "I think you're the most beautiful woman I've ever seen, Scarlet. Your passion and commitment to your goals are like catnip for a romantic like me."

I feel a blush crawling up my cheeks as I smile back at him.

"Thank you."

He swings the door open slowly.

"Please, please, please be careful in this neighborhood?"

I nod. "I promise. No more after-dark dinner runs."

That seems to satisfy him, and he steps through the door and into the alley.

"Goodnight," he says, then turns away.

My heart shoves my gut out of the way just for a moment.

"Andrew," I call out, swallowing the lump in my throat.

He turns back around to face me, and this feels like one of those moments I'll remember for the rest of my life somehow. Time seems to slow to a crawl as his beautiful brown eyes meet mine. I take a deep breath to quiet my racing mind.

"Would you like to have coffee with me…in a few weeks…when my project is done?"

He chuckles under his breath, smiling and nodding.

"It's a date, Scarlet. I'm just down the road when you're ready."

I grin. A big, stupid one.

I wave as I close the door and lock myself in, leaning against the door for a minute. I sigh under my breath and run a hand through my hair, looking around the quiet warehouse. I've stayed the night here quite a few times already and never felt alone until now. I find myself wondering exactly what that means as I wander back towards the library.

***

Andrew

Fire fascinates me in all forms, and now I've met a woman whose name literally means fire. A happy coincidence to most people, but I believe in signs. Fire is a big part of her personality, too. Passion. Drive. It's why I didn't try to charm her into taking my phone number after she clearly didn't want it. In more ways than I care to admit, I feel like I've met someone who is carved from the same stuff as me. She knows exactly what she wants, and she's going for it. She doesn't want distractions. I get it. I was the same way when I was much younger. I've learned to be more relaxed. I know how to let go now. Scarlet exudes control freak vibes. She reminds me of the way I saw life before it taught me I can't control everything.

I can't help feeling disappointed and even a little lonely as I walk back to the mini market. I was just about to pay for a bunch of stuff I was picking up for the guys at the fire station when I saw Scarlet's very recognizable figure running across the street. I left it all behind, yelling over my shoulder that I'd be right back as I bolted out the door and followed her into the alley.

I step back into the market and nod at Bill, the owner, as he pulls my purchases out from next to the register and starts ringing them up. Bill's not his real name. He says the real one is too hard to pronounce, and he likes Bill better anyway, so that's all I know about him. He's good people, and I worry about his safety almost as much as I'm going to worry about Scarlet's...now that I know she's living in a warehouse in this part of town.

"Was Jelly Jim causing problems again?" Bill asks with a sarcastic grin.

There's a local guy that Bill and some of the others call "Jelly Jim" because he gets triggered by something and starts going into every business on the street and asking if they sell jelly. It doesn't matter if it's Bill's little mini market or Handy's Hardware store down the street. He gets angry if he asks for jelly and there isn't any. He clearly has some mental health issues, and they're trying to get him some help, but it's going slow. Plus, like so many others, he doesn't want help. Some people don't trust authorities and healthcare professionals. Others don't think they need it.

This neighborhood has spiraled out of control in the time I've been at the fire station, and I've been here a few years. It's an event if the police aren't called at least once a night because of some disruption. Good people are leaving as fast as they can, and the others who can't afford to leave are scared. I wish there was something more I could do about it.

"No, I thought I recognized someone," I say as I swipe my card.

Bill hands me the bag of my purchases with a smile.

"Take care, Andrew."

I smile back. "Thanks, man. Have a good night."

I step outside and glance across the street, down the alley. All is quiet. I hate it, though. I admire her strength and determination, but I absolutely hate that Scarlet is living in that warehouse. I won't think about anything else the entire time she's living there. It's one of my most annoying qualities, according to Jake. He calls it Superman Syndrome, saying that I always have to run to someone's rescue. It's not in me to stand by if someone needs help.

But Scarlet doesn't want help. Or distractions. For several weeks, anyway. I'll just have to find something to do to distract myself. I head down the street, working the muscle in my jaw as I ruminate on this latest worry of mine. A worry that happens to have sunny blond hair and striking blue eyes. I think about that unbelievably gorgeous library she's created, and I'm so impressed. She has such a vision. I can't imagine the creativity it takes to conceive such a thing and bring it to life like that. I hope with all my heart that it pans out for her.

A phantom voice shouts something unintelligible in the distance, and worry comes washing back in like a wave. This is going to be the longest wait of my life. At least I told her how to find me, though. She can't call, but she does know where to find me if she needs help. It won't stop me from worrying, unfortunately. There's no way around that. On the bright side, though, I have quite a few weeks to plan the perfect coffee date.

***

Scarlet

Three days later, I'm still thinking about Andrew. I'm thinking of other things, too. I'm taking care of business. I get up at dawn, sit at my work table, and organize my day. Then, I leave the warehouse in the light of morning and walk three blocks to the coffee house. It's relatively safe in the morning around here, as most of the sketchy residents are passed out after a late night of doing who knows what. I feel fine about walking to the coffee shop, especially now that there is always someone in my peripheral vision who looks an awful lot like Andrew. He's usually walking across the street, keeping pace with me. I don't make eye contact, but it makes me smile that he's there.

I wouldn't take his number, but he's found a way to watch over me in a way that reminds me of myself. I am exactly like this. You can tell me no, but I'll find a way. Just like the eye contact we've shared in the coffee shop, I'm not creeped out that he's walking with me. I know for a fact that if I walked across the street, looked him in the eye, and told him he was bothering me, he would stop. Instantly. But he's not doing it because he wants to get his way. He's doing it because he's worried about me. I could see it on his face the night he left the warehouse. The fact that he's a fireman just fits. He lives his life to help others, and now that extends to me.

He keeps his distance at the coffee shop as well, but now we smile and nod at each other when we make eye contact. No words. But I get a bigger thrill out of that smile and nod than I got from the last guy I kissed. Which was a while ago. It makes me realize that things need to change, but I'm too busy right now. I'll tackle that later. After the contest is over.

Truth is...I like that he cares. I like that he's mature enough to step back and let me do what I want to do without taking it as an insult to his manhood or looking at it as some kind of challenge. And, as if all this isn't already enough to make me like him, he has started leaving a bag of snacks tied to the warehouse door handle every night. I have found one every morning since the night we met. His way of making sure I always have food.

The first morning I found one, I knew who'd done it. I kept smiling throughout the day, any time it came to mind. The next morning, I laughed out loud when I found another bag of snacks tied to the door handle. I found myself smiling before I even opened the door this morning. And there it was. Another bag of snacks. Chips. Fruit snacks. A granola bar. A chocolate candy bar. Nothing special, but the message is clear and very sweet.

I step back to admire my work, wondering what he'll think of my latest masterpiece. I'm going with a kind of magical faerie vibe in the bedroom, and I've just finished painting a cloudscape on the concrete floor. It's a dusky blue sky with wispy clouds blowing through, and I'm pretty thrilled with how it looks. I lean against the doorway with a stupid smile on my face.

"Oh my gosh, Scar," Sarah gasps as she walks up behind me. "This turned out so great!"

I turn my head and grin at her. "Thanks."

She shakes her head as she admires the floor.

"How's your space going?" I ask.

She grimaces. "I keep waffling back and forth on what I want to do. I can't seem to make up my mind."

I nudge her with my shoulder.

"You'll get there. Your designs are always beautiful. You have a way with color blending I really admire. I wish I could do it as well as you."

She laughs softly.

"Says the woman who just painted this gorgeous sky on the floor."

I wink at her. "I'll probably never be able to do this again, but I'm super happy with it."

"Whoa!" Kayla cries out as she walks up behind us.

She's holding her cell phone up to her ear, and both Sarah and I step out of the doorway so she can get a good look at the floor.

"Brad, you have to check out Scarlet's bedroom floor when you get here," she murmurs into her phone. "Yeah, hang on."

Kayla looks at both of us.

"Do you guys want lunch? He's stopping at Wong's on the way here."

I nod. "A number five and a number seven, please."

Sarah grins. "Same. Extra fortune cookies, please."

Kayla relays the orders, then hangs up and turns to me.

"You did good, girl. This is gorgeous!"

"Thanks, Kayla."

She shoves her phone in her pocket and claps her hands together.

"Right. We've got about an hour before Brad shows up with lunch," she says. "Let's get back to work."

I nod, and the three of us split off into our own spaces. I'm going to put a matte coat of clear sealant on the floor once it's dry, so I move to the library and sit at my work table. I've already measured the various sizes of ugly books I bought to fill the bookshelves. I have a huge pile of assorted scrapbooks and craft papers and a paper cutter, so I get to work cutting the large square sheets into the sizes I'll need. There are 317 books to cover. A shiver of panic trickles up my spine every time I think about that number. I just need to focus. That's how I tackle every problem life throws at me. Focus and no distractions. So, for the next hour, I focus on my paper cutter and getting this project closer to the finish line.

***

Andrew

I watch my colleagues, Todd and Leonard, bickering in front of the TV over a news story about our neighborhood, and I laugh under my breath. There's a local reporter by the name of Kevin Starbuck who's been doing spotlights on local businesses here, trying to get support from government officials to clean up the neighborhood. I have a soft spot in my heart for anyone trying to make the world a better place, so I'm all for it…but Todd says it won't make a difference, and Leonard says every little bit helps. Jake walks into the room and shakes his head.

"Why do you listen to these two?" he grumbles.

I prop my feet up on our beat-up old coffee table and grin up at Jake.

"I'm fully on Team Leonard in this case, Cap," I say with a smirk. "I just want to know how the argument ends."

Leonard looks up from under his baseball cap. "Thanks, man."

Todd tilts his head at me. "Do we all live in La-La Land now? A reporter writes a few stories, and the city council just magically cares about this neighborhood?"

I squint at Todd. "Have you ever met Councilwoman Bell?"

Todd shrugs but stays quiet.

"I met her at a city council meeting a few months ago. She seems like a good person to me. A nice lady who wants to do more, but without any funding, that's impossible. Do you know how you get funding?"

Todd rolls his eyes in surrender. "Attention from reporters?"

I raise my hand for a high-five, and he smacks it.

"That's one way, yes. Shining a spotlight on the situation gets politicians to act instead of waiting on the sidelines. The mayor, the city manager, all of these people want to be re-elected when it's time. People will remember if they helped, or they sat on their hands. So maybe we can get on the yes train instead of standing on the tracks and shouting that it'll never work, Todd."

"Or at least go make a sandwich or something," Leonard pipes in.

"You're hangry."

Todd opens his mouth to argue, then thinks better of it. Wordlessly, he shrugs, gets up, and moves into the kitchen. I hear cabinets opening and closing. Jake, Leonard, and I exchange bemused looks.

"Anyone want a grilled cheese?" Todd yells from the kitchen.

All three of us answer yes. I'm pretty sure Todd's grilled cheese sandwiches could bring about world peace. I never say no to them. I wish there was a way to preserve one for Scarlet so I could put it in my next nightly snack delivery, but that would be gross. I suppress a laugh as I wonder what she thinks of the snack drops I've been making at the warehouse. I've thought about dropping in a note, or even a flower, but it feels like crossing that line she drew in the sand.

I wonder a lot of things about her lately. I'd love to see how her project is coming along. I can't imagine what the library must look like with the hours she's putting in. I'd love to be able to cheer her on in person, but she thinks focus requires solitude, and I'm not going to argue with her. She feels the same connection between us that I do. She just thinks she can control it like everything else in her life. She wants to put it on the calendar and deal with it on a future date of her choosing. Neatly. Conveniently.

This was me five years ago. I thought I could calendar feelings, life events, and anything else that popped up at an inopportune moment. And then life taught me otherwise. I'd been putting off a visit to my best friend, who'd moved to Colorado, always thinking there was time. By the time I finally visited, he was in hospice care. He'd been waiting to tell me in person, but I kept putting him off.

I would never wish the awakening I had on anyone, but one thing is certain. Life will teach her that it can't be scheduled, controlled, or managed. Even if the connection we feel turns out to be nothing at all, I plan to be there as a friend to support her if anything happens while I'm around.

"What are you thinking about so seriously?" Jake asks as he plops onto the couch.

I smirk. "Why do you ask?"

"You're frowning."

I blink back my surprise and shake my head as if trying to clear my thoughts.

"Just thinking about a friend."

Jake eyes me suspiciously. He's good at sniffing out what's really going on with me. Too good.

"A woman."

I roll my eyes, and he laughs out loud.

"He sees all," Leonard pipes in. "Just tell him."

"There's nothing to tell yet," I explain. "Our first date isn't for about a month."

Jake's eyebrows hit his hairline, and Leonard shakes his head.

"Are you losing your touch, Andrew?" Leonard teases.

I shrug. "She has a project she's working on. She doesn't want devastatingly handsome distractions right now."

Leonard snorts. "She sounds just as serious as you."

Jake laughs, and I grin. "Thanks, buddy. I'll let you know how it goes."

"What kind of project?" Jake asks.

"She's an interior designer," I explain. "There's some kind of contest on the Home Network she wants to win. The prize is two hundred and fifty thousand dollars and a feature story about her on their TV show. It's a pretty big deal."

Todd comes back into the room with a dinner plate loaded with four giant grilled cheese sandwiches. It's anarchy for about three seconds as we mutter our thanks, and each grabs one off the plate, but world peace returns once we start eating.

Jake smirks at me. "And she doesn't want your pretty face

distracting her from the big prize. Now it makes sense."

I give Jake a good-natured shove. He's always teasing me about what he calls my "pretty boy face". I don't see it. Then again, I don't spend much time looking in the mirror. It doesn't stop me from teasing them right back, though.

"She's much prettier than me," I say with a wistful smile. "And probably more driven."

"More driven?" Todd chimes in. "Than you? How is that even possible?"

I laugh out loud. "She told me she and three friends have pooled their money together, and they've sectioned off one of the warehouses just down the street. Each of them gets two spaces to decorate. It belongs to someone in her friend's family, and he's letting them use it, but she's actually living there for the next few weeks, so she can get as much time on site as possible."

I take another bite of my sandwich and watch their faces as they come to the same conclusion I did the night we met.

"In this neighborhood?" Todd exclaims.

Jake shakes his head. "That's not smart. No wonder she's dating you."

I shove at him again.

"We're not dating. Yet. And I agree with the safety concerns, but she's an adult. She's not breaking any laws. She's just chasing her dreams. Can't fault her for that."

Jake nods thoughtfully.

"Well, there's no harm in keeping an eye on her," he grumbles. "Show us which warehouse when we're done eating, and we'll make sure we pay attention on your days off."

Chapter 5

Andrew

I'm speechless. My curious gaze roves over Jake's face, and he laughs.

"I know you, kid," he says as he sits back in his chair. "You've already got your superhero cape on. We can help, and we will help. Otherwise, you'll be here on your days off too. You know how I feel about that."

I grin. "It's important to take your time off and decompress."

Jake's expression is full of fatherly pride. He slaps me on the knee and takes another bite of his sandwich.

"So we've got a new neighbor to keep an eye on," Todd says. "Is she cute? Maybe she won't make me wait a whole month for a date if I make her one of my famous grilled cheeses."

I roll my eyes at Todd, a happily married father of two who will jump at any chance to goad me. He laughs under his breath and nudges my knee with his.

"No, we'll help," he says. "Finish your sandwich, and you can show us where it is."

We spend the rest of our break eating and trying to get Leonard to tell us about his new girlfriend. The man is notoriously tight-lipped. Soon, we're putting our jackets on and walking down the street toward the warehouse. I lead the guys up the sidewalk on our side of Larkin Street, then stop just outside Bill's little market and point across the street.

"See that alley?" I say to my friends. "She and her friends are working in the warehouse on the left. The door is almost at the end of the alley, but it has a white star painted on it."

Leonard and Todd nod together, eyeing the surrounding buildings. Jake is focused on the roof, looking from it to the direction of our fire station two blocks away.

"What are you thinking?" I ask curiously.

Jake points to the roof of the warehouse. "See that big red smoke stack coming out of the roof?"

I nod.

"None of the other warehouses have one. It's so tall I'll bet we can see it from our balcony."

I look seriously confused. "We have a balcony?"

He laughs. "Don't get too excited. It's not very big, but there's kind of a small balcony outside the third-floor window at the fire station."

I shake my head. "We don't have a third floor."

"It's an attic, really, but yeah, we do. I'll show you when you get back."

I turn us around and start walking back to the fire station, wondering how I've never known about this before.

"Show me now, man," I say quickly. "This sounds promising."

Jake laughs. "Careful not to catch your superhero cape on anything, Andrew."

***

Scarlet

"Dude, I'm done," I croak out. "I can't do another book. How are you still going?"

Brad pulls the iron away from the fabric he's working on and gives me a sleepy smile.

"I'm done too," he says as he fights back a yawn. "I just want to finish this one, and I'm out of here."

I lean against the door and watch as he swiftly moves the iron over the expensive fabric. The wrinkles disappear instantly. He sets the iron up on the ironing board and then folds the fabric carefully. Almost immediately, the rickety ironing board begins to fall over, and Brad drops the fabric to catch it before the hot iron hits anything valuable.

I rush forward and grab the fabric, shaking it out and folding it up for Brad as he leans the tilting ironing board against a wall of cardboard boxes. It looks sturdy enough for now. He checks to make sure the iron is steady as well, then comes to take the fabric from me.

"Thanks, Scarlet," he says with a sigh. "I'll be glad to be rid of that thing."

I smirk. "You know a new ironing board is only about twenty bucks? Pretty cheap."

Brad laughs. "I will not be bested by that beast. I will prevail."

I yawn loudly. "This was a long day. But I got a hundred books done."

"Oh, wow, I can't wait to see them."

I hold my hands up in surrender. "Tomorrow, okay? I'm beat. I need sleep."

Brad pulls me into a friendly hug.

"C'mon, gorgeous. Walk me to the door so you can set the alarm."

We start towards the door together.

"Where's your car parked?"

He smirks. "Right outside the door so I can hear the car alarm if anyone's messing with it."

"Smart."

We get to the door, and he pauses, turning to me.

"You're really okay sleeping here? You don't get scared?"

I roll my eyes. "Not if I don't talk about it, but now…thanks."

Brad winces apologetically. "Sorry."

"I'll move back home once I get most everything done," I say. "If I keep up this pace, I won't have to spend the whole time going at it like crazy."

He opens the warehouse door and steps out, then pulls a bag off the door handle and hands it to me with a grin.

"Prince Charming was here."

I smile as I look inside the bag. A protein bar, a bag of chips, a candy bar, and a little rabbit's foot keychain. I pull it out of the bag and hold it up so Brad can see.

"Oh, I love this guy," he gasps. "He's clever. He never leaves notes, but he does stuff like this to wish you good luck? Are you sure he's not gay?"

I laugh out loud. "Sorry, buddy. Pretty sure he plays for my team."

Brad sighs dramatically, opening the door to his car.

"Just my luck. All right, good night. See you tomorrow!"

I nod and wave, then wait to make sure he's inside his car before I shut the door. I lock up and set the alarm, then head straight for the bedroom. My fatigue level is so high the distance seems twice as far tonight. This warehouse is huge, and my section is on the side farthest from the door. Brad's is closest to mine and towards the middle, and Kayla and Sarah have sections in the corners behind his. I notice we left the lights on in his section, but I'm too tired to walk down there and turn them off. It won't hurt anything to leave them on tonight. I can't see it from inside the bedroom anyway, so it won't keep me up.

I head to the tiny bathroom near what used to be some kind of office inside the warehouse. I brush my teeth and wash my face, then head to the bedroom as a huge yawn rolls through me. I'm not even setting an alarm for the morning. I've earned the right to sleep in for once.

In under a minute, I've changed into my pajamas and plugged in my phone, then I climb into bed and stretch out with a sigh of contentment. I don't know that I've ever felt so exhausted. Every bone, every muscle is fully worn out right now, but I'm very happy with the amount of work I got through today.

I can't explain why. Maybe it's some kind of intuition, but I feel like I might really win this thing this year. My pulse happily quickens as I imagine receiving the news that I won the Decorator's Showcase Challenge. I imagine myself building my dream business with the prize money. Giving media interviews that I've watched so many winners give. Finally, having enough money to give my design firm a real launch.

Something clatters in the distance, and I laugh under my breath, realizing it's probably Brad's stupid ironing board that won't stand up straight. I should just buy him a new one so it doesn't scare me in the middle of the night. But I'm too tired for fear, so I close my eyes and dream of the beautiful, magical library coming to life in the next room as I drift off to a deep sleep.

***

Someone is calling my name, and I can't wake up. I hear them. They're frantic. I can't tell where they are, but they sound worried. I want to tell them I'm fine. I set the alarm on the warehouse before I went to bed. I'm fine. But I can't talk or really think right now.

"...thank God..."

I'm floating. I can't speak. I can't breathe. I'm floating...

"...stay with me, Scarlet..."

Who is that? I set the alarm. No one should be in here. I shouldn't be moving. I'm in my bed. Why am I floating? I finally get the strength to raise my head, and I see fire everywhere. It's up the walls. It's consuming my bedroom. I don't even have time to process what's happening before I fall and hit the ground hard. Pain shoots through my right arm, and then the world goes black.

***

Andrew

"She's gonna be okay," Jake mutters as he waits with me. "Are you all right?"

I nod, holding an ice pack to my cheek with one hand while keeping an eye on Scarlet. We're down the alley, a safe distance from the still-burning warehouse. She's still unconscious, and I don't know if her head was hit when part of the warehouse decided to collapse on us. The EMTs have her laid out on a stretcher, her right arm stabilized with a brace because she winced and moaned when they evaluated her. Better safe than sorry. I can barely see her face beneath the coat of ash covering her skin, but I can see her breath fogging the oxygen mask that sits over her nose and mouth. It's keeping the spark of hope alive inside of me.

"C'mon, Scarlet," I murmur, more to myself than her.

I'm so grateful I was here.

I hadn't been able to let go of worry ever since that night she showed me around the warehouse. I've spent most of my time on the small balcony at the top of the fire station after Jake showed it to me, sitting in a camp chair and reading a book when I have downtime. Listening for trouble. Watching for lights and activity. Just wanting her to be all right. And then I saw the smoke tonight...and I'll never forget it.

I sprung into action, activating the alarm and bolting downstairs to suit up. Jake was the first to get downstairs to meet me. I told him there was definite smoke coming from Scarlet's warehouse. The roof, with that unique smoke stack, is very visible from our balcony. Jake agreed to wait for the rest of the guys to come down, and then I grabbed an ax off the truck and ran. I couldn't wait another second. Flames were already shooting through the roof, and I wasn't sure how bad the inside of the warehouse was. I took down the door with the ax in two swings, then waited for the rest of the crew. My training and experience would never let me run into that building without the rest of the guys. The truck pulled down the alley seconds later, and I looked up to see Leonard's stoic expression through the windshield as he stopped the fire truck with trained precision.

Jake let me go in once I explained that I knew exactly where to look for Scarlet. The smoke was thick, making it impossible to see inside. My route was complicated by the fact that I'd only been in there once, but I found her unconscious in her bed with flames already eating up the wall between the library and her bedroom. She didn't answer me when I called her name, and I knew I had precious seconds to get her outside and into some breathable air. A glance upward showed me the roof was already severely compromised. I pulled her from her bed and threw her over my shoulder, stalking for the exit as if the fire was already burning at my heels. She must have woken up at some point because she started fighting me for a few seconds. Then, I felt a tremor run through her body. Her arms wrapped around me tightly, and I knew she understood what was happening. I was three feet from the door when part of the building collapsed and took us down.

One huge cough brings Scarlet back to us, and I heave a sigh of relief as the EMTs try to calm her. Her expression is panicked, eyes wild as she looks up at the burning warehouse. The fear and grief etched into her face are too much for me to stand by and watch. I step around the EMTs, careful to not get in their way, and move close to Scarlet's head. She calms as soon as she sees me. I see the realization hit her when she takes in my filthy, ash-covered coat. Her lip trembles, and she reaches out with her good arm. I quickly take her hand, reaching up to smooth her hair away from her face.

"You're okay," I say gently. "Everything's gonna be okay."

She tries to speak, but her voice is gone. A common issue with severe smoke inhalation. I shake my head at her.

"Don't try to speak, Scarlet," I say soothingly. "You're gonna be okay. I've got you. I'm here."

Spectators are already crowding the area, watching the blaze engulf the warehouse. The flames illuminate the alley, so bright it's like daylight. Fire hoses aimed at the warehouse are barely keeping the fire contained, so I feel relieved when I hear sirens blaring in the distance. More help is coming. Water falls like rain in the alley as my fellow firemen work with calm professionalism.

Scarlet's eyes well up, and her face crumples. Tears begin to flow as she watches her dreams burn to the ground. She buries her face in my shoulder and sobs as I wrap my arms around her. I can feel Jake's presence behind me, assessing the situation with a professional eye. I might be getting a lecture later. Something about getting too close to victims, but I'll take that if it comes.

I keep holding her, my heart cracking with every sob that shudders through her body. I hate this for her, and there's nothing I can do but feel grateful I got to her in time. My friend Craig is one of the EMTs assessing her, and he gives me a quick nod to confirm she has no other visible injuries. Another sigh of relief, but I'll feel better once she's been looked at by a doctor.

"You next, bud," Craig says authoritatively.

He yanks on my coat and helps me shrug out of it. I have to let go of Scarlet momentarily, and she clutches at me until I wrap my arm back around her. Jake gives me a look, and I answer back with an expression that tells him I'll explain later. He eyes me warily, then steps away once Craig starts checking me over.

"You got knocked pretty good," he says as his fingers gently move over my face. "You're definitely going to the ER. Probably going to have a black eye tomorrow."

I nod. No big deal. I don't even have a headache right now. My helmet did its job, but rules are rules, and I've learned to follow them. Mostly.

Scarlet's fist clenches in my shirt, and I look down to find her crying quietly. I wrap both arms around her, being careful not to move her or disturb her wounded arm.

"You know her?" Craig asks as he flashes a light in my eyes to check my pupils.

"Yeah," I reply, holding still until he's done. "Her name is Scarlet. She and a few others were working on a design project in there, and she was sleeping here so she could work as much as possible on it."

Craig nods, then lowers his face, so he's level with Scarlet's. The blue of her eyes is stark against the ash smeared on her cheeks.

"That's some dedication, Scarlet," he says warmly. "We're gonna get you checked out by a doctor, okay?"

She nods, still clutching at my shirt. Craig pats me on the shoulder.

"Well, we need to get her to the hospital asap," he says as he wraps his stethoscope around his hand. "And she's not letting you go, so you're gonna ride together. Quickly please. She needs a thorough check."

I nod, then look down at Scarlet.

"I have to let you go for a minute so they can put you in the ambulance, but I'll be right behind you, okay?"

Immediately, her grip tightens. I manage to get her to lay back on the stretcher, but she will not let go of my hand. I climb up into the back of the ambulance behind the stretcher, still holding her hand while Craig and his colleague load Scarlet in. The stretcher is secured, and we're locked inside. Moments later, an EMT jumps into the driver's seat, and we're moving.

I look down at Scarlet. Her tears have slowed, but the tracks have muddied the ash in long streaks on her face. I flip open a few drawers in the ambulance until I find some wipes. I gently pry her hand from mine and give her my arm to grip while I open the wipes.

"I'm just going to clean you up a bit, okay?" I say in a soothing tone. "You're covered in ash."

She nods, and I gently run the wipe across her cheeks and nose. I hold it up so she can see the ash-blackened wipe, and she shakes her head in disbelief. I get a new wipe and make another pass, carefully lifting the oxygen mask as I work, then placing it back against her face.

Scarlet squeezes my hand, then lets go. She feels around for the package of wipes until she grabs one, taking me by surprise, and then she lifts it to my face. I smile back at her and take it away, rubbing it over my face as her hand returns to mine. I finish that task and look down at her. She nods slowly as if satisfied that my face is cleaned up enough.

"I'm glad you're okay," I say, giving her hand a squeeze.

More tears come as she shakes her head and coughs some more.

"I know it doesn't feel like you're okay," I continue in a soothing tone. "You're alive, Scarlet. That's the important part. Everything else can be fixed."

The ambulance slows and then turns a corner. We speed up again, sirens wailing into the night. A few more turns, and we're pulling into the hospital lot. Scarlet coughs again, and I squeeze her hand.

"When we get inside, they're going to separate us to check us out," I explain. Her grip tightens. "I'll come right back to you as soon as I can."

Scarlet squeezes again, eyes pleading.

"I promise. I won't be far away."

She relaxes a little and nods at me. The ambulance barely slows to a stop, and the EMT is there to pull the door open and yank the stretcher out. Scarlet lets go as she's pulled away, and I heave a sigh of relief that she's in the doctor's hands now. Smoke inhalation is a serious thing, and I have no idea how long that fire was burning before I saw the smoke. If there were combustible materials that accelerated the progress of the flames, maybe I saw it fairly early. But if it was burning longer and she was breathing it for a while, she could have permanent damage to her lungs.

I scoot my way out of the back of the ambulance and follow them in, an ER nurse asking me a million questions as we walk. I explain what happened, and she escorts me to a bed two stalls away from where they've wheeled Scarlet.

The ER is busy tonight, but I can hear them giving Scarlet priority as they work to assess any damage caused by smoke inhalation. I hear chest and arm x-rays ordered STAT, and equipment is wheeled in quickly. One of my favorite nurses is with her, much to my relief. I can't hear what Sheila is saying. She's speaking to Scarlet in soft, compassionate tones as the x-ray tech manages the mobile equipment.

I close my eyes and try to imagine for a moment what it must have been like for Scarlet to be fast asleep one minute and then wake up while someone is carrying her over their shoulder the next. She must have been so frightened, which is why she fought me at first. Then, after she realized the warehouse was on fire, that must have just added to her panic. And then the roof fell on top of us. I've seen a lot of victims of fires go through various levels of PTSD, and my gut's telling me that's going to be something she has to deal with even after her body is healed. I just hope I can help in some way…and I still wish I'd gotten there sooner than I did.

Chapter 6

Scarlet

The emergency room is bright and loud, but none of it comes close to quieting the ever-present buzzing in my ears. Every cell of my body feels like it's on high alert. I dig my nails into my palms to the point of pain, desperately trying to control the horrible feeling that every piece of me will be consumed by the fire that's likely still raging through the warehouse.

In my head, I know I'm in a hospital bed…miles away from the fire. I can't explain why I feel the level of fear I do, like the fire is just outside the door, and it's about to burn through the building. Like it's a real, living thing, and it's coming for me. The only thing that makes me feel like I'm safe from it all is to hold on to the one person who was there to pull me from it.

A chill floats over my skin as the nurse says something to me. The pajama pants and tank top I was wearing when Andrew pulled me from the blazing warehouse are doing very little to protect me from the icy air of the hospital.

Someone pats me on the shoulder, and I hear them give instructions, but I don't comprehend anything. I'm taken through the motions of chest and arm x-rays. Nurses and technicians speak in gentle, sensitive tones, but I still don't really understand. The terror I felt when I woke up in the warehouse with the fire burning all around me replays on a loop in my mind. I feel Andrew's steps as he carried me over his shoulder. The reek of ash and smoke still scratches my throat, and I cough a couple times to try to clear my lungs.

A pinching pain in my uninjured arm stirs my thoughts, and I look down to find an IV has been started. People are talking to me, but everything sounds like it's far away. Under water. Everything is happening underneath that buzzing sound in my ears that just won't go away. Just as I'm ready to go looking for the only person who can make this buzzing stop, Andrew is here. The curtain is pushed back, and he's standing right in front of me.

The oxygen mask is placed over my face again, and a blanket is pulled over my legs, but I don't care. Andrew steps up to my bedside, and I turn immediately and grab at him, pulling him closer until his arms are around me and my cheek is against his chest.

Now. Now I feel safe. I feel the warmth of his hand on the back of my head as he holds me. The buzzing in my ears stops immediately, and a shudder rolls through my body. I'm vaguely aware of the nurse muttering something to Andrew. Maybe to me, actually, but I don't care. I don't care about anything anymore.

He smells like smoke and ash. Everything does, but the hard warmth of his chest against my cheek is solace enough. His voice vibrates against my ear as he speaks, and I slowly realize he's probably talking to me since the nurse left the room. I tilt my face up to look at him.

"What?" I rasp.

My voice is nearly gone.

Andrew looks down at me with eyes full of concern.

"I asked if there's someone I can call for you," he explains. "You mentioned your mom is on a cruise, but do you want anyone else to come and stay with you?"

My gaze flicks around the room until I find the clock on the wall. Two AM.

"I'll call Merry when I know she's up," I say hoarsely. "I don't want to wake her up in the middle of the night."

He nods, and I settle my cheek back against his chest. I feel like I should care about how hard I'm clinging to him. This isn't normal. This is the exact opposite of normal. I'm strong. Independent. I don't do things like this, and yet I absolutely cannot help it. I know it's irrational, but I feel a deep-seated fear that some hidden danger is coming for me. I'm more scared than I've ever felt in my whole life. The only thing that makes me feel safe is holding onto the person who literally carried me out of danger.

"I'm sorry," I strain to get out.

He looks down at me with a frown. "For?"

I squeeze my arms tighter around his waist for emphasis. "This."

He strokes a hand down my back and squeezes me tighter in response.

"Scarlet, you've just been through a terrifying experience," he says gently. "If this is what you need, I'm happy to give it."

I nod and settle against his chest again. His hands gently move up and down my back, their warmth radiating through the tank top I'm wearing. Another shudder runs through me, and he holds me tighter.

"I'm here," he says soothingly.

My brain keeps trying to drift back to the warehouse. To all my dreams on fire at this very moment. To everything I've lost. My chances of winning the contest, which seem funny to think about right now, but my mind is frantic. All my supplies. My laptop. Even my bed. It's all gone. I keep wanting to go over it in my mind, and then I'm overcome with relief at just being alive. That really is all that's important right now. I'm alive and safe.

"You saved me," I rasp out.

A large hand cups the back of my head, gently tilting my face up towards his. Andrew's all-consuming brown eyes stare deeply into mine.

"I'm glad I was there."

I manage a trembling smile as tears sting my eyes. "Me too."

That's all it takes for more tears to come. They fall freely, and I hold tighter to Andrew as a sob wracks my body. He lets out a half grumble, half sigh as he holds me through it. It was incredibly scary to wake up mid-rescue, not realizing that was what was happening. At first, I thought someone had broken into the warehouse, and I was about to be attacked. I started to fight him until I saw the flames mid-struggle and realized I was being carried to safety. Just as I wrapped my arms around him to hold on, something crashed on top of us, and that's the last thing I remember.

I give myself another minute, then pull away enough to see Andrew's face.

"Are you okay?" I ask hoarsely.

One of his eyes is swelling, and it's starting to look like he'll have a bad bruise. Probably a black eye. He's quiet for a moment as if he can't fathom my question, and then I'm rewarded with a beautiful grin that puts those dimples on full display.

"I'm fine, Scarlet," he says, giving me a little shake. "Thanks for checking on me."

I let out a soft laugh, which prompts a coughing fit. I lean over and try to force out the muck I can feel in my lungs. Nothing really comes, but eventually, the coughing calms down.

"They'll probably give you a few breathing treatments for that," he says calmly. "You'll be feeling better in no time."

I hope that's true. Better yet, maybe I'll wake up tomorrow, and this will all be a bad dream. Another nurse comes in, taking one look at Andrew and grinning like a Cheshire cat.

"Well, hello, my friend," she says lightly.

She pushes a wheelchair up to the side opposite Andrew, her gaze darting between the two of us.

"Scarlet Jackson?" she asks gently.

I nod.

"I'm Christine," she says. "I'm here to take you upstairs to your room."

"They've got you moving patients now?" Andrew asks as he steps back to give me room to swing my legs over the side of the bed.

"Not normally," she replies. "I'm just faster than those boys they've got helping us tonight, and I wanted the walk."

I step over to the wheelchair and sit down, letting Christine secure the footrests. She moves to push the wheelchair, and Andrew gets to me first.

"I've got it, Christine," he says, looking down at me. "Okay, if I drive?"

I smile and nod as Christine's gaze darts between us.

"Girlfriend?" she asks with a grin, wiggling her eyebrows at Andrew.

He laughs softly.

"I'm more like her emotional support animal," he replies. "Until another friend can be here."

"Well, let's go then," Christine says lightly, leading us out the door and into the hall.

It doesn't take long to get to the fourth floor, and I'm relieved to see there's no one in the other bed in the room. Christine helps me get situated in bed, securing the IV tubes and ensuring the call button is within my reach. I watch as she pulls a small tablet from a holder on the wall and starts poking around on it. Andrew steps over to my side and offers me his hand, which I immediately take. My hand practically disappears under his, but his touch and his presence are comforting in a way I'm not going to fight right now.

"Well, here's some good news," she begins. "No breaks in your arm or wrist. Looks like it's a severe sprain. We'll get you fitted with a better brace tomorrow when the doctor comes."

I heave a sigh of relief. That is good news. It doesn't feel like it's broken, but it is really sore. Having it confirmed that there's no break is great. Andrew squeezes my hand, and I look up to find him smiling down at me.

"First good news of the day," he says quietly. "And more to come."

My throat clogs with emotion over his optimism. Merry's going to love Andrew when they officially meet. He's just as reassuring and positive as she would be if she were standing here. And I need it now…because I definitely don't feel like everything is going to be okay. Not by a long shot.

Christine turns to me. "I'm going to go grab a pitcher of water for your room, but are you hungry?"

I shake my head. "Everything tastes like ash."

Another squeeze on my hand from Andrew.

"Eating a little something might help," he suggests. "Do you feel like trying?"

I throw my head back and close my eyes, considering whether I could even keep food down at this point. I feel disgusting. Dirty. Like it'll take a really, really long shower to get all the ash out of my hair and off my skin. I open my eyes and look at Christine.

"Can I take a shower?"

Christine pokes around on the tablet some more, then nods.

"Girl, I've got you," she says softly. "The admitting doctor put in your chart notes it's okay to take a shower. Let me go grab that drinking water, and then we'll get the shower going. With the IV and your arm, you're going to have to let me help you, but we can leave Andrew to order your snack while we're busy in the bathroom. Deal?"

I nod as Christine ducks out of the room, leaving us alone. I look up at him sternly.

"Please do not order me anything gross. That's all I ask."

He laughs softly.

"I was thinking along the lines of mashed potatoes," he says. "Or chocolate pudding. Tea."

I scrunch my nose at the mention of tea, and he laughs again.

"It really will help your throat," he says just as Christine comes back into the room with a plastic pitcher of ice water and a cup.

She hands them to Andrew, instructing him to pour, and leaves again. I watch as he pours some water into the cup and hands it to me. Without a word, he reaches out and gently removes the oxygen mask from my face.

"Thank you," I rasp.

I take a sip of water, and it feels like heaven as the cool liquid runs down my throat. A little moan escapes as I take another sip, and Christine chuckles as she comes back through the door with some things for the shower.

"I thought that might hit the spot," she says with a smile. "The shower will feel even better. You ready?"

She helps me out of bed, and we disappear into the bathroom as Christine instructs Andrew to order me some comfort food. I think she might just be my favorite person. We move slowly, but the shower does wonders.

Because my arm is wrapped and I have an IV, she has to wash my hair for me, but it's not long before I'm all dried off and back in bed with my hair in a towel. Christine whisks herself out of the room, mumbling something unintelligible. I already feel so much better. I still smell ash and soot in my nose, but it's not nearly as prominent, and my skin is clean. Unfortunately, it also means I'm wearing a hospital gown and a pair of bright yellow fuzzy socks with rubber treads on the soles. My walk from the bathroom to the bed was super glamorous.

"So, what did you order?" I ask Andrew quietly. "Are we still going to be friends when the food gets here?"

He laughs out loud, making me smile, the first real smile I've had since my whole life went up in flames. I mentally push away all the aftermath of it for now. I can deal with it tomorrow.

"I did right by you, Scarlet," he says with a grin. "Don't you worry."

Christine comes breezing back into the room and hands Andrew a set of scrubs. He looks at her quizzically.

"Go see Linda at the nurse's station," she instructs. "She'll show you to the staff showers, and you can clean up. I'll stay with Scarlet until you get back."

Andrew looks to me for approval, making me smile again. The way he cares for others is such a wonderful quality. I nod, and he moves toward the door. I feel my breath catch in my throat as he disappears from view, but I maintain a shaky kind of calm. Christine eyes me instinctively.

"You okay?"

I nod, forcing a swallow.

"You're staying?" I ask hoarsely, pulling the towel off my head and rubbing my hair with it to get it dry.

She nods, steps into the bathroom quickly, then comes out with another towel and begins drying my hair with it. I put mine aside.

"I've got this," she says. "It's too hard for you with that brace on your arm."

I manage a smile as she works the water out of my hair. I lift my good arm to comb through the damp strands, but I feel out of breath and have to take a break.

"It's perfectly normal to feel what you're feeling, Scarlet," she says, touching my shoulder lightly. "You've gone through some pretty serious trauma tonight. I can't imagine how scary it was. You were alone when it happened?"

I nod. "Asleep."

Christine nods solemnly.

"You may have a little fear and anxiety being alone for a while," she says. "And you may have a hard time sleeping. The doctor will assess you tomorrow, but don't be surprised if he recommends a few sessions with a therapist in addition to whatever medical treatments you'll need."

I give her a little smile as she works on drying my hair. I sit still, trying to quiet my mind while I experience the very strange sensation of someone else having to take care of me. It's hard to handle at first, because my fierce independence keeps wanting to take over, but I was getting pretty breathless trying to do it myself. Having my arm all bandaged up isn't helping either.

It doesn't take long for my short hair to dry, and Christine steps back and shakes her head.

"Well, there's a reason I'm not a hairdresser," she quips. "But at least it's dry."

I run my fingers through my hair, reveling in the clean feeling.

"It feels amazing," I rasp. "That's all that matters. Thank you so much."

She holds her hand out for a fist bump just as Andrew walks into the room, looking better than he should in a pair of blue scrubs. The sleeves are short, giving me a first look at his very well-muscled arms. No wonder I feel safe when I'm wrapped in those. Wow.

Christine grins. "Better?"

Andrew nods. "You're the best."

She nods and moves to the door, turning to smile at me.

"Just hit the call button if you need anything, Scarlet," she says kindly. "Try to keep the talking to a minimum until you see the doctor later today. You don't want to damage your voice, okay?"

I nod. "Thank you, Christine."

She disappears into the hallway, and I'm left alone with Andrew again. I can't help what happens next. I motion for him to come closer, and he immediately steps to the side of the bed and wraps his arms around me. I burrow into his side, holding back tears as I take the comfort he willingly gives. He moves a hand gently down my back.

"How are you doing?" he murmurs.

"Better now," I say, then feeling like an idiot for how desperate that sounds. "Especially since we don't smell like soot anymore."

He chuckles and gives me a little squeeze.

"That's the truth," he says. "I will never like that smell."

I stay attached to his side like a crustacean on a rock. I'm not in any frame of mind to deal with how far outside my normal this is. I'll find a way to snap back to it tomorrow. For now, I need him and it's enough that he's here.

"Do you smell like that at the end of every day?"

"No, it's not very common," he says quietly, his hand making hypnotic circles on my back. "Running into a burning building isn't an everyday occurrence."

I shake my head in disbelief. "I can't believe you do that for a living. It's so brave."

He scoffs, and I squeeze him a little.

"It *is*," I insist. "I wouldn't be here if it weren't for your bravery."

He pulls away a little and tilts my face up so I look at him.

"Completely selfish motives," he jokes. "You asked me on a coffee date. I don't want to miss out on the free cup of coffee."

I laugh, and it feels a thousand times better than it would on any other day. To be able to laugh after such an experience feels like a gift.

"You don't even drink coffee," I say with a smirk. "You're gonna make me buy that gross green tea."

He laughs again, and we fall into an easy silence. I lean into him fully, soaking up his warmth like a sponge. A knock on the door frame makes us both look up to find a hospital employee holding a tray.

"Snack time," he says with a little smile as he enters.

I clear my throat as if that'll get the soot taste out of my mouth. It doesn't. I watch as the man puts the tray down with all the flourish of a waiter in a five-star restaurant. I smile my thanks, then he turns on his heels and leaves us in peace.

Andrew reaches out and plucks the lid off the covered dish, revealing a grilled cheese sandwich, tomato soup, fries, and a little cup of chocolate pudding.

"You're so infuriatingly perfect," I say to Andrew as I shake my head in mock disgust. "You chose wisely."

He grins, and I get a lovely ticket to the dimple show.

"Eat up, Miss Scarlet," he drawls in a fake Southern accent.

I shake my head at the tray. "I can't eat all of this. You're going to have to help."

He plucks a fry off the tray, then pulls up a chair so he's right next to the bed. He helps me take off the oxygen mask so I can eat, then he sits. I pick up half of the grilled cheese, saying a silent prayer that one bite will bring my taste buds back to normal. I pick up the other half and hand it to Andrew, who begins to refuse until I give him a look...then he wisely takes it from me.

We eat in silence for a few minutes. It does help to get rid of some of the ash taste, but there's still a bit of it lingering. I turn the plate around so the fries are closer to Andrew, just in case he wants to steal more. The tomato soup is in a little mug, so I pop the lid off and take a sip. The hot liquid soothes my ravaged throat, and a little groan escapes me. Andrew chuckles, and I look at him curiously.

"Just basking in the glory of my great menu choices," he says.

I nod and take another sip. "Mad respect, dude. Thank you."

He steals another fry as I push the tray towards him.

"I'm full," I say, my voice still a little raspy. "Take whatever you want."

He shakes his head. "I was just eating to keep you company while you were eating."

I laugh softly. "That makes no sense."

He just smiles warmly, his eyes full of concern.

"Are you feeling a little better?"

I shrug. "I don't know how I feel right now. It seems to change every few seconds."

He leans forward, wrapping his warm, strong hand around mine. "Tell me."

I take a deep breath.

"Fear," I say first. "Anxiety. Denial. Loss. Devastation..."

My voice breaks up at the end, and Andrew quickly stands and wraps me in his arms again. I inhale him as I take another deep breath. His embrace is a balm to my frazzled nerves.

"Let's make a deal not to think about all that," he says gently. "Just for tonight. Okay?"

I nod against his chest, fisting my hands in his shirt.

"Deal," comes my hoarse reply.

I take another deep breath as his hand smooths over my hair and down my back. He's right. I don't know where I go from here, but it can wait until tomorrow. I take another deep breath, and a yawn escapes. Andrew pulls back enough to see my face.

"That yawn is encouraging," he says. "Are you feeling sleepy?"

I shake my head immediately. "No. I don't want to be alone."

He gently places the oxygen mask back on my face, then pulls the chair over again. He sits and laces our fingers together.

"I'm not going anywhere," he says gently. "I'll be right here while you sleep. You can keep hold of my hand. That way, you'll feel it if I try to sneak away for some of that gross green tea."

I look down at our laced fingers. This feels so good. Natural. As if sensing my inner turmoil, he squeezes our hands together.

"I'm here," he says warmly. "I've got you."

I press the control buttons on the remote to raise the head of the bed just a bit, because it seems to help the coughing. I lay back. Nope. I let go of his hand for a moment so I can adjust, turning on my side and facing him. I hold my hand up and wiggle my fingers, prompting a soft laugh from Andrew. He laces our fingers together again, and I give him a little squeeze.

"Talk to me," I say. "Please. Tell me something good."

Eating definitely helped my throat. I don't have to work so hard to be heard through the oxygen mask.

The bar on the side of the bed partially blocks our view of each other, and he wordlessly reaches up and pulls the bar down. I don't even think about worrying about the safety barrier being down. I have no doubt he'd catch me if I fell. He looks thoughtful for a moment, throwing his head back and pursing his lips.

"Okay, I'll tell you about a call we went on last week," he says. "Single mom, no one to help her with her hysterical five-year-old daughter... whose new kitten was stuck in the tree in their front yard."

I feel my eyes get as round as saucers. "No...poor thing."

He nods. "So we showed up, and I just kind of hit it off with this little kid. She was really sweet, and before I knew it, I was climbing that tree and making cute little pspsps noises at this little orange demon."

I smile, watching his face as he tells the story. Another yawn comes, making me cough a little bit.

"He looks right at me and climbs higher," Andrew continues. "So I climb higher. Then he climbs higher. So I go as high as I can go, but there are no more branches that can hold my weight. So I'm up in this tree, begging this kitten to come to me, silently praying that it doesn't fall…and that's exactly what it does, but I reach out and catch him."

"Oh my gosh!"

He nods.

"Little guy was so scared, so I pulled him close to my chest while I climbed down," Andrew explains. "As I was focusing on the climb down, the little demon got out of my hand and climbed inside my shirt…then latched onto my skin with his little kitten claws."

I stifle a giggle at his expression as he tells the story. I can only imagine him up in a tree with a scared kitten inside his shirt.

"I've never climbed out of a tree so fast in my whole life," he says with a laugh. "When I went to pull him out, his claw went right through my nipple."

I gasp and can't help the laugh that bubbles out of me.

"So painful," he says, letting out another laugh. "I finally got the little murder muffin out of my shirt, got down on one knee, and handed it to the little girl. She was so happy she gave me a little kiss on my cheek. Suddenly, I forgot all about my clawed-up chest. I felt like Superman."

I manage a tired smile, and another yawn escapes me. I blink at him tiredly, squeezing his hand.

"You *are* Superman," I murmur, drifting off to sleep.

Chapter 7

Scarlet

I wake up to an incessant beeping that's piercing my brain. I feel something hairy on my hand and open my eyes to find a sleeping Andrew using our still-clasped hands as a pillow. His lips are parted softly in sleep, and I feel a twinge of guilt when I notice the black eye blooming. Ouch. He got that black eye rescuing me. Saving my life.

I take a moment just to look at him. Except for the black eye, he still looks perfect, even after pulling me from a burning warehouse in the middle of the night and staying up with me in the hospital. I don't want to move and wake him up, but I am one thousand percent positive I don't look perfect this morning. It doesn't matter, though. I have a full day of very un-fun things ahead of me, including phone calls to Brad, Kayla, and Sarah to tell them we're all out of the running this year. Then I have to call Merry. Hopefully, she can come and stay with me so I can let poor Andrew off the hook. Although the thought of letting him go makes me sad in ways I'm not prepared to think about.

"What are you looking so sad about?" Andrew's voice wakes me from my spiraling thoughts.

I blink back my surprise. I hadn't even noticed his eyes had opened. I was so lost in thought. I don't have the energy to try to force a smile, and he'd see through it anyway.

"Life," I say vaguely. "And all the unpleasant tasks it brings me today."

He sits up and stretches his back, not letting go of my hand. Brown eyes full of concern settle on me.

"We'll work it all out," he says softly. "How are you feeling this morning?"

"Okay, I guess."

He watches me curiously, waiting to see if I'll offer more detail. I cave.

"My head hurts," I say, still hoarse but sounding better than last night. "Wrist aches. Still hurts to breathe. Basically, I'm still a mess... and I'm not looking forward to making the phone calls I have to make this morning."

He looks thoughtful for a moment.

"Is there anything I can do to help?"

I consider, then shake my head.

"You've done plenty already," I reply. "You saved my life last night. How did you even know the warehouse was on fire? Don't tell me you just happened to be walking by at two AM and noticed the flames."

He looks a bit chagrined as he considers his reply, and now I'm curious.

"I was...watching over you," he confesses. "It really bothered me that you were there all by yourself in such a sketchy neighborhood. When I was on shift, I'd go sit up on this tiny little balcony we have at the fire station. I could see the roof, part of the side of the warehouse, and even the top of the door if I stood in the right spot. When I didn't have anything to do, I'd go sit up there with a book. It made me feel better about things to be up there. And, for some reason, I just couldn't settle down last night."

My eyes drift over his face as I take in his words. The words of my friend. I think I can call him that now. He had my back even when I tried to push him away. He watched over me and pulled me to safety when I needed it most.

"Andrew," I whisper in a voice thick with emotion. "I think you might just be the kindest human being I've ever met in my whole life."

He laughs softly and squeezes my hand.

"I'm not sure I deserve all that," he says quietly. "I'm just glad I was there."

I look up at the clock on the wall. It's just after eight in the morning, and it's safe to call Merry without waking her up. I look back at Andrew.

"It's time for me to call Merry and tell her what happened," I explain, pushing the button on the bed controls so I can sit up. "You may hear a little hysteria on the other end, but please don't be alarmed."

He laughs and nods. "The feral one. I remember her."

I pull the rolling table close enough so I can reach the phone and dial Merry's number on speaker. I say a silent prayer in the hope that she picks up a call from an unknown number, and it works.

"Hello?" Merry's voice sounds on the other end of the line.

"Hey, Mer," I say calmly. "I have to tell you something, and I need you to not freak out."

Andrew waits expectantly, squeezing my hand in encouragement.

"Girl, that is not the way to get me to not freak out," Merry replies. "That is exactly the way to get me to freak out. What's happened?"

And so I tell her the whole story, all while having to tell her to stop freaking out until it's all over and she knows everything. I give her the name of the hospital and all the information she needs to find me, then hang up. I feel like I've just gone a round with Mike Tyson, and that was only just telling Merry. I don't even want to think about what it'll be like to deal with Marina and Ashley. Or my mom.

I look at Andrew.

"I'm sorry you're about to witness Merry in full-out panic mode," I tell him. "She'll be here in about twenty minutes, and she is not happy with me."

Andrew nods. "She's the friend who knew you were living in the warehouse?"

I nod. "Knew and disapproved. Then I doubled down by asking her to keep it a secret from our other friends."

He makes a face, and I laugh softly.

"When she gets here, please feel free to make any excuses you need to in order to get away," I say, already regretting the moment he leaves. "She's the best, but she's going to be a lot."

He focuses those gorgeous eyes on me.

"I will be here as long as you need me to be here," he says gently. "Do we need to come up with a code word? Then you can say it if you need me to give her a tranquilizer."

I laugh out loud, which prompts a coughing fit.

"Whatever happens, I've brought this on myself," I tell him. "I'm the one who created this mess, so I'll listen. I'll apologize. I'll apologize again. And then I'll try to figure out how to make this up to everyone."

He gives me a confused look.

"Make it up to everyone? You didn't do this on purpose."

"No, I know that, I just..."

I drift off, not sure what I want to say.

"Do you?" Andrew asks. "I'm not sure about that."

I smirk at him, but he holds my gaze.

"You don't have to put the whole world on your shoulders, Scarlet."

Something in his words hits home. I do that. I do put the whole world on my shoulders. I pride myself on never needing help, and I have the feeling that life is about to humble me...big time.

"How do you know that about me?" I ask.

I've never met anyone who seemed to understand me so quickly.

The corners of his mouth twitch into a little smile.

"I told you before…you remind me of myself. Of the me I was before, and the me I am now."

I sit back, trying to let my thoughts play out in my head. I'm used to setting a goal and just running towards it at full speed. If something gets in my way, I jump over it or go around it. I never stop. I just go, go, go all the time. Slowing down, asking for, or needing help…that's not in my wheelhouse. I don't know how to do that. I realize now that the fire has done something that will have repercussions for a long time. It wiped out my goal. It destroyed my project, along with all the supplies and tools I needed to accomplish that goal. None of it exists anymore. I have to rethink everything.

"What are you thinking with that very serious expression on your face?" he asks, dipping his head at an angle that prompts me to look at him.

I shake my head. "I guess I'm just wondering what I do now," I say honestly. "Once I get out of the hospital, I need to figure out where to go from here. My project is gone. There's no hope of me winning the contest now. What do I do? Other than go bed shopping…"

I let out a bitter laugh as Andrew regards me soberly.

"I hate to hear you say there's no hope," he says, rubbing a thumb over the back of my hand. "Are you sure? Maybe we can find a way."

I shake my head. "Assuming the warehouse is a total loss, that means my laptop is gone," I say firmly. "My cutting machine. All my supplies. Even if I had the budget to replace all the equipment and supplies, which I don't, I have no place to create the spaces now. It's done. It's over."

A muscle ticks in his jaw as he gets lost in thought while I stare blankly at our joined hands, wondering how my life has come to this.

I know the inevitable realities that are lurking in the wings now. I just don't want to admit it's happening. So I keep staring at our hands, trying to work out a way for this to not be as bad as I know it is.

I'm not sure how long I was lost in thought, but it feels like seconds before I hear Merry's distinct voice down the hall.

"...I don't know any more than that, I'm just telling you what I do know, I'll—"

She stops in the doorway to my room with tear-filled eyes, her gaze landing on me in relief. I feel my lower lip quiver when I see her. I'm so happy to see my friend, whose support I desperately need right now.

"I found her," she says into her phone quickly. "We'll talk more when you get here...just get here."

She hangs up and launches herself at me, wrapping her arms around me as a low sob escapes her throat. It's all I need for my own tears to start up again. I wrap my arms around my friend and let the tears come.

"Thank goodness," she whispers through her tears, squeezing me hard. "You're okay, Scarlet."

I open my eyes briefly and see Andrew watching our embrace carefully. I smile at him to let him know I'm all right as Merry loosens her grip on me and lets me go. She stands back to look me over.

"You're really okay?" she asks. "What's the oxygen mask for? Why is your wrist wrapped up like that?"

I feel Andrew's hand on mine again, and I grip it tightly. Merry's eyes dart over to him, then our joined hands, back to him again...and her jaw hits the floor.

"Whoa!" she says, pointing a finger at Andrew. "Black Leather Jacket!"

Andrew's mouth tightens as he suppresses a laugh, and he lets go of me to extend his hand to her.

"Andrew, actually," he says.

Merry extends her hand in slow motion, shaking Andrew's hand slowly as her gaze drifts over to me. Her eyes are huge, and I steady myself for a whirlwind of questions.

"Is he the one who saved you?" she asks excitedly. "Are you even freaking kidding me right now? How did this happen? I—"

I hold my hand up, and Merry stops mid-sentence, pulling her hand from Andrew's and raising her eyebrows at me in question.

"Not kidding. Yes, he saved me...because he's secretly Superman and was watching over me," I say as I smile at Andrew. "Turns out he's a fireman, and he works at the fire station right down the street from the warehouse."

Andrew clears his throat. "Why don't I go see if I can round you up some of that gross black coffee while you and Merry catch up," he offers. "Will you be okay?"

Anxiety flutters through my heart and all around my stomach at the mere thought of Andrew leaving the room, and I know I'm going to have to find a way to come to grips with this. Very soon. It's one thing for him to make a joke about being my emotional support animal and another thing altogether if it's really true, and I can't let him go without freaking out.

I nod at him and reach for Merry before he even gets to the door. Merry grabs my hand and gives me a worried look.

"I can't seem to be without people right now," I say shakily. "I start to panic whenever someone tries to leave me alone. I get...scared."

Merry nods and wraps her arms around me.

"Of course you are," she says gently. "I can't even imagine what it was like to be in that warehouse while it was—"

Her voice breaks up, and she squeezes me harder.

"We don't even need to talk about that right now," she says. "We just need to get you well. And feeling safe."

Merry lets me go and stands back up, and I realize she's wearing a backpack. I point to it.

"What's that for?"

She shrugs out of it, and it hits the floor with a loud thud.

"I came to camp, girl," she says with a wink. "My cousin is working at Nonno's for me. I'm all yours."

A lump forms in my throat. Of course, she's mine. And I'm so lucky to have her and Marina and Ashley. My three ride-or-die girlfriends would do anything for me. I know I always try to not need anyone and control everything myself, but it's a comfort to have them in my life now...when I'm very likely going to need some actual help.

Merry nods at my arm. "So, what's up with your paw, tiger?"

I laugh, which is exactly what she was trying to make me do. Merry's sense of empathy and humor is a treasure to everyone who loves her. We don't call her the unicorn of the group for nothing. She brightens any room she's in.

"It's just a bad sprain," I say. "It's sore more than anything else. They said the doctor will give me instructions when he gets here."

Merry nods, then taps her nose. "And the oxygen?"

I shrug. "I got a chest x-ray last night and some other tests. I'm sure the doctor will talk to me about it. I keep coughing, which Andrew says is the smoke inhalation from the fire."

She sits on the edge of the bed.

"Yeah, about him," she murmurs as Andrew re-enters the room. "Wow, girl."

"Everything okay?" Andrew says as he heads over to the side of the bed with his hands full.

I mentally thank a higher power for sending Andrew into the room at just the right moment. I'm not ready to answer questions about him yet. He sets a cup of black coffee on my tray table while making a face at me, then offers Merry a cup.

"I wasn't sure if you're the gross black coffee type as well, so I opted for hot cocoa," he says, taking a seat in the chair that he slept in. Guilty twinges tug at my heart for that.

"Thanks," Merry says, taking the cup with a grin. "Good guess."

I can tell by the look in her eyes that Merry is absolutely bursting with questions for me, which she'd rather not ask in front of Andrew. I also realize that I need to let the poor guy go home and get some real sleep. I take a sip of my coffee, audibly sighing as the hot liquid goes down my throat.

"Thank you so much," I say to him. "That really hits the spot."

He laughs softly. "Ew, but my pleasure."

I smile at him, hating what I have to say but knowing I have to say it.

"If you want to go home and get some sleep, Merry can stay with me."

His beautiful brown eyes rove over my face, assessing.

"And you'll be okay?"

I force a smile.

"Merry's got me," I reply. "And I'll feel so much better about you staying with me all night if I let you go and get some rest. I've monopolized you enough."

The muscle in his jaw feathers while he considers my words.

"Will it be okay if I come and check on you later this evening?"

There is no question as to whether it'll be okay. Yes. It'll always be yes. But something in Andrew's expression tells me he's not sure whether I'll want to snap back into a world where I'm holding him at arm's length. I smile and nod at him.

"I would love that," I reply. "Text me—Oh. Never mind."

Merry nods. "Your cell phone's gone, remember? We'll fix that."

Andrew stands and wraps me in a hug. I bury my face in his chest, not even caring that it'll prompt another dozen questions from Merry when we're alone.

"She was unconscious when I picked her up," he explains to Merry. "She wasn't able to grab anything."

I don't want to, but I loosen my hold on Andrew and turn to Merry. "Can you give him your cell phone number?"

She nods, and Andrew hands over his phone. She types in her info and hands it back to him. He looks at the new contact info.

"Thanks, Merry," he says, then looks down at me. "I don't really want to let you go, but I know you're in the best hands possible."

I laugh softly. "You won't feel that way once you climb into your own bed."

He shakes his head. "I'll be back around two. Let me know if you want me to bring anything."

I nod, then grab him just as he steps away. Immediately, his arms wrap around me again.

"Just one more hug," I mumble into his shirt as a chuckle echoes through his body.

I hold on as long as I feel I can before forcing myself to let him go. I force a smile onto my face as I look up at him.

"Get some rest," I say quietly. "You've more than earned it."

He nods, then reaches out to cup the side of my face with his palm. The gesture, not to mention the tenderness in his eyes, is more than enough to make me get all swoony. My heart feels like it's doing backflips in my ribs.

"I'll be back soon," he says. "I might even bring you some more of that gross black coffee."

I laugh, then reach up to brush my fingers lightly across the bruise around his eye.

"Put some more ice on that," I say in a wobbly voice. "And thank you for saving me."

Andrew's expression softens, and I feel tears threaten the backs of my eyes.

"Okay, Scarlet," Merry says softly, wrapping an arm around my shoulders and giving me a comforting squeeze. "Let's let the hotness take a nap, all right?"

Andrew blinks back his surprise and laughs. "What?"

I put a hand over my face and shake my head.

"No, don't ask her," I say through my mortification. "Just go while you can."

Merry shakes me a little, and I laugh out loud. Andrew looks hesitant as he heads toward the door, turning just before he steps into the hall and waving at me. I wave back and watch him leave, then look back over at Merry.

"Thanks for being here, Mer."

I'm rewarded with a hug...and silence. No judgment. No "I told you so". Just love. We sit together for just over an hour. First, she stays by my side, as I call Brad, Sarah, and Kayla. At Merry's suggestion, I did a group video chat, so I didn't have to tell the story three times. All three of my friends were alarmed at first but ultimately just glad I was okay.

None of them wanted to continue pursuing the contest, and I can't say I blame them. We all lost everything, and we were helping each other because we all had limited budgets. None of us have money growing out of our ears. They all ask if they can come visit me in the hospital, but I'm not up for all the chaos that many visitors would bring. I feel a little fragile right now, so we make arrangements to meet up for lunch in a few weeks, and that's that.

Merry gives me another hug when the call is over, which I accept gratefully. I see a flash of Marina's red hair as I'm looking over Merry's shoulder and let out a choked sob as she and Ashley burst into the room.

Ashley gasps. "Are you okay?"

I open my mouth to speak, but I'm cut off by Marina's arms wrapping me in a fierce hug. Emotion clogs my throat as Ashley comes in from the other side with a hug, and I let out another sob.

"I'm okay, guys," I say in a wobbly voice. "Really. I'm just so glad to see you."

They pull away, and Merry grabs another chair from the corner so Ashley has a place to sit. Marina takes the chair Andrew was in, and Merry just climbs onto the bed with me like she does this kind of thing every day. Ashley dabs at her eyes with a tissue as we all settle in.

"So what on earth happened?" Marina asks, eyes wide.

I look at Merry to try to gauge how much she told them.

She shrugs. "It wasn't my story to tell, so start from the top."

I force down a swallow and nod, taking a deep breath.

"First of all, I owe you guys an apology," I begin softly, voice wobbling a bit. "Especially Merry. I put her in a tough spot."

Merry reaches over and squeezes my hand as Marina and Ashley look from one of us to the other in confusion. So I explain. I air out all my dirty laundry to my friends. And then I apologize one more time.

"Hey," Marina says softly as she leans forward and squeezes my arm. "I'm just glad you're all right. That's the most important thing. Everything else is fixable. Starting with this."

Marina pulls a small box out of her bag and hands it to me. It's a new cell phone. I look at her with huge eyes.

"Merry said you lost everything," Marina explains. "I assumed that meant your phone as well, so we stopped on the way."

"Marina—"

Marina points a finger at me.

"Before you rant on about how I shouldn't have spent the money, I got that from your cell provider. They said if you have insurance, they can retroactively set this one up as your replacement. All you have to do is go in there and give them your account information. See? Everything else is fixable."

I scoff. "That's what Andrew says."

Merry perks up. "Yeah, wait 'til you guys see him."

She lets out a low whistle, prompting big grins from Marina and Ashley as I shake my head.

"No, it's not like that," I say quickly.

Merry frowns. "I thought we were done with lying. Hmm?"

I open my mouth to object, but Merry's not done. She looks at Ashley and Marina, her hands making gestures as she talks.

"He is gorgeous," she blurts. "Like...drop dead. And he definitely has feelings for her."

I close my eyes in defeat. When Merry starts talking with her hands, there's no point. You have to just let her go until she runs out of steam.

"He does?" Ashley chimes in.

Merry nods. "He has the most beautiful brown eyes I've ever seen on a man, and when he looks at Scarlet with them...wow. He's intense."

I actually feel heat crawling up my neck as Merry describes him. It's one thing to feel these things are true and keep them inside, but when your friend starts openly pointing them out...well, they're harder to keep inside. Andrew does give me all the feels. There's no point in denying it. All eyes turn to me, and I can't help the smile that spreads across my face.

"He is the sweetest guy I've ever met," I say softly. "And yes, before you guys start grilling me, I like him. A lot. But things are complicated right now, and it's probably not smart to—"

Marina holds up her hand to silence me, and it works. My eyebrows shoot up in surprise.

"As much as I'd like to argue with you about the ridiculous notion that the sweet, kind, drop-dead gorgeous fireman has come into your life at the wrong time," Marina says with an obvious roll of her eyes, "the first priority here is you. What does the doctor say?"

I shake my head. "Hasn't been here yet. But I feel better today than I did last night, for sure. Mostly."

Ashley leans forward. "Mostly?"

"I have a cough," I explain slowly. "Andrew says that's the smoke inhalation. But I keep feeling this overwhelming sense of fear."

Merry nudges me. "Of course you do."

Marina nods. "It's understandable. I can't imagine how scary it must have been, Scarlet. How terrifying."

I feel a lump start to form in my throat as a flash of memory hits me. The sight of the warehouse on fire as I woke up being carried over Andrew's shoulder. I shiver a little.

"I don't understand what's wrong with me," I confess. "It's not logical. Last night, I literally felt like the fire was going to come through the wall of the emergency room."

"Oh, honey," Marina says with a sigh. "Definitely tell the doctor this is happening. I think this might be some fallout from the fire. Waking up like that had to be terrifying. It makes sense that it made an emotional impact on you."

I nod my reply. I'd planned on sharing everything with the doctor, anyway. I'm one of those people who walks into the doctor's office with a list of questions to ask so I don't forget anything. I make a mental note to write those down before too long.

"Were they able to save anything at all," Ashley asks. "Or did everything burn?"

I manage a tight smile. "When I woke up, the fire was huge. I have to assume it's all gone. No bed. No laptop. No cutting machine or supplies," I hold up my new cell phone and look at Marina. "Thank you for this. I'll pay you back as soon as I can do the insurance claim."

Marina nods with a smile.

Merry nudges me again. "I'm so sorry."

"Thanks, Mer," I say softly. "I'm sure the tears will be coming for a while, and I'll mourn it all several times over, but I'm so grateful I'm alive it feels wrong to dwell on losing the contest."

Ashley frowns. "You didn't lose. You lost everything in a fire, but the Home Network people don't know that."

Marina nods. "And besides, there are no rules for this kind of thing. You're allowed to be sad that you lost your whole project."

"Not just my project," I say with quiet emphasis. "Everything I needed to make this happen."

"No, you didn't," Merry argues, then she reaches up and thumps me on the forehead. "You still have all that creative genius in that amazing brain of yours."

I choke out a laugh.

"I appreciate the vote of confidence, but my whole life is a dumpster fire right now. Tell me how I come back from this."

Merry looks at me as if I've just issued a challenge. She raises her chin in my direction.

"Even a dumpster fire can be a good thing," she says defiantly. "The strongest steel is forged in the fire of a dumpster."

I look at Marina and Ashley, who are both looking at the floor and trying not to laugh. It does absolutely no good because as soon as I see their faces, I start to smirk, and then I burst into laughter. They quickly follow, and Merry begins to giggle. The four of us are rolling in hysterics in no time, with me coughing as much as laughing. I pull Merry over to me for a hug.

"I love you so much, dude," I say, wiping a tear off my cheek.

I really needed that laugh.

Marina composes herself, then narrows her gaze on me.

"All right, I'm not buying it. Let's talk hypothetically for a minute. If the doctor discharged you from the hospital today," she says, "and you had infinite funds in your budget…would you still give up?"

"I'm not giving up," I argue. "I'm facing facts. Everything is gone, and I have to use what savings I have to buy a new bed and replace my laptop and my cutting machine. It's time to stop chasing this stupid contest and find a job. I can't do this anymore. I'm out."

Chapter 8

Scarlet

"I don't believe that for a second," Ashley says incredulously. "If you had the money, those words would never have escaped your lips. You'd be barking orders at us to take you to the paint store as soon as you're discharged."

I laugh out loud at that. She's right. I would have. Something about this has knocked the wind out of my sails. I've lost my fight. I don't know why.

"The fact of the matter is…I don't have the money," I say plainly. "The money I've saved will need to go towards replacing my bed, then it'll have to sustain me until I can find a full-time job."

Merry's eyes go round as saucers.

"A job?"

I smirk at Merry. I've been incredibly privileged to be able to pursue my passion and live rent-free with my mom, and that's only because she's the absolute best. It's time for me to pull my weight, just like most people do every day.

"I was thinking I'd start applying at some interior design firms," I share. "I have a small list of past clients who will give me recommendations, and I can always share the footage of my corbel bookshelves that made it into the Home Network's TV special that time. But I'd even take a spot as a receptionist at a design firm if it meant a steady paycheck at this point. I can't afford to pinch pennies anymore."

Merry squints at me.

"Who are you, and what have you done with our friend Scarlet?"

I shrug. "Someone that life finally took down a peg or two. Still the same friend, just more…realistic."

Ashley frowns. "If I could smuggle Chinese food in here right now, I'd call an emergency conclave on your behalf. This just doesn't sound like you."

I slide open the cell phone box and go about setting up my new cell phone. Maybe they have a point, but I don't want to think about it right now. It feels like a time to carry on and push forward, just not toward the contest I've spent the better part of my adult life pursuing. And for what? I barely escaped with my life last night because I was so focused on winning.

It's time to find my new normal. I just have no idea what it's supposed to look like.

***

Andrew

I hear the knock on my apartment door just as I get out of the shower, so I throw a towel around my waist and pad to the front door. I see Jake through the peephole, so I open it and let him in. I keep back so that sweet little Miss Kelly across the way can't sneak a peek at me. It happened last summer, and since our bathrooms share a common wall, she has a habit of knocking on my door to borrow sugar… salt… you name it, any time she hears my shower running. Even though she's about eighty years old, it's a little sus.

Jake steps in with a shake of his head, gesturing at my bare chest.

"Put some clothes on and stop making your elders feel bad," he grumbles.

I laugh as I head back to my bedroom.

"Make yourself at home, grandpa!" I yell, shutting the door so I can towel off and dress.

I finish drying off, then slip on a pair of jeans and a t-shirt before heading back out to the living room to see what Jake's visit is all about. He's sitting on my couch with a diet soda in his hand. There's another one on the coffee table for me.

Hmm.

So it's a heart-to-heart, then. I'm betting it's something to do with Scarlet seeming so attached to me right after I pulled her from the warehouse.

"What are we talking about today, boss?" I say with a grin as I flop on the other end of the couch and grab my soda off the table.

Jake sits back against the back of the couch and dips a chin at me.

"How's the eye?"

I shrug. "It's fine. I've had black eyes before. I'll probably have more again. The doctor cleared me, right?"

Jake nods. "Yep. Just making sure you're feeling all right. I also heard you spent the night at the hospital with the girl."

There it is. Now I get it. I nod.

"She was showing classic signs of PTSD, Jake," I begin calmly. "You know it causes more stress when they're left all alone, which is quite possible in a busy hospital."

Jake nods and takes another swig of his soda.

"Why'd it have to be you?"

I tilt my head at him. "Because I know her," I say incredulously. "She's a friend. Might have been more than that if we'd gotten to have our coffee date in a month, but I'm not sure that's gonna happen now."

He stays quiet to let me continue.

"What if I'm suddenly a reminder of that horrible night for her...and she can't see me without remembering it?"

Jake chuffs. "That would suck for you."

"Yep," I say simply. "I like her, Jake. Nothing wrong with that. I'm not breaking any fire department rules. I knew her before the fire. We had plans before the fire."

Jake gives a quick nod. "I know you did, kid. I just wanted to know where your head was at."

I hold up my soda. "Screwed on straight like always," I joke.

Jake laughs and pulls a small gift bag out from the other side of the coffee table, handing it to me.

"Got you something."

I set my drink down and take the bag. I reach inside and pull out something soft that's wrapped in tissue paper. I unwrap it and hold up a black t-shirt that says "You should see the other guy" on it. I bust out laughing.

"That's awesome, Jake. Thank you."

Jake laughs as well. "Figured you could use something interesting to explain that shiner."

I pull off my t-shirt and slip this one on.

"I love it so much I'm gonna wear it when I visit Scarlet later," I say. "It'll make her laugh."

"How's she doing?" Jake asks with genuine interest.

I shake my head.

"Not sure, if I'm being honest," I say quietly. "She was a thousand percent latched onto me right after I pulled her from the warehouse. Over time, she lightened up. She seemed okay when I left, but she's been through serious trauma. Psychologically, she might be dealing with this long after her body has healed."

Jake considers my words, then claps me on the back.

"Well, we both know about that."

I nod soberly. "Occupational hazard."

Jake takes another sip of his soda.

"Well, let me know if I can help in any way," he says. "I'm happy to."

I level my gaze at him. "Actually, I might need help. I have an idea. I'm just not sure if it's necessary at this point."

Jake reaches over with his bottle, and we clink the bottle necks together in a sort of belated cheers.

"I'll be at the ready," he says, offering me a half smile.

"Thanks, man," I mumble.

Jake sighs loudly.

"I'm just glad to have you back at the station tonight. Leonard and Todd are about to drive me insane."

***

An hour later, I'm walking through the halls of the hospital and making my way to Scarlet's room. I silently hope the doctor has been here and she'll have news to share. I also hope her feral friend is still with her. The idea of Scarlet being left alone in her current state of mind...well, I don't want that for her. As I round the corner and step into the doorway of her room, I see my fears are completely unfounded. The feral one is sitting on the bed with Scarlet, and now there are two more friends as well. All eyes turn to me, and I suddenly feel like I'm under a microscope. My eyes dart nervously to Scarlet's.

"Hi."

She smiles. "Hi."

I hesitate at the door. Can they smell fear? These women look pretty serious. As if reading my mind, Scarlet beckons me with her hand.

"Come in, they don't bite."

I step into the room, moving to Scarlet's left. As I approach the bedside, she leans over and reaches for me. I pull her into a hug, relishing the way her arms feel when they slide around my waist. I'm glad to see her smiling and talking with friends. I plop the teddy bear I'd been holding into her lap, and her whole face lights up. The bear is wearing a fireman's uniform. We give them to kids at special events, but I snagged one for Scarlet earlier. She runs a dainty hand over the bear and smiles up at me.

"This is the best thing ever," she says, making my whole day. "Andrew, these are my best friends. Marina, Ashley, and you already know Merry."

I nod at Merry and shake Marina and Ashley's hands. Marina looks familiar, but I can't place where I've seen her before.

I gesture at the bear.

"I thought you could use a backup emotional support animal for those times when I can't be there."

She grins up at me. "Thanks, Superman."

I hold my hands up. "Not a superhero at all, I promise. But it looks like you're feeling a little better?"

She nods, then proceeds to bring me up to speed. The doctor has been to see her. She has some minor concerns about the smoke inhalation and wants her to stay one more night just to be safe. She'll be on regular oxygen, so there's no more mask on her face. Just the clear tubing under her nose. Her arm will heal naturally. She just has to keep it in a brace for six weeks and limit use. And the doctor arranged an appointment with a therapist for Scarlet's anxiety. Since she doesn't have a bed and her mom is still blissfully unaware on a cruise, Scarlet will be staying with Ashley at her apartment for a while. All good news.

The corner of my mouth twitches up in a half smile.

"I told you more good news was coming."

She smiles. "You sure did."

I notice the phone in her hand. "Hey, you replaced your phone. More good news."

Scarlet nods at Marina. "More like I have the best friends in the universe. Marina stopped by and picked it up on her way here."

I look at Marina. "What a good friend," I say, still unable to place where I've seen her before.

"Hey, Andrew," Merry says from the other side of the bed. "Are you staying for lunch? We haven't eaten yet."

I look at my watch. It's past two now, so I'd say it's a safe bet. I don't have to be at the fire station until later this evening. I nod at her, and she wiggles her eyebrows at me.

"Do you like Italian?"

"Shouldn't we ask him if he even wants to have lunch with the whole group? We can be a lot," Marina asks.

Ashley gasps. "That's a great idea!"

Merry winks at her. "Right? He's totally breadstick-worthy."

I do a double take as Scarlet scrubs a hand down her face in embarrassment.

"I'm sorry," I say, trying not to laugh. "I'm what?"

"Please ignore them," Scarlet pleads.

"Oh, but it's okay when you're accusing me and Rick of having a moment and embarrassing me to death in front of him?" Ashley teases.

Scarlet gasps. "You *were* having a moment…and the proof is right there on your left ring finger, dude."

"I recommend the spaghetti," Marina chimes in.

I feel like there are thirty-seven different conversations going on at the same time, and I'm part of all of them. What is even happening right now? I decide to focus on the original topic and nod at Merry.

"Actually, that sounds really good," I say, still wondering what *breadstick-worthy* means.

Merry types away at her phone and then looks up at all of us.

"Order in! It'll be here in thirty minutes."

Scarlet wiggles excitedly in the bed.

"You're the best, Mer," she says excitedly. "Nonno's is exactly what I need."

"Oh, that little Italian bistro over on North Street?" I ask. "I love their food."

"That's my Nonno's place," Merry says, beaming with pride.

"Nonno is Italian for grandfather," Marina leans forward to explain.

"Wow, that's my favorite place to get Italian," I say with a huge grin. "And the cookies are even better."

Merry's expression sobers. "The cookies? At Nonno's? You like them?"

All of a sudden, I have a feeling my answer is going to make or break Merry's whole day. Marina, Ashley, and Scarlet all watch me with expectantly, and I decide the only way out is with the truth.

"Uh...yeah," I reply. "Those little Italian wedding cookie things? They're covered in powdered sugar...so good."

Merry throws her arms in the air, yelling, "He's a keeper!"

I can't help it, I laugh out loud. Poor Scarlet looks like she wants to crawl inside the mattress on the bed and disappear. Marina and Ashley are laughing as well, and I slip my arm around Scarlet.

"Hey," I murmur close to her ear. "It's okay. I can take it. It's all in good fun."

Scarlet moves her hand enough so she can look up at me with one eye. She's blushing, and it's so adorable.

"If you only knew," she says, then lets out the cutest giggle.

I squeeze her around the shoulders again.

"While we wait for lunch," Ashley leads, propping her feet up on Scarlet's bed. "Maybe you can help us talk some sense into Scarlet."

I frown down at Scarlet. "What's this?"

She rolls her eyes. "They think I should stay in the contest," she explains. "But even if I had unlimited funds, I still don't have two rooms to design and decorate. I've already done every room at my mom's house. I did Ashley & Marina's apartment. Marina's offices. There's no space to decorate and no time to find a space. It's done."

I glance around at Scarlet's friends, then back at Scarlet.

"We can help you find a place if you still want to do it," I say. "Is that all that's holding you back?"

She shakes her head. "I also do not have unlimited funds, and I am not going to leech off my friends."

Marina throws Scarlet a pouty look, and it hits me like a lightning bolt. I snap my fingers and point at her.

"You're the mermaid!"

Marina laughs. "I was wondering when you were going to get it," she tells me. "You kept looking at me like you've seen me before."

I nod excitedly. "That was such a cool video of you singing and the three sailors—"

I stop abruptly as I look from Ashley to Merry to Scarlet. They're all grinning.

"Were you guys the sailors?" I ask excitedly.

Scarlet laughs softly. "Guilty."

"Wow, that's amazing if you think about it," I say, gleaming at Scarlet. "All that time ago when I was watching it on the news…I never knew I'd be pulling one of those sailors out of a warehouse fire someday."

Scarlet beams up at me. "And I never knew Superman was watching me."

I nod. "I never knew one of those sailors was going to be the sole focus of my attention every time she walked into my coffee house and ordered a gross black coffee."

Scarlet laughs again, and it's almost musical. I can't believe she was a small part of a viral video that had the city spellbound about a year and a half ago. There was a huge traffic jam on the Golden Gate Bridge. I don't remember why, but Marina was dressed as a mermaid, and the other friends were in sailor suits. They were singing to pass the time, not knowing The Royal Rebels were on their tour bus in the very same traffic jam. Their lead singer actually got out of the bus and sang with them, and the video went viral. Suddenly, the whole city wanted to know who that mermaid was. It was a big deal at the time. I make a mental note to look at some YouTube videos of it later so I can see Scarlet in that sailor suit.

I pull my cell phone out of my pocket and hand it to her.

"Can I ask you to put your number in there, or are you going to give me a hard time again?"

She smirks at me and takes my phone.

"Part of me wants to give you a hard time just because you said that," she says, but I watch her type her information into my contacts. "But you still get a pass for saving my life."

She hands my phone back to me, and I smile back at her. "Thanks."

"Whoa!" Merry exclaims, prompting all of us to look over at her.

She's riveted by something on her phone.

"What is it, Mer?" Marina asks.

Merry looks at me and Scarlet with a slow smile. "You guys are famous."

"What?" Scarlet and I reply in unison.

Merry holds up her phone and shows us a photo someone took of us when Scarlet was on the stretcher in the alley. In the photo, she's clutching onto me, face crumpled in grief, and my arms are wrapped around her. Both our faces are smudged with ash, illuminated by the glow of the fire coming from the warehouse. Just above the photo, the headline reads:

THE PHOENIX AND THE FIREMAN

I take Merry's phone when she offers it to me, and I sit on the edge of the bed so we can read it together. The article talks about the neighborhood and all the troubles it's seen lately, as well as giving a golden review of the fire department...which, of course, I totally agree with. The picture is stirring. The photographer managed to capture Scarlet's grief and terror while providing a touching commentary on the role first responders play in the community. I look down at Scarlet to see how she feels about it, and she smiles up at me.

"Thank you," she says simply, leaning into my side.

I frown slightly as I wrap an arm around her. "For what?"

She points to the picture. "For running to my rescue."

I squeeze her closer to my side and smile down at her.

"Always."

***

Scarlet

The next morning, I try to ignore the funk hanging in the air between my friends and me as I wait for Christine to come in, hopefully, any minute, with the wheelchair. Dr. Arledge has already thoroughly checked me over and was very happy with my progress. I'm to follow up with her at her regular office in a week. I'm free to go... and I'm thrilled... but the girls are still not happy that my mind is made up about this year's Home Network decorating contest, and they think I'm making a huge mistake. So there's a funk.

Andrew had to leave for work right after we devoured the order from Nonno's yesterday. He's been checking on me via text messages that always get my pulse hopping. They, along with that stirring picture of Andrew holding me after the fire, provide a momentary distraction from the ire I seem to have provoked in my friends. To be fair, they've watched me work myself to the bone for years and years just trying to be a finalist on the Home Network's decorating challenge. They're just as invested as I was, and they want to see me succeed. But all the wishes in the world can't create more money in my savings account than what is actually in there, and so tough choices must be made.

It's time for me to let go of this dream and face facts. That means using what's left of my savings to buy a new bed. I don't need the dresser, nightstands, or even a headboard...but I'm going to replace my actual mattress.

Yes. Absolutely.

I plan to save the rest of it for essentials while I go about finding a job. A real job. I have no idea where, but it's time for me to earn a steady paycheck, and the jobs I get from my fifteen minutes of fame being the Corbel Queen aren't enough to pay all the bills.

Okay, yeah, maybe I'll regret this decision in the future. I have to admit that. I can't explain it, but I had this sort of intuition that this was my year for that competition. It was my year. I knew it. But it all burned up. Marina and Ashley already offered to bankroll my supplies and everything I need to design a project, but where? I have no space to design something worthy of this contest. And, even though they're my very best friends, there is no way I'm comfortable with them spending all that money on my project. At some point, common sense must prevail.

I look down at my cell phone for what feels like the hundredth time. Still no text from Andrew this morning. I don't know why I'm expecting to hear from him so often. I know he's working. I just...miss him. I'm not even sure if that's okay to say. We went through something extraordinary together, that's for sure. I'll add it to the list of things to discuss with the therapist.

For the third time in about thirty minutes, Marina checks her watch. The little hairs on my arms stand up as if they're trying to warn me something's going down. I narrow my gaze at her.

"Why do you keep checking your watch?" I ask.

Marina looks at me, and then her gaze flicks to Ashley and Merry.

"Me?" she says with feigned innocence. "Just bored. I mean, how long does it take to discharge a person? We've been here for ages."

"If you want to distract yourself, maybe you can finally show me what you bought," I offer, gesturing at the bag on the floor next to her chair.

I asked her about it when she and Ashley arrived this morning, but she blew me off in a way that only made me suspicious.

Marina scoffs. "I'll show you when we get you settled at our apartment."

Ashley looks up from her phone. "Hey, married lady," she says with a smirk. "It's not *our* apartment anymore."

I laugh softly and reach over to nudge Marina.

"Well, thanks for getting married, so there's a spare bedroom for me to crash in."

Marina winks at me just as Christine comes whizzing into the room with the wheelchair. Merry quickly picks up her cell phone, her thumbs flying across the screen.

"And what are you doing over there?" I ask her.

Maybe there's not a funk. Maybe I just feel like these three are up to something.

"It's called texting," she says.

"Sarcasm much?" I ask, laughing.

"Ready to escape?" Christine asks with the sunshiny smile I've come to appreciate so much.

"Absolutely," I say, throwing my legs over the edge of the bed.

Christine removed my IV a few hours ago, and now she reaches over and gently takes the tubing from the oxygen off my face.

"Thank you," I say with a smile. "Let's roll, girl."

Christine laughs and helps me into the chair. Merry had an extra pair of leggings and a t-shirt in her backpack that she loaned me, so I'm thankful not to have to wear a hospital gown on the ride home. Too bad, though, that the t-shirt features a dancing cookie with sexy legs and a message that says "Kiss me, I'm delicious" in bright pink letters.

Ashley, Marina, and Merry follow behind as Christine guides the wheelchair through the halls, into the elevator, and out into the San Francisco air. I look around for Ashley's car, but I don't see it. Just as I'm about to ask her about it, a huge fire truck pulls up to the front of the hospital. Andrew sits in the passenger seat with a huge, beautiful grin on his face and I feel laughter bubble up and out of me.

"What's going on?" I ask, turning in the chair to look up at my friends.

"No idea," my three friends say in unison, huge grins on their guilty faces.

Andrew jumps out of the fire truck, followed closely by his colleagues. Two are maybe in their mid-thirties and the other man looks to be in his mid-fifties. They all smile at me like we're old friends. Andrew motions for them to step closer.

"Scarlet," Andrew greets me, giving me a quick hug. "I'd like you to meet my colleagues. This is Leonard, Todd, and this is our Captain. Jake Scheffler."

One by one, they each step forward so I can shake their hands. I steal a glance at Marina, Ashley, and Merry, and it's obvious they know about whatever this is.

Captain Scheffler steps forward.

"Scarlet, we heard about what you were doing in the warehouse," he begins. "And we hate that you lost your whole project, so we came to help."

Tears sting the backs of my eyes as I shake my head.

"Captain, that is so generous, but I've lost—"

"You haven't lost anything that can't be replaced, Miss," Captain Scheffler counters, looking over my shoulder at my friends.

Marina steps forward with the suspicious bag, pulling out a brand new laptop and gently placing it in my lap while muttering, "You're not allowed to say no to this. You can pay me back when you win the two hundred and fifty thousand dollars."

My jaw drops open as she steps away, and a tear falls down my cheek. This is too much. Captain Sheffler motions for Todd to come forward, who is holding a slightly different version of the same cutting machine I use.

"This is on loan from my wife," Todd says as he puts it in my lap on top of the laptop box. "I'm grateful to you for needing it, actually. The thing drives me nuts. She makes labels for everything. Even the toilet paper."

I laugh out loud as he steps away and takes position next to Leonard.

Captain Scheffler steps forward again.

"I don't think Andrew ever told you this, but our firehouse needs a massive re-do," he says. "We'd be honored if you would consider using our kitchen and living room as the two rooms you need to decorate for your contest."

My lower lip quivers as more tears fall. This is absolutely the sweetest thing ever. I can't believe this, and I have so many questions about how they orchestrated all of this. I'm barely aware of Merry taking pictures of the entire exchange.

"Oh! I almost forgot," Captain Scheffler says, pulling a large slip of paper from his back pocket. "Handy's Hardware has donated any paint and paint supplies you'll need."

The last shred of my resolve crumbles to dust, and I let out a sob. I move to try to get up, and Andrew steps up quickly to take the laptop and cutting machine away. I get up out of the wheelchair and turn to my friends. I'm instantly wrapped in hugs, and then I turn and find my way to Andrew, who has set down the laptop and cutting machine and is watching me with so much emotion in those remarkable eyes. I wrap my arms around his neck and hug him tightly. He holds me until I let go, then I turn to take a tissue that Ashley offers me.

"So what do you say, Phoenix?" Andrew says. "Ready to rise from the ashes?"

I smile at him, Captain Scheffler, Andrew's colleagues, and my friends and nod slowly.

"Let's do this."

Chapter 9

Scarlet

I don't think I realized just how much of a control freak I am until life taught me I'm not really in control at all. Last night was hard. Before they left the hospital parking lot in the fire truck, Captain Scheffler and I scheduled time this morning for me to get a tour of the fire station with my new friends. Then I hugged Andrew another dozen times before Ashley, Marina, Merry, and I came back here to the apartment.

Since the four of us were all together, we had some good healthy girl talk. Even though I didn't want to worry my mom, my friends helped me come to the right conclusion…and I called her. Well, I sent her a text message to call me when she was available because I wasn't sure when she would have cell phone service. She called fairly quick, and we did a video call so that she could see I was with the girls and everything was fine.

Mom was worried, of course, but I answered all her questions, and she felt better knowing that I was not alone. I convinced her to stay on her trip, and she agreed on the condition that we would talk every day. It seems a small price to pay to avoid the horrible guilt I would feel for ruining her vacation. My mom works hard, and she's the best mom ever. I would feel terrible if she came running home early when I'm perfectly fine and have a great place to stay where I'm not alone.

Marina's room isn't being used because she married Zach and moved upstairs to his apartment. He owns the whole building, so it works out fine. He refuses to charge Ashley any rent because he's just a freaking nice guy, so Ashley doesn't need a roommate. Marina's old room is basically sitting empty. I absolutely could have just gone home to the four-bedroom condo I share with my mom, but then I'd be all alone. No one thought that was a good idea, including me, so I'm staying here with Ashley until my mom gets back from her cruise.

I really thought I would be all right last night, especially after the absolute joy Andrew and my friends brought me when they plotted the ultimate surprise and helped me rally after I lost everything in the fire. But when Marina and Merry left, and Ashley and I got tired, things went south pretty fast. I tried my best to put on a brave face when it was time to say goodnight, but once I walked into the bedroom by myself, I started sweating. I felt like the fire was on the other side of the wall, and it was just a matter of minutes before it was in the room with me. I tried to tell myself it was just anxiety, but it didn't work. I lasted exactly ten minutes before I was yelling Ashley's name at the top of my lungs. The panic attack scared the daylights out of her, but once she realized it was some kind of anxiety I was experiencing because of the fire, she pulled me into her room, and we had a sleepover. I slept through the night, but I felt like an idiot being a grown woman who can't sleep alone. A grown woman with a teddy bear dressed like a fireman.

"Hey, how did you sleep last night?" Ashley asks as she takes a seat at the kitchen counter next to me.

I nod. "Okay, all things considered."

She places a gentle hand on my arm.

"I hope you're not giving yourself too much grief because you had to sleep with me last night."

I smirk. "Of course I am."

Ashley shakes her head. "Why? Certainly, it's understandable. When's your appointment with the therapist?"

"This afternoon," I say quietly. "I wish it was sooner, honestly. I have so many questions."

"Well, be prepared," she replies softly. "Therapists love to give vague answers."

A very rhythmic knock sounds at the door and keeps going, and we both break into laughter. Merry. She likes to bang out song lyrics when she knocks and then makes us guess what it was. We never get it right.

I slide off the bar stool and head to the door, opening it and immediately get pulled into a hug by Merry.

"Two guesses," she says as she rushes into the apartment.

"Michael Jackson's Billy Jean?" I reply.

"Nope! Ashley, what's your guess?"

"Bad Romance, Lady Gaga."

Merry clicks her tongue at both of us.

"How did you guys not hear Sweet Child of Mine?"

I shrug. "I don't know, dude, maybe because Axel Rose wasn't standing out there with you?"

Merry rolls her eyes at me, then glides into the kitchen to hug Ashley.

"You going with us, girl?" she asks.

"Nope," Ashley replies, digging in her purse and handing me her car key. "I've got a date with a Viking god. We're looking at wedding venues, then we're going out to lunch."

I grin. "Tell Rick I said hello."

Ashley grins back. "I will, but he might still be here when you get back. He was pretty upset when I told him about the fire. He wants to make sure his Corbel Queen is okay."

"It's always good to see my favorite Royal Rebel," I say, then turn to Merry. "Ready to go?"

Merry nods. "Born ready. Let's go see some firemen!"

I hug Ashley goodbye, then follow Merry out the door. We head downstairs to Ashley's car, which is parked on the street. I beep the locks, then walk around to the driver's side to get in. Merry plops into the passenger seat beside me, we buckle up, and I pull away from the curb.

"Do you mind if we stop at the coffee house on the way?" I ask Merry. "I'd like to buy the guys coffee and breakfast."

Merry gives me the side-eye. "You're not buying them any of those disgusting cookies, are you?"

I giggle as I turn a corner.

"Nope. I wouldn't dare. They make pretty amazing breakfast burritos. I was thinking of doing that."

Merry nods her approval and pulls a small bakery box from her bag to show me.

"I actually made Andrew some Italian wedding cookies to say thanks for saving my friend. Way better than anything at that coffee house."

"Merry, that is so sweet! Thank you for doing that."

I turn the car up California Street, which always makes me nervous, but it's the most direct route to get where we're going. This street has some of the most famous views of San Francisco, but it's full of steep hills. It can be a challenge for someone like me who doesn't drive every day. I focus on the task of steering the car around the city and pulling into the small parking lot next to the coffee house in less than fifteen minutes.

Merry and I get out and head inside, and my eyes immediately dart to Andrew's regular table. It's currently occupied by two police officers who are drinking coffee and starting their day just like the rest of us. I step up to the counter when it's my turn and smile at Rosa.

"The usual?" she says with a pretty smile.

"No, actually. I need an order to go. Can I get a carafe of black coffee, along with cups, cream, and sugar? A dozen of your egg and sausage breakfast burritos. And one green tea latte."

My heart does a few stupid little flips when I order Andrew's gross green tea. I'll have to find a way to keep my thoughts under control now that I'm designing the decor for his workplace. Avoiding him was easy before, but now…not so much. And I don't want to avoid him. Not really. Lots of things changed in the blink of an eye.

Rosa nods, takes my payment, and Merry and I find a table to sit at while we wait for the order to be filled. Merry drums her fingers on the tabletop.

"So what are you going to do about Andrew?"

I laugh softly. "Can you read my thoughts? I was just thinking about that."

Merry points to herself. "Superhero!"

"I'm not sure what to do about him," I say honestly. "I'm a little worried about the why behind my feelings, if I'm being honest."

Merry frowns. "What do you mean?"

"Well, are my feelings for him rooted in the fact that he saved my life?" I ponder. "Or are they real? And what are they? Everything is all jumbled. I think I'll feel better when I talk to the therapist."

Merry nods. "Solid plan. And I'm glad you're going to see someone so you can deal with everything. Talking to someone who doesn't know you personally will help you more than you know."

"I agree."

"But I say it's real," she says, almost smirking.

She's got that all-knowing look about her.

"Oh?"

She nods. "You wouldn't have had me come out to the coffee shop to gawk at him if you didn't have feelings for him. And that was well before he saved your life."

I scoff at her. "I just wanted to see if you thought the looks he was giving me were creepy."

Merry grins at me. "You liked him back then, and you like him now. Don't try to make it less than it is. You found your person."

My eyes nearly bulge out of their sockets. "That is ridiculous! I don't even know him."

Merry wiggles her eyebrows at me. "He's got an energy about him, and I have a sense about these things. He's your person."

My phone starts chiming in my pocket, and I pull it out to see a call from Brad. I show Merry who it is before answering.

"Hello?"

"Hey, my friend," Brad says. "How are you feeling?"

"Okay, all things considered," I say. "I'm about to tour the fire station with Merry."

He texted me last night to check on me, and I brought him up to speed on the fire station project.

"Take some pics of hot firemen for me."

"No problem," I reply in a voice dripping with sarcasm. "What's up?"

"I wanted to let you know the insurance guy called my dad about the cause of the fire," he begins. "I should have listened to you and bought a new ironing board. I was so tired that I apparently never turned the iron off, so when the board fell over, the hot iron landed in those cardboard boxes. Some of them contained my spray paint. That's what started the fire. I'm so sorry."

I close my eyes for a moment, feeling terrible for Brad and then realizing something.

"Oh wow…I heard something fall over right before I fell asleep," I murmur into the phone. "I'll bet that was it. If I'd only checked—"

"Nope," he interrupts. "This isn't your fault. But I know you, and I thought you might be subconsciously putting this on yourself. I wanted to let you know it was me."

I laugh softly. "I did wonder," I admit. "I'm just trying to process a lot right now."

"One less thing to worry about then," he says. "I've gotta run, but please call if you need anything. Love you, girl."

"I love you too, B. Bye."

Merry is watching me expectantly, so I relay Brad's news. She nods and reaches over to squeeze my hand just as Rosa calls my name.

We get up and retrieve my order from the counter, then head to the car and load it up. We buckle ourselves in, and I drive us the short distance to the fire station. When we pass the alley where the warehouse was, I turn my head away on instinct. Out of my peripheral vision, I can tell there's a big shell where there should be a warehouse…but that's it. A couple walls are standing, but I can't bring myself to look directly at it. A little shiver runs through my body as I pull the car into the long driveway beside the fire station.

Merry and I are just pulling the takeout order from the car when Captain Scheffler steps outside to greet us with a friendly smile. I look around for Andrew, but he doesn't follow. Half of me is a little sad that he didn't come to greet me, half of me is telling the other half to calm down.

"Good morning," I say to Captain Scheffler. "I brought you coffee and breakfast."

He looks genuinely surprised and steps forward to help Merry with the carton of coffee.

"That's very kind of you," he says. "Andrew's inside with an unexpected guest. Shall we?"

Before I can ask who it is, Captain Scheffler steps over to the door and holds it open for us. Merry and I exchange quizzical glances as we move to the door. The Captain smiles at me and nods.

"The kitchen is to your left as you walk in," he says as we step through the door.

I follow the Captain's directions and find a decently-sized kitchen with appliances that look like they're from the land that time forgot. Andrew is leaning against the counter and talking to another man whose back is to me. Andrew's whole face lights up when he sees me. I smile back, and it's one of those smiles you feel through your whole being. Every cell of my body is happy to see him.

"And here she is," Andrew says as he pushes off the counter and comes to greet me.

Merry and I place the takeout packages on the counter, and I turn to Andrew just in time for him to wrap me in a hug. Oh, how I've missed this. I've missed him.

I look up at him with a glint in my eye. "Are you talking about me?"

The man turns around and steps closer, a friendly smile on his face. He's older than we are, but not by much. He has short brown hair, nice blue eyes, and he's laser-focused on me right now.

Andrew steps back and places his large, warm hands on my shoulders.

"How are you feeling today?"

"Good," I say with a nod. "This is a little surreal still. Who is our new friend?"

Andrew lets go of me and steps to my side, gesturing to the man.

"Scarlet Jackson, I'd like you to meet Kevin Starbuck," Andrew says. "The reporter from the San Francisco Times who wrote the Phoenix and the Fireman article."

I feel my eyebrows shoot to my hairline.

"Oh, hello," I say with a grin. "That's you? That was a great article.

Thanks for spotlighting the guys here at Engine 14. They deserve all the kudos we can give them."

Kevin steps forward to shake my hand.

"It's a pleasure to meet you, Scarlet," he says warmly. "I'm glad you liked it. And I'm happy that circumstance is favoring me today."

I look at him curiously. Andrew's hand cups my elbow, and I can't help but lean into his touch.

"He just happened to stop by this morning," Andrew explains. "Looking for me to talk about the warehouse fire. Cap told him you were on the way, and it kind of escalated from there."

As if on cue, Captain Scheffler steps into the kitchen with Todd and Leonard.

"Was I supposed to keep it a secret? That article has already generated a lot of positive attention for the fire department. The Chief even sent me an email this morning."

I notice Todd's focus is locked on all the bags.

"Oh! I almost forgot," I exclaim nervously. "I brought you guys some coffee and breakfast burritos as a thank you. Please dig in."

I'm lost in a sea of thank yous and a flurry of activity as the guys make short work of unpacking everything. I pluck the green tea latte out of the beverage holder and turn to Andrew.

"One gross green tea latte for my favorite fireman," I say quietly.

He laughs softly and pulls me in for another hug.

"Thanks, Phoenix."

I roll my eyes. "I am sooo not like a phoenix."

Andrew's warm gaze scans my face as a smile plays at his mouth.

"I disagree completely."

I wish we could spend some time alone, but there's too much to do this morning. Before I know it, we're all seated in their living area on couches that have seen much better days. They really *do* need my help. I desperately want to take photos and measurements of the kitchen and living room and start sketching in my book, but I'll have time for that later. I focus on the conversation, which is currently all about the photo Kevin took of Andrew holding me after he pulled me out of the fire.

"I took that picture with my cell phone," Kevin is telling Andrew. "I can't believe it came out so perfect. Although I am sorry for the reason behind it."

Kevin nods at me, and I offer a feeble smile.

"Andrew tells me you lost everything?" he asks.

I nod. "Material things. I'm just grateful Andrew was there."

Andrew smiles at me from his spot on the end of the couch next to me.

"I was able to get the most valuable thing out safely," he says. "That's all that matters."

Be still my freaking heart.

Merry leans over to whisper in my ear. "He's sooo your person."

I nudge her with my elbow and fight the blush I feel crawling up my cheeks.

"And now I get to do something for them by freshening up their living space."

Kevin swallows the bit of breakfast burrito he was chewing and nods.

"About that," he says excitedly. "I was wondering if you guys might let me write a weekly series of articles about the whole thing."

Andrew and I exchange interested looks as Kevin continues.

"I'd stop by a few times a week," he explains. "You can show me what you're up to, I'll interview you. Take pictures. That kind of thing."

Oh. Whoa.

"This contest is highly competitive," I say warily. "If you publish—"

Kevin holds up a hand. "I wouldn't publish any pictures that would reveal too much of your project. And you would get final approval on what pictures I include with each article."

My gaze darts to Andrew, who is watching me carefully.

"Look," Kevin says, leaning forward. "I've lived in this city a long time, and I hate to see neighborhoods like this one start to struggle. There's been a stellar response to the Phoenix and the Fireman article. If we build on the attention it's getting, we could really do something."

"What kind of stellar response?" Andrew asks.

"People are calling my office every day," he explains. "They're very moved by what they saw in that picture. They want to know how the Phoenix is. Who she is. They want to know you're all right. They want to know more about the fireman in the photo. The emotion on both of your faces is incredible."

Merry nudges me, and I look in her direction.

"You okay?" she asks in a low voice.

I nod. "Yeah, but I want to talk to Andrew about it before I agree to anything."

She nods. "Go on then. I'll keep these boys entertained."

I laugh under my breath. I have no doubt. Merry is awesome, and these guys have no idea what's about to hit them. I look over at Kevin.

"Do you mind if Andrew and I talk about it for a few minutes?"

Kevin grins ear to ear. "Not a bit. I'm stoked you're thinking about it."

I look at Andrew, and we both stand up, walking toward the door. He opens it for me, and we step outside. We walk away from the fire station a bit, coming to a stop on the sidewalk. He immediately pulls me into another hug, and I sink against him. I wrap my arms around his neck tightly, and he rocks us slowly a few times before letting go enough so that we can look at each other.

"So what do you think?" I ask him, resting my palms on his forearms.

"The hug? I love your hugs," he answers with a silly grin. "Five stars. Highly recommend."

I laugh and give him a playful push. "C'mon."

The muscles in his forearms flex under my fingertips as I wait for his answer.

"I think it's a great idea," he says with a shrug. "I've been reading his stuff for a couple years now. He seems like a good guy who really cares about this city. But this is your call. I'll back you up whatever you decide."

His last words bring a smile to my face. He'll back me up. Of course, he will. It's what he's done from the moment we met. I wrap my fingers around his arms and shake him a little.

"I know you will, Superman."

Someone starts shouting obscenities in the distance, and I close my eyes like I'm listening to the sweetest symphony.

"Aww. I'm back in the old neighborhood."

Andrew rolls his eyes at me.

"Except this time, there will be no late-night Dinner Dash runs down the street or sleeping in sketchy warehouses."

"I'm probably never going to live that down, am I?"

He grins, and the dimples come out to play.

"Oh, I'm sure you'll give me at least another twenty heart attacks over the course of our…oh. I almost said your least favorite word: relationship. I guess I don't know what to call us."

I chew on my lip for a minute, thinking. His deep brown eyes scan my face.

"If I'm putting you on the spot, feel free to kick me right in the shins."

"I would never," I say, laughing softly. "We should probably figure this out, huh?"

He works a muscle in his jaw, holding that grin. Holding me. I should step out of his arms, but I don't want to. I should be able to put a label on this thing between us, but I can't. I have so many feelings. I just can't decipher them all right now.

"It's okay to ask for what you need, Scarlet. I'm not going anywhere."

Of course, he isn't. He's my…rock. Part of me feels like I should fight that, but it's the old me. Some of my rules burned up in the fire, or at least they don't apply to Andrew. Maybe they never did.

"I think whatever this is between us doesn't have to have a standard label," I say pensively. "But I want to be sure I'm doing the right thing. Not just for me but for you too. So, just for now, I say we're friends with potential."

His face lights up when I say potential.

"Potential, hm?"

I squeeze his arms and smile up at his handsome face.

"Sooo much potential," I reply, making myself step out of his arms. "I just need a little bit of time, that's all."

He reaches a hand out as if he's going to cup my cheek, then thinks better of it. I feel an insane level of disappointment when he lets his hand fall, but until I figure out my feelings, it's probably better to avoid that. It wouldn't do to have Merry have to scrape a Scarlet-shaped puddle off the sidewalk after he melts me with those eyes. Not to mention those lips. I have to fight not to imagine what he'd be like to kiss. It crosses my mind far too often.

He clears his throat. "So seriously…what's the decision on the article series?"

I chew on my lower lip for a moment.

"My first instinct?" I begin, shuffling my feet. "I want to do it. I think, just like us, it has a lot of potential."

Andrew laughs out loud and follows my lead as I head back to the fire station.

"I agree, Nix," he says, giving me a wink.

I stop dead in my tracks. "Nix?"

"I love calling you Phoenix, but I also have a habit of shortening names," he explains. "If I shorten it to "fee" it makes you sound like some kind of pampered poodle. But Nix? That's you."

I grin up at him and fold my arms across my chest. "It is?"

He nods. "Yeah. It's scrappy. Sassy. It's you."

I continue walking up the driveway to the front door, Andrew stepping ahead of me to open it. Just as I walk through the door, I lean over and whisper into his ear.

"I like it."

When he steps in behind me, I swear I hear him mutter a prayer for help, and I try to suppress an evil grin. We return to the living room to find Merry holding all the men in a thrall, and I am soooo not surprised. As soon as we sit back in our seats, Todd looks over at us.

"Merry was just telling us you guys were the sailors dancing around the mermaid in that viral video," he says.

"We were," I say lightly, then I shoot a sobering glance at Kevin. "I would really appreciate it if you didn't share that in your articles. No need to kick that mess up again."

Kevin nods. "Don't worry. My goal is to shine the spotlight on the neighborhood. I don't want to distract anyone from the stories here."

I let out a sigh of relief. The viral video of us singing on the Golden Gate Bridge never had any negative repercussions for me personally, but it felt like the entire city was on the hunt for Marina when it was happening. She was dressed as a mermaid at the time, and the city was obsessed with finding out who she was. Bringing all that back would cloud the light we're trying to shine on my new friends.

"So does that mean you've decided you're in? With the article series?"

I glance at Andrew once more, who gives me that "I'm on Team

Nix" look again, and then I turn back to Kevin and nod.

"If you can promise me I get a final veto, you've got yourself a deal, Mr. Starbuck."

Chapter 10

Scarlet

"That's great!" Kevin exclaims, shaking both our hands again.

"Well, let's get started then, shall we?" I say, unable to contain my excitement a moment longer.

Focusing on this project feels like a step back to normal.

I stand up and pull my cell phone out of my pocket. I look to Andrew and his colleagues.

"Show me what I'm creating a design for, as well as anything that's off limits."

Captain Scheffler stands up and waves a hand around the room we're in now. It's a sort of combination living and dining room. I take a series of pictures to capture it all. I'll take measurements later.

"This is our common living area," he explains. "The city would have to approve anything we're spending department funds on, including furniture or whatever else."

"Let me worry about that," I say cryptically. "Anything else I need to know?"

These people save lives. They run into burning buildings when others are running out. I have zero intention of them having to pay for a single thing, but I have to get some good solid think time in on this. I have a plan, but I need to organize it into workable chunks.

Captain Scheffler thinks for a moment, then blurts. "No pink."

Everyone laughs at that, and I pat him on the shoulder.

"Duly noted. How about the kitchen?"

He motions for me to follow, and I do, but so does everyone else. As soon as I step into the kitchen, I get a better look at the appliances and my spirits fall right into the dirt. Actually, about six feet under. Go ahead and bury my morale right now. These appliances look like they're a thousand years old. They're dented and scraped like they went five rounds with Mike Tyson.

"Wow," Merry says. "It's like the land of forgotten, mismatched appliances."

Leonard and Todd snicker. Captain Scheffler looks around, trying to put a positive spin on things.

"Maybe a little paint will—"

Merry laughs out loud. "Hey, Cap, I don't think there's enough paint in the world to help this along."

He smirks and points a finger at her, then me. "I thought I told you two to call me Jake."

"Well, Jake," I begin with a gleam in my eye. "There's an old saying, you can put lipstick on a pig, but it's still a pig."

Everyone laughs as I pull out my phone again and take pictures of everything. I shake my head.

"This will be a challenge for sure," I say. "But I've had bigger challenges. I can handle this."

I literally have *no* idea how I'm going to handle this. I'll figure it out. I always do.

I check out the cabinets next to the stove and notice a framed photo of a fireman. I take a step closer to get a good look at it.

"Uh, that should stay. If at all possible," Captain Scheffler, or Jake, says.

I nod. "Who is he?"

Jake purses his lips together. "Firefighter James MacLachlan. Died in the line of service June 7, 2001. He was my best friend. And he was Andrew's dad."

My gaze flies to Andrew, who is leaning against the counter and focusing his gaze on the floor. A muscle ticks in his jaw. I instinctively cross the kitchen and move to his side as Jake continues.

"We went through training together and became fast friends."

I reach my hand toward Andrew's. As soon as our hands touch, he wraps his hand around mine, and I give it a little squeeze.

I'm here.

"Our first assignment was here. Engine 14," Jake continues. "He was a good man. A great friend. And a very proud dad."

I squeeze Andrew's hand again, and he rubs a thumb across the back of my hand.

Jake smacks a hand lightly on the stovetop and smiles at all of us.

"And he loved to cook," he says. "He put love into everything he did. You could've had the worst day ever, but if Mac was in the kitchen, you knew everything was gonna be okay. He had a way with food, so I like to keep his photo right here. Where it all started."

I nod at Jake. "I think that's a wonderful way to remember him."

Merry smiles. "If he liked to cook, he sounds like a good guy to me."

Andrew squeezes my hand again. My heart breaks for him as I do the math in my head. He must have been around five years old when his dad died.

"Oh, hey," Merry says lightly, grabbing the box of cookies from her bag and handing it to Andrew. "Something to say thanks. For saving my friend."

Andrew takes the box and looks excitedly at Merry.

"Are these what I think they are?"

She nods proudly, and Andrew gives her a huge hug.

"Thank you, Merry, so much. I'm not sharing these with anyone."

Jake makes a grumbling noise, then turns to me.

"So, do you still want to take this project on? This kitchen's almost as old and busted as me."

More laughter from the group, including me, because if I don't laugh, I may actually cry at the state of this kitchen. I really have my work cut out for me. But I feel the familiar pull of a challenge rising in my chest. I'm beginning to feel inspired, and that's a welcome thing.

Andrew lets go of my hand and wraps an arm around my shoulders instead, giving me a little side hug.

"I saw what Scarlet was creating in that warehouse," he says. "It was amazing. If she can create a gorgeous library inside a beat-up old warehouse, I know she can handle this."

I beam under Andrew's praise, and I already have a few great ideas bubbling to the surface for this project. The funny thing is I'm more excited about doing this for the firefighters of Engine 14 than I am about winning this contest. It's kind of liberating. I slide an arm around Andrew's waist and smile at the guys.

"Gentlemen, I'm going to give you a kitchen and a living space worthy of Engine 14."

The guys are all grinning ear to ear, and I feel honored that they're putting their faith in me. I just hope I can come up with a miracle. Actually, I need about three miracles for this job.

Alarm bells sound in the station, making me nearly jump out of my skin. Instantly, the guys go into alert mode. I'm vaguely aware of Andrew squeezing my hand and saying something to me as he rushes away.

There's a very organized flurry of activity as they prepare themselves. Merry, Kevin, and I all step back and out of the way as we watch them. It's almost like a choreographed dance. I hear snippets of information coming from a speaker somewhere, either in the fire truck or somewhere else in the station.

....Bush Street...structure fire...

Fire. *Fire.*

I look up to see the fire truck pulling away from the station, lights flashing and sirens blaring. A familiar buzzing noise is in my ears and suddenly, I'm back in the warehouse. Merry steps in front of me, forcing herself into my line of sight. She's talking to me, but I can't hear her. The buzzing is too loud. I can see her mouth moving, but I can't hear her. I feel like I'm going to be sick. Hands are on my shoulders, trying to move me somewhere...but the fire is on the other side of that wall. It's coming. It's coming, and I can't get away.

...sit down, girl....

I can feel the heat seeping through the wall as the fire gets closer. I can smell the smoke, feel it clawing its way down my throat. I feel myself trembling.

Scarlet, look at me!

My eyes flick up, and I see Kevin Starbuck's worried expression filling my view. I feel Merry's presence beside me. Her arm is around my shoulders, and she's holding one of my hands while I pant out anxious breaths, just trying to get some air.

"Scarlet, can you hear me?" Kevin asks gently.

I nod.

"Take a breath," he says. "Big inhale."

I do as he says, and this time, my body actually does what I want it to. I inhale as deep as I can, but I feel like my lungs are fighting me. The buzzing has gotten quieter in my ears, which helps me relax.

"That's good, Scarlet," I hear Merry say next to me.

I turn my head to look at her. Her face is lined with worry as she rubs a hand up and down my arm. A shudder quakes through my body, shaking me to the core.

"I'm sorry," I croak out. "Sorry."

Merry squeezes my shoulders, and I take another jagged breath.

"No need for that," she says softly. "Just breathe."

I take another deep breath and exhale.

No one says a word. They just sit with me while I catch my breath. Finally, I look up at Kevin.

"He's gone?"

Kevin nods solemnly, and I look at Merry as my face crumples.

"He's gone to a fire."

My voice is so hoarse I barely recognize it.

"He'll be back," she says calmly. "It'll be okay. Just keep breathing."

A tear falls down my cheek, but I ignore it. I take another shaky breath. Then another.

Kevin gets up and goes to the kitchen, then brings back a bottle of water. He unscrews the cap, then hands it to me.

"Thank you," I rasp.

More silence. More waiting, giving me space to calm down.

"Well, I guess we can all be glad I have my first appointment with the therapist this afternoon," I say quietly.

Merry fumbles around in her purse and then shoves a tissue into my hand. I offer her a weak smile.

"Thanks."

Kevin seems relieved that I'm breathing normally again, and he sits back against the couch.

"Are you feeling a little better?" Merry asks.

I nod. "Obviously, I know what Andrew does for a living, but it's a different thing altogether when he has to run out of here right in front of me."

I swallow hard.

"How brave they all are…" my voice breaks up, and I can't finish the sentence.

I take another deep breath and smooth my palms over the tops of my thighs a few times. I feel my heart rate returning to normal. I look between Kevin and Merry.

"Okay," I say lowly. "So what should we talk about while we wait for them all to come back… unharmed?"

***

Andrew

As far as I'm concerned, we can't get back to the fire station fast enough. We're trained to move whenever a call comes in, so that's what I did. It's what we all did. Like so many calls, we weren't needed at all. In this case, someone reported a building was on fire when it was really just a grill that got out of control for a minute. By the time we arrived, it was out completely.

Once we were sure there was no danger, we loaded back into the truck, and Leonard started driving us back. Now I'm sitting here wondering what effect the alarm, not to mention the lights and sirens, had on Scarlet. I *did* tell her we'd be fine and would be back soon, but I'm not sure she heard me. At least she wasn't alone when we left, but I'm still worried.

As soon as the truck pulls into the station, I jump out and head inside. I find Scarlet sitting with Merry and Kevin in the living area, all calm. Too quiet. I know it was bad as soon as I see the look in her eyes when she sees me. Her lower lip quivers, and she stands, then she walks straight into my arms. She puts her cheek to my chest as her arms wrap tightly around me, and I look over her head at Merry and Kevin.

Merry gives me a nod and a look as if to say Scarlet is fine now. Kevin's expression is full of empathy. I lower my lips to Scarlet's ear.

"Are you all right?" I murmur.

"I'm okay," she says quietly, nodding. "Just wasn't expecting that."

She pulls away and looks up at me, then buries her nose in my shirt and sniffs me. I laugh softly.

"You don't smell like smoke," she says, trying to smile a little. "No fire after all?"

I shake my head. "Not one that needed us. So how's it been going here?"

She smirks, then turns, and we walk back to join the others as Jake and the guys file in as well.

"You mean other than my massive anxiety attack?" Scarlet jokes shakily. "We're good."

I feel like there's a crack beginning to form right down the center of my heart.

I give Scarlet a gentle nudge. "I'm sorry."

She shakes her head. "Not your fault, but I'm really glad I'm seeing that therapist today."

"Have you ever practiced meditation?"

"Never needed to," she says. "I'm pretty tough."

I nudge her again. "Even tough guys practice meditation."

She raises her eyebrows at me, and I nod.

"Working out helps too," I share, then laugh when she rolls her eyes and groans.

I lower my voice and lean over so only she can hear me.

"Actually, for you, maybe direct confrontation would work."

Jake, Leonard, and Todd are keeping Merry and Kevin busy for now.

"What?" she whispers.

"What if we went down to the warehouse?" I suggest. "Would it help to see that it's gone? If even the thought of another fire gives you anxiety, it might help to confront the place where it all started."

She shakes her head nervously. "No, I don't think so."

I think she's wrong, but I keep my opinion to myself. We're so alike, and I know, without a doubt, I'd need to confront the situation head-on. I think Scarlet does, too, but she doesn't want to hear it right now.

Kevin leans forward and looks at Scarlet somberly. "You're doing better?"

Leonard flops down on the sofa across from us. "What happened?"

Scarlet gives him a half smile.

"Had a little anxiety attack watching you guys run off to fight fires."

He smirks at first, like he thinks she's joking, and then he sobers.

"Really? You okay?"

Scarlet nods. "I just need to get back to normal."

I hope she's right. More than that, I hope she realizes that normal may look different after going through something like this. She survived a terrifying thing. That changes a person. Hopefully, it doesn't change her so much that she decides she can't deal with a fireman in her life. My biggest fear is that we form an even deeper connection, but she can't deal with the idea of me running off to a burning building when the call comes. Because who could blame her for that after what she's been through? The dread of it lurks in the back of my mind, and I can't seem to shake it.

***

Scarlet

I've never gone to a therapist before, so I have no basis for comparison, but I already love mine. Kate is awesome. She's around my mom's age, and, like me, she doesn't pull any punches. She's direct when she needs to be but also infuriatingly vague at times. I feel great just sitting here talking to her, and I can't believe it's almost been an hour already.

"So let's go over your homework before our time is up," she says with a kind smile. "In the next day or two, you're going to look closer at different methods of meditation."

I nod. "Even if I don't think it'll help?"

She laughs under her breath.

"Even then," she replies. "It's okay to question or even disagree, Scarlet. There aren't usually cut-and-dried answers here. But I'd love it if you'd give it a good solid try before throwing out the idea of meditation."

I nod. "I can do that."

"I know you can," she says. "And you might be surprised at the result. The anxiety attack you had today, for example. Meditation can help you to become less reactive in these situations. It's a valuable tool."

"I had a question about that, actually. Andrew, my..."

Kate smiles. "Your friend, for lack of a better term?"

I nod. "Yes. Andrew suggested that seeing the warehouse might help me."

"Judging by the look on your face, I'm guessing you disagree with him?"

I shrug. "I wanted to know what you thought."

She smiles at me. "What do *you* think, Scarlet?"

I make a face at her, and she laughs softly. I consider my feelings for a moment. I think about how it felt to drive by the alley and feel, rather than see, that huge empty space where the warehouse should have been in my peripheral vision. I think about what I felt when Andrew suggested I go and look at it.

"I'm afraid."

Kate raises her eyebrows as if she's surprised I actually said it.

"I'm afraid of the memories that might flash back," I continue. "I'm afraid of seeing pieces of my work lying in the ashes. And I'm afraid of having another anxiety attack."

Kate nods. "That's good work, Scarlet. It takes courage to admit our fears. And also to confront them. I think it's enough homework to explore meditation before our next session. If you do feel like visiting the site of the fire, then I'd recommend making sure you have a friend with you for support."

I nod in agreement. We spend the rest of our time discussing the frequency of our sessions, finally settling on twice a week for now. I'm grateful for that since I want to get through this and get back to normal. I book my next appointment with her and head out to the lobby, where Merry is waiting for me. We walk to the car together, and I sit behind the wheel for a moment.

"I just want to say thank you, Merry," I say to my friend. "For rearranging your whole life just so I don't have to be alone right now. You're a great friend."

She scoffs. "Okay, first...you're welcome. And second, I'm not sure how much of a life I have to re-arrange, anyway. You'd do the same for me."

She's right. I'd find a way. But I really hate inconveniencing my friends, and Merry is being a real trooper.

"So, how did it go?" she asks as I turn the car onto the street.

"Okay, I think," I begin. "It felt good just to talk to someone neutral about it all. And, of course, I have homework before our next visit."

"Yeah? What homework?"

"I am supposed to research meditation and self-soothing methods," I explain. "She gave me a few video recommendations to watch. And then I'm supposed to try to sleep alone. If I get stressed, I'm supposed to try to meditate to calm myself down."

"And what if it doesn't work?"

"Then I can bother Ashley," I reply. "Lucky her."

"Hey, you can bug me too. Don't give Ashley all the love. Call me any time."

I laugh out loud and turn the corner. "Aren't I already bugging you enough? Isn't Nonno ready to kill me for taking up so much of your time?"

"I told you my cousin is filling in for me," Merry says. "He doesn't need my help, and maybe if he misses me a little bit, he'll soften up and let me open Nonna's old bakery."

I give Merry a sideways glance as I pull the car up the street towards Ashley's apartment.

"Really?"

She laughs. "No, I think it'll take more than that to get him to say yes. I'm not giving up, though."

I nod. "Good. I would be sadly disappointed if you gave up."

I park the car in Ashley's preferred spot, and then Merry and I get out and walk upstairs to the apartment. I take two steps inside, dying for a bottle of water, and I hear one of my favorite voices.

"Corbel Queen!" Rick shouts from the kitchen.

I grin like crazy and head in the direction of his voice. He rounds the kitchen island with his arms wide open, and I run right to them. Rick is well over six feet tall, and he wraps me in a hug and lifts me straight off the ground. I scream when he slightly tosses me in the air, then he catches me and puts me down. I step back to catch my breath and see Ashley leaning against the counter, laughing hysterically.

"You doing okay?" Rick asks me as he steps back.

I nod. "Alive, safe, grateful for my friends, and a big hot mess."

Rick laughs. "You're not a hot mess, Scarlet. And I'm glad you're safe."

Ashley is giving him the sweetest looks, and she's melting my heart. If anyone would have told me last year that she would be madly in love with Rick, I wouldn't have believed them. We called her the Dragon Lady because of the way she would just roast any guy who tried to hit on her when we were out. I can't imagine these two being any more in love with each other, and it makes me so happy. They're definitely made for each other.

"Me too," I say as I grab a bottle of water from the fridge. "And I have homework tonight, so we may not need the sleepover this time, Ash."

She raises her eyebrows at me as Rick steps behind her and pulls her back against his chest. Merry and I each pull up bar stools at the kitchen island, and I fill them in on my homework assignment. I'm kind of excited to try it, which surprises me.

"Well, I think I'm gonna make like a baby and head out," Merry says, making me choke on my water.

I laugh out loud as Ashley stands there and shakes her head. Rick is just blinking like he can't believe what he heard.

I walk over to Merry and wrap her in a hug.

"Thanks for coming today, Mer."

She hugs me back, then heads for the door.

"Any time, girl. I'll see you in the morning."

Merry lets herself out, and I head back to the kitchen.

"So, what are we doing for dinner tonight?" Ashley asks, looking from me to Rick and back to me again.

"I'm going to attempt to be alone in my room," I say with all the grandeur I can muster. "I was planning to watch some meditation videos and just kind of go from there."

Rick grins at me. "Going after your homework super fast, huh?"

I nod. "I want to feel normal again, guys. I should be able to be alone without feeling like I'm going to die."

Ashley nudges me on the shoulder. "You'll get there. This is only your second night here."

"I know. I'm not very patient with myself. We know this."

Ashley laughs and looks at Rick.

"Yep! You should see her when she wants to learn something, and she can't get it."

Rick winks at me. "You got this, Corbel Queen."

I nod and head down the hall.

"Thanks, Rick," I call out. "Wish me luck."

"Good luck," both Ash and Rick yell as I disappear into my room.

I hate this. They're staying in because of me. Ashley is staying here because of me. Because just being alone cripples me with fear. I have to get a handle on this. I hate feeling this needy.

I set the bottle of water down on the nightstand, pop my shoes off, and climb onto the bed. I grab the TV remote and bring up one of the videos Kate recommended, then hit play. Thirty seconds later, I pause it because I wasn't paying attention. I was thinking of how badly I wanted to go back to normal. My brain is super squirrely right now, racing all over the place and just nuts. I back it up and hit play again, hoping I can relax enough for this to sink in. Please, please, please.

An hour later, I feel a thousand times more stressed out and no closer to healing. Every time I try to close my eyes and relax into meditation, my brain goes crazy. Instead of focusing on my breathing, my thoughts immediately turn to the project at the fire station, what to get Merry as a thank-you gift, or Andrew's hugs. Or, heaven forbid, the fire. The scratch of the ash in my throat. The heat of the fire in the warehouse as Andrew carried me to safety. The crippling fear of waking up and not knowing what was happening, then the horror of realization.

I feel my skin heating up and my breathing getting shallow as the memories begin to hit me. Somehow, I remember Kate's words to me. When I feel panic rising, I close my eyes. Breathe in deep. Breathe out slowly. Focus on my body. The feeling of the bed underneath me. The sounds around me. Tell myself I'm safe. I'm all right. Andrew's safe.

Everything is okay. Everything is fine. Another breath in. Another out. I am safe. I'm at peace. Nothing can harm me.

A shudder rolls through my body, and my eyes flutter open. They're wet, and I realize I was crying. But I'm okay. I pull a tissue from the box on the nightstand and dab at my eyes before swinging my legs off the bed. I'm supposed to celebrate my little wins, so I try to give myself credit for the fact that I can be in this room alone for an hour, and I don't have a panic attack. I mean, I almost did…but I stopped it. That's something, I guess. I cling to the hope of that as I grab my bottle of water and head out to the living room to join Ashley and Rick.

They look up as I come skulking into the room, hopeful expressions on their faces. I shrug.

"Meditation is a challenge," I say as I plop into a chair. "But I felt an anxiety attack coming on, and I think I stopped it with some deep breathing."

Ashley gasps. "Hey, that's great!"

I nod. "Baby steps, I guess. Even if I'd rather run at full speed."

Rick nods in my direction. "It'll happen, Scarlet. I believe in you."

"Thanks, my friend."

Ashley picks up the TV remote and brandishes it at us. "Anyone up for a movie?"

"Actually," I reply as I give my friend a conspiratorial grin. "Can we chat about the fire station project for a minute?"

Ashley nods. "Sure. How's it going?"

I tilt my head. "Early stages, but I need a favor."

Ashley and Rick await, curiosity painted on their faces.

"I need you to talk to your dad for me," I say to Ashley.

Chapter 11

Scarlet

I can't keep the smile off my face as I drive through the city this morning. Alone. I'm in the car alone. It is weird to be this excited about such a simple thing, but it's progress. After I hung out with Rick and Ashley last night, Rick bid us goodnight and headed home, and I felt too raw to even try to sleep by myself. I spent the night in Ashley's room again. But I woke up this morning feeling like I could maybe drive to the fire station alone. I called Merry and asked if she'd mind meeting me there. We agreed she would meet me at 9 AM.

That gives me time to walk to the coffee house with Andrew and get back in time to start work when Merry arrives. I'm not confident enough to risk being alone at the fire station when the guys could be called away at any moment. As much as I'd love to be able to handle that, I must allow myself the time to get there. Rome wasn't built in a day. Neither will Scarlet 2.0.

I'm so grateful that Merry will continue her trips to the fire station for at least this week. I'm going to have to think of something I can do for her as a thank you, like a new car or a puppy. Or, really, if I could have a heart-to-heart with Nonno about that bakery, but I'm not brave enough to try it.

I pull the car into the driveway at the fire station and find a very handsome Andrew waiting for me, grinning ear to ear.

Hello, Mr. Dimples.

"Good morning," Andrew greets me as he opens the car door for me. "Driving all alone? I'll bet that felt good."

I step out of the car and straight into his arms for a hug. Driving alone didn't just feel good. It felt great. But not as good as this. The best thing ever, I think as I wrap my arms around him and give him a good squeeze.

"The amount of pride I feel over it is probably ridiculous," I say as I reluctantly step out of his embrace. "But my therapist tells me I should celebrate all my wins. Even the little ones."

Andrew nods. "This is definitely a win. Ready?"

I decide to leave my stuff in the car until we return, so I beep the locks and tuck the key fob into my purse. Andrew and I fall into an easy pace as we walk together, but I feel a nervousness come over me as we near the site of the warehouse. It's on the other side of the street, but there's a pull. Like an energy that's begging me to look in that direction. I don't, but I feel like every hair on my body is standing at attention…trying to pull me over there.

Wordlessly, Andrew reaches over and wraps his hand around mine. I take it gladly, compulsively squeezing his fingers. Our pace doesn't slow, but I glance over at him to find him watching me.

"How did you know I needed that?" I ask.

"Something about you changed," he replies. "Call it your energy or…aura…whatever. I could feel you tensing up without even looking at you. But then I looked, and I could tell it's bothering you to be so close to the area where it all happened."

"I'm not even sure it's bothering me," I say, even while trying to sift through my emotions. "I actually feel drawn to it. There's curiosity but also fear. Or dread. Everything is so muddled up."

He gives my hand a little squeeze. "You need time to figure it out. You'll get there."

I heave out a frustrated sigh. "I don't want time. I want to fix it. Now."

Andrew doesn't reply, but I feel him watching me. He's probably wondering what kind of a hot mess he's getting involved with. We walk in silence for a while longer until I can't take it anymore.

"Sorry," I mutter as we stop at a corner and wait for the light.

He lets go of my hand and turns to face me, concern etched into his face.

"For a person who always wants to be in motion," he begins, "and always doing something, I can imagine how frustrating this is. But you can't force yourself to heal, Nix. Please be patient."

My spirits lighten considerably at the sound of his nickname for me. I adore it. And, for some reason, being compared to a fiery bird that rises from the ashes gives me a feeling of empowerment. It's refreshing since I've been feeling pretty powerless lately. I look up into those beautiful brown eyes of his.

"I'm not good at it," I say, prompting a slow smile from Andrew.

"Nope. You're not."

I nod and give him a playful shove as the light turns green, and we start walking again.

"So the only question is...what will you do about it?" he asks.

I frown. "What will I do about the fact that I lack the ability to have patience with myself?"

"Yep," he replies. "Knowing you as I do, I would say your first instinct is to *make* yourself have more patience. Force it. Just do it."

I don't even try to suppress the laugh that bubbles up over his words. He does know me far better than he should.

"Am I right?" he asks in a teasing tone.

"You're not wrong," comes my coy reply.

"So, will you do that now? Try to force it?"

I focus my gaze on the coffee house that's now just a half block away, and I smirk at him.

"Do I sense some advice coming my way?

He shakes his head. "I would not presume."

I stop in my tracks and put my hands on my hips, now curious.

"What would you do?" I ask seriously. "I feel like you've been down this road before. What would you do?"

Andrew's intense gaze lands on me.

"You have two options, Nix," he says with a calm that soothes me. "You can do what fear is trying to make you do. You can try to grab control. Stomp your feet. Throw a tantrum if you want to. None of that will change the fact that you have a hard time being patient with yourself."

I consider his words. Something about the way he's sharing this makes me feel I hit the nail on the head without a doubt. He's been down this road before. Part of me wants to step back into his arms and beg him to make it all go away, but even Andrew doesn't have the power to do that.

"And the other option?" I ask.

"Run straight towards it," he says confidently. "Stop avoiding it. Stop dancing around it. Admit it. You can't be perfect at everything, right? Tackle it. Look it in the face and own it."

"Own the fact that I'm impatient with myself?"

He nods. "Yep. Every time you try to force yourself to just get on with things, you give up more power. Looking at your weakness and being honest about it will help you get stronger."

Part of me thinks this sounds absolutely ridiculous. But the other part of me is realizing that nothing else has worked for me. And I know in my gut that Andrew is right. Every time patience is required,

I do the emotional equivalent of stomping my feet and throwing a little tantrum in my head.

I nod, then roll my neck like I'm limbering up to go into a boxing ring with Mike Tyson.

"All right," I say with renewed determination. "I suck."

Andrew blinks back his surprise. He seems unsure of how to respond, but there was something freeing about those words just now. I feel a little tease of liberation, so I dig in my heels and then dive in.

"I suck at being patient with myself. I am terrible at it."

Poor Andrew just stands there, and the look on his face gives me the giggles. I start to laugh at how ridiculous all of this is. It's just somehow very funny that someone like me, who is usually so confident in everything, feels empowered by admitting a flaw. But I do feel empowered.

"When it comes to being patient with myself, I am the weakest link," I continue. "I have zero game. But yeah…wow…Andrew, that feels good to say."

I start laughing again, and this time, I'm rewarded with a beautiful grin on his handsome face. The poor guy is probably seriously worried about how unhinged this crazy woman is in front of him, laughing on the sidewalk, but it just makes me laugh harder. I laugh until I'm short of breath.

"Are you okay?" Andrew asks, barely holding in his own laughter.

I shake my head and blurt. "I have no idea!"

We both break down into laughter, and I throw my hands up in the air.

"I have absolutely no idea what I'm doing," I sputter. "None! It's both funny and frightening in equal measure."

A muscle ticks in Andrew's jaw. His eyes gleam as he reaches for me, then his hand falls away as if he thinks better of it. I decide to throw caution to the wind, and I step into his space and wrap my arms around him. His strong, muscular arms wrap me in a cozy Andrew cocoon, and I am instantly at peace. I sigh against his chest.

"Thank you for not running away from me, even though I'm a walking dumpster fire," I say quietly.

"You're not," Andrew murmurs. "You're just going through some stuff."

I can feel his lips moving against my hair as he speaks...and I'm tempted, just for a moment, to turn my face up towards his and touch those lips with my own. What would that be like? I have a feeling it would start another sort of fire. One that could not be extinguished.

Somehow, I gather the strength to step out of his arms and shake off my mania.

"Right," I say determinedly. "Let's go get some awesome coffee and gross green tea."

Andrew laughs softly and falls into step beside me. "I think you've got that backward."

"Impossible."

We cross the street, and I step through the door when Andrew holds it open for me. Rosa looks up with a quick smile, one that doubles as she realizes Andrew and I walked in together. She points a finger between the two of us.

"The usuals?" she asks.

We both nod, and she gives us a thumbs up. We walk over to Andrew's usual spot and sit down. I drum my fingers on the table a few times.

"So...if I'm going to try running at all of my problems," I begin, "I feel like I should think through visiting the warehouse."

Andrew nods. "Okay. What's that look like to you?"

I trace my finger along the faux wood grain on the table, focusing on identifying all the emotions roiling through my heart. Everything still feels so churned up.

"It's scary," I reply honestly. "Every time I think about it, I want to recoil from it. But that's what makes me think I should just do it. Rip off the bandage."

"What does your therapist say?"

"She said the meditation was enough homework for now and that if I decided to go out there, I should make sure I go with a friend. Not alone."

"I'm happy to go with you if you want," he offers. "How did the meditation go last night?"

I purse my lips together. "Not awesome."

He reaches for my hand and laces our fingers together.

"You'll get there, Nix. I know you will."

I revel in the feeling of our hands linked together. It grounds me in a way I don't fully understand.

"Have you ever tried it?" I ask.

He nods slowly. "It can be tough to get the hang of at first, but yes. I still practice meditation occasionally."

I raise my eyebrows in question. "Only occasionally?"

"I get a better sense of calm from swimming."

"Ah, so that's where you get those amazing shoulders," I say with a grin. "And arms. And...everything else."

Andrew laughs. "I do lift some weights and do other cardio. Right now I'm training for a race, so I spend a lot of time in the water."

"You race?" I ask incredulously. "Like...in a pool?"

He grins widely. "In the bay, Nix."

"Wait, what? You swim in San Francisco Bay? Andrew, there are sharks out there."

He shrugs like it's no big deal at all.

"They stay away from me, and I stay away from them," he says, and then he laughs out loud. "Don't look at me like I'm crazy."

I smirk. "No wonder you're not afraid of running into burning buildings. You swim with sharks."

"Will it make you feel better if I tell you that I do most of my workouts in a swimming pool? Shark-free?"

"Yes, a little."

Rosa calls Andrew's name, and he gets up to grab our drinks, then he comes back to the table. I don't miss the cringe on his face as he hands me my coffee. I laugh softly.

"Thank you," I say with a smile. "So tell me about this race."

Andrew blows on his gross tea, then sets it down.

"I do the Alcatraz Swim every year," he says with a wicked grin.

My face falls in shock. The Alcatraz Swim is a challenging event where swimmers begin at Alcatraz Island, the historic prison, and swim just over two miles to a yacht club in the bay. You have to be a very experienced swimmer to even entertain the idea of participating.

"You swim in that thing?" I ask incredulously.

Andrew laughs out loud and nods.

"Every year. I love to see if I can decrease my time each year. It's my favorite personal challenge."

I sit back in my chair and take a sip of my coffee. Heaven.

"Well, I am officially impressed," I say. "That is amazing, Andrew."

"Thanks, Nix," he says with a wink. "For me, there's peace in the water. Calm and quiet. I love the feeling of pulling myself through the water. The way my body feels weightless. But I also love to just swim down to the bottom of the pool and listen to the water all around me. It's like nothing can touch me."

I heave a sigh. "That sounds nice."

"You're welcome to come with me any time," he says as he takes a sip of his drink. "If you can swim, that is. I promise there won't be sharks in the swimming pool."

I roll my eyes. "Yes, I can swim. My mom and I have taken countless trips to Hawaii over the years. I wanted to take paddle boarding lessons when I was a kid, so I had to learn to swim first."

Andrew smirks. "You know, there are sharks in Hawaii."

I give his rock-hard shoulder a playful shove. "Whatever."

He laughs, then sobers. "So will you try meditating again?"

I nod. "Definitely. I promised to give it a good try, and I don't think I can say that at this point. Besides, I did feel the start of a panic attack last night…and I feel like I was sort of able to calm myself down a little with the breathing stuff. So I want to try again."

"Well, let me know if you want to try the pool too," he says. "I'm off on Saturday, and I have some guest passes for my gym that you can use."

The thought of seeing Andrew in swim trunks, with all those muscles rippling in the water, brings a heated flush to my cheeks. I'm not sure how much it'll do to calm me down, but it would be worth it just to see that. Although when my therapist told me to be open to new things, I don't think she was talking about a half-naked Andrew in a pool.

"I may take you up on that if I can't figure out meditation," I say. I take another sip of my coffee, and Andrew's phone beeps.

He pulls it from his pocket, and his expression grows more and more curious.

"What is it?" I ask quietly.

"Kevin Starbuck is on his way to the fire station," Andrew shares. "And he wants us to meet him there."

Andrew stands, and I follow. We both grab our drinks and head for the door.

"Does he say why?"

Andrew shakes his head. "He says he has something you might find very interesting."

I feel my eyes bulge, and I pick up the pace a little.

Andrew laughs and catches up.

"Let's go, shark bait," I tease. "I want to know what it is."

"Shark bait?" he parrots. "I reject that nickname. I like it when you call me *fireman*."

I scoff.

"I would argue that I wasn't allowed the opportunity to reject Nix, but I like it too much."

"Of course you do," Andrew eases. "You can't mess with perfection."

I laugh, then get lost in my thoughts as we continue down the sidewalk towards the fire station. The closer we get to the site of the warehouse, the more I feel that pull. And the fear. However, the novelty of the situation is wearing off, and that fear is now followed by a hint of defiance. Anger. The more I think about it, the more I don't want to let fear win. I know I can't control what I feel, but I can control how I respond to it.

When we arrive at the fire station, Kevin is already parked in the driveway, and he's not alone. There's a man with him who, for lack of a better description, looks like some kind of lumberjack. Big boots, blue jeans, flannel shirt, beard. As soon as he sees us, his face lights up in recognition. Kevin gives Andrew a handshake and a quick back slap, but I go straight in for a hug.

"So what's going on?" I ask excitedly.

"This is Nick Sanchez," Kevin replies, gesturing to the lumberjack dude. "He reached out to me through the newspaper. He's an artist who works with metal."

Nick steps forward to shake both our hands, grinning.

"It's really you," he says as his gaze darts between Andrew and me. "It's so cool to meet the Phoenix and the Fireman for real."

We both look at each other and smile back at Nick, waiting for more information.

"I'm a blacksmith," he elaborates. "I saw the story in the paper and wanted to help."

Out of my peripheral vision, I see Andrew's head turn so he can look at me. A blacksmith. Now, this is interesting. He could create some unique elements for the design that'll really make it pop.

"I'm all ears, Nick," I say as I take a step closer.

He shrugs self-consciously. "Well, I have a small business and sell custom-made signs and other architectural elements in my spare time. I thought maybe I could make something for the fire station as a thank you."

Andrew claps a hand on Nick's shoulder. "That's really nice, man," he says genuinely. "As a thank you for what?"

Nick shrugs again. "For being here," he says. "For all of us. You saved the phoenix, but it could have been any one of us. My studio is in my garage not far from here. Naturally, I work with a forge…and fire. It could have been me you rescued. It kind of hit home."

I step forward and loop my arm through Nick's.

"Why don't you come inside and show me some pictures of your work? I'll bet you've done some amazing stuff."

Nick nods. "Oh yeah, for sure," he says as he pulls his phone from his pocket. "Let me find a picture of this towel rack I made for a lady in Nob Hill."

And just like that, I have a new friend in the neighborhood.

***

Andrew

Scarlet is a force of nature. I'm sitting at our tired old kitchen island with Leonard and Todd, watching her chat with Kevin and Nick in the living room. Kevin is mostly observing, but Scarlet and Nick are sitting close to each other. Her sketchbook is in her lap, and the pencil in her hand flies furiously across the page as she sketches ideas that pop into her head. Sometimes, he grins and nods along with her. Sometimes, he leans over and takes the pencil from her so he can add something. The minds of creative people are fascinating to me, mostly because I don't have a creative bone in my body.

It's not really in me to be a jealous man, but I have felt a little ping of it here and there when Nick leans in too close. It's childish and stupid to feel any kind of jealousy. Nick doesn't give off any kind of vibe like he has romantic intentions. He seems like a decent guy. And she isn't mine to feel jealous over. I don't know what she is right now. To me, at least. I know I've never felt this kind of connection with a woman before, even at this early stage. Given that Scarlet has just been through a huge ordeal, she gets to decide the pace. And the direction. She has enough to deal with.

It's wonderful that Nick reached out through Kevin to see if he could help on this project. The second article in his series was just published yesterday, and it was good. It delved into a little information about Scarlet and me, including her project burning out and the fact that her friends and our station made it possible for her to continue. I don't mind admitting I had a tear in my eye as I read it, so I can understand someone like Nick being moved enough to try to help.

A knock on the door rouses me from my thoughts. I shove myself off my seat and head to the door, opening it to find an elderly woman smiling up at me. A boy, looking to be about eighteen years old, stands beside her, holding a shopping bag that appears a little heavy.

"Oh! You're the fireman from the paper," the lady exclaims with a bright smile, prompting me to laugh out loud.

"Good morning," I greet her, extending a hand. "I'm Fireman Andrew MacLachlan, ma'am. How can I help you?"

Her eyes light up, and she points to the bag the boy is holding, then takes my hand in both of hers and shakes it slowly.

"I had my grandson Wesley bring me right over," she says excitedly.

"I just finished it, and I want you to have it."

The boy holds the bag open for her, waving it in front of her a bit.

"Show him, Grandma," he says gently, then he looks up at me with a shy grin. "She made this for you."

She reaches into the bag and pulls out a folded item that looks like a blanket as Leonard and Todd come up behind me. Her grandson helps her unfold it, and they each hold up a corner as a beautiful quilt unfurls. Several different fabrics were used in its construction, most of them fireman-themed. The intricate design and precision stitching have resulted in a breathtakingly gorgeous piece.

"You made this? It's amazing," I tell her. "How long did this take you?"

She gives her corner to her grandson, and he folds the quilt back up for her.

"Oh, not too long," she replies. "I've been retired for years. Got nothing but time on my hands now."

Her grandson shakes his head and laughs softly.

"She's being modest," he tells me. "She's won a lot of ribbons at the California State Fair and the county fair."

I love how proud this kid is of his grandma.

She laughs. "Well, if you asked me how to do all that social media stuff, I'd be slower than slow. But quilting? I'm pretty good."

The city is warming up out there, and I realize she's standing in the sun, so I step back and invite them both in. I usher them to the living room, where a curious Scarlet is now watching from the sofa.

"Oh, how wonderful!" the lady exclaims when she sees Scarlet. "You're here too. I'm Sarellen Davis, dear. I'm so excited to meet you."

She shoves herself right between Nick and Scarlet, and I have to fight back a laugh as Nick looks up at the rest of us with a huge grin. He scoots over to give her more room. I motion for her grandson to have a seat as well, and he takes a seat across from her.

"Wesley, look," Sarellen says. "It's the Phoenix. How pretty you are, dear!"

Is Scarlet blushing? Something squeezes at my heart watching her.

Wesley grins and nods, but he seems to be a quiet kid. Scarlet looks up at me in curiosity, wondering what on earth is going on.

"Mrs. Davis made something for the station," I explain to Scarlet.

"I made it for *you*, handsome," Sarellen says with a wink. "You deserve a reward for being so brave. But if you want to share it with these other brave young men, you won't get any trouble from me."

I laugh out loud as Sarellen motions for Wesley to show off the quilt again. He unfurls it and tries to hold it up himself, but he struggles with the width. I reach over and grab a corner and we hold it up together.

Scarlet's face lights up in amazement as she takes it in. She's positively beaming as she gets up and steps closer so she can observe the workmanship.

"This is so beautiful!" she exclaims, reaching out to run her fingers over the stitching.

Leonard comes into the room with bottles of water for our unexpected guests as Scarlet returns to her seat on the couch next to Sarellen.

"You're next, dear," she whispers to Scarlet, winking. "Your quilt is going to take a bit more time, but it's going to be a real showstopper. Oh, what a pleasure it is to see you in person. Your name is Scarlet? Are you well? Recovered from the fire?"

Scarlet smiles sweetly at Sarellen and nods, holding up the arm with the brace on it.

"Mostly."

I don't worry so much about the strain on her arm. It will heal over time. But I do worry about the wounds to her spirit. Sometimes, the ones you can't see are the hardest to heal.

"Well, please take care and get some rest, dear girl," Sarellen says gently.

Scarlet nods. "I will."

Sarellen clicks her tongue.

"That picture of you right after the fire nearly broke my heart. When I saw it, and I saw how he was comforting you, I knew I had to do something. So I got right to work and made that quilt for Andrew. A bit of comfort for one who gave the same to you."

When Scarlet's eyes meet mine, they're glassy with unshed tears. I want to pull her into my arms right now, but I don't want to make a scene in front of everyone. Not with so many unanswered questions between us. She manages a shaky smile in my direction. I smile back at her, hoping my expression communicates enough.

You're safe.

I've got you.

I'm here.

Chapter 12

Scarlet

I sigh loudly for the tenth time and look Kate square in the face.

"Can't you just give me the procedures for this?"

Kate raises her eyebrows and gives me half a smile.

"It doesn't work that way."

"As my Nonno would say, 'We can put a man on the moon, but we can't do this?' I don't understand what you mean when you tell me to set my intentions. I already do that every day."

Kate nods. "Yes, but I'm not talking about something as simple as making a list of the errands you want to run for the day or a shopping list for decor items. Set your intentions for healing."

I slide my hands under my thighs so I don't throw one of the pillows on her couch. This is so frustrating. I flop back against the cushions and close my eyes.

"I just don't want to be afraid anymore," I say in a voice thick with emotion. "I hate it."

"Scarlet," Kate says softly.

I open my eyes to find her watching me. There's compassion in her eyes, and I know she gets it, but I am still tired of the relentless back and forth that this session has turned into.

"Yes?"

"You want the procedures for healing only you can do," she says. "Healing is a very individual thing. I can't tell you what steps to take, but I can help you figure out which steps might work for you. In order to do that, we talk. About what you're feeling."

I chew on my lower lip for a second, trying to nail down just one of the feelings I have right now. My feelings are all over the place.

"I feel like my emotions are in a fish tank," I say quietly. "And someone just reached in there and stirred it all up. I can't see anything. The water's murky. It's just a lot of muddy chaos."

Kate nods. "Okay, let's go back. Before the fire. Can you make sense of your feelings then?"

"I was solely motivated to win the contest," I say firmly. "I woke up, I had a list of tasks to do for that day, I did those tasks, I went to bed."

She smiles at me. It's a smile I'm quickly learning I don't like because it's usually followed by words I'd rather not hear.

"I asked you about your feelings, and you gave me your to-do list."

I think about it for a minute, then burst out laughing. She's right. I did that. I really am a certified hot mess. I close my eyes and think back to a time that feels like it was so long ago, but it's really only been a week since the fire. I feel like I'm living in some kind of weird wormhole where time is something completely different.

"Feelings before the fire," I muse. "Love for my mom. For my friends. Gratitude that my mom supports me chasing this dream of mine. Purpose. I felt a sense of purpose over my professional goals. Excitement about the Decorator's Showcase competition. I really felt like this was my year. And a little hopeful curiosity."

Kate's expression lights.

"Curiosity?"

"Andrew," I say, unable to stop the smile from blooming on my face.

"First, I kept seeing him at the coffee house at the same time, and then we met that night in the alley. He's...well, he's one of the best people I know."

"So what were you curious about?"

"Before the fire? Him."

Kate tilts her head at me. "And now?"

I shrug. "Everything feels more complicated. You should see him, Kate. He's gorgeous. And sweet. And funny. I was attracted to him before the fire, but I wanted to wait to get to know him until after my project was done."

Kate nods. "No distractions. I remember."

"Something changed in me because of the fire," I share.

It's the first time I've said it out loud and it's kind of liberating. Looking at it is just another thing I've been avoiding. I didn't want to look too close, but the fact is my priorities have changed.

"Life feels more precious," I explain as emotions clog in my throat. "So does time. Part of me wants to grab hold of him and not let go."

"And the other part?"

"The other part wonders if my attachment to him is because of all those things or because he saved me and I have some kind of weird hero worship thing going on."

Kate considers my words for a moment. "Does that *feel* true?"

I don't have to think about it much. "No."

She offers me half of a smile, her eyes full of compassion.

"This whole experience is going to teach you to check in on your feelings more often, Scarlet," she explains. "It's not good to shove them aside and make time for them later. Check in on your gut. And your heart. What do they tell you?"

The words are on the tip of my tongue, but I fight to get them out. Saying them makes it real. Gives it weight. Fear curls in my gut, motivating me to get it out. I'm tired of fear and apprehension nipping at my heels.

I nod and swallow hard. "That he's my person," I reply, almost a whisper. "I don't know why. I barely know him."

"Sometimes your head gets it the way and sometimes your heart does," she says cryptically. "It's up to you to be diligent and make the best decisions you can. That being said, you haven't been sitting here asking obsessive questions about getting into a relationship with Andrew. That seems to be a good sign."

I can't help the smile that blooms on my face at her words. I also realize the truth of them. I'm attracted to Andrew, not obsessed with him. If I was ever obsessed with anything it was winning the contest, which now seems to have fallen down my priority list a few spaces. Getting normal back is at the top now. Being able to be alone without being afraid. Things that are far more important than any contest.

"I guess I'm really just beginning to realize that I'm going to need to lean on the people in my life to get through this."

"Good," Kate replies. "Think about the times when you've been there for your friends. Were you keeping a tally? Were you keeping a log of your service to them so that they could pay you back some day?"

I scoff. "Never."

"Right. So why do you believe you don't deserve the same energy and effort from them?" she asks. "You have people who care about you and want to be there to support you. You don't need to feel guilty about accepting their support or asking for help."

I consider her words carefully. She's right. If the tables were turned, I would never hesitate to give my friends whatever they needed. I realize something profound and look at Kate excitedly.

"This is all about letting go, isn't it?" I ask, not waiting for a reply. "Letting go of my fears. The fire. Leaning on my friends. Exploring possibilities with Andrew. It's all a form of fear."

Kate grins at me and nods. "Keep going."

"My panic attacks are just unrealistic fears that the fire is going to magically reappear and hurt me," I share. "My need to push through this whole process is just fear that I'll exhaust the patience of my friends, which I know is never going to happen. They love me and care about me. And the Andrew thing…I'm just afraid to risk my heart."

"So what do you plan to do with all of that now that you've had this realization?"

I laugh softly. "Well, my immediate response is to say that I'll just push forward and tackle my fear…but I know it's not that easy. It hasn't been that easy. But I think I see now that I have a big tool to get the upper hand over that fear. Meditation did work the other day when I started to have that panic attack. So I think my plan should be to focus on trust when my fears rise up and give me doubt and to keep trying meditation."

"That sounds like a good plan."

"Andrew shared something with me the other day," I say excitedly. "That I could run *at* my challenges. The emotional ones. I'm really good at other challenges, but I tend to avoid them when they involve emotions or what's going on in my mind. I feel that this applies to all of it. I've been sort of dancing around everything, wanting to avoid it. Telling you to give me the procedures instead of getting my hands dirty and picking through it all. I think I get it now."

"Great work, Scarlet," Kate says. "Just remember not to rush yourself. Don't push yourself too much. If you keep checking in with yourself on how you're feeling in your gut, your head, and your heart, you'll figure it out. Do what feels right."

I nod, and I'm surprised when a tear rolls down my cheek. I wipe it away, feeling an almost foreign sense of pride in myself for having worked through these emotions and now at least see a path ahead. I realize I'm not back to my normal self yet, and I probably won't be for a while, but at least I can see the road ahead. I know which way to head on this new journey.

"Thank you, Kate."

She grins. "Thank yourself. You did the work."

I smooth my palms across my jeans, excited that I've made this connection. I feel the swift and familiar return of my motivation, like a little tease of things to come. My normal, or my new normal, is coming into focus, and I feel hope building in my heart. I feel like I'm back in the driver's seat. For now, it's more than enough.

***

Andrew

I blink at my phone screen, wondering what Scarlet's cooking up in that beautiful head of hers.

Nix: Hey...when are you working next?

Andrew: Are you implying you won't be seeing me on my days off? Because nothing could be further from the truth. I'll be there in the morning.

Nix: Really?

Andrew: I will be at the station on my days off until your project is done. Consider me an extra set of hands.

Nix: If you're trying to get on my good side, it's too late...you're already there.

Andrew: Oh?

Nix: Facts. So I'll see you in the morning? Coffee and gross green tea run?

I'm grinning like a fool. She's adorable when she teases me.

Andrew: What a perfect way to start the day, Nix

Nix: I couldn't agree more, Fireman...xoxo

Did she just type little kisses and hugs? I feel a familiar surge of hope rush in, and I do my best to stifle it. I would love to explore a romantic relationship with Scarlet. I've wanted that from the moment I saw her in the coffee house the first time, with her determined little walk and that fire in her eyes. Not to mention that musky, slightly spicy perfume of hers. Lately, though, I see hesitation behind those eyes. She's been through a lot, so I don't necessarily believe it has anything to do with me directly but I do think I need to step back and give her the support she needs. I just need to find a way to do that while suppressing the urge to pull her into my arms and kiss her senseless because that's all I think about when that beautiful little mouth smirks at me.

I glance at my watch. My shift is over in ten minutes, so I'll head down to Handy's Hardware to pick up the paint Scarlet ordered for the project. She wouldn't tell me what color she chose, but I chuckle to myself as I remember her indignant expression when I asked if she was going to paint flames licking up the walls. She lightly punched me on the arm, insisting that any self-respecting interior designer would never do anything so obvious. I think back to the beautiful library she was in the midst of creating before the fire and I can't wait to see what she has planned for the station. Whatever it is, I know she'll pour her whole heart and soul into it.

Jake comes thudding down the stairs and smacks me on the shoulder as he heads for the kitchen, throwing a small duffle bag on the counter.

"If you're looking for more brownies, Todd got the last one," I tell him, then laugh at his wounded expression.

"Really? They're all gone?"

I nod, feeling equally sorry they're gone. A very nice lady named Mrs. Edwards dropped by last night with a foil pan full of the most delicious brownies any of us have ever had. Like so many others, she was moved by Kevin's article series and wanted to do something for us. I had three of them before bed last night, and I don't even want to think about how many Leonard had.

"Hey, I know you're planning to help Scarlet on your days off," Jake begins. "Just make sure you're taking time for yourself."

I grin widely. "Do you really think I'm gonna waste time on station chores just because I'm here? On my days off, I'm Scarlet's to command. I promise I won't do anything remotely fireman-ish."

Jake laughs out loud. "Fireman-ish is not a word, kid."

I shrug. "Is now."

"I've never seen you like this," Jake shares, his eyes studying me. "She's special, isn't she?"

"Yes. I've never met anyone like her."

Jake looks like he has a thousand words on the tip of his tongue, but he remains silent. He turns his attention to the walls around us.

"What color do you think she picked out?" he asks.

My gaze flicks to the boring white walls covered in scuffs and nicks from years of abuse.

"I know two things for certain: first, I will not attempt to guess what she has planned for us. And second, whatever it is, it's going to be amazing."

Jake nods. "All right, kid."

"Actually, when I'm off the clock, I'm heading down to Handy's to pick up the paint she ordered. I told her I'd help with that."

"Oh, then I'm going with you," Jake says.

I look at him to see if he's serious, and he is.

"You don't get to be the only one who knows what color she picked out," he says with a huge grin.

I laugh out loud and stand up, pulling my keys out of my pocket and jingling them at him.

"All right, old man," I tease. "Let's roll."

***

The following morning, I have to fight not to keep giving Scarlet the side-eye as we walk to the coffee house together. There's something different, and I can't figure out what it is. She has a very sweet, slightly smug expression on her face. She slows to a stop when we get to the spot directly across the street from the warehouse. She turns her head to look down the alley, stepping closer to me as she does. Instinctively, my hand finds hers.

"I decided some things yesterday," she says in a near whisper, eyeing the alley with a guarded expression. "I want to see it."

I look into her eyes, searching. "You're sure?"

She nods. "Yes, but not right now. Sometime soon. Will you come with me?"

I reach up and tuck a strand of hair behind her ear, unable to stop myself. I ache to just hold her, but for now…friends.

"You know I will," I say quietly. "Anything you need, I'm here."

Her eyes are full of emotion as she studies my face. She opens her mouth as if she's going to say something, then decides otherwise. She looks away, then tugs me farther down the sidewalk. I don't miss the fact that she keeps hold of my hand. I'm not sure what to make of it. My thoughts float back to the "xoxo" in her text last night.

"So, what do you think of the color?" she asks as we stop at a corner and wait for the light.

"It's nice."

The light turns green, and we walk through the crosswalk, continuing towards the coffee house ahead.

"Nice?" she scoffs. "Please tell me you weren't expecting something red or orange."

I laugh out loud.

"Honestly, I'm not sure what I expected…but a yellow beige wasn't it."

She stops in her tracks and pulls her hand from mine, placing both hands on her hips and gawking up at me as if I just told her puppies are ugly.

"There is no beige in that paint color, Andrew," she says adamantly, looking adorably fierce.

I can't help it. She's asking for this. I shrug.

"Looks beige to me," I say with a smirk.

The corner of her mouth curves up, and she jabs a finger into my chest.

"Take it back."

I shake my head. "Nope."

"Take it back, or you won't get the present I brought you," she says, turning on her heel and continuing down the sidewalk.

I keep up with her. "You got me a present?"

"Sure did."

I run ahead of her and block her path, flashing her my best smile.

"I take it back. It's the most beautiful color I've ever seen. And there's no beige in it. I don't know what I was thinking."

Scarlet laughs, and we finish closing the distance to the coffee house. I'm about to open the door for her, and she pushes my hand away. I step back and wait for an explanation.

"I promised you a coffee date," she says. "So please allow me to be a gentleman and open the door for you."

I chuckle to myself as she steps forward and opens the door with a dramatic flourish. I nod my thanks and step inside.

"Nix, if you were a gentleman, we wouldn't be on a date," I remind her. "Coffee or otherwise."

She smiles up at me.

"Fair enough, but please go take a seat. I'll be right there."

I do as she asks, picking the table she usually prefers and watch her as she orders our drinks. She comes back to me as soon as the order is in and takes a seat opposite me.

"This isn't really our coffee house date, is it, Nix?" I ask. "You didn't give me any warning."

"You need a warning to go on a coffee date with me?" she asks with a frown.

I laugh softly. "No, but I usually make myself all handsome before I go on a date. You didn't give me the chance to get ready."

Scarlet rolls her eyes, making me laugh again.

"Andrew, have you looked in the mirror? You're the most handsome man alive. There is nothing you can do to improve that face."

I lean forward and flash her a devilish grin.

"Do you like my face, Nix?"

She smirks, and my heart skips a beat. That's all it takes...just a little of that sass of hers, and I'm completely under her spell. Scarlet's name is called when our order is ready, and she darts over to the counter to grab them.

I take this moment to gather my wits. I don't know what's happening with her, but I am resolved to be the friend she needs, and she's making it nearly impossible. I *want* to flirt with her. I want to tease her with little touches and whispers in her ear. And I absolutely want to kiss her. None of these things are something I should do when she just needs the support of a friend. And that is exactly what I intend to be.

***

Scarlet

I am having way too much fun messing with Andrew. I'd almost feel guilty about it, but he loves messing with me just as much. I walk to the order counter slower than usual, taking a moment to check in with myself. Do I still want to move things along with Andrew? Yes. Do I plan to mess with him just a little more? Also yes.

I thank Rosa and take our drinks, then turn back toward the table. Andrew's wearing a tight-fitting t-shirt and old jeans today because I told him we're going to spend all day painting the kitchen and living area. I thought maybe he'd show up in some old, baggy, torn rags, but no. While his jeans have likely seen better days, they still look amazing on him. And the t-shirt is doing everything in its power to make sure I don't change my mind about the message I'm sending to Andrew today. I can see every contour in that muscled chest of his, and I am dying to run my fingers over it. Just not quite yet.

"Thank you," he says, then laughs out loud when I place his tea in front of him with a disgusted scowl.

I sit, then blow on my coffee. I scowl at his cup once more for good measure.

"I don't even know how you can drink green tea," I say. "It looks like broccoli water or something."

He chuckles under his breath, then takes a quick sip of his tea and lets out an exaggerated sigh like it's the most delicious thing he's ever had. I hate to admit it, but I love it when he messes with me.

"So really," he begins with a serious tone, "this isn't our coffee date, right?"

I nod slowly. "It totally is."

He frowns and gestures at his clothes.

"I would have dressed much nicer if you'd have warned me," he grumbles. "What happened to all the rules?"

I blow on my coffee and hold his gaze.

"Do you mean all the rules I had about distractions like handsome firemen?"

He grins, and every cell of my body awakens in response. He has such a beautiful smile. Those dimples could bring about world peace,

I'm sure of it.

"Yes, those rules."

I take a sip of my coffee.

"I threw them out," I say simply. "The fire taught me a few things."

He raises his eyebrows, watching me curiously. Waiting for me to explain.

I shrug. "Life is too short not to take every chance to kiss a handsome fireman. If you're lucky enough to come across one."

That grin again. It'll be the death of me. His gaze dips to my mouth and lingers. I take another sip of coffee and smile back at him, watching him process my words. He has that look on his face that I love. The one that says he's about to start pushing all my buttons just to get a reaction.

"I don't know," he says coyly. "Maybe that fireman is afraid of coffee breath and won't make a move."

I laugh, which makes Andrew laugh. The energy between us is now fully charged as we hold each other's gaze. Without missing a beat or looking away, I reach into my bag and feel around for the small tin of mints I keep on hand. I pull it out with a little flourish and place it on the table, loving the absolute delight on Andrew's face as he watches me. I open the tin and pop a mint into my mouth, giving him a look that's as much of a challenge as it is an invitation.

That's all it takes for Andrew to stand up.

"Okay, we're going," he says with the look of a man on a mission.

I laugh softly as I stand as well, grabbing my coffee. He reaches for me and wraps his hand around mine, then we head to the door together. Andrew opens the door for me, and we both wave goodbye to Rosa as we step out into the morning air.

I take two steps and then stop cold with a gasp.

"Oh wait! I didn't give you your present," I say quickly.

I was too busy flirting and completely forgot. I let go of Andrew's hand and set my coffee down, then slip my hand into the inside pocket of my bag, closing my fist around it so he can't see. I look up to find him staring at my mouth, his eyes darkened and so incredibly sexy.

"It's not wrapped or anything," I explain, "but I saw this and wanted you to have it."

Someone walks by, and Andrew wraps a hand around my elbow, ushering me into a shady spot closer to the building so we're not in the middle of the sidewalk. He looks down at my hand as I open it to reveal a small gold pin in the shape of a phoenix. The golden bird is in flames, its wings spread wide and looking fierce.

Andrew's expression sobers as he reaches out to take it from me. I smile up at him as he looks it over.

"The clasp on the back is the same as a tie tack," I explain. "So I thought you could use it if you ever dress up. Or not. You don't have to wear it or anything. I just thought it was neat. A reminder of me."

The corner of his mouth slants in a half smile as he looks at me.

"I can't imagine ever needing to be reminded of a woman who never leaves my thoughts," he says slowly. "But I love it. It's beautiful. Just like you."

This man is bent on showing me that Marina and Ashley were right all along. It's easy to reject the wrong guys. I can do that all day long. But I can't keep Andrew at arm's length anymore. I don't want to.

I take a step closer to him, looking up into those gorgeous brown eyes. I can feel the heat of his body, and a little shudder ripples through me. I want him to wrap me in his arms and never let me go, but he stays still. Watching. My eyes lower to his perfect lips. I want his kiss more than anything I've ever wanted before, but he holds back. Like some invisible tether is keeping him from kissing me.

I raise my face closer to his, and our eyes lock. The warmth of his breath caresses my cheek, and a little shiver runs through me. All I have to do is move just slightly to touch my lips to his, but I don't. I wait for him, giving him half a smile as I get ready to push his buttons in return.

"Andrew..."

"Nix?"

I smirk. "Are you going to kiss me, or do I need to pop another mint in my—"

And that did it.

Chapter 13

Scarlet

Andrew's warm, strong hands caress my face as he walks me backward until my back is against the building and I have nowhere to go. Not that I'd ever want to escape this. He presses close, and I revel in the feeling of his hard, muscled body pushed against mine. My heart hammers against my ribcage as I nod...yes...*please*. He lowers his mouth and claims mine without hesitation, and I wrap my arms around his neck to press myself even closer.

His kiss is reverent, as if he can't believe we're finally at this moment. His firm lips caress mine softly. Slowly. A low moan escapes his throat as I arch against him. His thumbs caress my cheekbones as he holds my head exactly where he wants me. We taste each other with such passion I have to lean into him to keep standing. Again. And again. And again. Finally, we pull apart just enough to look into each other's eyes.

Andrew smiles the most beautiful smile I've ever seen, and I can't resist it. I bring our mouths together again, raining soft little kisses across his lips, his chin, and those freaking sexy dimples. I rub our noses together and inhale his scent, so clean and citrusy. I pull back to look at him, and he presses our foreheads together with a grin.

"I knew it would be like that," he says in the sweetest tone. "You're going to ruin me for all other women, Nix."

I nod, drinking in his beautiful face.

"Good."

His gaze drifts down to my lips, and I steal a few extra kisses before pulling away and heaving out a sigh.

"I wish I could kiss you all day," I confess. "But we have some painting to do."

Andrew wraps his arms around my waist and pulls me close, nuzzling my neck and sending shivers of pure bliss down my spine. He moves his lips to my ear.

"I'm all yours, boss lady."

I pull away just enough to beam up at him.

"I love the sound of that."

He smiles lazily. "Mmm. Especially now that we've kissed. I won't be able to get enough of you, Nix. I'm hopelessly addicted."

I laugh softly and give him one more soft, slow kiss in reply.

"You're sure about this, though?" he asks gently. "It's not too soon for you?"

I nod and kiss him again just to drive home the point.

"Honestly, now that I know you're such an excellent kisser, I'm a little mad at myself for waiting this long."

Somehow, we manage to separate and start the walk back to the fire station. Andrew laces our fingers together as we walk, and we keep stealing glances at each other. Merry pulls up to the station just as we're walking up the driveway. She looks pointedly at our joined hands and shoots me a look over the top of her sunglasses that tells me we're definitely having a catch-up conversation as soon as possible.

Two of the other firefighters I met in the first days of the project walk towards us. Bruce and Amy, who hug Andrew and wave at me as we all converge.

"Good morning," Amy greets. "We're able to lend a hand today. We're on duty, though, so give us something we can drop quickly if we get a call."

I think for a moment. The painting absolutely has to be done today, or the entire schedule will be thrown off.

"Well, Merry is very capable and a little scary with power tools," I begin, earning a nudge from my friend. "I was going to have her label all the kitchen cabinet doors and then remove them and sand them down. Can either of you help with that?"

Amy throws a hand up, and the two women high-five each other as they head into the kitchen. I look at Bruce with a hopeful grin.

"That leaves you to help tape the kitchen and living areas with Andrew and then start painting. That sound good?"

Bruce nods and pulls Andrew away from me, which is just as well because I really need to focus, and it's impossible when I'm within touching distance of that man. I follow, grabbing my tape measure and a pencil from my tote bag. I move to the main wall of the living area.

"I'm going to make the first mark for you, then you'll understand where I'm going," I say. "I need a tape line three-quarters of the way down all the walls in the living area. We won't have to tape the kitchen. We'll use the countertops as the line."

I run my measuring tape up the wall, then use the pencil to make a mark where I want the tape line. The guys watch and nod. Easy peasy.

"We're only painting the walls above the tape," I explain.

Andrew frowns. "So the bottom of the walls are going to stay this ugly, scuffed-up white?"

I shoot him a fiendish grin.

"Nope," I answer cryptically. "But that's all the information you're getting today, Fireman."

Andrew leans forward and moves his lips close to my ear.

"I'll get it out of you later, Nix."

A delicious shudder rolls down my spine as he moves back into the living area. I laugh and shake my head, then head out to the car to grab my laptop. I set it all up on the kitchen island and prepare to organize my day. It isn't long before I'm lost in the busy work of checking my emails and completing all the project manager tasks I like to get out of the way at the start of my workday.

An hour later, the guys have finished taping, and the painting has started. The buttery yellow color looks wonderful on the walls of the fire station's living area. So much so that Andrew has stopped teasing me about it looking beige. It provides the perfect base for more. It's neutral enough to not overwhelm the space, but it's too plain to be left alone. I plan to put various pieces of art on the walls to break up the space and provide more visual interest.

My phone vibrates in my pocket, and I pull it out, finding a text from Kevin Starbuck.

Kevin: Hey, Scarlet, I took the liberty of reaching out to a few electronics stores, and the VP of Community Relations for the Tech Mart chain would love to provide our friends with a new big-screen TV with surround sound for the fire station.

I gasp, and Andrew and Bruce look up to make sure I'm okay. I give them a big, stupid grin and wave them off.

"Top secret design stuff, guys," I say quickly. "You wouldn't be interested."

They continue painting, and I duck into the kitchen to reply.

Scarlet: That's amazing! When do they want to deliver?

Kevin: They're ready when you are, I just wasn't sure what day to tell them.

I do a little happy dance in my spot in the kitchen before I type the reply. This is absolutely perfect.

Scarlet: Any time tomorrow between noon and five would be perfect. Nick is coming to install the metal panels, and then we can move furniture around. Will it be wall-mounted, or do I need to be sure I get a console in here for the TV to stand on?

Kevin: I'll check back with you later to confirm...I'll ask.

Scarlet: Thanks so much, Kev, this is great! Either way, I'll be ready.

I slip my phone back into my pocket and step over to the fridge to refill my water bottle just as Jake comes downstairs. I grab the water pitcher and step out of his way.

"I gotta say," he begins as he grabs a soda from the beat-up old fridge. "I wasn't expecting yellow."

I tilt my head towards the living room.

"But it looks good, right?"

He nods enthusiastically.

"So good. I obviously should not be picking out paint colors, which is why my wife always does it."

I grin at him, and my gaze wanders to the photo of Andrew's father behind Jake.

"Can I ask you something?"

"Sure," Jake replies. He leans against the counter and waits.

I quickly turn my head to make sure Andrew is occupied, and he is, then I turn back to Jake.

"Do you think it would be upsetting to Andrew if there was something in the kitchen that memorialized his dad a bit more than that tiny picture?"

Jake works a muscle in his jaw as he thinks it over, but he shakes his head pretty fast.

"Nope," he replies. "He's been without his dad for most of his life. He doesn't tend to get emotional about it, but I know it means something to him. This kitchen is where I feel most connected to Mac since we worked here together and he loved to cook so much. We talked about it once, back when Andrew was first assigned here, and he told me that he likes the fact that we keep Mac's memory alive."

I nod, contemplating an idea rolling around in my head. It's just an idea right now, but I feel like I could turn it into something really amazing.

"Can you tell me more about him? What did Mac like to cook most?"

Jake grins. "Anything spicy," he replies. "The guy had a cast iron stomach, I swear. He loved anything with heat. He even made his own hot sauce."

"Oh wow, really?"

"What's this about hot sauce?" Merry pipes in, grabbing a bottle of water from the fridge.

"Apparently, Andrew's dad used to make his own," I tell her.

Merry suddenly looks very interested. Any talk about food, cooking, or especially baking will do that to her.

"Believe it or not, I still have a bottle of it in the back of my freezer," Jake says with watery eyes. "Mac was more of a brother than a friend. It's probably stupid, but I can't seem to let go of that hot sauce."

Merry nods. "I think that's really sweet."

Strong arms wrap around me from behind, pulling me backward against a very muscled chest. I grin at Jake as I relax against Andrew's warmth.

"Are you talking about Dad's hot sauce again, Jake?" Andrew asks with a grin.

Jake laughs. "Don't bust my chops, kid. That was the best hot sauce I ever had."

"Yeah, it was pretty good," Andrew agrees. "From what I can

remember, anyway. It wasn't as hot as most other people said, but it was pretty tasty."

Jake jabs a finger in the air towards Andrew as Merry waves goodbye and heads back outside.

"That's because you got your old man's taste buds," he says with pride.

Andrew's body shakes behind me as he chuckles, and it's nice to see the bond between him and Jake. I turn my head to get a peek at Andrew.

"Did you always want to be a fireman?"

Andrew squeezes me a little as he takes a minute to form his reply.

"That first time my dad brought the fire truck to our house, I was hooked."

Jake laughs and nods at the memory.

"His eyes were huge," Jake shares. "Mac was so excited to show Andrew that truck."

I return my gaze to Andrew, who smiles at Jake affectionately.

"I always thought it was cool that my dad was a fireman," he says. "But after we lost him, I wasn't sure how I felt about it all for a while."

I step to Andrew's side so I can see him better, and he wraps an arm around my shoulders.

"It stayed with me, but it felt different," he shares. "As I got older, I realized I wanted to do more with it."

I look back at Jake, who is still gleaming at Andrew with fatherly pride.

"More?" I ask.

Andrew nods. "I love the work I do, but I want to get into arson investigation someday."

Jake nods, then looks at me.

"He's got the head for it," he says. "I keep telling him when he finally puts his hand up and applies, they'll be stupid not to take him."

I smile up at Andrew, but it somehow feels like the questions in my head should be asked when we're alone. Why hasn't he applied? What's holding him back? It seems like he does everything for those he cares about, but does he do things for himself?

"So when are we painting these sad old appliances, Nix?" Andrew asks.

I don't miss the fact that he's abruptly changed the subject on us. There's definitely more to unpack here. I shrug and give them a sly look.

"Ask me that same question tomorrow."

Jake's eyebrows raise in surprise, and I silently pray that he leaves it there. I'm not very good at keeping secrets when I'm excited about something, and I'm extremely excited about tomorrow...because I've actually managed to pull off one of those miracles I needed. My new friends are going to have a great day, especially now that we're adding a big-screen TV to everything being delivered. I can't wait to see their faces.

My excitement wanes when Merry steps back inside with a look on her face that says something's up. We all wait for her to share.

"Hey, uh, there's a lady in the driveway who wants to see you guys," she says, smiling slightly.

Andrew looks at me and I nod, stepping away from him as we all make our way outside. A young woman, about our age, is standing in the driveway chatting with Amy as she takes a break from sanding the cabinet doors. This reminds me, yet again, that we're in danger of being behind schedule if we take too many breaks today. But I can't exactly bark orders at the good people giving me free labor.

"Hey, guys," Amy says, jabbing a thumb in the woman's direction. "Meet Nancy Kolby."

I step forward and shake Nancy's hand, then Andrew and Jake follow. Merry comes to a stop on my right, watching me expectantly.

"It's nice to meet you, Nancy," I say lightly. "How can we help you?"

"I'm actually hoping I can help you," she says, gesturing at a rather bulky book she's holding in one arm. "I'm an artist, and I read the latest article in the San Francisco Times. I saw the guy who does metal work had donated some of his art, and I was hoping to do the same by donating a piece or two of mine."

My heart pounds eagerly as she pulls the book out and opens it. This could be so great if she's any good. If she's not, this is going to be a really awkward conversation…but if she's good, my budget is going to be so happy.

Please be good. Please be good. Please be good.

Nancy steps forward with the open book and tilts it towards me. Ohhh, hello. She's not good. She is *great*.

"Wow," I gasp. "Nancy, these are amazing."

Her whole face lights up as Merry steps to the side, making room for Nancy to get closer as I flip through the book. Page after page, her art comes to life before my eyes. A lot of it is gritty, but beautiful. They almost look a little abstract, but then an image forms as you look at it and then you're entranced. She also has some examples of watercolor and mixed media pieces.

"I'm sure you probably already have a plan for what you're going to use on this project," Nancy hedges. "But I also thought, well, nothing ventured, nothing gained. So here I am to show you what I can do."

"These are incredible," Andrew says from over my shoulder.

I smile over at him, and then I'm reminded that all the work has stopped so everyone can look at Nancy's incredible paintings. I nod in agreement, then step away from the book and level my gaze at Nancy.

"Would you like to come inside and get a look at the wall space?" I ask. "I'd love to talk to you about something for the living area."

Nancy beams at me. "Really? That would be incredible. Yes, let's go."

I motion for her to follow me, and Merry and Amy get back to work. We step inside the station, and I show her the main wall in the living area.

"I'm going to need something for either side of the television and something on this other wall here as well."

Nancy looks around, training her artist's eye on the space involved.

"I love this color," she says. "I was thinking you'd probably go with a gray or blue, but that's why I'm not the interior designer."

I nod. "I didn't want to go with something predictable or too masculine. There are female firefighters at this station as well, and I didn't want it to feel too impersonal. They live here when they're on duty. I want it to feel and look comfortable and pleasant. I wanted something that brings light, and I felt that the usual grays would make this space look like an auto shop or a garage. Not what I'm going for at all."

Nancy nods. "So you're thinking of something for either side of this TV?"

Andrew has gone back to work with Bruce, and Jake has disappeared again, so I lean over and lower my voice.

"They don't know it, but they're getting a new TV tomorrow," I say excitedly. "Bigger than this one. I'm waiting to find out if it'll be a wall mount or tabletop installation. So for art, I'm thinking thirty-six inches width-wise would be the max."

Nancy fixes her gaze on the wall space ahead of us.

"Are you putting wainscotting on the bottom of the wall? Is that why it's not painted?"

I nod. "Not wainscotting, but there are panels our metalworking friend is bringing tomorrow. They don't know about those either."

Nancy chuckles.

"They're lucky to have you and your bag of surprises."

My gaze softens as I watch Andrew and Bruce working together. Jake walks in and flops on the couch, giving me a wink as he sits. I look at Nancy.

"I'm lucky to have them too," I whisper, feeling a little emotion lumping in my throat. "And I'm determined not to let them down."

Nancy turns to me and folds her arms across her chest.

"I know we just met, but how much do you trust me?"

I laugh out loud at her question. It's another reminder of how much I've changed because it wasn't too long ago when I wouldn't have given anyone artistic license over any part of my project. Now? I'm definitely going with my gut a lot. And my gut says I can trust Nancy and her artistic vision.

"If you can stay within a certain color palette, I'm prepared to trust you a lot."

Nancy grins conspiratorially. "It's a deal. When do you need the pieces?"

***

Four hours later, Andrew snatches my laptop away and shoves a plate with a piece of pizza on it in front of me. I look up with a frown, and he's giving me a look that definitely tells me I'd better not argue. I roll my eyes and take a bite of the pizza just as my stomach lets out a monstrous growl.

I'm camped in my usual spot at the kitchen island, so Andrew pulls up a stool next to me and digs into his pizza as he bobs his chin at the kitchen cabinets. Most of the appliances are now taped off and covered in plastic. I'm really hoping we don't end up keeping them, but until I'm sure, I don't want to get paint on them. Merry is busying herself with taping off the floors before I turn her loose with the paint sprayer. Heaven help us all.

"So?" Andrew says as he gestures at the living area walls. "What's the plan for the bottom of the walls?"

I shake my head at him, refusing to share, and take another bite of my pizza. He laughs.

"C'mon, Nix," he teases. "Out with it."

"It's a surprise," I say simply. "But you'll find out tomorrow, I promise. Does that make you feel any better?"

His eyes dart over my face, landing on my mouth. He leans forward and presses a sweet kiss to my lips, then on the tip of my nose.

"No," he says quietly. "But that did."

I laugh softly and take another bite. We eat in relative silence for a bit. A glance at the clock tells me I don't have much time left before I have to pack up and get out of here for the day. Unfortunately, that means Merry will be able to paint the base cabinets, but the doors won't be back on until morning now. These little interruptions keep chipping away at my timeline, even though they've all managed to bring us some great surprises.

"When we're done for the day, can you do me a favor?" I ask quietly.

"Anything," he replies without missing a beat.

"Will you go to the warehouse site with me?" I ask quietly as if the warehouse might hear my plans. "So I can see it?"

Andrew wraps his hand around mine. "Of course I will. Are you sure?"

I nod. "I can't stop thinking about it."

A muscle ticks in Andrew's jaw as he considers my words.

"I'm ready whenever you are," he says.

I take a deep, calming breath and let it out slowly. Andrew squeezes my hand.

"You okay?" he asks.

I nod. "Just mentally fighting with Old Scarlet…the one from before the fire."

"What does she want to do?"

I smirk.

"She wants to schedule this confrontation for a more convenient time and then skip the whole messy part where I actually have to deal with it."

Andrew nods in understanding. "And what does Nix want to do?"

I beam at the sound of my nickname.

"Nix wants to run at it full speed so she can feel all the feels and get on with her life."

Andrew laughs out loud, prompting me to join in.

"I think the actual solution is probably somewhere in between," I say.

I take another bite of pizza. Andrew reaches over and pulls on my bar stool to scoot me closer. I chew my pizza with a half-smile on my face as he drags me so I'm basically seated between his legs and then wraps his big, strong arms around me. I lean into his embrace and lay my head on his shoulder, sighing in contentment. I feel the stress melt away as Andrew plants a light kiss on the top of my head. For now, this is enough. It's more than enough, actually. And as I sit here being held by this man with a huge heart and such a lovable, noble soul, I wonder how on earth I never made time for this before.

The revving of a drill announces Merry's presence as she breezes into the room, compulsively pulling the trigger and making crazy eyes at me. I laugh but don't move from Andrew's embrace, and she wiggles a finger at us.

"Like, get a room."

Andrew grins at Merry.

"Are you jealous?"

Merry makes a face at him, then nods.

"I'm ninety percent happy for Scarlet, ten percent jealous," she says with another rev of the drill. "I never used to be, but now my friends are all settling down and leaving me."

I scoff. "Not me."

Merry gives me a look of pure disbelief and points to Andrew. "He's your person. It's only a matter of time."

I look back at Andrew.

"This is why we call her the unicorn," I share. "She's all rainbows and kittens and unicorn positivity."

Andrew laughs behind me, making me smile from the inside out, and then Merry points that finger of doom at him.

"And she is your person, buddy," Merry says. "Hurt her, and I'll shank you with my unicorn horn."

I bust out laughing, and so does Andrew. Merry laughs under her breath and sets the drill down.

"Whatever." She pulls up a bar stool and sits. "So when's quittin' time, boss?"

I look around the kitchen, mentally calculating how much work we can get done today. If it were up to me, I'd be here until late tonight... but I've made multiple promises that involve me not working myself to the bone and not encroaching on their living space for more than eight hours a day. I intend to honor those promises.

"Do you think you can get the base cabinets painted in two hours?" I ask Merry. "We can put the doors on in the morning, but I would love to give them time to dry overnight before...stuff happens tomorrow."

I give Andrew the side-eye and giggle. He's leaning over, trying to gauge my expression to see if I'll give anything away. It's killing me not to tell him, but I'm a no-spoilers kind of girl.

Merry nods and spins on her heel, trotting back outside and calling out, "It will be done, boss lady!"

My phone vibrates in my pocket, and I pull it out to see a text from Ashley, which is likely top secret. I look at Andrew and nudge him with a grin.

"Back to work, young man."

Andrew plants a sweet, light kiss on my cheek and heads back to the living area to finish the baseboards with Bruce as I check my messages.

Ashley: Full steam ahead, Scarlet. Delivery scheduled by eleven in the morning.

I breathe a huge sigh of relief. Miracles do happen. That's miracle number one.

Scarlet: I don't know how I'll ever repay him, but please thank your dad for me.

Ashley: I will. He said to say how proud he is of what you're doing. We all are.

Scarlet: Thanks, girl. See you tonight. Love you!

Ashley: Love you too.

Two hours later, the living area is completely painted, the base cabinets in the kitchen are drying, but the doors are still off. And they need paint. We'll have to get caught up in the morning before deliveries begin to arrive. Hopefully. I try to push it all out of my mind as I walk down the sidewalk toward the warehouse site with Andrew on my right and Merry on my left.

"Doing okay, Nix?" Andrew asks, squeezing my hand gently.

I take a deep breath.

"So far, so good," I say quietly.

We stop at the intersection and wait for the light. Merry is a silent ball of energy beside me, but I can feel her keeping watch. The light turns green, and we cross the street, and soon, we're looking down the alley. Or what was the alley. Without the warehouse, it's pretty open on the left side now.

I take another deep breath as we head down the alley. Memories begin to flood my mind. So many afternoons making a quick run to the mini-mart for something before dark. All those hours I spent inside, toiling away over my cutting machine to create that beautiful library. Andrew's incredibly sweet snack drops.

I stop in my tracks and turn to Andrew.

"I never thanked you."

Andrew looks at me, shaking his head. "For what?"

I take both his hands in mine. "All those late-night snack drops you made, trying to keep me from needing to go out after dark."

He grins widely. "I did what I could."

I wrap my arms around his neck and step into his embrace. I love the feeling of his arms wrapping around my waist as he looks down at me with those beautiful, searching eyes.

"Thank you."

I bring our lips together for a soft, quick kiss and then pull away. I look from Andrew to Merry.

"Okay, let's do this."

Chapter 14

Scarlet

Merry puts a reassuring hand on my back and gives me a little pat as we move down the alley. Part of the exterior walls are still standing, but most of the warehouse burned to the ground. A clean-up crew has been here. That much is obvious. There are large dumpsters scattered around. The interior walls are all gone, burned up in the fire to the point where only the steel support beams are visible. The dumpsters are filled with ash and rubble.

I step up to the edge of the warehouse floor. There should be a wall here…and the door was here. It's all gone now, including whatever piece landed on Andrew as he was carrying me to safety. I look around the footprint of the warehouse, shaking my head.

"I can't believe it's all gone," I whisper. "We all spent so much time here."

Movement out of the corner of my eye catches my attention, and I look over to see Kevin Starbuck trotting down the alley toward us. I give him half a smile as he draws near.

"Hi guys," he says. "I stopped by the fire station, and Jake told me you came down here. Can I join?"

Merry looks at me to make sure I'm okay, and I nod quickly. I feel a squeeze on my hand from Andrew.

"Sure," I say, then gesture at the ruined warehouse. "Just confronting an old ghost."

Kevin gives me a sympathetic look. "Are you doing okay with it?"

I swallow and nod, then look back at the ruined warehouse. My thoughts drift to my library, now completely gone. All that work. All the help from my friends. Gone. As if guided by some internal force, I take a step forward onto the concrete slab floor of the warehouse and begin walking towards the area where my rooms were. Andrew remains by my side, my friends following close behind. My heart fills with gratitude that they're here with me. Ready to support me however I may need it.

I pass through the area where our makeshift table and chairs were, stopping to offer Andrew a half smile.

"This is where Andrew and I had our first conversation," I share. "Sitting on paint buckets and eating chicken kebabs after he followed me down the alley to make sure I was alright."

Andrew wraps an arm around my shoulders and pulls me against his side. I slide my arm around his waist and let his warmth seep into me.

"So this is where you first met?" Kevin asks softly.

I shake my head. "We'd been noticing each other at the coffee house down the street for a couple weeks."

"But she wouldn't talk to me," Andrew clarifies.

Merry smirks. "You could've talked to her."

"Nope. Her whole vibe was very much stay-away. Do not approach."

Merry thinks about arguing, then thinks better of it. I laugh under my breath.

"I was really hungry one night and didn't realize I had no food in here until after it was already dark," I explain. "So I ordered dinner on an app, and Andrew saw me running down the alley with it. He followed to make sure I was okay."

Kevin nods in understanding, and I flinch as Merry points a finger at me.

"You promised you wouldn't go out after dark, young lady."

"I know, I'm sorry," I tell her. "I never did it again. Mostly because Andrew kept leaving bags of snacks tied to the door handle every night."

He beams at me, then presses a sweet kiss to my temple. Kevin notices but says nothing.

I take another brief moment, then continue further into the warehouse. The steel beams inside the walls are still standing, allowing me to find my way even with the drywall burned away. I slow to a stop at the doorway that led to my bedroom and step away from Andrew. I can't help it. I have to get a closer look.

The floor. My beautiful painting of billowy clouds in a sun-kissed sky is still here. Parts of it are gone, where the furniture was that burned up, but the open spaces remain untouched. I kneel down to run my fingers over it. It really was the best painting job I ever did, I realize as my throat closes up with emotion. I let out a low sob as I remember that last night here.

Andrew immediately appears at my side. He kneels and wraps an arm around me as Merry steps to my other side. I feel the warmth of her hand land on my back in a reassuring gesture.

"It's really beautiful, Scarlet," she says reverently.

Only when I look up at her do I realize my eyes are lined with tears. I blink and one falls down my cheek, giving more tears permission to follow.

"Thanks."

"Which room was this?" Kevin asks softly.

"Her bedroom," Andrew replies. "The room I pulled her out of."

Something in Andrew's words sends my heart straight up into my throat, and my lip quivers. I sink to the floor as even more tears fall. I barely register the fact that Andrew immediately sits and pulls me into his lap. I lay my head on his shoulder and just let it out. And it *pours* out. The grief. The pain. Every ounce of loss.

I'm vaguely aware of Merry's voice saying soothing, comforting words as I cry. Her hand smooths my hair as she talks. I bury my face in Andrew's neck.

"Thank you," I murmur. "Thank you, thank you."

Andrew rocks me in his lap, his arms a protective cocoon. He presses his lips to my temple. No one moves or says anything, and I find myself so grateful that my friends are just here for me. Letting me process. I inhale a shaky breath and just cry.

I don't even know how much time passes before I'm finally ready to stand up and deal with this. Merry pushes a tissue into my hand, and I blot my eyes as I look at the remnants of my painting on the floor.

"It's harder than I thought it would be," I say to no one in particular. "To be back in the space where Andrew pulled me to safety. A place I thought would bring me my greatest dream in life, and it ended up being a nightmare I had to survive."

Kevin looks around the remnants of the space.

"I can't imagine what it was like to live in here at night," he muses. "Were you able to hear the yelling and car honking on the streets?"

I manage a feeble smile.

"Not really. You'd think the metal walls would amplify the sounds of all that chaos out there, but it really didn't. It was pretty quiet but still scary to spend the night in here because I knew what the neighborhood was like at night."

Kevin nods. "You've got some crazy passion, Scarlet. It took a lot of courage to go after it like that."

I take a moment and realize something profound that I need to confront.

"It doesn't feel like courage now," I share. "It feels like carelessness."

Merry watches me with concern.

"I was so focused on winning that I jeopardized my own safety," I say with a shake of my head. "I forgot something really important. I am a highly capable, *formidable* woman. I didn't need to sleep here to get my project done."

Andrew pulls me into his side.

"Hey," he murmurs. "You did what you thought you had to do. Looking back at it now won't change anything. Don't beat yourself up."

I nod and move toward the area that once held my beautiful library. The floor wasn't done in here yet, so there are no remnants to see. The space is completely empty. Everything was burned away. A clean-up crew has already been through here, so it's been swept clear. Ashes and debris are scattered throughout the space in dumpsters.

Something glints in the corner of my eye, and I look over against the wall to see a bit of gold sticking out. I walk over to it and crouch down to pick up a six-inch piece of that beautiful wallpaper I had planned to use. I let out a sad sigh and hold it up to show my friends.

"This is all that's left of a two hundred dollar roll of wallpaper."

I run my fingers over it. It really is beautiful. The edges are singed from the fire, but the paper in the center still looks new. So elegant and pretty.

"I'm never going to be this reckless again," I say with a shake of my head. I turn to Merry. "I'm sorry I worried you because of what I did."

Merry lets out a sigh and steps over to me, wrapping me in a hug. I wrap my arms around her, too, squeezing my friend. So grateful for her.

"We're okay, girl," she says in my ear. "And you are still a highly capable, formidable woman."

I nod as I pull away.

"You bet I am," I say, tucking the piece of wallpaper into my bag as a reminder of what's important. "I'm just not going to be an idiot anymore."

Merry opens her mouth to protest, but I shake my head at her. I *was* an idiot. But the time to focus on all of this is over. It's time to move forward. I take one last look around the skeleton of the warehouse and mentally say goodbye.

"Right," I say with fresh determination. "Shall we get out of here? I've had enough of the past."

Andrew grins widely and steps into my path. I let him pull me into his arms and I bury my face in his neck, inhaling his clean scent. It washes through me, soothing all my rough edges. He moves his mouth to my ear.

"I'm so proud of you," he murmurs.

I wrap my arms around his waist and place my hands on the back of his broad shoulders. His muscles ripple under my fingertips as we hold each other. I can't believe I ever thought keeping this man at a distance was a good idea.

I step out of Andrew's arms, and we link our hands together as we all walk toward the area where we entered. In so many ways, I really do feel like a phoenix. I survived this fire. I'm safe and well. I have wonderful people in my life. And I didn't freak out here. I cried. I grieved. But I wasn't overcome with anxiety. I'm handling this and coming out stronger, which just gives me one more thing to be grateful for.

***

Andrew

My heart hurts. After seeing Scarlet sobbing on the floor of the burned-out warehouse and scooping her into my arms, I'm devastated for her. Oddly enough, she seems to have been reborn after confronting it all, but I am still clearly affected by how hard it hit her. I know it didn't happen very long ago. I just hate to see her in pain over anything.

There's almost a bounce in her step as we walk up the alley and make our way back to the fire station, but the whole experience has left a stain on my spirit. It's in my nature to want to make everything better, no matter the cost. Right now, all I want to do is find someplace quiet, hold her in my arms, and kiss her until that warehouse is the furthest thing from her mind.

Kevin leans over and whispers something to her, but the only word I can discern is "tomorrow". There's definitely something happening, but I know better than to ask. If she wants it to be a surprise, then that's what it'll be. From the look of things, Merry knows, too, because she's dancing around like a ball of energy. For now, I'm just content to walk beside Scarlet, our fingers entwined.

We walk up the driveway to the fire station and gather around Kevin's car. He holds his camera up with a sheepish expression.

"Um, I took a few pictures in the warehouse," he confesses. "I didn't want to steal the focus by asking if I could at the time, so if you'd like me to delete these I have absolutely no problem doing that...but they're really good."

I look to Scarlet, who doesn't look upset at Kevin's revelation. I don't mind at all. I'm well aware of his work. His photos are a huge part of the stories he tells. I watch as he pulls the images up and holds the viewing screen so we can see.

He's right. These are amazing. The best ones are of me and Scarlet on the floor. She's in my lap, and I'm holding her. Her face is against my chest, and I have my head dipped over hers. Merry is standing at my side with her hand on Scarlet's back. With most of the exterior walls gone, the afternoon light puts us in a near silhouette. The image is as moving as it is dramatic.

Scarlet shakes her head slowly. "Kevin, these are so beautiful."

He watches her carefully. "You're okay if I use them?"

She nods. "Yeah. I'm okay. Thanks for checking, though."

Merry smiles at Kevin. "It's grief. It's healing. It's love and friendship. It shows so much."

Kevin nods his thanks and tucks the camera in a black bag on the seat, then turns to the group of us.

"Thanks, guys. So I guess I'll see you guys in the morning for the big moment," he says excitedly. "If I drop in around nine, is that plenty of time?"

Scarlet nods. "I may put you to work while we wait for the delivery," she says. "We're behind schedule, and I need to provide an update to the Home Decorators Showcase in a few days. This is when I share the before photos and talk about the project, so I want to be sure I have everything ready."

Kevin gets into his car and smiles at us through the open window.

"I'll arrive ready to help," he promises. "And with a new article for you to review as well."

Scarlet gives him a fist bump through the window as he backs out of the driveway. I wave at him, then turn to find Merry hugging Scarlet.

"Want me here at nine, too?" she asks, giving Scarlet's shoulders a squeeze.

"Yep," she replies. "I need those cabinet doors painted and back on the cabinets by the end of the day. Then, hopefully, we'll go shopping if I get my furniture budget from the city."

Merry jumps up and down, cheering, and I wonder if she ever runs out of energy.

"My favorite!"

I step aside with Scarlet as we watch Merry get into her car and back down the driveway as well. Alone at last. I turn to Scarlet and join our hands as she heaves a great sigh.

"Long day?"

She lets her head fall back, and her eyes close for a moment. I take a moment to admire her. From the sunny blond of her hair to the blush on her cheeks to those gorgeous lips. So beautiful. She opens her eyes and nods.

"Long day," she repeats. "But a good one. Except for being behind schedule. People are being so amazing, but every time we get a random act of kindness from a stranger, it sets my timetable back. And then I feel like an ungrateful jerk."

I steal a soft kiss from her.

"You're not an ungrateful jerk," I argue. "Even if you do keep insisting on not sharing any info with me."

Her face lights up, and she grins up at me.

"I love surprises," she says excitedly. "I'm not even sorry about keeping you in the dark. It's the first of many, hopefully."

"What are you doing for dinner?" I ask quietly. "I'm not ready to say goodbye to you yet."

Scarlet smiles softly. "Me either. But I'm not sure I'm up for going out."

"No?"

"Want to come over to Ashley's and order in?" Scarlet offers. "She'll probably be glad to have some time off babysitting duty."

I pull Scarlet into a hug. "No one's babysitting you."

She laughs softly. "I know, I know. I just need to get used to all the help."

I give her a quick kiss, then reach into my pocket for my keys.

"Let's go, Nix. Lead the way."

Scarlet nods and gets in her car as I get into mine. I back out and wait for her, getting ready to follow her and realizing I'd follow her anywhere. I'm completely hooked.

Traffic in the city is heavy at this time of day, so it takes just less than thirty minutes before I pull my car up to the curb behind Scarlet in a much nicer neighborhood than our usual spots. I get out and look up at the four-story building. From our conversations, I know the ground floor houses the offices of The Mermaid Foundation, a charity run by Scarlet's friend Marina. As far as I remember, the second floor is a short-term apartment that The Mermaid Foundation uses to help families in crisis. The third floor is where Scarlet is currently staying with Ashley, and the top floor is where Marina lives with her new husband Zach…who just happens to be one of the biggest rock stars in the world. I haven't met him yet, but Marina is pretty great, so I hope I'll feel the same about Zach if I ever meet him.

Scarlet waits for me to join her at the front door, then we step inside and immediately climb the stairs to the third floor. She unlocks the front door, and we step into an open entry that gives me a full view of most of the apartment. There's a very large living room with a nice exposed brick wall and a connecting wall covered in bookshelves, followed by an open kitchen at the back with a large island…where Marina and Ashley are currently laughing and talking with two very recognizable members of The Royal Rebels, an indie rock band.

Marina squeals and runs for Scarlet, followed closely by Ashley. I laugh under my breath. I love their friend group. They're more like sisters than friends, and it makes me happy that Scarlet has such a strong support system. Scarlet is surrounded in hugs, then she turns to me and laces our fingers together before pulling me towards the kitchen where Zach Adams and Rick Archer are waiting.

Zach steps forward and offers a hand, which I shake enthusiastically.

"Andrew, right?" he says in a very British accent. "I'm Zach."

I nod, then take Rick's extended hand for a shake.

"And I'm Rick, Andrew. Nice to meet you."

"It's nice to meet you both as well," I say, feeling a little star-struck if I'm honest.

These guys have been on my playlists for years. I love their music.

Scarlet comes up beside me and wraps an arm around my waist, which makes me stupid happy. I wrap an arm around her shoulders and squeeze her into my side as I press a kiss to the top of her head.

"We were having a kind of impromptu catch-up," Marina explains. "Zach was visiting me at the office when Rick and Ashley pulled up, so we came up here to chat. We were thinking of going to Nonno's for dinner. Did you guys want to join?"

Scarlet looks at me, then back at her friends. "Normally, I'd love that, but I'm exhausted. We were thinking we'd just order something in."

"I'd offer to bring something back for you guys, but you'll probably want to eat sooner than that," Ashley says sweetly. "Text me if you want anything, though."

Scarlet nods, and we spend the next few minutes gathered on the sofas in the living room…visiting. I'm surprised at how down-to-earth Zach and Rick are since they're so famous. I mean, these guys have won World Music Awards for their albums. Zach has a street named after him in Los Angeles. But here they are, sitting around the living room like regular people and asking Scarlet about her project.

"That's all I can say in our present company, guys, sorry," Scarlet tells Rick and Ashley while giving me a gentle nudge. "I want Andrew to be just as surprised as everyone else."

"When's the big reveal?" Zach asks.

"Well, the really *big* reveal is about two weeks away," Scarlet shares. "But there are some nice surprises being delivered tomorrow that I won't be able to keep a secret from my new friends."

"Do we get to be there for the really big reveal?" Marina asks excitedly. "We're so proud of you."

Scarlet smiles at her friend.

"That's my plan. I want to do it before the judges come so it's more of a party and less nerve-wracking. I'm inviting our gang, plus everyone from the community that's pitched in, to help. And, of course, all the firefighters stationed at Engine 14."

"When do the judges come?" Ashley asks.

Scarlet shrugs. "They haven't said yet. I'll have more information after I file my check-in paperwork with the network."

Rick winks at her.

"I'm sure you will, Corbel Queen. Then we can celebrate your big win."

Scarlet laughs softly and winks back. "My favorite Rebel, always."

Zach feigns a hurt look, and Scarlet breaks into a full giggle, which is absolutely adorable. I smile down at her, relishing the fact that she's tucked into my side on this couch like it's just any other day. I've quickly realized that our relationship has had a very unconventional start. I need more quiet, normal moments with her. And definitely more kissing.

Rick clears his throat, jolting me out of my thoughts. Was I staring at Scarlet's lips?

"Well, we're heading out," Rick says, dragging Ashley behind him as she grins at us.

Yep, I was staring at Scarlet's lips. I'd feel more embarrassed about it, but it looks like they're going to give us some space, and I'm excited about that. The foursome waves goodbye, and Scarlet promises to text them if we want dessert. The door snicks shut behind them…and we're alone.

Scarlet turns her head and grins up at me.

"I love my friends, but I kind of felt like I was in high school waiting for my mom to go to bed so I could kiss my boyfriend."

Every cell of my body lights up at Scarlet's words. I lean in and bring our foreheads together, looking into those beautiful blue eyes of hers.

"You can kiss me any time you want, Nix."

She offers me a shy smile.

"Good."

And that's all it takes. She raises her lips, and I gladly lower mine. Her mouth opens to mine, and we explore each other lazily. Passionately. I raise a hand to cup her cheek, and the sexiest little moan escapes her throat. Her lips are so incredibly soft. I feel myself getting lost in her kisses, and I don't really care if I'm ever found. Let me just drift away with her.

I don't even know how long we kiss before we mutually pull away for a little air, which is highly overrated. Her words from before finally hit home, and I grin down at her.

"Did you just call me your boyfriend?"

She bites her lower lip, and my stomach dips at how cute that is.

"Is that okay?" she asks, taking a playful nip at my bottom lip. "Apparently, Scarlet 2.0 is very brazen and just goes for what she wants."

I smirk because it's the way we are together, but I am over the moon ecstatic about this whole boyfriend thing.

"I think the original Scarlet was probably just as brazen."

"True," she admits. "But she had a strict no-relationships policy, so I had to kick her to the curb."

I reach up a hand and smooth my fingers across the softness of her cheek. Her eyes flutter closed for a moment. I could really, really fall hard for this woman. She's so beautiful, smart, and incredibly sexy without even knowing it. I'm in big trouble.

"Well, as your boyfriend," I begin, my voice husky with longing. "I wholeheartedly approve. I don't want to live in a world without your kisses."

That earns me a beautiful smile. I rub my thumb across her lower lip, which is plump from being thoroughly kissed.

"I just have one question for you," she says cryptically, her gaze dipping to my mouth.

I raise my eyebrows and wait for more details.

"What's your dinner order?" she asks, stealing a quick kiss.

I laugh under my breath. "Whatever you want is fine," I murmur. "The only thing I'm really hungry for is you, Nix."

Her eyes darken considerably, and she brings our lips together in another soft, exploratory kiss. She pulls away too quickly, then pulls her phone out and begins feverishly thumb-typing something. I flop back against the sofa cushions and watch her with a stupid happy grin on my face.

"What are you doing?"

She stops typing, then pivots herself into my lap in one deft move. I wrap my arms around her as she tosses her phone onto the couch.

"I ordered dinner," she replies, snaking her arms around my neck. "We have a whole hour before it gets here. What do you want to do in the meantime?"

I laugh out loud and put my hands on either side of her beautiful face, slowly drawing her mouth down to mine.

"Come here, and I'll show you, gorgeous."

And I'm lost again.

Chapter 15

Scarlet

I let my foot off the gas after a glance at the speedometer, which tells me I'm going ten miles over the speed limit again. I mutter a curse under my breath and try to focus on being calm, but I'm just so excited for today. I got a text from Nick Sanchez just as I was leaving the apartment. He's already at the fire station, parked down the street, and waiting for me. I can't wait to see what he's created for the station.

Andrew should be arriving shortly as well. His shift starts today, so I'm happy that he, Jake, Todd, and Leonard will all be present to see the installation. And they'll be the very first to enjoy the other surprises being delivered this morning. It's going to be a great day. I can feel it.

I turn the last corner and spot Nick's truck parked on the side of the street. I pass him and pull into the driveway at the fire station as he pulls away from the curb and follows. I notice Andrew's car is already here, and my heart starts racing in anticipation.

That man can *kiss*. I'm surprised I don't have dark circles under my eyes this morning. Not just from being up way too late kissing and talking and kissing some more. When I finally did go to bed, I couldn't sleep. I felt like a teenager crushing on her first boy.

Ashley texted me once the gang got to Nonno's last night, letting me know that she'd stay away as late as I wanted her to so Andrew and I could be alone. The girl is a loyal friend. I didn't keep her away too long, but I kept her up for hours after Andrew left so we could talk about him.

I grin at Nick as he gets out of his truck. He looks excited and proud, so I'm taking that as a very good sign. I rush over to him, giddy with excitement.

"Okay, let me see!"

Nick nods quickly.

"Yeah, come on to the back of the truck, and I'll show you," he says.

I follow him, and he pulls a pair of work gloves from his back pocket and then puts them on. He reaches up and pulls a gleaming copper panel out of a custom rack he has built into the bed of his truck, and I gasp as soon as I see it.

"Nick!" I cry out. "This is beautiful!"

He's beaming with pride as he pulls out a second panel, and I literally squeal. I don't think I've ever made a sound like that in my life, but now it's a thing. Movement out of the corner of my eye gets my attention, and I look up to see Andrew coming out of the fire station with a huge, handsome smile on his face. I look at Nick and hold up a finger.

"Hang on just one sec, okay?"

Nick nods and shoves the panel back into the rack as I run towards Andrew and straight into his arms. Heaven. I give him a quick kiss hello and then start dragging him toward the back of Nick's truck as he laughs out loud.

"Come on! Time for the first surprise."

Andrew lets me drag him to the back of Nick's truck, where Nick is removing the first panel. Nick has cut thin panels made of copper to cover the lower third of the walls in the living space. Each panel has been intricately engraved with scenes of firefighters in the line of duty. Each panel has a different scene on it, from firefighters doing chores at the station to engaging with the community and then, of course, fighting fires.

I watch Andrew's expression go from one of excitement to absolute wonder as he marvels at Nick's beautiful work. My heart fills with something more than pride, more than joy, as I see how much this art means to him. Jake comes jogging out as well, and I step aside so he can get a good look at the panels. His expression mirrors Andrew's, and I trade grins with Nick as we watch their reactions. I reach up and pat Nick's shoulder.

"Look what you did," I whisper to him. "You made their day."

Nick grins at me. "All because of you, Scarlet. This wouldn't have happened without you."

I shake my head and am suddenly pulled into Andrew's embrace. I put my hands on his shoulders and squeal as he kisses me soundly.

"This is amazing, Nix," he says, spinning me around. "You're amazing."

I shake my head again. "This is all Nick!"

Nick holds his hands up quickly.

"But you can't kiss me like that, dude. I'll take a handshake."

We all laugh, and Andrew lets me go long enough to shake Nick's hand. Jake follows suit, and then the guys help Nick carry three of the panels into the fire station. I quickly grab my bag from the car and run inside to join them. When I get there, Leonard and Todd are oohing and aahing over the panels, and it looks like Leonard actually has tears in his eyes. My heart squeezes a little at their reactions, and I'm absolutely overjoyed at the end result. Nick recruits the entire group to go back out and grab more panels, and I move to the living area to get ready for the installation process.

When they return, I ask the guys to lean each panel against a portion of the wall so I can get a look at all the different scenes. Nick gave me a vague idea of what he was doing, so I knew the panels would be different, but I want to see how they look before I decide what order I'd like Nick to put them in. Nick comes to stand beside me as we look at the panels together.

"Did you sign them?" I ask Nick.

He nods. "I signed them and engraved my logo into the design on each piece somewhere. I personalized each panel for the station, though. Look closely."

I step forward to get a better look, and now it's me who's pushing back tears. Every fire engine in every scene has Engine 14 on it. It doesn't take me long to realize these aren't just generic images of firefighters. It's Jake...and Andrew...Amy...Bruce...Leonard...Todd. Every firefighter assigned to this station is represented. I step back and cover my mouth with a trembling hand as the tears come.

"This is so incredible," I say quietly, just as the guys are realizing they're part of this beautiful art.

Nick looks a little choked up at my reaction. He rubs the back of his neck and shrugs.

"Well, I wanted them to have something worthy of the job they do," he says humbly. "I'm happy you like it."

I shake my head. "I love it. I couldn't imagine anything more perfect than this, Nick."

I can't help it. I don't even ask if he's a hugger, I just pull him in for one. Thankfully, he gives me a good hug back.

"I'll make sure you get credit for this," I tell him. "I'll include your name and business in the brief I'll submit to the judges for the competition, and you know Kevin will mention it in his article."

"Are you taking my name in vain, Phoenix?" Kevin's voice sounds from behind me.

I turn to greet him, but his gaze falls on the panels, and his face freezes.

"Whoa."

I jump up and down. "Right? Aren't they amazing?"

He nods. "Completely. This is better than anything I imagined in my head, Nick."

I grin at Nick and start pointing to panels.

"So I was thinking it might be nice to go from the one where they're working around the fire truck to the one where the truck is driving down a street to—"

"Nix," Andrew says from his spot on the other side of the room. "I think you want to see this one."

Nick watches me with a secretive smile as I cross the room, and Andrew steps back away from the panel.

"What? No way!" I exclaim, squatting in front of the panel to get a better look.

Nick has perfectly recreated the photo of me wrapped in Andrew's arms on the night of the fire, but it's engraved into the panel. The detail of it is absolutely breathtaking. I run my fingers over Andrew's face. There's no mistaking it's us. The artistry is perfect.

I stand and turn, looking at Nick with tear-filled eyes. I cross the room to him and wrap him in another hug.

"You are amazingly talented," I say, not letting him go. "Thank you so much for all this work."

Nick's arms wrap around me, and he pats me gently on the back. I let go and beam up at him.

"How can I ever repay you?"

Nick grins at me. "There's no need. You're giving back to them by managing this whole project and bringing your vision to life. This is my way of giving back. I'm grateful to be a small part of this. Thanks for letting me help."

Merry comes inside, barely stopping to hug me hello before heading over to inspect the panels. I walk over to the end panel, which is the only one I haven't had the chance to check out yet, and there's an instant lump in my throat. This one. This is the panel that will be front and center in the living space. I'm sure of it. Nick has engraved this panel with an image of every firefighter currently stationed at Engine 14. They're standing so they're facing away, but their hair and physical traits make it clear who they are. They're standing arm in arm. Family. It's a beautiful message. It'll be perfect under their new flat screen, which will be wall-mounted by the end of the day today.

"All right," I say excitedly. "Let's hang these, shall we?"

Everyone bolts into action, ready to move panels around according to my directions. Merry makes her excuses and heads out to get started on the kitchen cabinet doors. I have Andrew move the one I selected for the center into place. Then, I begin deciding the positions of the other pieces. Before long, Nick is ready to get to work mounting them in place, and I drift over to the kitchen island to boot up my laptop and get going with the rest of my task list.

I check my phone for messages. The automated delivery system the appliance store uses indicates that our delivery is approximately three hours away. Kevin told me the TV delivery would happen around eleven. A lot is going on this morning, but no email from the Home Decorators Showcase producers yet. I should be hearing from them soon. I never withdrew my application for this year, and contestants weren't required to give any details about our project when we originally signed up. So, at this point, they have no idea whether I'm doing two rooms in a warehouse or a firehouse. The next step involves them reaching out via email with a link that I'll use to fill them in on the details of my project. After that, things should ramp up rather quickly.

I hope I'm ready for it. I think I am. It's weird, though, because I'm not experiencing the same apprehension, anxiety, and all-out obsession that I have in previous years. I'm not sure that's a bad thing, either. My priorities have changed, and the amount of joy I'm getting from giving something back to these firefighters and engaging with people in the community who want to do the same is outshining anything I've ever gotten from the contest.

***

"No, you can't come down yet!" I exclaim at the crew of Engine 14 as they hover on the stairs.

Kevin stands there as a babysitter after Andrew tries to sneak a peek. Merry and Amy are still outside working on the cabinet doors.

I'm standing in the kitchen with the appliance delivery men as we all suppress our laughter, and they try to finish a few final touches on the brand-new appliances they've installed. The hideously old refrigerator with plastic handles so old they were yellowed and cracked is gone. Hauled onto the truck and ready for disposal. So is the range, the microwave, and the dishwasher that Andrew told me hasn't worked properly in more than a year. All gone. There are beautiful new matching stainless steel appliances in their place. Not the best of the best, but definitely better than what they had. And they'll look beautiful with the newly painted cabinets, especially when the doors dry and we can put them back on.

"I hear plastic ripping," Todd says to the rest of the guys. "Is that plastic ripping, Scarlet?"

"I'm not telling you," I reply, watching the delivery guys ripping the protective plastic off the fridge. "Less than five minutes, and you'll get to see."

Finally, the installation is complete, and I quietly say thanks as

I scramble to grab the refrigerator contents off the kitchen island and put them into the new fridge. I grab a paper towel to wipe the condensation off the counter and toss it in the trash, then step back to give the kitchen a final look. It isn't completed. There's still a lot to do. But the appliances make it look so much better, and that's the big surprise for the guys today.

"Scarlet, c'mon," Jake whines. "I want to see so I can go back to watching the new TV!"

I laugh under my breath. Such babies.

"Okay, Kevin, can you please come to the kitchen?" I request in my calmest voice.

Kevin gives the guys one more warning, then joins me in the kitchen. His face lights up when he sees everything, and we jump up and down together. We're both so excited to see the reactions. He grabs his camera off the nearby dining table and signals to me that he's ready.

"Okay, guys, come on in!"

Todd comes running in, trying to push Andrew behind him, and the rest of the team isn't far behind. I laugh out loud as I watch them try to push each other out of the way, all in good fun. Suddenly, they stop, and all jaws fall open.

"Nix!" Andrew cries, reaching for me.

I step to his side, and he pulls me into his arms.

"Surprise!" I say excitedly.

"Amy, Merry!" Jake calls. "Get in here!"

Todd walks over to the new stove, laying his palms reverently over the burners.

"I'm gonna make so many grilled cheeses on you," he whispers to it.

I barely hold in a snicker at how serious he is. It's adorable.

Jake comes over and gives me a huge hug before pulling open the fridge and looking inside. Wordlessly, he runs a hand over the ice and water feature in the door. He smiles and sighs with the air of a man who's been lost in the desert without water. The ice maker in their old fridge had been broken for years. I'm smiling so much my face hurts.

"How did you manage this?" Jake asks. "We were told there wasn't a budget for any replacements this year."

I nod. "When you shared that with me, I reached out to a family friend for help," I share. "Given the age of the appliances you had, it felt like bureaucracy to me…not truth. So, my friend Ashley's dad is actually friends with the Mayor of San Francisco. I asked him to have a little chat with him."

Bruce's eyes are huge. "What? Wow!"

I hold up my hand to quell his excitement.

"I do want to share that the city ordered the models that are standard for any city government office," I explain. "I wanted to be sure that no rules were broken or anything. I just asked Ashley's dad to talk to his old friend. And the publicity Kevin's articles have generated were definitely a plus."

Kevin nods. "And, thanks to my superior journalistic skills, I was able to learn that Engine 14 was actually due for replacement appliances four years ago. You guys were long overdue."

"There were quite a few fire stations that had been bumped ahead of you and shouldn't have been," I explain. "I don't know all the details, but they simply fixed that issue and ordered you new appliances immediately."

Andrew turns me to face him.

"You are so smart and so talented," he murmurs as his beautiful eyes rove over my face. "And scrappy. You always find a way."

I put my hands on either side of his face and bring him in for a kiss, not even caring about the hoots coming from his friends. Judging by the way he's kissing me back, he doesn't care either. We break off our kiss, and I pull myself up to sit on the kitchen island's counter while everyone checks out the new appliances.

"Oh wow, we don't have to wash dishes by hand anymore?" Jake gasps when he notices the new dishwasher. "My only regret is that I didn't get to kick a bunch of dents in the old one before you took it away."

I giggle and give myself these few minutes to enjoy watching them. Kevin is stepping around them all, finding the best angles to take photos for his articles, which gives me a fun idea. I pull my cell phone out of my pocket, open the camera app, and turn so my back is to the kitchen.

"Hey, everyone," I say loud enough to be heard over their chatter. "Selfie time!"

Everyone turns around and smiles for the camera as I check to make sure I have everyone in the frame. Kevin is taking a photo of the whole thing, and I yell at him to get in here too. He puts his camera down and gets in the frame, then I realize we're missing Merry.

"Merry! Selfies!!"

I don't have to worry about whether she'll come. She loves a good selfie. She runs into the kitchen from outside, and Andrew comes up behind me and brings us cheek to cheek just before I click the shutter button.

Best. Selfie. Ever.

Andrew spins me around on the counter so I'm facing him, making me squeal in the process. I wrap my arms around his neck as he gives me a quick kiss.

"You are so amazing," he murmurs. "Look at what you've done."

I grin and shrug.

"All while spending zero dollars. Handy's Hardware donated the paint and painting supplies, Nick donated the panel art, and you were due for these appliances…I just moved things along with the city."

Merry pulls herself up on the counter next to me and gives me a shoulder bump.

"That's my amazing friend," she says affectionately.

Jake points to the picture of Andrew's dad, which still hangs on the side of the cabinet.

"And you kept Mac right here," he says happily. "Thanks, Scarlet."

Andrew turns in my arms so his back is to me, but since I'm perched on top of the kitchen island, I can see over his head. I pull him back against me and kiss the top of his head, then look over at Jake.

"I'm still not done in here," I remind him. "Today was more about the big reveal of all your new toys. There's more coming, and that includes an upgrade for Mac."

Merry leans over to me. "Actually, I have an idea for that, too. Chat later."

"Oooh, yeah? Definitely."

I am super curious what Merry's thinking.

"What are you two whispering about?" Andrew asks.

"More surprises," Merry says as she reaches over to squeeze his shoulder.

She pulls her hand away and gives me a look, mouthing the word *Wow*. I stifle a laugh.

"Maybe we should get back to work before we get behind schedule," Andrew pipes in, giving me a wink.

That's my guy. Helping every way he can.

"Okay, Andrew's right," I say, "we need to get back to work."

"And I need to watch the game on our new TV," Jake says, gleefully treading over to the living area.

Andrew turns around and grasps my waist, helping me jump down from the counter. I give him another quick kiss and then point him back to the living area, where he needs to remove all the painter's tape.

"Dude, his muscles are very…muscular," Merry whispers from her perch, making me laugh.

I lean back to steal one more glance at him before grinning over at Merry.

"He's pretty perfect," I say quietly.

"You guys are cute," Merry says, jumping down off the counter. "I'm gonna go check the cabinet doors, but I wanted to tell you that Nonno offered to cater the big reveal party if you'd like him to."

"Oh my gosh, that's so sweet," I reply. "I am definitely taking him up on that. I'll stop by sometime this week to thank him in person and invite him to the party."

"Oh, he'd love that!"

I reach for my laptop as Merry heads back outside. I need to figure out what we're going to do about new furniture in the living area. They just need the basics, but I want something that's going to hold up well, and I definitely want to get them an area rug to go under the couches. The whole first floor is tiled. An area rug is a must, to soften things up a little.

I look over at the living area space, which already looks so much better than it did a week ago. The light, buttery yellow wall color brings in cheer, and then Nick's beautiful metal panels take up the lower third of the walls. Since this is a fire station, I originally planned to use diamond plate along the bottom third of the walls, but when Nick showed up with his offer, and we talked about what he could do...well, this is more perfect than anything I could have imagined.

The large flat-screen TV delivered today takes up a good amount of wall space, so it breaks up the yellow. Nancy's art will break it up further when she brings her finished pieces. Curtains are a big no here, so I plan to get new blinds for all the windows, and I'll have to think of some kind of unique window treatment to trim the windows with.

"Hey, Jake?" I call from the kitchen.

"Hey, Phoenix?" he answers from his spot on the couch.

I look over at him and laugh.

"Do you have any old fire hoses lying around?"

Andrew pulls the last of the painter's tape from the baseboards and pops up, walking over to join the conversation.

"Getting another brilliant idea, Nix?"

I grin. "Think so. Maybe."

"Yeah, we've got a couple out back," Jake answers. "Why?"

I wiggle my eyebrows. "Can I have them?"

Andrew laughs and watches Jake for his reaction.

"Sure," Jake replies with a shrug. "They're just going in a recycling bin. We can't use them for anything."

"Perfect!"

This is great news. I know exactly what I want to do with those, but I'll need to get them back to the apartment so I can experiment.

Merry comes back inside with the first of the cabinet doors, but she's not revving the drill like she normally does, and her expression is...hmm. Something's wrong.

"Merry? What's up?" I ask.

She glances out to the driveway and then steps closer to me.

"There's a man outside," she whispers. "He's talking to Amy right now, but he's wearing a suit and seems pretty peeved about something."

I step around the island to get a look. He's an older man. Judging from the suit and the very annoyed look on his face, I'd say he's here on some kind of business.

"What's going on?" Kevin asks, peeking out the window. "Who's that?"

I shrug just as Amy turns and motions for the man to follow her inside. The three of us scramble away from the window and act busy as they enter. Amy presses her lips together and gives me a look that seems an awful lot like a warning as she escorts the stranger to the living room. I don't miss the fact that he gives me a dirty look as he passes. Like he knows exactly who I am, and he's not thrilled that I'm here.

"Captain Scheffler?" Amy calls. "We have a visitor."

Now I know something's up. Jake doesn't like formalities, so his people never call him Captain Scheffler. Kevin, Merry, and I exchange curious glances.

Jake turns off the TV and stands, shaking the man's hand as Amy introduces them. They're far enough away that I can't really hear what they're saying, but the look on Jake's face is not giving me a super warm and fuzzy feeling. Finally, Jake motions for the man to accompany him to the kitchen, and Amy heads back outside.

"Uh, this is Mr. Mercer from the City Auditor's office," Jake says, rubbing the back of his neck. "We have a problem."

Andrew comes to stand next to me as I extend my hand to Mr. Mercer.

"I'm Scar—"

"I know who you are, Miss Jackson," he says curtly, pulling a document out of the folder in his hand and smacking it on the counter next to me. "I have an injunction ordering you to stop your work immediately and leave the premises."

Chapter 16

Scarlet

"What?" I exclaim.

My pulse hammers against my wrist as Andrew's hand wraps around mine and gives me a little squeeze.

"Why?" Andrew asks bluntly.

"This entire project is inappropriate and unauthorized," he huffs. "You are not an approved city contractor, ma'am. You haven't been vetted through our formal bidding process."

Andrew scoffs. "She's working for free. Who's going to outbid that?"

Mr. Mercer throws Andrew a withering look. My morale is spiraling lower by the minute. He's shutting us down? My nervous gaze flicks to the very official-looking document on the counter. He's shutting us down.

What am I going to do...

Jake looks at me apologetically.

"I did clear this with the Chief before we even offered the project to you. He didn't think it would be a problem."

"My office was never informed," Mr. Mercer goes on. "There is a process for this kind of work, and none of our procedures have been followed. Anyone working on city property must have a completed background check, be insured, and have a proper identification badge displayed at all times. Not to mention the questionable way you've procured your equipment and supplies."

We're all speechless. No one says a word or moves as Mr. Mercer's face gets redder and redder.

"If you were never informed, then how did you even find out about it?" Kevin asks.

Mercer does a double take, then looks Kevin up and down.

"And who are you?" he sputters. "Are you Fire Department personnel?"

Kevin smirks, and I kind of love him for it.

"No."

Mercer points to the injunction document.

"This injunction officially puts an end to all the work you're doing here, effective immediately. Anyone who is not a city government employee must leave these premises," he declares.

"But—" Merry tries to interject.

"No buts," Mercer interrupts. "You're done here. And now I have to figure out this mess."

Kevin reaches out and slides the injunction closer so he can read it.

"Mr. Mercer," I say carefully, "this seems like a simple misunderstanding if Jake, er, Captain Scheffler cleared this in advance."

He levels a stare at me that might be intimidating to some, but not me. He's rude. Dismissive. And annoying. Intimidating? Not to scrappy little ol' me. I'm ready to punch this guy right in his pocket square.

"The proper channels were not used to request or approve this work," he argues. "And, again, not to sound like a broken record, but how did you procure this equipment? These appliances look brand new."

He looks over at the living room, then back at me.

"What about that television? Where did it come from? What kind of unethical perks did you get from the vendor? Not to mention the fact that you are not an official contractor with the city. You may leave, Miss Jackson. Now."

"Now, wait just a minute—" Andrew says, stepping forward.

Mercer takes three steps back, looking suddenly fearful of Andrew and all those muscles. I wrap a hand around Andrew's arm and pull him back.

"Andrew, wait," I say gently, pulling him away. I lean closer and whisper, "I don't want you to get in trouble on my behalf. We'll figure this out."

"Mr. Mercer, this injunction is not permanent," Kevin interjects. "It's for a maximum of two weeks."

Mercer squints at Kevin. "And who are you again?"

"Kevin Starbuck," he replies with a sarcastic grin. "Columnist with the San Francisco Times."

Mercer gulps. "You're a reporter?"

Kevin nods. "The very reporter who wrote the story that probably made you aware of this project."

"Yes, possibly. My secretary told me about the articles. I don't read."

Merry snort-laughs, and I lightly smack her on the arm. Mercer glares at her.

"I don't read *the newspaper,*" he sneers.

"So you have two weeks to find evidence that something is..." he leans over the paper to read an excerpt, "ethically unsound, and she has two weeks to get vetted and approved by the city. Would you say that's correct?"

Mercer smirks at him. "Not quite. We have to allow others to bid on the project."

My heart soars when Kevin smirks right back at him.

"How many interior design firms do you expect to go through the city's bidding process in order to work for free?"

Mr. Mercer scoffs. "That's not the point. There is a process that must be followed without exception. Until then, all work must stop, and everyone who is not a city government employee must leave."

"Scarlet, I'm sorry," Jake says. "I'll get to work figuring this out on our end."

I nod at Jake. "Thanks. I know you will."

I close my laptop and slip it into my bag, feeling my entire project crashing down all around me as Merry retrieves her purse from the living room. How did it come to this? Today was such a great day until this dude showed up and shut me down with a piece of paper. Emotion starts to clog my throat, and I fight it back. I will not show this man any vulnerability. He's just a bully in a suit.

"You're free to go as well, Mr. Starbuck," Mercer says coldly. "If you're writing any kind of story, please reach out to the city's Public Relations office."

"Oh, I'll go," Kevin says. "But I'm going to walk Scarlet and Merry to their cars so we can talk about you all the way down the driveway."

Mercer smirks again, and I want to wipe it right off his face. I can't stand people like him. People who go out of their way to throw a wrench into things instead of pitching in to help, or at least being professional. There are ways to handle things. He could have shown up and asked questions with an interest in finding out the truth instead of being rude and throwing around ridiculous accusations.

Mr. Mercer pulls another copy of the injunction out of his folder and holds it out to me with a self-satisfied smile.

"Here is your copy, little lady."

Oh, that does it. I set my jaw and give him my very best glare before taking two very slow, very calculated steps forward. I make sure I end up way too close, encroaching in his space, as I snatch the paper out of his hand. He flinches just slightly, and it brings me a ridiculous amount of joy. Bully, indeed. He expected to have me in tears and running to my car with my tail between my legs. Not *this* little lady.

"Thank you, Mr. Mercer," I say, giving him a cold smile. "Did you see how easy it was for me to be courteous, even to someone like you?"

His eyes dart around my face in confusion.

"I said thank you, and I used your proper name," I explain. "Mine is Miss Jackson, as far as you're concerned. You used it previously, so I'm not quite sure why you have the audacity to address me as *little lady*."

He begins to sputter a reply, but I have no intention of letting him get it out.

"I will go," I say, holding my hand up in his face. "And while you're working your ridiculous investigation, I will be gathering all the evidence I need to show that there have been no 'ethically unsound' decisions here and certainly no unethical perks offered or received by anyone. And then I will return to finish this job."

He scoffs. "Not without my permission, *Miss Jackson*."

I don't miss the sarcasm with which he says my name this time. I reach into the depths of my self-confidence and raise my eyebrows at him, nodding.

"Oh, Mr. Mercer. I will absolutely be back here, and you will not only *invite* me to return...you'll apologize as well."

His jaw drops open, no doubt at my gall. I hear Leonard smirk in the background, and I want to hug him for it. I move to the door, where Merry and Kevin are waiting with smug expressions as they watch me. I turn back and wink at the jerk.

"I'll see you soon."

I turn and walk out of the fire station with my friends, feeling a surge of pride as I hear Andrew behind me.

"Mr. Mercer, sir, I don't think you're ready for the fight you just started," he says as he follows me out the door.

***

Andrew

I am barely hanging on to the last of my composure as I watch Jake walk Mercer to his car, parked on the street. Scarlet, Merry, and Kevin are now gone, and the driveway looks lonely. I walked Scarlet to her car and told her I'd text her as soon as Mercer was gone. I'm sure she went somewhere with Merry and Kevin to talk about what just happened, but I'm on duty. I can't just get in a car and go to them.

I pull my phone from my pocket and open a text message.

Andrew: Are you okay? I'm so sorry this happened.

I wait, but there's no immediate reply. She's probably not even looking at her phone right now. I can picture her gesturing with her hands, venting to Kevin and Merry with that razor-sharp tongue of hers, all while coming up with a plan to defeat this jerk. Spoiler alert: whatever the plan is, I'm on board.

Nix: I'm okay, just steaming mad right now. Call me when you can and I'll catch you up, but this guy will NOT defeat me.

Andrew: I have no doubt. The guys and I have some chores to get done, which will include getting the rest of the cabinet doors put back on for you. I'll call you tonight. xoxo

She responds with a heart emoji that fills up my entire screen, and suddenly, I feel like ten-year-old me did when Jennifer Roberts kissed me in the sixth grade. I head out to help Jake and the guys with our task list for the day, and I can't wait to call Scarlet later.

***

Scarlet

"I love how it took you about thirty seconds to go into battle mode, girl," Merry tells me. "I want to be you when I grow up."

I giggle, then drop another scoop of mint chip ice cream into my bowl as Merry squirts caramel syrup all over her bowl of vanilla.

"Thanks, girl. I say we enjoy this ice cream, and then I'm going full speed ahead with my plan."

Merry nods. "Self-care rocks."

I laugh out loud as I put the ice cream container back in the freezer. "Right!"

We head to the living room and plop onto the couch. I feel some of the tension in my shoulders release as soon as the first creamy, minty spoonful of ice cream hits my tongue.

So good.

"So, are you gonna call a conclave?" Merry asks.

I nod. Whenever one of us has a crisis, we call an emergency conclave, and all our friends come running. We grab some takeout, get together, and work out the problem. I already have some ideas, but I need all my girls for this. I put my bowl on the coffee table and whip out my cell phone.

Scarlet: Emergency conclave tonight at Ashley's right after work.

Marina is typing...

Ashley: I'll be there!

Marina: I'll order a delivery from Wu's!

I hold my phone up to Merry.

"That didn't take long."

"You wanna fight this guy, we're ready to help," Merry says around a mouthful of ice cream. "I thought he was a real jerk."

A knock on the door has me looking at the clock, wondering who it could be. It's definitely not Andrew. He's on duty. Merry and I shrug at each other as I get up and head for the door. I open it and squeal with delight.

"Mom!" I cry, pulling her in for a hug.

"Hey, baby girl," she says as she squeezes me tight.

Forget Mercer. This is still the best day ever. I got to surprise and delight everyone at Engine 14, and now my mom is back. I step back to get a look at her.

"Wow, Mom! Gorgeous tan!"

She laughs a little as she spins for me and Merry, who applauds from the sofa. Nothing could pry that girl away from a bowl of ice cream. It's never happened.

Mom steps inside, and I shut the door, pulling her into the living room. She heads to the couch and pulls Merry up to give her a hug, then sits with me. She looks wonderful. Her shoulder-length blond hair is loose and wavy. Her tan really sets off her blue eyes. She's wearing a pair of jeans and a black long-sleeved top with a scoop neck. It's a nice change from the designer suits I usually see her in when she's heading to work or coming home, but that's life as a successful attorney.

"I thought it might be late enough in the afternoon for you to be here," she explains. "If I was wrong, I planned to go downstairs and hang out with Marina until you showed up. I'm so glad to see you, honey. And so glad you're safe."

I frown for a moment as I try to figure out what she means.

"Oh, the fire!" I exclaim. "Yeah, I have some new drama that's replaced that. But I'm sorry, Mom, that I had to call you and tell you all of that when you were on vacation."

She reaches over and puts her hand on mine. "Baby girl, I'm just grateful you're safe. I'll talk some sense into you another time. But what's the new drama?"

"Some jerk from the city government showed up with an injunction and kicked me out of the fire station today," I reply. "Something about not going through a proper bidding process and me possibly getting some kind of perks out of all of it."

Mom purses her lips. "Sounds like good old-fashioned politics to me. Who's going to bid on a project for free?"

"That's what Kevin said," I answer. Mom looks confused. "The reporter who's writing the articles about the project."

"Ah, yes," Mom says with a proud grin. "I've been reading them online since you called and told me about what was going on. He's very passionate about the city. I like his column, and I am so incredibly proud of you. The response from the community is like nothing I've ever seen, and you inspired that."

Merry nudges me with her foot and smiles around her spoon. I nudge her back.

"It's weird, but I care less about winning the competition and more about just doing a great job," I share. "Surviving the fire changed something in me, and I'm not so obsessed with the singular goal of winning."

Mom reaches over to give my hand a squeeze but stays silent to let me continue.

"I know I'd already decided that this was my last year competing for the grand prize," I elaborate. "But, since the fire, I'm just not as obsessed as I was in previous years. I'm still determined to do a great job, but that's just me anyway. The competition is no longer the center of my existence. It's liberating."

"Good girl," Mom says. "You're a wonderful designer. You'll be able to focus on building your business, which will take longer without all that prize money if you don't win it, but I have absolutely no doubt that you'll be successful."

"Thanks, Mom."

"And this...Andrew?" Mom says with barely contained excitement.

"Tell me about him."

Merry makes a gulping sound, and we both turn to look at her. She smiles at my mom around a mouthful of ice cream.

"He'th her perthon."

I laugh out loud.

"Dude, don't talk with your mouth full," I scold.

She makes a face at me. Typical.

It doesn't deter my mom. Her eyebrows shoot straight up to her hairline as Merry nods at her.

"He's your person?" Mom says, looking at me with a sweet, hopeful look in her eyes. "Tell me about him."

I sit back against the soft cushions of the couch and grin at her.

"You'll love him, Mom. He's…amazing."

"Well, since he literally saved your life, he's already one of my favorite people."

I grin. "Me too."

"So, what's your plan to deal with this city guy?" Merry asks.

She gets up and grabs my bowl on her way to take her own to the kitchen.

"Well, Jake says he cleared it with the Chief," I begin, then turn to Mom. "Jake is the captain of Engine 14. I think my next step is to reach out to Ashley's dad again. He knows so many people in the city government. He can help me figure out if any steps were actually missed."

Mom nods in approval.

"Good. Dave's a good guy, and this was never an official contractor job that required the city to open a bidding process to ensure fairness. This is a one-off project that fits more under community outreach than anything else. This guy is barking up the wrong tree."

"I agree. I'll also ask whether they'd like me to go through a background check, which I'm happy to do in order to comply with whatever rules they need me to follow. Hopefully, I can get some quick answers."

Mom grins proudly. "That's my girl. So when are you coming home?"

I look at the clock. It's already getting towards dinner time, and I don't want to dash out of here without thanking Ashley. Besides, I don't have a bed anymore.

"How about this weekend?" I purse my lips. "I don't exactly have a bed anymore. I'm going to need to go shopping."

"Yes, your bedroom looks so strange with no furniture in it," Mom replies. "I got home from the airport, dropped off my bags, and peeked in your room. Thank goodness you told me what happened first."

"It's pretty empty," I say with a sheepish grin.

"Since you're unable to do any work at the fire station for now, why don't we go out to lunch tomorrow, and then we can go shopping for a new bedroom set and mattress for you?"

One corner of my mouth turns up as I consider my words carefully. If we go shopping together, Mom is going to want to pay for everything, and I'm a grown woman who should not be leaning on my mommy for everything.

"I'd love that, but I'm paying for it."

Mom scoffs at me.

"Scarlet, you have many wonderful qualities, but you're too thrifty when it comes to spending money on yourself. I'll buy the furniture."

Merry sits back on the couch, looking like she's watching a tennis match, eyes moving from one of us to the other and back again.

"I think being budget-conscious is a good quality," I counter.

"Yes, absolutely," Mom says. "For any project or just in general, but you are a little too budget-conscious. I know my daughter. You'll end up buying some low-budget torture chamber for a bed. So I'll make you a deal: I'll buy the mattress, and you can buy the rest of the furniture."

I laugh under my breath. She's right. I can't argue with her for calling me out on exactly what I would have done.

"Deal. Thanks, Mom."

"You guys are so cute," Merry says, a hint of longing in her tone. "I love your relationship."

Mom smiles fondly at Merry. She's more of a mother to my friend than her own mother is, and it's been that way for years. Merry's parents are Silicon Valley executives. They live and breathe the tech world and are extremely wealthy. It ended up causing a rift with their daughter when she didn't embrace the ultra-rich lifestyle they wanted her to have. She moved in with her grandfather, Nonno, years ago and now only sees her parents during the holidays.

"How is Nonno?" Mom asks Merry. "I don't think I've seen him since Marina's wedding."

"He's doing great," Merry replies. "Yelling at my cousins, and sometimes me, but still making amazing food and not letting me open my Nonna's old bakery."

Mom gives Merry a sympathetic look.

"You are too talented to just sell cookies out of the bakery case at Nonno's," Mom says. "If anyone can talk some sense into him, it's you. But if you need help to form your argument, I'm happy to help."

"Thank you," Merry replies. "It's tragic. He uses Nonna's old bakery to store extra stuff for the restaurant and equipment he doesn't use every day. And he won't even go over there. He makes us do it."

I chew on my bottom lip, squinting while an idea hatches in my brain.

"What if you showed him what it *could* look like?" I say slowly. "Clean it up and decorate it like a real bakery, but not like your Nonna had it set up. Make it look like something that doesn't break his heart and remind him that she's gone."

Merry jerks straight up and sits at the edge of her seat.

"Hey…that could work."

I nod, a slow smile spreading across my face. "Right?"

Merry grins at me. "Would you help me? I mean with the paint colors and stuff. You'd pick something way better than what I'd pick."

"Mer, I owe you so much," I say softly. "Of course, I'll help you. A thousand times."

Merry holds up a finger.

"One, you don't owe me a thing," she says with a wink. "Two, I accept the help. But I need time to figure out some details, so…more to come. Just not yet."

I smile at my friend. "I'll be ready. Whenever you need me."

"Sweetie, you better call Dave before too long," Mom reminds me. "It'll probably take time to figure out what the actual issue is."

Normally, I just have Ashley speak to her dad for me. He's so busy, even though he recently retired from running the investment firm he owns. But Mom's right. This is urgent, and I need to get going. Mr. Roberts is like a dad to all of us girls. We all have his number.

I dial it, and he picks up on the second ring. After the usual pleasantries, which includes him telling me how excited he is that Ashley is getting married, I get to the problem at hand. He promises to check in with both the mayor's and the fire chief's offices because it turns out he's golf buddies with both. I thank him, and we say goodbye after he makes sure to tell me how proud he is of me. That's just how he is with all of us, and it's exactly why we love him.

"Well, you heard my side of the conversation," I say to Mom and Merry. "He'll call me when he talks to some people."

Mom nods. "And in the meantime?"

"I have plenty to do," I reply. "I can work on the window treatments, for one. And I have to figure out what to do if the city decides they're not going to give me a budget for all the furniture."

Mom's brows raise in curiosity.

"That bad?"

Merry laughs.

"They have duct tape covering the rips in their fake leather chair, and there are so many stains on the couches it's hard to tell what color they were originally."

I nod. "Yep. It's that bad. But I do have plan B if they decide to play hard to get."

Mom grins proudly. "Of course you do. Because what are we?"

"We are formidable women," I say, loving the mantra Mom raised me with.

She gives me a fist bump, and I find myself wondering how I got so lucky to have such a mom. She's always been amazing. Always supportive. And she's taught me to embrace my power as long as I can remember, even back to when she'd stand me on the bathroom counter so I could smile at myself in the mirror and say positive affirmations. I am smart. I can run fast. I read a new book today. Whatever it was, my mom was helping me celebrate it.

"I'm so glad you're home, Mom," I say softly.

My voice cracks at the end, and she gets up from her seat immediately. Her arms wrap around me, and suddenly, everything is all right because I have my mom. I close my eyes and absorb all the positive, one-of-a-kind energy that only my mom can give. I am a formidable woman...because I come from one. And I don't know how I'm going to do it, but it doesn't matter. I know I'm going to clear up this mess that Mercer started and come out on top.

Chapter 17

Scarlet

The rev of the blender makes me grateful I don't have to drive home. Ashley's margaritas are as powerful as they are delicious, and I definitely want another one. Maybe a third one is a bad idea, but it's not like I have far to go. In fact, maybe it'll help me sleep all by myself tonight. Just like a big girl.

"I can't wait to see these window treatments you're talking about," Marina says from her perch on the couch. "You're so creative."

I pull my head up off the floor to wink at my friend.

"You're not the only one with crazy talent, my mermaid friend," I say, making her giggle.

Marina looks over her shoulder to yell at Ashley in the kitchen.

"Hey, Ash, tone down the tequila a little bit," she says. "We've got a phoenix on the floor in here."

I push out a pouty lip.

"I just really like your floor," I throw back. "This area rug is downright cuddly."

Merry's face pops into view as she leans over me from her seat in the chair.

"Wow, girl."

Ashley's face appears as well, and she squints down at me.

"What are you doing?" I ask with a frown.

"Assessing."

I frown more. "Assessing what?"

"How many fingers am I holding up?" Ashley asks, wiggling four at me.

"Four."

She nods curtly.

"Very well," she says as she passes me what I've already decided is my final margarita.

I sit up and take it from her. "Thank you!"

I pull the large bowl of tortilla chips over to my side of the coffee table and grab a few.

"The next time I call an emergency conclave, I want Ashley's margaritas and some *tacos*," I declare. "Chinese and margaritas make my tummy a little..."

Marina leans forward, eyes big.

"Sick? Get in the bathroom and away from the couch."

I burp. Loudly.

"Gassy," I say over Merry's laughter. "Not sick. And I'm nowhere near your couch."

Merry flicks me on the head.

"It's literally right behind you."

I laugh out loud, then shrug.

"Girls," I say sweetly, taking a big sip. "I truly appreciate you. Thank you for coming to this emergency conclave and thank you for being my friends."

"We love you, Floor Phoenix!" Merry cries out, making me giggle.

Marina shakes her head at Merry and laughs, and Ashley comes back to the couch with a fresh margarita. A knock on the door silences all of us. I look at Marina.

"Don't look at me," she says defensively. "Zach knows never to disturb an emergency conclave."

"So does Rick!" Ashley chimes in.

Merry flings herself from the sofa and stomps toward the door. I tilt my head back so I can watch her upside down. I get a full view of upside-down Merry as she swings open the door…and reveals a very handsome Andrew. With a massive fire hose wrapped around his body.

"What is even happening right now?" I ask loudly.

Andrew's eyes instantly find mine, and he fights back laughter as I struggle to control my traitorous limbs. I stop trying to get up and just gaze at him in his upside-down form.

"That is so hot," I say.

I mean, c'mon. I just watch, still upside down, as Andrew steps inside and walks slowly over to where I'm lying on the floor.

"Hi, Nix," he says quietly, the corner of his mouth twitching upward. "You okay?"

I hold my hand up in a silent plea for help, and he takes it, gently pulling me up. I lean my back against the couch and on his hand.

"Thanks. Come down here."

"Wait a minute!" Merry all but shouts, her eyes huge. "There's a man in the conclave."

Ashley fights back a smile. "Yes, that's true."

Merry nods dramatically, then proceeds to walk around Andrew in a slow circle.

"So if your men-folk aren't allowed at conclave, then why is Scarlet's? Shouldn't we discuss this before we allow this… breach?"

I frown at Merry. "What are you…the conclave police?"

Merry smirks at me. "This is sacred girlfriend time."

I point up to Andrew. "He's brand new. He doesn't know."

Marina nods. "I vote we grant a one time exemption."

"I concur," I say, possibly a little too loudly.

Merry points at me. "Someone has to second the motion."

Mercifully, Ashley grabs Merry and pulls her over to the couch. "I second the motion."

Merry lands on the couch next to Ashley and lets out an "Oooof!"

Andrew looks around at all of us.

"I'm sorry to interrupt, ladies," he begins. "I wanted to check on Scarlet and bring her the fire hose she asked us for."

He starts pulling the looped hose off of his broad shoulders, biceps bunching and flexing as he manipulates the heavy material. My mouth goes instantly dry. He is so beautiful. His eyes keep darting to mine as I watch him, and I check the corner of my mouth for drool. All clear, but...wow.

"Aren't you on duty?" I ask breathlessly.

Andrew curls the fire hose on the floor next to the chair and sits next to me on the rug.

"Leonard took my shift when he heard what happened with Mercer," he replies, reaching an arm around my shoulders and pulling me into his side. "I think he wanted me to check on you just as much as I wanted to."

I rest my head on Andrew's ample shoulder. "That's so sweet."

My slightly intoxicated heart melts as Andrew presses a kiss to the top of my head.

"You have been fully adopted into Engine 14. We're all pretty angry over what's happened."

I see movement out of the corner of my eye and look over to see Merry motioning at Marina and Ashley while pointing at me and Andrew. Not so subtle. I give her a look that says *knock it off*.

"What happened after I left?" I ask.

"Jake made it clear to Mercer that he didn't appreciate the drama he's causing, and Mercer left pretty fast," Andrew replies. "He called the chief before Mercer even had his seatbelt buckled."

I raise my head to look at Andrew, and everything spins a little.

"Oooh," I mutter, leaning over and putting my margarita on the coffee table. "No more for me."

"Andrew, would you like anything to drink?" Ashley asks.

"I'd love a water or a diet soda, thanks," he replies.

Ashley heads to the kitchen. The arm that's wrapped around my shoulders gives me a little squeeze, and I look up into Andrew's deep brown gaze.

"You okay?" he asks.

I nod. "What did the chief say when Jake called him?"

Andrew shakes his head slowly. "Not much, but he said he'll look into it immediately. Apparently, the chief knows exactly who Mercer is, and I get the feeling he's not well-liked."

"What's to like?" Merry chimes in. "Marina, Ash…I wish you could have seen our little phoenix. She kicked his butt with just her words."

I try to fail to suppress a giggle.

"I just wanted him to understand that my leaving wasn't a sign of defeat, that's all," I say determinedly. "He doesn't get to win just because of a piece of paper."

"So now…we wait?" Andrew asks.

I nod. "I don't have a choice. I have to give Ashley's dad time to see if anything can be done."

A slow smile spreads seductively across his lips.

"If you feel yourself getting impatient, I'll be happy to think up something to distract you."

I smile back and lean in, whispering, "Like what?"

I could dive into those deep brown eyes and never return. They're so warm. So incredibly sexy. And the way he looks at me makes me want to stay in all day and just kiss him.

"First on the list is taking you on an actual date."

"Ooh, I would like that."

Andrew's gaze moves from my face to something just over my shoulder. I turn my head to find Marina and Merry watching us from the couch. They look so love struck they could be watching a Hallmark movie. Andrew lets out a soft laugh beside me, and I squint at my friends.

"What?"

Marina tilts her head and gives me a look that screams I told you so.

"You guys are adorable," she says from behind her margarita.

Ashley comes back into the room with a diet soda for Andrew.

"Thanks, Ashley," he says as he twists off the cap. "I feel bad that I interrupted your girls' night."

I nudge him and shake my head. "I'm glad you came."

Andrew brings our foreheads together. "Yeah?"

"Yeah."

"Well, if you feel bad, there's a way to make it up to us," Merry says with a frightening amount of mischief in her eyes.

Uh oh.

Poor, sweet, innocent Andrew doesn't see it.

"Just tell me how, Merry," he says.

"Submit to questioning."

Marina chokes on her margarita, and Ashley clicks her tongue.

"Oh, stop! We're not making him do that. He's outnumbered."

Merry is undeterred. She levels her gaze at Andrew, a challenge sparkling in her eyes.

"Scared?"

"Merry..." Marina hedges.

To my surprise, Andrew's delight in Merry's challenge is almost feral. He squints his eyes at her in what I can only describe as a mock threat.

"Scared?" Andrew teases. "Me? Do your worst, unicorn girl."

I hold up my hand. "Wait! I am putting a cap on this insanity, Merry. You're allowed three questions."

Merry scoffs.

"Take it or leave it, unicorn girl," I say authoritatively.

"Fine. Three questions."

Beside me, Andrew makes a show of readying himself for Merry's interrogation. I lean over and plant a kiss on his cheek.

"You're such a good sport."

His hands come up to cup my face, and he kisses me lightly.

"Anything for you, Nix."

He turns to Merry and raises his chin.

"Bring it."

Merry looks absolutely delighted. Ashley sits next to Marina, a rapt expression on her face.

"I feel like we should make popcorn," she murmurs.

Marina shushes her.

"Question number one," Merry begins with all the dramatic flourish of a ringmaster in the circus. "What's your favorite food?"

I heave a sigh of relief that Merry's question is a playful one and not something embarrassing like diving into his dating history. Or, knowing her, medical history. Yikes.

Andrew gives Merry a smug grin.

"Italian wedding cookies from Nonno's."

Oh, he is good.

Merry laughs out loud.

"Seriously…favorite food?" she insists.

Andrew considers for a moment. "Strawberries."

Merry nods. "Okay. Question two: what's your dream job?"

He shrugs. "Easy. Arson investigator."

Ashley and Marina look suitably impressed. Merry tips her head to acknowledge his answer.

"Are you ready for the final question?" she asks with a look designed to intimidate him.

Andrew laughs. "C'mon, Merry. Don't keep me waiting."

"Describe the perfect woman."

I laugh out loud at Merry's boldness and turn to Andrew.

"You do not have to answer that," I say.

But he does answer. In fact, I get a front-row seat to the dimple show as he looks away from Merry, and his eyes find mine. He reaches up to brush a stray strand of hair away from my cheek.

"The perfect woman is about five-foot-seven," Andrew begins, not breaking his gaze from mine. "Sunny blond hair. Brilliant blue eyes. Very determined walk. Lots and lots of sass. Whip-smart. Independent, but very loving. And absolutely beautiful."

The corner of my mouth tilts up in a smile as I plant a little kiss on one of those incredible dimples.

"You are too sweet," I whisper into his ear.

"Aww," Ashley purrs.

She puts her head on Marina's shoulder.

"How cute are you two." Marina sighs.

Merry grins triumphantly.

"You're welcome," she says to me, then whisper-yells, "He's your person."

"Andrew, that was incredibly brave," Ashley says. "Not many men would dare face Merry's questioning."

He gives her a thumbs up. "My pleasure."

"So what's the fire hose for?" Marina asks. "I'm sure you have some incredibly creative use for it, Scarlet."

"I'm thinking about using it for a window treatment," I share. "I'll have to find a way to cut pieces of it, though."

"We have a hose cutter at the station," Andrew offers. "I can cut it for you if you tell me what length you want the pieces."

"That'd be great. I feel bad that you lugged it all the way up here, though."

Merry snorts. "I don't."

All heads turn to her.

"I'm sorry, but that whole walking in with a hose wrapped around your muscly muscles was a thing of beauty, Mr. Hotness."

And I'm dead.

Marina and Ashley giggle as I plant my face firmly in the palm of my hand. Oh, the embarrassment. Merry's one-liners get me every time. Thank goodness Andrew is laughing.

"Ladies, can we have a minute, please?" I ask my friends.

I don't need to explain. They get it. Ashley nods and drags Merry to the kitchen with her, Marina following closely behind. I wait until they're far enough away that they can't hear me whisper.

"Hey, I'm sorry about that," I say quietly. "I hope that didn't make you uncomfortable."

Andrew cups the side of my face with his hand.

"It's Merry," he says sweetly. "Who would feel uncomfortable around her? She's only teasing."

I nod. "Thank you for coming to check on me."

He brings his lips to mine, and I sigh against his lips. He is such a good kisser. I could live here, just kissing him. We pull apart, and he rubs our noses together.

"I'm going to let you guys continue with your night," he says. "Can I pick you up at six tomorrow? Does that work?"

My stomach dips in excitement at the idea of going on an actual date with Andrew.

"Yes, but I'm so sad that I won't get to see you until then. I've gotten so used to spending all day with you."

Andrew nods. "Me too. But I have faith that it'll be dealt with quickly."

It will if I have anything to do with it.

"What should I wear?"

He thinks for a moment.

"Dinner is definitely involved," he says. "Do you have a favorite restaurant?"

"Hmm. I know better than to subject you to Nonno's right off the bat," I say with a smirk. "The food is great, but Nonno would be grilling you with questions the whole time."

"What about seafood?" Andrew asks. "There's this little grotto down in Fisherman's Wharf that has the best scallops. Have you ever been to Jack's?"

"I love that place!"

He wraps his hand around mine and squeezes.

"Then dress for Jack's and we'll have a nice dinner on the water," he says. "Sound good?"

I give him a soft kiss...and then another. And another.

"Perfect."

He stands, then extends a hand to me and pulls me up. I wobble a little, and he steadies me. Little sparks of heat shimmy up my arms where his strong hands are holding me. I can't bring myself to step out of his embrace and let him go.

"I was going to try to sleep in my own room tonight, but now I want to make sure I look well-rested for our date," I tell him. "Maybe I'll just sleep in Ashley's room."

Andrew looks at me with concern.

"I hate that you're still having trouble sleeping. Is therapy helping at all?"

I run my fingers up his muscular forearms.

"It's definitely helping," I share. "And not just with the anxiety from the fire. I find I'm more able to let things go and relax about the stuff I can't control. I didn't expect that."

He nods. "That's good to hear. You can call me anytime you need me, you know. Even in the middle of the night if you can't sleep or you're scared."

"You're the sweetest. I'll keep that in mind."

There is no limit to this man's sweetness. He bends down to pick up one end of the fire hose.

"How long do you want the pieces when I cut this?"

I think for a moment. "Let's do 48-inch lengths. As many as you can cut."

He nods and starts wrapping the hose around his shoulders.

"Merry," he calls to her. "Mr. Hotness is heading home with the fire hose. Don't miss the show."

I laugh out loud as he winks at me. Merry squeals and runs over to get a better look.

She makes a show of watching, and he makes a show of wrapping the hose up. Merry reaches out to give Andrew a high-five, which he returns enthusiastically.

"You're a good man, Andrew," she says. "Thanks for checking on our girl."

He waves at my friends as I follow him to the door.

"Thanks for letting me crash your party, ladies."

Marina and Ashley wave from the kitchen. I open the door for Andrew, and he leans down for one more kiss.

"I'm serious," he murmurs against my lips. "You can call me anytime you want. I want to help."

I nod. "I'll remember, I promise."

Andrew steps out into the hall. The smile he gives me nearly melts me into a puddle on the floor.

"See you tomorrow, Nix."

And with that, he turns away and I close the door before I'm tempted to follow. I turn and lean against the door as all three of my friends squeal in excitement.

"You guys are so cute together!" Ashley cries out.

I laugh and head to the sofa, my head a little fuzzy from the margaritas and Andrew's presence.

"Stop," I chide her.

Marina plops down next to me and beams.

"Remember when you didn't want anything to do with a relationship?" she teases.

"Hush, you," I say back, stifling a giggle.

A low vibrating sounds nearby, and I look around for the source. We all look for it, and then Ashley gasps and grabs my phone off the end table near her. She holds it up as she tosses it to me.

"It's my dad!"

I swipe the screen immediately, hope rising in my chest even though it's too soon to get any real answers.

"Hey, Daddio," I answer, using the nickname I gave him years ago. He's always insisted that Merry, Marina, and I call him Dad.

"Hey, sweet girl," he replies. "Don't get too excited because I don't have any official answers for you yet. I wanted to let you know that Dirk is not happy at all that this has happened, and he's promised to look into it first thing in the morning."

Right. The Honorable Dirk Jansen, the mayor of San Francisco, who is on first-name terms with Ashley's dad.

"I also wanted you to know that he went on and on about the Phoenix and the Fireman story," he shares. "He looks forward to every article, and he spoke to me in detail about the good that's coming from it. He loves the stories of people in the community coming forward to help, and so I'm positive that he's going to do whatever he can to solve this in your favor."

I let out a huge sigh.

"That gives me hope," I say into the phone.

He chuckles on the other end.

"Hey, kiddo, try to relax about it," he says. "If all goes well, he assured me you'd be getting a call from his office before five tomorrow. I have faith this is gonna work out."

"Thank you so much, Mr. Roberts."

"Uh uh," he scolds.

"Daddio!"

He laughs, and we say our goodbyes. I look up to three very excited, expectant faces.

"No definitive answer yet, but the mayor is not pleased with what's happened, and he's investigating tomorrow. They'll call me soon."

Merry scoffs. "I hope the mayor gives that guy an atomic wedgie."

I grin at Merry as I sit back against the cushions and try not to get too hopeful.

"Me too."

With any luck, by this time tomorrow, Mr. Mercer will be firmly put in his place.

***

Andrew

I let out a long, tired sigh as I weave my way through San Francisco traffic on my way back to my apartment. Scarlet seems okay, and that makes me happy. It's a stark contrast to the wounded version that suffered through the aftermath of the fire. I know she's still recovering and will be for quite some time, but when I see her rallying like this, it lifts me up. Her scrappiness is one of the things I adore most about her.

There are times, though, when I worry about how often she's

triggered by working at the fire station. I see it far too often: a flinch when a radio flares to life or that far-off gaze that comes over her face when I find her staring at the fire truck sometimes. There's a fragility still hanging in the air that I can't seem to reach. I'd love nothing more than to clear it all away for her so it never bothers her again, but I know that's not how this works.

I pull into my parking space and head upstairs to my apartment, with Scarlet consuming every thought. Tomorrow is our first official date, and I want to be sure it's a good one. Jack's is a nice restaurant, but not so fancy that there's a dress code. I still wouldn't mind seeing Scarlet in a dress, if I'm being completely honest, although I'm not sure I could handle it. Would I be able to compose an intelligent sentence with her looking extra gorgeous? Before the fire, she was so concerned about keeping distractions away, but she is definitely a distraction from my point of view. A gorgeous one.

I'll play it by ear after dinner. There's a lot to do down by the wharf, including just walking along the water or sitting someplace and enjoying the lights on the bay and the view of the Golden Gate Bridge.

Once inside my apartment, I turn on the lights and flop on the couch so I can text Leonard. He was good enough to take my shift, and I know he was concerned about Scarlet, so he gets an update.

Andrew: Scarlet's doing well. Surrounded by her closest friends and was tipsy on margaritas when I got there. She's being the phoenix we've all come to admire. Already has a plan for handling Mercer. She was touched by the fact that you took my shift so I could check on her. Thanks again.

Next, I call Jack's and reserve my favorite table by the fireplace for tomorrow night. The view of the bay is beautiful from that side of the dining room, not that I'll be able to tear my gaze away from Scarlet. I can't wait to spend time with her outside the fire station and away from interior design projects. Most of the time we've spent together has been because of her project, and I just want to get away from all of that for a little bit.

Leonard: Good to hear. Now you owe me a favor next time I need to take off, dude.

Andrew: Absolutely. Thanks again.

I grab the remote off my coffee table and turn on the basketball game, needing a distraction. My brain just wants to think of Scarlet all the time. How funny that I need a distraction from the woman who has been the most wonderful distraction I've ever experienced. I force my focus on the game, but it's not too long before I feel fatigue setting in from the craziness of today. The last thing I remember is a three-pointer shot by my favorite player as I drift off to sleep.

***

Two hours later, I jolt awake at the sound of my phone ringing.

Scarlet.

I grab it quickly and swipe it open.

"Nix?"

I hear a soft sigh on the other end of the line.

"Yeah, I'm sorry," she says quietly. "Did I wake you up?"

"I fell asleep on the couch," I confess. "I wasn't in bed. Are you okay?"

"Yes and no," she says. "The good news is that I'm in my bedroom alone. The bad news is every time I lay my head on the pillow, I start freaking out again."

"I'm glad you called me. How can I help?"

She doesn't answer right away, and I wonder if she might be more upset than she sounds. Is she crying? How bad is her anxiety right now?

"Can we just talk? I feel less alone, and I don't want to bother Ashley."

"I'm sure she wouldn't think you were bothering her, but of course, we can talk."

"She would say exactly the same thing, but I'm still not used to needing to lean on people as much as I have been. I want to give her a break. So it's your turn."

I laugh softly. "Lucky me, Nix. Now...may I ask you a favor?"

"Of course," she replies with a sweet edge to her voice.

"Can we make this a video call so I can see your beautiful face as we talk?"

I hear a sharp little intake of breath.

"You're so sweet. I love that idea," she says. "Yes, please."

"Okay, hang up, and I'll call you back on video. See you in three seconds."

She laughs and hangs up, and I dial her right back with a video call request. Scarlet answers quickly, and I'm looking at a new version of my favorite person. One with a freshly scrubbed face, free of makeup, and tucked into her bed.

"Hello, beautiful," I say with a huge, stupid grin on my face.

She smiles brightly, and my pulse pounds in response.

"Hello, Superman," she says with an adorable grin.

Chapter 18

Andrew

"Hey, I was so tipsy earlier that I forgot to tell you I got to see my mom today," she shares happily. "She's home, and I got some mom hugs. It was amazing."

I'm stupid happy for her. She loves to be independent, but I've felt like she might need her mom after everything has happened. I knew she'd be back but wasn't sure when, so this is great news.

"That's great, Nix," I say. "Does that mean you'll be moving back home soon?"

She nods. "Probably this weekend. We're going out to lunch tomorrow and then shopping to replace my bedroom furniture since I can't move back without that unless I want to sleep on the floor. I'll move back whenever it's delivered."

"I'll bet it felt great to see her."

"It really did," she shares. "She is my biggest cheerleader. I really missed her."

I smile at her, happy to just listen.

"Are you close to your mom?" she asks. "I just realized I know about your dad but not your mom."

My stomach grumbles. I purse my lips together as I get up and head to my kitchen, carrying my phone so we can still video chat.

"Fairly close," I reply. "She lives across the bay in Alameda and doesn't really like to come into the city, so I go over there to visit."

I prop my phone up on the counter as I pull a French bread pizza out of the freezer and pop it into my air fryer. I grab a bottle of water from the fridge and turn back to find Scarlet's eyes tracking my every movement.

"How about an apartment tour?" she asks. "Do I get to see where you live?"

I laugh softly. "Sure, Nix. My pleasure."

I put my water on the coffee table, then flip the camera and head back to the kitchen.

"This is my tiny kitchen," I say, feeling a little ridiculous. I'm not great at this kind of thing.

I turn around and point the camera at my living room.

"You're probably cringing at my decorating ability right now, so I'm glad I can't see your face."

I hear her laugh. "It's actually pretty cute, Andrew. I'm not judging."

I smirk as I head into my bedroom. "That's exactly the vibe I was going for when I moved in here: pretty cute."

She laughs again, and I move the camera around my bedroom and then my bathroom. Then I flip the camera to the front so I can smile at her on my way back to the couch.

"That's all there is of my little apartment, I'm afraid," I say. "Pretty boring."

She smiles sleepily. "Nothing about you is boring."

This woman. She's a gut punch of love right in the feels, I swear.

"Likewise, gorgeous," I say huskily. I clear my throat. "You're starting to look sleepy. Why don't you snuggle down under those covers and get comfortable."

"Oh," she says excitedly. "You're right...I am feeling a little sleepy."

I fight back a grin. "Well, don't get all excited or you'll scare away all the sleepy vibes. Stretch out under the covers."

"I'm not ready to say goodnight to you, though."

So freaking adorable.

"Me either, Nix," I say gently. "Prop the phone up on the nightstand and stretch out. I'm not going anywhere."

She nods, then turns and tries a few positions with her phone until she finds one she likes. I watch as she lays down and turns on her side so she can see me.

"Better?" I ask.

"Yep," she replies, stifling a yawn. "You have the best ideas."

I laugh again. "That's quite a compliment coming from the woman who's going to make a window treatment out of a fire hose. So creative."

She smiles at me from her pillow, and my stomach flips in response.

"It's gonna be so great," she says faintly. "You'll see."

"I have no doubt, Nix."

I watch in fascination as she fights against her heavy eyelids, weighed down by sleep. She doesn't want to give in, but sleep claims her. The sense of joy I feel that she was able to fall asleep without someone else in the room is almost overwhelming. A stupid, silly grin spreads on my face as I watch her breath even out. Her lips part softly, and I know she's gone, but I can't bring myself to hang up.

A few seconds later, she jolts awake. Her eyes dart around the room until they land on her phone. On me.

"Are you okay?"

Scarlet smiles. "You're still there."

I nod. "Not going anywhere. I felt bad about hanging up without saying goodnight."

"Did I really just fall asleep all by myself?"

"You did," I say soothingly. "Now go back to sleep, Nix."

She lets out an adorable groan. "Still not ready to say goodnight."

"You don't have to," I say, watching her eyelids fall. "I'll stay right here."

"M'kay..." she whispers against the pillow.

And she's out again.

I smile at my screen for a few minutes before turning the TV on. I lower the volume so it doesn't disturb Scarlet. When the air fryer beeps, I trot quickly to the kitchen to put my pizza on a plate, then bring it back to the couch. I take one of the accent pillows off my couch and put it on the coffee table, leaning my phone against it so I can eat and still be visible to Scarlet if she wakes up again. I wish I could reach through the phone and turn the light off for her, but it doesn't seem to be bothering her at all. I say a silent prayer to ward off all nightmares, wishing her a sweet, dreamless sleep.

***

Scarlet

It's morning.

What?

It's morning...and I slept alone last night. No nightmares. No anxiety. I slept alone!

I bolt upright with the biggest smile on my face. Wow. This is such huge progress. Maybe not to others, but it is to me. I got a huge chunk of my normal back last night.

Last night. Memories trickle in through my foggy pre-coffee brain. Merry and Marina left, and then I told Ashley I was going to try to sleep alone. I came in here and was able to be alone for a while before...I called Andrew. I look at the nightstand for my phone, and that's when I see him. My heart turns into a giant ball of goo. Our video chat is still open. Sometime during the night, he went to bed and took his phone with him. I'm sure he was thinking of me panicking if I woke up. He's just that sweet. And now I'm looking at him as he sleeps.

He's on his side, facing the camera. He's not wearing a shirt, so I am treated to the sight of the beautiful, sculpted shoulder and bicep that are peeking up from the covers. I take a moment to stare unabashedly at his beauty. Because he *is* a beautiful thing. His gorgeous dark hair is tousled and falling across his forehead. And those thick, black eyelashes that plenty of women would kill for sweep across his cheek. Not to mention that beautiful mouth of his. The best kisses come from those lips. I wish I could teleport myself through the phone right now and kiss him awake.

I pick up my phone and steal one last glance before disconnecting the video chat with very conflicted emotions. I don't want to wake him up. He is always thinking of others, especially me. I want him to rest, so I decide not to send a text message right away to thank him for this latest amazing thing he's done for me. I'll wait an hour or so, and then I'll send it. I get up and skip the shower for a minute, heading into the hall to see if Ashley's awake yet. I hear her thumping around in the kitchen, so I race out there to celebrate my victory.

As soon as she sees me, she starts jumping up and down. I run into the kitchen and join her, heart full of gratitude not just for my victory but for such an amazing friend who's always ready to celebrate me.

"You slept all on your own!" she exclaims, still jumping.

I throw my arms up like Rocky Balboa in the movie Rocky.

"Victory!"

We both stop jumping, and she grabs me for a hug.

"I'm so happy for you," Ashley says.

"This is amazing," I say excitedly. "I can't wait to tell my therapist."

Ashley beams at me. "I'll bet!"

"I'm going to take a shower," I say as I head back to my room. "I just wanted to see if you were up because I knew you'd understand."

"Of course I do," she says sweetly. "I'll put some coffee on. Come right back when you're done."

I grin and pad back to my room. I'm so excited it feels like my body is humming from electricity racing through my veins. I head into my bathroom and start up the shower, then go back into the bedroom to grab my phone. I open up the group chat that I share with my besties.

Scarlet: I slept all by myself like a big girl!

I laugh under my breath and go grab a pair of jeans and a light sweater for today. I'll play with my sketchbook this morning and flesh out the idea for the window treatments. Then I'll head over to meet Mom for lunch and shopping. And later tonight...dinner with Andrew.

I know exactly what I'm going to wear for my first official date with the sweetest man on the planet. I can't wait for tonight, and now we have my little victory to celebrate. I know it'll be a perfect evening.

***

"This is definitely the one," I tell Mom hours later as I lie on a mattress in the middle of a huge furniture store. "It feels like I'm laying on a cloud."

The salesman, who can't seem to take his eyes off my mom, glances over his shoulder at me.

"And would we like the Lux 3000 power base for our new cloud? It's thirty percent off today."

Before I can open my mouth to say no, Mom nods.

"You can put that on my part of the bill," she tells him, giving me a look that I know all too well. No arguing with that face.

I pull myself up off of the mattress and join Mom as she follows the salesman to a kiosk where he'll ring us up. I would argue more with her about it, but she will definitely get her money back. Whenever she needs to decorate a room or her office at the law firm, she calls her favorite designer…because I'll do it for free, of course. Bottom line, we just take care of each other. We always have.

We finish our transactions, and I'm delighted to hear that everything will be delivered on Saturday. That works well for me, and I get to hang out with Ashley for a bit longer. We head to Nonno's for lunch, which I'm excited about since I haven't seen him in a long time, and I'll get the added bonus of seeing Merry.

"What are you so quiet about, my fearless daughter?" Mom asks from the driver's seat as she pulls the car into the small parking lot behind Nonno's.

I smile to myself as I unfasten my seatbelt and then turn to face her. I really missed having my mom around, and this is just one of the reasons why. She knows me better than anyone.

"I really missed you, Mom."

"Oh, come here," she says as she gently pulls me close enough to kiss my forehead. "Now, what's on your mind? I missed you too, baby girl, but that's not it."

I shrug. "Nothing major. I just hate waiting. I like to be busy, and I like to have control. But Mercer derailed my project, and I am temporarily…unbusy."

Mom laughs under her breath as we both get out of the car. She walks over to my side and wraps an arm around my shoulders, giving me a supportive squeeze.

"I have faith it'll be worked out very soon," she says. "First, because I have faith in my amazing daughter. Second, because there's nothing Dave wouldn't do for you. You're like another daughter to that man. And third, if all of that fails, you have a mother who is a pretty terrific lawyer."

I throw my arm around her waist and squeeze back.

"I'm sure I won't need a lawyer," I say as we round the building and hit the sidewalk that leads to the front door. "I have a secret weapon named Kevin Starbuck."

Merry spies us through the large front windows as we near the door, and I wave at her as she runs to open it for us. She steps outside with a bright smile.

"Hello, Jackson girls!" Merry calls out.

"Hello, sweet girl," Mom says as we step inside. She turns immediately and hugs Merry.

Merry gestures at the nearly empty dining room.

"Take your pick," she says. "You missed the lunch rush today. That must mean you found some good stuff, huh?"

I nod as she walks with us to a table near the window.

"I found a great bedroom set in the clearance section," I begin. "Some minor scrapes on the side of the dresser, but I know how to fix that."

"And I bought the mattress with a power base," Mom shares with a smug grin. "Since my too-frugal daughter would compromise her spinal health to save a buck, and I am too bougie to care."

Merry and I laugh.

"I'll go grab some menus," Merry says. "What can I get you to drink?"

"Water with lime, honey," Mom replies. "I'm driving."

I smile up at Merry. "Same, girl."

Merry runs off to get our drink, and Mom gestures at me quickly.

"So, what's going on with you? You're quiet."

I shake my head. "Nothing important. I hate waiting for things, that's all. I'm really hoping Ash's dad calls me today, but even if we get that sorted out, I still need a budget number from the city for the furniture. I don't want to overspend, and I need to get moving. I don't have much longer."

Mom nods. "Understandable. But what else? That doesn't seem like everything."

I take a deep breath. Some things don't feel real until I say them out loud, and I haven't said this one out loud yet. I run my fingers over the napkin that holds my silverware.

"I don't care about the competition anymore."

Mom's eyebrows shoot straight up to her hairline.

"You don't?"

I shake my head violently.

"No, I do," I stammer. "But I don't. Up until the fire, I was completely consumed by the competition. I didn't allow space for anything else in my life."

Mom chuffs. "Oh, I know, honey. I've watched you go for this thing every year."

"And there's Andrew..."

Mom flashes me a feline grin.

"Yes, let's talk about him."

Merry brings our waters and two menus, then looks at my mom with a conspiratorial grin.

"You talking about Andrew?"

Mom laughs out loud when I roll my eyes.

"Scarlet, you can't blame us," she says. "You were so against any possibility of a relationship for ages. This is refreshing to see."

Merry nods. "He's her person."

I look up at Merry. "Will you stop saying that?"

She shakes her head. "Nope. I was right about Marina. I'm right about you too."

I look down at the table, unsure of what to say. I feel drawn to Andrew in a thousand ways, but what if I'm wrong? My silence doesn't stop Merry from continuing.

"And now you'll run off and get married, and I'll be the only single one left," she drawls dramatically. "Just go ahead and get me my crazy cat lady kit right now. I'm going to end up a spinster."

"Oh, stop!" I yelp, taking a swipe at her as she giggles and runs back to the kitchen.

I turn back to Mom, who waits patiently for me to continue.

"Part of me worries that Andrew caught my eye, and then he saved my life, and now I'm throwing aside my goals because I'm crazy about some guy."

Mom considers my words carefully.

"But he's not just some guy, is he?"

The look in her eyes tells me she knows without me having to answer the question. No, he's not just some guy. Andrew means a great deal more than any other man I've ever known.

"No, Mom, he's not," I say, feeling almost breathless. "I just have this underlying fear that I can't shake. That I'm somehow abandoning my goals because of him. And I know in my heart that's not true, but sometimes my head gets in the way."

"Oh, my beautiful ladies!"

I turn at the sound of the very Italian, very sweet Nonno's voice as he comes barreling into the dining room from the kitchen. His chef's whites are pristine looking as he takes my hand and pulls me out of my seat for a hug, which I give more than willingly. I love Nonno like I'd love any grandfather by birth. He's the best.

I stand back and watch him do the same to Mom, and then he gestures for both of us to sit as he pulls a vacant chair over for himself. He flips it backward and straddles it so he can lean over the chair back.

"Scarlet, I'm so proud of you," he gushes sweetly. "Are you well after the fire? All better? Merry tells me nothing."

Merry scoffs as she comes up behind him.

"No," she argues. "Merry tells you it's not her story to tell, and

Scarlet will fill you in when she visits."

Nonno shoots her a mock glare, and then they both laugh.

"I'm okay, Nonno," I reply. "Thank you for asking."

"And this fireman," he prods. "He's very handsome in his pictures, but the news articles don't say if you're romantic and—"

"Merry tells me nothing!" Merry interrupts in her best Nonno impression, prompting a giggle out of both Mom and Nonno.

I grin at Nonno. "We're dating," I say excitedly. "And he was already a fan of Nonno's when I met him. He loves Merry's Italian wedding cookies."

Nonno grins proudly at Merry, then puts his meaty hands on either side of her head and gives her a loud kiss on her forehead.

"My girl Merry, she's a big baker like her Nonna."

Almost immediately, I see a wistful, far off look in Nonno's eyes. Merry looks at me in frustration. We both know if she chimes in right now and tries to get him to let her re-open her Nonna's bakery the answer will be no. But something has to give, for Merry's sake.

"She's certainly very talented," Mom pipes in.

Nonno shakes his head like he's trying to clear out the memories, then offers us all a polite smile.

"And what have you decided for lunch, my beautiful ladies?"

I don't even have to think about it.

"Lasagna for me, definitely."

Mom grins. "Make that two."

Nonno claps his hands.

"Excellent choice! Prepare to be spoiled, ladies," he says flamboyantly. "I'll come see you before you go. Enjoy your lunch."

We wave goodbye as Nonno retreats to the kitchen, and Merry shrugs.

"I don't know what else I can say to get him to let me try," she says defeatedly. "I'll be right back."

Merry heads off toward the kitchen again, leaving me alone with Mom.

"Honey, honestly, I think you're overthinking this one," Mom tells me quietly. "You spent so long with those fierce anti-dating boundaries up. It's nice to see you interested in someone."

I feel myself relax a little at her words. And I know she's right because it *feels* right. I sit back in my seat and grin like a lovesick goof.

"Tonight is our first official big date."

Mom's eyebrows shoot up in curiosity.

"Exciting! What are you going to wear?"

Merry comes galloping back to our table with a generous basket of Nonno's garlic bread sticks, and I'm already drooling. She sets it down between us and gives us each a small plate.

"Thanks, Mer," I say as I grab a bread stick. "Mom just asked me what I'm wearing on my date tonight. We're going down to the wharf, so it'll be cold."

Merry snaps her fingers and points at me. I know exactly what she's thinking because it's what I'm thinking too.

"Pink sweater dress," we say in unison.

Mom grins. "You always look beautiful in that dress. Great choice."

I blow a kiss at my mom in thanks, then take a bite and feel the endorphin rush immediately. Mmm. These things are heaven, and I'm starving.

"I'm gonna let you gals chat," Merry says with a wink. "Just yell if you need anything."

Mom eyes me quietly, reminding me of the nagging feeling I have lately…of needing to explain myself. More for me than for others. I'd become so used to being focused on one thing I feel like I don't fit in my own skin at times. I give her a reassuring nod.

"I'm all right, Mom," I say gently. "I'm just adjusting to my new normal, which is apparently a new Scarlet who is no longer obsessed with winning a TV network contest and has a boyfriend who gets her out of the house and takes her on dates."

Mom raises her glass. "Well, cheers to that, my beautiful daughter."

I beam back at Mom just as my phone vibrates. I swipe the screen and see a notification that I have a new email, so I check the sender and gasp out loud.

"I got an email from the fire department!" I exclaim, frantically poking around on the screen to get to it.

Mom waits patiently for me to relay the message, and I gasp again.

"It's from the Chief!" I say quickly, then skim through the email and feel my heart slide down through my ribs and drop into my stomach.

No. This can't be happening.

"Uh oh," Mom says lowly. "What's wrong?"

I look up from my phone and smirk.

"I finally got my furniture budget," I say in disgust. "They're giving me a whopping five hundred dollars to replace all the furniture in the fire station."

Mom's eyebrows shoot straight up to her hairline. "The fire chief emailed you to tell you that?"

I scroll back to the beginning of the email and read it to her.

"Dear Miss Jackson, let me first begin by telling you how very sorry I am about this latest confusion with the City Planner's office. You have my assurance that we're working to resolve the matter quickly. I received clarification that Engine 14 is due for furniture replacement at the standard budget of $500. The City Planner's office made it abundantly clear that we cannot exceed that amount. I'll be in touch again as soon as we have a resolution to the remaining issue. Sincerely yours, blah blah blah."

Mom watches me with sympathy in her eyes. "What now?"

I sit back in my seat for a moment and nervously bite at the inside of my cheek. There is no way I can squeeze living room seating, end tables, a coffee table, and a dining set out of five hundred dollars. The Swap House and all its bargaining glory can't even get me out of this predicament. I need another miracle.

Soon.

Chapter 19

Scarlet

After lunch with Mom, which also involved planning the big reveal party's catering with Nonno, I head straight back to my temporary home. I park Ashley's car on the street and walk into the building, but not up to the apartment. Instead, I open the door to the Mermaid Foundation's offices and go on the hunt for the two people I need to pull off the miracle of miracles. Fortunately for me, they're both in Marina's office, and the door is open. Marina looks up in surprise as I walk in and hug her hello.

"What's this all about?" she asks with a huge smile.

Her events manager, Hillary, smiles up at me from one of the chairs in Marina's office and I smile back at her.

"I need a huge favor."

Hillary stands from her chair. "I'll leave you to it."

"From both of you."

Hillary sits back down and grins. "I love a challenge. What's up?"

Marina motions for me to sit with them at a small conference table in her office. I take a deep breath to calm my nerves and sit.

"The city gave me a whopping five hundred dollar budget to furnish the fire station," I deadpan. "The whole thing."

Marina gasps, and Hillary's expression goes sour. They get it.

"And you need us for...what kind of favor?" Marina asks.

I place my palms on top of my thighs and rub them over my jeans, gathering my thoughts.

"If I remember correctly, the Rebels are on a break right now?"

There's an immediate glint in Marina's eye, telling me she sees where I'm going.

"Not only are they on a break," Marina shares, "but they're all coming to dinner at our apartment tonight."

I grin at Marina. "Perfect."

She nods. "Just to make sure my mind-reading skills are still accurate, are you suggesting the guys do some kind of performance to help you raise more funds?"

Hillary gasps and claps her hands together. "I love this idea!"

I nod. "Yes, but there's a real jerk in the city government who'll try his best to muck it up however he can. We need to think two steps ahead of him. He shut me down for not having a background check and some other red tape."

Hillary begins making notes on the pad in front of her.

"Well, when people hear that this is for Engine 14 where *the* fireman is stationed, this performance is clearly going to raise more money than what you need for furniture," Hillary surmises. "Why don't we advertise it so that people know all excess funds will go to the fireman's retirement fund? That way all firefighters in the city will benefit."

I jump in my seat and point a finger at Hillary.

"See...that right there is exactly why you're on my miracle team," I say excitedly. "They can't stop us from fundraising for that, and it's such a great cause."

Hillary beams with pride at my compliment, but it's one hundred percent true. The woman is a miracle worker. She's done amazing things in her job as Marina's events manager. Hillary's in full thinking mode now, tapping her pen against her lip. Marina paces.

"You need this to happen pretty quickly, right? Your deadline for the decorating contest is getting close," Marina asks.

I nod in response.

Hillary shrugs. "So we call it a pop-up concert and find a venue that we don't need to fill. A stadium that seats a hundred thousand people would be a huge mistake if we want something to happen in a matter of days, and we'll need to make sure we have a permit for the event."

My stomach drops. "I didn't realize we needed that."

Hillary winks at me with a cocky glint in her eye.

"It shouldn't be a problem," she says sweetly. "I've organized so many events for the Mermaid Foundation that the guy in the permits office has a little crush on me. I can get it done. How do you feel about the concert venue in Golden Gate Park? That feels right for something like this."

Marina is grinning ear to ear as she watches Hillary plan this out. She really is amazing.

"You're incredible, Hillary," I say in complete awe. "I think that's perfect."

"To get maximum attendance, we'll need it to be on a weekend," she muses. "Is next weekend too late?"

"Not at all," I reply quickly. "I can window shop and make all my choices in advance, so I'm ready to go when we have the funds."

Is this actually going to work out? My imagination runs rampant with images of Mercer crying in his cornflakes because he wasn't able to stop me.

"So if we have the concert next Saturday, does that give you enough time?"

I pull up my calendar on my phone and nod excitedly.

"We do the concert on Saturday, and if I can get the funds for the furniture pretty quick, it gives me three or four days to shop, order, and get it delivered. It'll be tight, but I can do it."

Hillary's pen flies feverishly across her pad, making note after note.

"Give me twenty-four hours, and I should be able to confirm that we have the permits and the park is available," Hillary says, then she turns to Marina. "You'll need to talk to Zach and the guys, of course."

Now it's Marina's turn to wink.

"That man is putty in my hands," she says. "And he's upstairs. Why don't we go talk to him right now?"

I jump up out of my seat. "Let's do it."

Hillary laughs.

"She forgets it works both ways," Hillary teases. "She's putty in his hands as well."

She gets up and puts a hand on my shoulder.

"Don't worry about a thing, Scarlet," she says calmly. "I could do this in my sleep. I've got this."

I give her a huge hug and follow Marina upstairs to the apartment she and Zach have together. Zach has a huge heart, so I doubt we'll have to sweet-talk him very much at all. If they can do it, I know they will. Otherwise, I'm betting that he can help me find some other bands to perform. Either way, my next miracle is well in hand, and I feel pretty good about how this is going to go. I almost wish I could see Mercer's face when he realizes he hasn't beaten me.

***

Andrew

I check my reflection in the visor mirror one last time, then grab the bouquet of flowers I picked up for Scarlet before heading inside to pick her up for our date. The sun is still shining, sort of. There's no heat from it as a thin layer of fog rolls over the city. That's life in San Francisco, though. I checked the weather forecast in case we want to walk around Fisherman's Wharf after dinner. No rain is predicted, and the fog isn't expected to stay long.

I find myself racing up the stairs to Ashley's apartment door. I'm just that excited for tonight. Getting to have a normal date with my girl is priceless in a million different ways. She makes me as giddy as a teenager going to his first dance sans the angst and acne.

I knock on the door and wait. It feels like forever, but I'm rewarded with a stunningly beautiful smile from Scarlet as she opens the door wearing a dress that hugs her in all the right places.

Wow.

Scarlet swings the door open to welcome me in. I step inside and take a moment to admire her. She's wearing a sweater dress in a soft pink color that brings out the blush in her cheeks and the blue of her eyes. If I looked in a mirror right now, I'm sure I'd see hearts floating out of my eyes like a cartoon. Her earlobes are dotted with dainty pearls, and her usual straight bob has beautiful waves in it. I am spellbound.

"You look absolutely beautiful," I say in a near whisper.

Somehow, I manage to remember the flowers in my hand and present them to her.

"For my Nix."

My stomach dips like I'm on a rollercoaster as she smiles. So gorgeous. And that smile is for me.

"Andrew, thank you. They're beautiful."

She leans in and places a soft kiss on the corner of my mouth, and I'm tempted to pull her into my arms. She pulls away quickly and motions for me to follow as she heads to the kitchen for a vase, and I look around to see if Ashley or any of her other friends are here. I see no one.

"We're alone," she says with a sweet smile as she fills a vase with water. "You don't have to deal with anyone but me tonight."

She unwraps the bouquet and drops it into the vase, taking a moment to arrange the flowers. As soon as she's satisfied, I step into her space and pull her into my arms. Something primal in me stirs at the little gasp she lets out just before she wraps her arms around my neck.

"Trying for another kiss?" she teases.

I let my gaze drop to her sumptuous mouth and nod.

"Don't make me break out the dimples," I tease back. "I know your weakness."

She laughs softly and raises her lips to mine. That's all the permission I need to take possession of those lips with my own. She leans into my body, and her softness melts against me. Our kiss is soft and slow, and I'm tempted to cancel dinner and order in just so I can keep kissing her like this. She feels like she is made to fit in my arms, molded just for me as I am for her. She ends our kiss with a little nip at my lower lip, but she doesn't pull away.

"How was your day?" she asks, those bright blue eyes roving over my face.

I shrug. "Uneventful compared to this."

She laughs softly, and I cup the side of her face with my hand. Her eyelids dip closed for a heartbeat, and she leans her cheek against my palm.

"How was your day, beautiful?" I ask.

"Eventful," she says with a heavy sigh. "Even stressful."

I frown. "What's wrong?"

She steps out of my arms and reaches over to the entry table for a small evening bag, then loops her arm through mine with a smile that seems a little forced.

"I'll tell you on the way," she says as we cover the short distance to the door. "But after that, let's forget about the project and everything else for a few hours. I just want to spend time with you and forget about all the problems in my world."

It's incredibly hard to do, but I ignore the part of me that wants to stop us in our tracks and demand the truth so I can fix those problems. But if Scarlet needs to forget about things for a while, then that's what we'll do. I'll do everything I can to make this a perfect evening for her. For us. Starting with a delicious dinner in a romantic spot on the wharf.

By the time I pull my car up to the valet stand in front of the restaurant, Scarlet has unloaded the gritty details of her stressful day. I absolutely hate that there's really nothing I can do to help things along with our city government. Part of me wishes I could aim the fire hose at Mercer on full stream the next time he shows his face at the station, but that will have to remain a fantasy. Still, the mental image of his scrawny body getting propelled down the street on a giant spout of water makes me grin as I take the ticket from the valet and step around the car to escort Scarlet inside.

Within minutes, a hostess greets us and walks us to the table I specifically requested when I made the reservation. Positioned against the window near a long, glass-enclosed gas fireplace partition, this table has a gorgeous view of San Francisco Bay and part of the Golden Gate Bridge. Dusk is just beginning, so it's still fairly bright in the restaurant, but once the sunset really begins, they'll dim the lights in the dining room and light the fireplace in the glass partition...and we'll have a beautiful view of the bay. I brought my mom here on one of her visits to the city, and I've always thought this was the perfect place for a romantic date.

The look on Scarlet's face as she sees the view fills me with pride. I chose well. She smiles at me as I hold her chair out for her, then I take my seat across the table.

"This is perfect," she says quietly. "It's so beautiful."

I keep my eyes locked on hers, ignoring the bay.

"Absolutely beautiful," I agree.

I'm rewarded with a slight blush that creeps up her cheeks.

"You're going to lay on all the charm tonight, aren't you," she teases, laughing softly.

I grin at her. "Just telling the truth, Nix."

A sharply uniformed server whisks up to our table, smiling brightly.

"Good evening," she greets us. "I'm Carrie. I'll be taking care of you tonight. What can I get you to drink?"

I look to Scarlet, who is scanning the menu.

"Just a Diet Coke for me, please."

I smile up at Carrie. "Same."

She nods politely, and her gaze lingers a moment between me and Scarlet before she heads off to fill our drink orders. I turn my full attention back to the breathtakingly gorgeous woman seated before me.

"So what do you plan to do once this is all over, Nix?" I ask. "Once the project is done and you've won the contest, what does that look like?"

Scarlet beams at me.

"I love how confident you are that I'll just run away with the whole thing."

I stretch my hand across the table, palm up, and she places her delicate hand in mind.

"I have no doubt."

"Assuming you're right, I'll get to work building my interior design business in earnest," she replies. "I'll have all the funds I need to set it up the way I want it, so there won't be any more bumps in the road. The publicity from winning this contest is insane. There will be lots of media interviews. I won't be praying for clients anymore…they'll be landing in my lap."

"You've worked really hard, Scarlet," I say proudly. "You deserve to win this."

She surprises me with an indifferent shrug.

"The thing is…it doesn't matter to me in the same way it did before the fire," she says, squeezing my hand when I look surprised. "Don't get me wrong. I'm still passionate about wanting my own business, but the contest is starting to make me feel like a prize show dog having to jump through a bunch of hoops."

I nod slowly. "I guess I can understand that. It's a lot of pressure."

Scarlet gives me a half smile.

"It is. And I think you should prepare yourself because the other designers are all working on projects that didn't get derailed by a raging warehouse fire or an uptight city clerk. I'm proud of the job I'm doing at Engine 14, but it's not going to win this contest for me. I don't want you to be too disappointed when someone else wins."

I shake my head at Scarlet.

"Don't even speak that into existence, Scarlet. You're going to win."

She laughs softly and squeezes my hand again.

"Remember the library I was creating in that warehouse?"

The mental picture immediately appears in my mind. It was truly incredible. I nod.

"Think about what it would look like now if it hadn't burned down," she says. "I would have had all this time to build layer on layer of beauty and elegance in that space. I—"

Her voice breaks up, and she closes her mouth, suddenly stricken by emotion. I'm sure she's picturing that beautiful library and mourning its loss all over again. Frustration lodges itself in my chest at the knowledge that there's nothing I can do to bring that library back and give her a bigger space to offer the judges.

"I'm sorry," Scarlet murmurs, shaking her head. "I don't know where that came from."

I lace our fingers together and wait until her gaze locks back with mine.

"It's okay to feel all that emotion, Scarlet. You've been through a lot."

Carrie comes back to our table just at the wrong moment, and Scarlet buttons up completely.

"Have you decided?" Carrie asks as she sets our drinks down.

Scarlet offers up a polite smile and orders the shrimp and scallops, handing the menu to Carrie.

"I'd like the Kobe beef and scallops, please, Carrie," I say with a quick, polite smile. "Can we also have the crab cakes for an appetizer?"

She asks a few questions to make sure our orders are just right, then takes our menus with a nod and disappears.

Scarlet squeezes my hand to get my attention.

"Let's talk about something else, okay?"

Her eyes look like she might be fighting back tears, and I consider persisting a little bit…just so she can let her feelings out. I study her for a moment, the quiet stretching out between us like a long, taut string. I give in before it breaks.

"Whatever you want, beautiful," I reply quietly.

I lean over and pull her hand closer, brushing my lips across her knuckles before lacing our fingers together again.

"How are you still single?" Scarlet asks sweetly.

I blink back my surprise. "What?"

She laughs, and it feels like little sparks dance around my ribs and settle in my stomach.

"You're just…perfect," she says, blushing again. "I find it hard to believe some woman hasn't snatched you up and dragged you down the aisle."

I laugh out loud and shake my head.

"We're too similar, Nix," I tell her. "Would you ever let some man drag you down the aisle?"

She scoffs. "Nope."

Carrie comes back to the table with two appetizer plates and a heavenly-smelling plate full of crab cakes.

Scarlet pulls her hand from mine, unrolling her napkin and placing it in her lap.

I do the same.

"I know I shouldn't say anything," Carrie says quietly, "but you're the Phoenix and the Fireman, aren't you?"

Scarlet looks up from the crab cakes in surprise, and we both laugh.

"We are," she answers for us both.

Carrie barely contains her excitement, and I stifle another laugh. She acts like she's talking to an A-list celebrity couple instead of two regular people experiencing a fleeting moment of fame.

"I knew it," she says excitedly. "I won't bother you all night, I promise, but I just wanted to say how much I love your story. You guys make a beautiful couple."

Scarlet's eyes drift to mine, and her gaze softens, making me want to reach across the table and kiss her until her lipstick's gone. She looks back up at Carrie.

"Thank you so much."

"Okay, I'm going to go away and leave you alone for now. Enjoy your crab cakes."

Carrie disappears again, and I nudge the crab cakes towards Scarlet.

"Phoenixes first."

She laughs softly and moves a couple to her plate, then I serve myself.

"I love it when you call me Nix," Scarlet says quietly. "It makes me feel special."

I feel a ridiculous amount of pride from that and I smile back at her.

"You *are* special, baby."

She sits back in her chair. "And what makes you feel special?"

I don't even have to think about it. "You chose me."

She eyes me suspiciously. "That doesn't feel like it should count. You chose me first."

I light up at the challenge. "Ah, yes, but you didn't *want* to choose me. We know this. And eventually, you saw sense."

Scarlet laughs out loud. "Okay, what else?"

I think for a moment.

"Interacting with kids when we do community outreach stuff. They love that truck. They're so full of questions and energy. They make everything fun."

Carrie steps in to deliver our plates, staying long enough to make sure we have everything we need. Everything smells delicious, and I laugh at the absolute feral expression on Scarlet's face as she eyes my steak.

"Regretting your choice?" I tease lightly.

She shakes her head, eagerly looking down at her own plate.

"I stand by my selection, but that does look incredible."

I hover my fork over my plate. "I'll share. How big of a piece should I cut?"

She waves me off with a sweet smile. "No, I'm not stealing your dinner. Let's dig in."

I cut a bite-size piece for myself as she dives into her plate.

"Okay, but just say the word if you change your mind."

She nods her thanks, and I know she's not going to stop thinking about my steak until she tries some. I stifle a laugh and cut a decent-sized piece to share later.

"Oh wow," Scarlet murmurs against her fork. "This is so good."

The conversation slows a bit while we eat, but it never falters. Scarlet tells me about her close relationship with her mother, and how hard she worked as a single mom to make sure Scarlet had a wonderful childhood. Maybe that's one of the reasons why we fit so well together. We were both raised by strong women.

I laugh as Scarlet shares the story of that viral video she and her girlfriends were all part of about two years ago. Apparently, Zach literally walked away with Marina, dressed as a mermaid, in his arms and rescued her from a mob of unruly fans while Scarlet, Ashley, and Merry watched helplessly from their car. Marina was strictly against any kind of romance at the time and had no idea her three girlfriends were plotting against her in the car, trying to come up with any way for Marina to have to see Zach again once they were all safely away from the chaos.

"Well, she isn't the only one of you who was against romance, Nix," I tease.

She rolls her beautiful eyes at me, then gives me a playful nudge across the table.

"I came around a lot faster than Marina did," she says in her defense. "You're too perfect to resist for long."

I laugh out loud at that. "I'm nowhere near perfect."

We're having so much fun chatting away that I almost fail to notice her nearly clean plate. I stab the piece of steak on my plate with my fork and move it to Scarlet's, giving her a knowing look as she grins.

"Um, you're sharing your steak with me," she says as she cuts into the piece. "That's pretty perfect."

"I just want you to be happy, beautiful."

Scarlet's eyes close, and she dips her head back as she savors the steak. A little moan escapes her throat, and I find myself having all kinds of not-so-perfect thoughts all of a sudden. She opens her eyes and shakes her head at me.

"Andrew, thank you," she says, beaming. "How did I get so lucky... finding a man who's so giving."

Be still my heart.

"I don't know how I got so lucky, Nix," I murmur. "I pride myself on always being prepared, but I was unprepared for you and everything you make me feel."

Without a word, Nix gets up from her side of the table, takes three steps over to me, and sits right in my lap. She wraps her arms around my neck and kisses me sweetly, then places her hands on my face and looks into my eyes.

"And I was definitely not prepared for you," she says quietly. "You make me so happy, Andrew. I can't imagine my life without you."

Always surprising me, my girl. Talk about unprepared.

I'm also completely unprepared for Carrie stepping in with a long lighter, flipping the gas switch on the glass-enclosed fireplace next to our table, and lighting it up. Scarlet jolts in shock as flames erupt against the glass, and I wrap my arms tighter to keep us both from toppling over.

Her breathing is instantly panicked, and she fights wildly to get out of my lap. I let her go, trying to steady her with my arms, and I get up from my seat. I rush to her side as she quickly backs away, and she steps into my embrace once we're far enough away. My gut lurches as she trembles in my arms. The stupidity of my actions tonight comes crashing down around me. How could I be so insensitive...I didn't even think about the fireplace as anything but romantic.

Scarlet inhales a shaky breath, and I hold her tightly against me. Her hands clench in the back of my shirt, and she buries her face against my chest. I feel like the worst person alive right now.

"I'm so sorry, Nix," I murmur against her hair.

I rock her gently, rubbing a hand down her back in soothing strokes. "It's all right, baby. You're safe. I'm right here."

She nods her head quickly, pulling away enough to look into my eyes. She's fighting back tears and takes a self-conscious look around us to see if anyone saw.

"I'm okay," she mutters.

She gives herself a shake, her fierce spirit taking charge, and then blinks away the tears before they fall.

I rub her shoulders gently. "You sure?"

She nods again, then steps close and plants a kiss on my cheek.

"Thanks to you."

Carrie steps over into our view, looking incredibly guilty.

"I am so, so sorry," she says quietly. "I didn't expect the fireplace to flare like that."

Scarlet offers her a soft smile. "No, it's okay," she says, then she looks at me. "I'm okay."

"Would you like me to move you to a different table?" Carrie offers.

I'm about to take Carrie up on it when Scarlet answers for us.

"No, this is great," she replies. "I'm okay now."

Carrie gulps down her embarrassment, then clears our plates and retreats as Scarlet and I head back to the table. I hold her chair for her while she sits, then take my place again. I don't miss the fact that her eyes are darting nervously towards the fireplace.

"Are you sure you're okay? It's no trouble to move to another table."

Scarlet takes a deep breath, her eyelids fluttering closed for a moment before she levels her gaze at me.

"I'm feeling a little shaky," she admits, "but I want to try to deal with it first."

I reach across the table, and she puts her hand in mine.

"Whatever you need, Nix."

Without letting go of my hand, she slowly turns her gaze to the fireplace, and her lip trembles. I give her hand a squeeze, and she squeezes back but keeps her eyes on the fire. I hate how powerless

I feel as I watch her trying to deal with the lingering fear from her scare. Instinctively, I know she's trying to find the resolve to stay at this table, but it's needless. Or maybe it just seems needless to me as the man who wants to shelter and protect her from every bad thing in the world. When I allow myself to think about it for half a second, I realize that I would do the same exact thing if the tables were turned. I would face the thing that scares me and try to find the resolve to overcome it.

"I used to think fires were so pretty before," she murmurs, turning back to face me.

My heart breaks at the lost look I see behind her eyes. I struggle for words at first, but then I decide to try something.

"They are pretty," I hedge. "It's only bad when they get out of control. There are so many good things about fires…like s'mores."

The corners of Scarlet's beautiful mouth twitch just a bit, and I know I'm onto something.

"I guess I can't argue with that one," she says quietly.

"Campfires, too," I continue. "Grilling outdoors. My favorite campfires are on the beach with the ocean air…it's a whole vibe."

She nods. "Toasted marshmallows are the best."

I pull her hand to my lips and graze a kiss along her fingers.

"And fireplaces are a good thing, too," I say. "Stormy nights. Curled up on the couch with a cup of cocoa and a good book."

Scarlet raises her eyebrows in surprise. "Cocoa, huh?"

I nod, flashing her a grin. "I really hate not having a fireplace in my apartment. We always had a fireplace growing up."

Scarlet begins to smile, but her eyes dart back to the fireplace again. She takes a deep breath and frowns, shaking her head.

"Can we move?" she asks with a tremble in her voice. "I know I should be brave, but—"

I wave Carrie down immediately, standing with Scarlet and wrapping her in a hug.

"You are brave, Nix," I murmur against her ear. "Being brave is also knowing when to ask for what you need."

She grabs her evening bag, and Carrie escorts us away from the fireplace to a booth. I try to fight against it, but an overwhelming sense of failure begins to creep in. I should have thought about the fireplace. I should have realized it might be a trigger, but all I saw was a chance to impress Scarlet with the perfect evening...which I've now thoroughly ruined.

Chapter 20

Scarlet

I slide into the booth Carrie escorts us to, scooting far enough in so that Andrew can join me. He moves in close enough so that our thighs are touching, and he wraps an arm around the back of the booth as I sink into his side. The trembling in my body starts to subside, and I take a deep breath.

Carrie, looking thoroughly sorry, brings our drinks over and makes herself scarce. I know she didn't mean to do that, and if it had happened to around 99% of the other patrons in the restaurant, it would have been no big deal at all. It was just bad luck. I feel Andrew watching me carefully, and I lean my head on his broad shoulder.

"I'm all right, Superman," I tease in a tone a little lighter than what I feel. "You can put your cape away."

His fingers trace a lazy circle on my shoulder.

"I am so sorry, Nix," he says quietly. "I should have thought about the fireplace. It was incredibly insensitive."

I pull away from his side and frown at him.

"It wasn't," I argue. "Not a bit, Andrew. Please don't take

responsibility for this. It was just an ugly coincidence. You couldn't have known this would happen."

His eyes roam over my face. "I feel terrible about it."

I run my fingers across his smooth cheek and pull his face closer to mine, pressing a long, soft kiss to his lips.

"Please don't," I plead. "You can't put the whole world on your shoulders."

He leans down and nuzzles my neck, sending a flash of goosebumps all over my skin. Lordy! I move my lips close to his ear.

"Let's just go back to having a wonderful evening, okay? Because that's what it was before I freaked out. I really am fine."

Andrew pulls away and looks into my eyes, and I hold his gaze. I don't want to dwell on the fact that a stupid fireplace scared me right now. I just want to have a nice night with him. He remains silent, trying to assess whether I'm just trying to be brave or if I really do feel fine.

"You're the boss, Nix."

I smile up at him, but he doesn't smile back. I lean in and kiss the corner of his mouth gently.

"Thank you."

Carrie reappears with a large piece of scrumptious-looking cheesecake and two forks. She sets it down between us as I look at her in surprise.

"I tend to apologize with cheesecake," she says with a sheepish grin. "I am really very sorry that scared you so much."

I shake my head at her. "There's no need, I'm fine, really."

Andrew forces a smile. "This is very kind, Carrie."

"Well, something you should know about me right away," I say as I pick up my fork and dig in. "I never say no to dessert."

Andrew laughs softly as I hold the loaded fork up to his mouth.

"You first, Superman," I say quietly.

He holds my gaze and opens for me, closing his mouth around the fork and closing his eyes. He lets out a low moan that I feel all the way down to my toes.

"Wow," he says, picking up the other fork. "That is really good."

He puts a bite of cheesecake on his fork and holds it up for me. His eyes are dark as they dip to my mouth.

"Your turn, Nix."

This is more like it. I want this man's attention, but I want the good stuff tonight. I know I've been through a lot lately, but there's something to be said about just being on a date with the most handsome guy on the planet. I want to enjoy myself tonight.

I close my mouth around the fork and pull away as my tongue and taste buds do the happy dance.

Oh wow.

"Mmm," I murmur. "This is the best cheesecake ever."

Andrew nods slowly, his eyes melting me into a Scarlet-shaped puddle of goo. I shake my head at him.

"Do you want to know a secret?" I ask coyly, loading up my fork and holding it up for him.

He looks between the fork and my eyes, trying to decide whether to answer or eat the cheesecake first. So cute. He gulps at the fork in my hand and then nods as I laugh.

"I am absolutely crazy about you, Andrew MacLachlan," I confess. "You make me so glad I threw all those stupid rules out the window."

Andrew puts his fork down and pulls me into his arms without a word. He looks into my eyes with so much feeling it takes my breath away.

"And I'm just as crazy about you, Nix," he says hoarsely. "I can't imagine my life without you. I can't wait to go on a thousand more dates with you."

His hands come up on either side of my face, and he brings me in for a gentle kiss. Yes, please. Andrew's kisses are even better than cheesecake.

The evening falls back on track as we continue feeding each other cheesecake and stealing kisses. I don't know when, but Carrie dropped off the check at one point, and Andrew took care of it when I went to the ladies room. On the way back to the table, I pulled Carrie aside and made sure she wasn't beating herself up over the fireplace thing. Sure, it scared me, but I feel totally fine again.

I loop my arm through Andrew's as we make our way to the front door. We step outside into the San Francisco night air, and I'm glad I'm wearing a sweater dress. It's a bit chilly out here. There's a beautiful low fog rolling in under the Golden Gate Bridge, lending a kind of magical feel to the wharf.

We stop walking for a moment, and Andrew smiles down at me.

"Would you like to walk around a bit, or is it too chilly?"

I consider, then step close and wrap my arms around his neck. I'm instantly wrapped in his arms and pulled against his hard, muscular form. I steal a kiss before giving my answer.

"I don't want this night to end yet," I tell him. "Let's walk around a little. It is a little chilly, but I love it when it's like this."

Andrew runs his hands up and down my arms to warm me. "Would you like my jacket?"

I smile up at him. "Not right now, but I might take you up on that later. Which way should we walk?"

He takes my hand and tucks it into the crook of his elbow.

"I have a great idea, Nix. This way."

Andrew leads, and I follow. We walk through the small parking lot adjacent to the restaurant until we get to the sidewalk, then head for the crosswalk at Hyde and Beach Streets. I steal more kisses as we wait for the light to change, but Andrew doesn't seem to mind.

When Andrew turns us up Beach Street towards Larkin, I get

suspicious and stop in the middle of the sidewalk. He looks at me curiously, waiting for an explanation.

"Are you kidding? Are you going to eat ice cream after that amazing cheesecake?"

I get another ticket to the dimple show when he grins widely.

"First of all, their ice cream is amazing and could totally compete with that delicious cheesecake," he quips. "But I have another idea if you'll indulge me."

I start walking again. "Well, I can't wait to know what it is."

Ghirardelli Square, a haven for chocolate lovers, looms in the distance as we continue walking. They have an incredible ice cream parlor, which is where I thought Andrew's head was, but now I'm curious to see what else he has planned. Sure enough, he leads me up the steps of the red brick plaza and straight to the famous chocolate and ice cream parlor.

We step inside, and the smell of chocolate is a delicious assault on my senses. I haven't been here in ages, and I'd forgotten how good it smells in here. I think it might be possible to get a sugar rush just from inhaling the air in this place.

A hostess escorts us to a small booth against the wall and leaves us with two menus just as a server walks by with a tray laden down with decadent-looking ice cream sundaes. I nod at the tray as it passes and raise my eyebrows at Andrew.

"You sure we're not here for ice cream?"

He grins to himself as his eyes dart across the menu.

"You're very welcome to get ice cream or anything else on the menu, Nix, but I thought this would be just the thing."

He flips his menu over to me and taps his finger to a section that shows all the hot cocoa drinks they serve.

"Ooooh! Oh my gosh, this does sound perfect."

He sits back in his seat with a nod. "Thought so. But you really can get whatever you want, baby. I'm never going to tell you no."

Oh, that's interesting. Time to play.

"Really? Never?"

He smirks at me. Game on.

"Never."

"Let's put pickles in our cocoa."

"That sounds really gross, Nix," he says with a healthy dose of sass in his tone. "But I'm game to try it if you are."

Hmm. I think again.

"You know, I've been thinking of shaving my head lately."

The sense of triumph I feel when he raises his hands in surrender is fabulous. I laugh out loud, and he joins in.

"I give up," he croaks. "I have no doubt you'd be the most beautiful bald woman in the world, but please don't shave your head."

A waitress drops by and takes our orders for hot cocoa, then Andrew whispers something to her, and she nods. She disappears again.

"What was that about?"

He grins mischievously. "It's a surprise. Now promise me…you won't shave that beautiful hair."

"I promise I won't," I say with a grin.

He reaches for my hand across the table, and I gladly slip my fingers into his.

"So tell me something," I say, changing the subject. "About the arson investigator dreams. There was something Jake said…you haven't applied yet? Can you just do that any time?"

Andrew shakes his head. "No, there has to be an opening. He wanted me to put in for it last time, and I didn't, and he has some feelings about that."

"Oh?"

"Jake's like a father to me, and I know he looks at me like a son," Andrew explains. "I think he just wants to see me in a less dangerous role, and he was disappointed that I didn't put myself forward when it was open."

I nod. "And why didn't you?"

"I was still going through training," he says plainly. "In addition to working at Engine 14, I was studying fire investigation at the National Fire Academy at the time. It's important to me to build a strong foundation in specialized education, and I didn't feel like I was there yet, so I didn't apply."

"And how do you feel about it now? How long ago was that?"

He thinks for a moment. "Almost a year ago," he replies. "I've gotten a few certifications now, but there are still more classes I'd like to take. If a spot opened up now, I'd definitely feel more qualified. I'd consider it."

I squeeze his hand. "I think you'll be brilliant at it when you do."

Our waitress returns with two massively decadent hot cocoas like I've never seen before. She also sets a small platter of chocolate-covered strawberries between us. Oh, yum. The hot cocoa is something else. It's in a giant dark blue ceramic mug the size of my head. The rich, heady scent of pure chocolate steams up from under a mile-high swirl of freshly made whipped cream. Chocolate sprinkles decorate the top. I look up to find Andrew watching me with the sweetest smile on his face.

"Well, Nix? What do you think?"

I lean forward and take a nice long sniff of the chocolate aroma.

"It smells like it's about six thousand calories, and I'm gonna drink every single one."

I'm rewarded with a deep laugh that sounds like it's coming all the way from Andrew's toes. He throws his head back and just lets it go. My heart feels a familiar tug again.

I know I'm falling for him. I'm not surprised at how easy it is. He's the kindest man I know. He has such a giving nature. And, well, he's beautiful. But I've been alone for a long time, and it's still scary to put myself out there. It feels like I'm walking in completely foreign territory. Sometimes, if I let myself think too much about it, I get really afraid of getting hurt again. And I'm already dealing with too much fear.

***

Days later, I'm sitting in the passenger seat of Andrew's car with my mouth hanging open in shock. I can't believe what I'm seeing. This is…wow.

I take Andrew's extended hand, and he helps me out of the car. Hillary told me not to worry about getting to Golden Gate Park too early, so I didn't, but there must be at least ten thousand people already in the concert area, and it doesn't start for another hour. I've never been to a concert in the park, nor have I really paid attention to how many people it can hold. This is insanely bigger than I realized, and I can't believe Hillary has pulled this off in the amount of time I gave her.

My project is still paused while the city runs my background check at a snail's pace, but I did receive a call to tell me that I've been cleared to continue my project as long as said background check comes back clear. Which it will. Because I'm the most boring person ever. I've gotten several texts from Nancy Kolby, the artist working on the living room art. Her pieces are beautiful, and I'm so eager to hang them. I promised to get back to her as soon as I know when I'm allowed back to work.

Being dead in the water has allowed me more time to do other things, though. I've moved back in with Mom. Andrew and I have been able to see each other every day, including a lovely dinner with my mom, where he brought her flowers and basically swept her off her feet. She's a big fan, but who wouldn't be? He's perfect.

My heartbeat hammers against my ribcage, and my stomach is in knots as my imagination goes wild with all kinds of what-if scenarios. I know Hillary is amazing at organizing events, but I silently pray there won't be any negative repercussions from this. It's just so much bigger than I expected, mostly because The Royal Rebels came running to my rescue and are giving a pop-up concert of their ten greatest hits. What's more, they asked a local band they've been admiring to open for them. And both major radio stations local to our area have picked up the news and run with it. One of them is hosting the event today. Ticket sales skyrocketed as soon as the news hit the airwaves. They always do when it's The Rebels. The event has already raised so much more than I'll need to furnish the fire station, and I'm excited to see how much we raise for the fire department's retirement fund.

"You okay, Nix?" Andrew asks beside me, pressing a kiss to my temple.

I lean against him, soaking in his warmth, and try to relax.

"I think so," I say, but I'm still a little breathless. "There are so many people. It's more than I expected."

Andrew laces our fingers together, then brings my hand to his lips and kisses the back of it. My tummy dips in response, and I smile despite all the pressure I feel over this concert. I lean forward and steal a kiss.

I watch as Andrew surveys the crowd that's gathered in front of the stage. Food trucks are parked on the grass all around the concert area, and I smell at least half a dozen foods I'd love to try. I'm not sure my nervous stomach would tolerate it, but it smells amazing out here today. Two large fire trucks are parked in a v-shape at the entrance to the green where concert patrons are gathered. They have their ladders extended up, forming an arch for everyone to walk under. At the entrance, volunteers from the Mermaid Foundation scan tickets with barcode scanners as people file in. All around the trucks, firefighters in uniform are engaging with families. They're passing out red plastic fireman hats and letting kids check out the fire trucks up close.

"Hey," Andrew murmurs against my ear.

A delicious shiver runs through my body, and I turn towards him as he pulls me into his arms.

"All of this," he says as he nods at the craziness before us, "is because of you."

I shake my head. "All of this is because of Hillary and The Rebels. I just asked if they could help."

He laughs and pulls me into a big, wonderful bear hug that I never want to get out of.

"Someday, I'm going to get you to admit how awesome you are."

"Oh, I'm awesome," I tease. "But my awesomeness had about two percent to do with this."

I squeeze Andrew closer and inhale his wonderful citrus and spice scent. The stress melts right out of my muscles. This is the cure right here. Andrew. I'm so incredibly grateful for him and the fact that he and I just fit together in all the important ways. My friends have already accepted him into the inner circle. Rick and Zach, too. I'm sure the other two Rebels, Jimmy and Sam, will do the same when they meet him. And me? Well…I'm falling so hard.

He is my person. I have no doubt now. Andrew is who I run to when I need a rescue, and I pray he always will be. I can't imagine life without him.

"Okay, let's get down there and check in with Hillary," I say after taking a deep breath. "I know she's going to want me to speak on stage, and I'm dreading it."

Andrew takes my hand, and we begin walking across the grass to the fire trucks marking the entrance.

"Are you nervous, Nix? Really?"

I glance over at him as we walk.

"Are you surprised at that?" I tease. "I wouldn't say I'm super nervous, but I wouldn't normally choose to get up on a stage and speak on a microphone in front of several thousand people. But I'll do it for you and your firefighter family."

Andrew grins widely, and I nearly trip because I'm staring at those confounded dimples.

"Surely, by now, you can see that they're your family, too," he replies. "I think we need to see about getting you an honorary firefighter badge."

I laugh under my breath and swing our hands between us as we walk. Even with all the stress of this project, the contest deadline, Mercer's roadblocks, and my anxiety after the fire...I feel like I'm happier than I've ever been. There's an ease about my life I've never felt before, and it's largely to do with the very handsome, very dimpled man at my side. I can't really make sense of it, but when he's near, I can't just help but feel that everything will be okay. He's got me. I've got him. It's like our own little brand of magic.

One of the volunteers scanning tickets waves at me, and I recognize her from some of the Mermaid Foundation events I've attended.

Jackie, that's her name. Phew!

I head in her direction and stifle a laugh when she can't stop staring at Andrew.

Me too, girl.

"Wow," she says, still staring at Andrew. "That's *the* fireman."

"Andrew, this is Jackie. She's on Marina's team at the Mermaid Foundation."

My stomach flips as he flashes those dimples at her and offers his hand for a handshake.

"Nice to meet you, Jackie."

Jackie shakes his hand, then clears her throat and has to visibly gather herself together. I get it.

"Nice to meet you," she replies. "Hillary is backstage right now. The security team has been briefed, so they'll let you right through."

I nod and pull Andrew away.

"Thanks so much, Jackie."

We start walking again, moving at a leisurely pace towards the stage. One of the local radio stations is involved today, so they're playing music on the stage speakers, and I can hear a DJ talking to the crowd periodically. It definitely gives off festival vibes.

Even from this distance, I get fleeting glimpses of the walking miracle that is Hillary. She's off to the side of the stage right now, speaking animatedly to a woman we all call Hella Bella. Her actual name is Bella, and she's married to one of The Royal Rebels, as well as being their manager. Marina told me Bella has a pretty fierce reputation in the music industry, but today she just looks excited about the event.

"Oh my gosh, it's them!" a young woman's voice exclaims to my right, and I turn just in time to see two teenage girls rushing in our direction.

I smile at them as they approach, their eyes wide with excitement.

"I can't believe it," the other friend gasps. "You're the Phoenix and the Fireman!"

"It's nice to meet you," I say as I extend my hand. "I'm Scarlet."

Both girls barely look at me as they shake my hand. They're staring at Andrew so hard I'm surprised I don't see heart emojis in their eyes. I fight to hold my laughter at their enthralled expressions as he extends his hand to them.

"And I'm Andrew."

They're both completely spellbound. One girl pops her gum, and the other laughs nervously.

"Can we get a selfie with you guys?" one of them says. "Oh, I'm Kaley, and this is Jude."

"Yeah, let's take a picture," Andrew says, offering to hold Kaley's phone and take the picture.

Because let's face it, he does have longer arms. Longer, muscular, completely spectacular arms.

We all pose together, and Andrew lets the girls check to make sure they're happy with the photo before we say goodbye and move on. We make it exactly ten feet before we're stopped by a couple about our age, thrilled that they've spotted The Phoenix and the Fireman. We oblige them when they request a selfie as well, and that sets a precedent. The walk to the stage should take five minutes, but it takes us thirty because we're stopped by strangers so many times. We meet so many kind people, all here to support the firefighters of San Francisco and all eager to tell Andrew and me how much our story has touched their hearts. By the time we actually reach the stage, I'm so moved that I have tears in my eyes.

I make eye contact with Hillary, and she waves me over. Bella notices and waves at me as well. I lead Andrew over to the side of the stage, and a security guard moves a barrier so we can go through. Hillary trots down the stairs off the stage, followed closely by Bella, and wraps me in a hug.

"Andrew, this is Hillary and Bella, two of the miracle workers I'm proud to know," I say with a huge grin.

Andrew shakes both their hands as Bella nods in my direction.

"Takes one to know one," she counters. "I'm thinking about redecorating our cabin up at Big Bear. I'd love to talk to you about that sometime soon."

"Oh, I would love to do a cabin, especially for you and Sam!" I exclaim. "Is it okay if I reach out when the competition is over?"

Bella nods excitedly. "That sounds perfect."

Hillary nods eagerly at the gathering crowd. Indeed, as I look back at the entrance, there are throngs of concertgoers entering the venue.

"We sold out last night," she informs me. "Even I was shocked at how quickly this amped up, but we're prepared. The facilities team here is so great. Between them and Bella, I've barely had to lift a finger."

I laugh loudly. "I highly doubt that, but wow...sold out?"

Bella gives us a proud grin. "It's The Royal Rebels, ladies. I'm not surprised one bit that fifty thousand fans came through at a moment's notice."

My heart lurches into my throat.

Fifty thousand?

I inhale sharply, then choke as my nerves kick in. Andrew runs a large, warm, comforting hand across my back.

"You okay, Nix?"

I nod slowly, even though I'm not sure it's true. Fifty thousand people. I am not okay. I step over to the stairs that lead up to the stage and take a seat for a minute. Andrew watches me carefully while the unflappable Bella and Hillary begin listing all the positive things that are coming from this event in an effort to calm me down.

"Did you even hear me, Scarlet?" Hillary asks, prompting me to look up into her face.

She looks positively thrilled over something, but I keep hearing the words *fifty thousand people* echoing in my head. Andrew leans forward.

"Nix..."

Andrew's voice snaps me from my trance, and I shake my head for a moment.

"Sorry, Hillary...what?"

Hillary squats down in front of me with a huge grin.

"We've raised more than five million dollars."

I gasp. "That's incredible!"

Andrew pulls me up off the steps and crushes me in his arms. I wrap my arms around his waist and hold him close. His lips move tantalizingly close to my ear.

"There's nothing you can't do," he murmurs, sending little shivers down my spine.

I reach my hand up and wipe a tear off my cheek. Five million dollars. It's incredible. And I can't imagine a more worthwhile group than first responders. This is absolutely incredible. I pull away from Andrew enough to wipe away more tears.

"I'm a mess," I say with a laugh. "Hillary…Bella…thank you so much for everything you've done."

Andrew reaches up and gently wipes another tear away, looking at me with a sweet smile. Bella and Hillary stand together, grinning at me. I shake my head.

"It wasn't long ago that I was shutting everything else out of my life so I could obsess over a contest," I sputter. "And now here I am in the middle of Golden Gate Park with fifty thousand people where we just raised five million dollars for a great cause, and I don't give a rat's behind about that contest. I don't care at all. I'm so proud of what we've pulled together. Thank you so much."

I step out of Andrew's arms to hug Hillary and Bella, and then Andrew pulls me back in for another hug. I smile against Andrew's chest as the sound of someone's nasally, obnoxious laughter sounds not too far away. I pull away from Andrew to see Bella rolling her eyes in disgust. Hillary leans close to me.

"I forgot to warn you," she says in a near whisper. "The radio DJ we got to emcee the concert is hideous."

"Heyyyyyyy!" the aforementioned DJ calls out as he descends the stairs towards us. "I spy the Phoenix and the Fireman, my babies!"

Eeew. This guy is smarmy. He has all the charm of a game show host from the seventies, and he over pronounces all his words. Bella makes a gagging sound as she steps away from him, and he laughs a little too hard.

"Dan Tanna, and yes, that's my real name," the schmoozer coos at me as he extends his hand. "Are you ready to rock the park, Phoenix?"

I shake his hand and have to pull hard to get him to release my hand.

"You can call me Scarlet," I say, hoping he gets the hint.

It makes my skin crawl when he calls me Phoenix. Major ick.

Andrew quietly steps forward and shakes his hand.

"And you can call me Andrew."

Dan nods and offers our group a sickeningly fake smile.

"All right, so show time is at three, yeah? And we have the Howdies opening with three songs, and then The Royal Rebels with their ten greatest hits. Can I get you two on stage with me for a bit before The Rebels come on?"

Oh boy. I knew I'd be expected to get up on stage for a bit, but I wasn't anticipating the massive crowd of people or the very, *very* fake and smarmy dude I'd have to be on stage talking to. I might be able to say whatever words are appropriate for the setting, but my facial expressions are always going to tell the truth. How am I going to be on stage with this guy without either laughing or looking like I'm going to barf?

"Uh, yep," I say quickly. "Happy to."

Dan studies my face for so long that I wonder if there's something wrong with it. I brush my hand over my face to make sure there isn't dirt or who knows what on there.

"You look so familiar," Dan says, scrutinizing me further. "Have we met before?"

"Absolutely not," I reply. "I'm sure I'd remember it."

The look on his face tells me he takes it like a compliment, which it isn't.

"Hmm, maybe you just remind me of an old girlfriend," he says back, then he slaps Andrew on the shoulder. "You know how it is, right, buddy?"

Andrew looks like he wants to punch Dan, and I can't say I blame him.

I see Zach and Marina standing in the wings across the stage and smile. She turns to look out onto the stage and sees me, waving excitedly, and I blow her a kiss. The obnoxious DJ looks from Marina to me and back again. He snaps his fingers and then points right at me.

"I've got it! You're one of the mermaid's sailor girls, aren't you? Oh my gosh, we're gonna have some fun with this today, Scarlet. We need a command performance!"

Chapter 21

Scarlet

I stare at the DJ and feel my mouth fall open in shock.

What?

What?

Hillary, Bella, and Andrew are all grinning at me like this is the best idea ever.

Me? No.

I feel like I'd rather die. This is insane. Dan steps into my field of vision with that stupid fake smile. I want to punch him so hard right now.

"Even if your other friends aren't here, I know we've got the mermaid and the most important sailor," he drones on. "Tell me you'll do it. The crowd will go crazy for this."

My gaze flicks to Andrew's. He's obviously excited by the prospect.

"I can't believe *you* think this is a good idea," I scold. "This is not about me. This is about raising money for the fire department's retirement fund."

He dips down and plants a quick kiss on my lips.

"Which you've done to an amazing level," he says gently. "But today is also about fun and celebrating the community spirit our story sparked. These people came to see The Rebels, but they've also come because of what you started."

I give him a look as he jumps to correct himself.

"What *we* started," he says quickly. "You saw the response we got just from people who saw us walking together, Nix. They're going to want to see us on stage together, and I agree with Dan in this case. They'd love to see the mermaid and the sailors. To know that our Phoenix was part of the mermaid craze will just make it extra fun."

Hillary winces sympathetically and chimes in. "I agree. Sorry."

"Scarlet, do it," Bella orders. "It'll be over before you know it, and, from a PR perspective, it'll be gold. You've got to do it."

I sigh heavily and level my gaze at Dan. "I'll talk to Marina and the girls and see if they want to do it. Then, and only then, if they all agree…I will do it."

Dan jumps into the air and squeals so loudly that I nearly jolt out of my skin. I mutter a curse under my breath and excuse myself from the group, heading across the stage to where Marina is talking to Zach in the wings. She turns as she sees me approaching and pulls me in for a hug.

"Scarlet, are you okay?" Zach asks quickly. "You look pretty peeved."

Marina looks at me worriedly. "What's wrong?"

I purse my lips as I try to find the best way to break the news.

"The smarmy DJ has figured out that I was one of the sailors in the famous mermaid video."

Marina rolls her eyes. It's old news to her, and the hysteria died down long ago, but now that she and Zach are married, the city has fully fallen in love with their story. Any time that mermaid video comes up, it's a high point of conversation. People still love it.

"He wants us to perform together on stage, Marina," I say somberly.

Marina's expression remains open, which isn't really a surprise.

She performs with Zach occasionally in front of crowds much bigger than this one. It's not really a scary prospect for her.

"Okay, I'm in," she says simply.

Because it is that simple to her.

Good Lord.

"Hey, friends!" Ashley says as she breezes backstage, hugging Marina, me, and Andrew. "Scarlet, the turnout is amazing. You must be so excited!"

My momentary panic subsides when I'm reminded of the reason we're all here. I am excited. I'm thrilled, actually. I need to just hold on to that perspective. This isn't about me and whether or not I want to sing on a stage with my friends. This is about pulling off a miracle for our first responders. And I'm all about miracles these days.

I smile at Ashley. "I am…this is amazing. And now I need another favor."

Ashley nods, waiting for me to ask and ready to deliver. Because that's how my girls are. Ready to back me up whenever I need it.

"The local DJ-slash-smarmy dude has realized that I was one of the sailors in the mermaid video," I begin. "Obviously, he knows who Marina is and that she's here with Zach, so he wants a command performance."

Ashley throws her head back and laughs just as Rick steps to her side. He pulls her back against his chest and grins at me.

"Hey, Corbel Queen, what's up?"

Zach slaps Rick on the shoulder. "The DJ wants the girls to sing The Wellerman on stage."

Rick's eyes get as round as saucers. "Oh, wow, they'll go nuts for that. You're gonna do it, right?"

I laugh at how this is no big deal for most everyone else, and I know it won't be a big deal for Merry when she hears. The girl doesn't care what anyone thinks. She just lights up the world.

"I'll totally do it," Ashley says. "I think it'll be fun."

Marina clicks her tongue. "It's too bad we didn't think of this sooner. We could have worn the costumes too."

I balk. "You'd wear that dreaded mermaid tail for me?"

Marina giggles and waves her hand like it's no big deal. "For you? Yes. For firemen? Also yes. But I'm also glad we didn't think of it because that thing sucks."

Zach pulls her against him with a growl. "I think you look beautiful in it."

Marina giggles again. "So much so that you kidnapped me in the thing."

Zach rolls his eyes at her. "I literally saved you from a throng of crazed fans, my love."

Andrew wraps his arm around me and moves his lips to my ear.

"So you're really doing this? I get to watch my Nix perform on a concert stage?"

I squeeze him around the waist. "Don't say things like that. It makes me nervous."

Andrew chuckles lowly and kisses my cheek. "You're going to be great."

Zach and Rick step away to chat with the band that will perform three songs as an opener, while the rest of us discuss logistics. I look behind us, searching for the smarmy DJ, and see him trotting towards us with Merry in tow. He grins when he spots Ashley, and then his gaze flicks to me.

"So we're good? Looks like you're all here," he says as he sets a hand on Merry's shoulder.

She shrugs him off immediately. "Dude, don't touch."

I don't even try to hold back the laugh that bubbles up at the sight of her putting him in his place. I love it.

"Merry, are you okay performing The Wellerman on stage today?"

I ask, already knowing the answer. "Dan here thinks the crowd will love it."

"Duh," she says, holding her hand up for a high-five.

I give it to her.

Andrew chuffs. "This is gonna be great. I can't wait to see it."

I smirk at him, and he pulls me into his arms and dips me backward, looking into my eyes with the sweetest expression.

"You are amazing," he says as I clutch onto his shoulders for dear life. "You're going to do an amazing job. This whole day is going to be a wild success."

His lips meet mine in a sweet kiss as I hang there in his arms, feeling completely safe. Treasured. My heart fills with…love. Oh, man…it's happening. I'm hopeless to stop it.

Andrew pulls me back up, and I wrap my arms around his neck, kissing him again. I take a minute to drink him in. So handsome. So very sweet. Mine.

"I am so crazy about you, Fireman," I murmur with a little smile. "You make my heart so happy."

Andrew's eyes dart over my face, his expression one of…love, maybe. I'm smiling so hard my face actually hurts as I realize he's looking at me the exact same way I look at him. I'm his person, and I'm sooo here for it.

He rubs our noses together and turns us so that none of my friends can see our faces. He brings our mouths together in a kiss that is savagely passionate, literally making me weak in the knees. I hold on for dear life as he kisses me thoroughly, sending wave after wave of shivers through my body. When we finally break the kiss, he moves his lips to my ear.

"Mine," he murmurs.

And suddenly, I'm mentally cursing the fact that we're spending the day with fifty thousand of our closest friends instead of finding somewhere to be alone together. I am done. Give me a quiet corner somewhere with Andrew, and the rest of the world can fend for itself.

Unfortunately, or fortunately...depending on how you look at it... Hillary pops up in my view with a very apologetic look on her face. Just like that, I know we're close to show time. I step out of Andrew's embrace and smile at her.

"Sorry to bother you, but there's someone here to say hello, and I think you'll want to meet him."

I raise my eyebrows in curiosity just as Kevin Starbuck appears from behind her...and he's not alone. The very honorable and very near Mayor Dirk Jansen steps out from behind Kevin, flashing me a perfect smile. Wow. I didn't even think we'd have dignitaries here. I'm sure this is all Hillary.

"Miss Jackson, I'm Mayor Jansen," he says as he extends his hand. "I'm so happy to meet you."

I take his hand, feeling like this entire moment is happening in slow motion. I smile warmly.

"It's an honor to meet you. Welcome to our fundraiser, sir."

He nods politely, then shakes Andrew's hand, and I introduce him to my friends. It's a surreal moment as I stand in the wings of this stage with fifty thousand people filling in the audience area as my friends and the Mayor of San Francisco meet the world-famous indie rock band I know. While I hold hands with my boyfriend. How is this my life right now? Let's just chalk it up to another miracle I worked.

I take a moment to hug Kevin hello, then delight in watching him turn total fanboy as he meets The Rebels. I love it. When all the pleasantries are exchanged, the Mayor turns his attention back to me.

"So, Scarlet, I wanted to bring you some good news personally," he says, clapping his hands together. "Your background check has come through, and I'd like to officially invite you to return to your project at Engine 14."

"Oh my gosh!" I cry out as my friends cheer.

Before I even know what I'm doing, I grab the Mayor and hug him hard around the neck. He laughs and gives me a good squeeze before releasing me.

Andrew pulls me into his arms and lifts me off the ground, spinning me like crazy. I squeal and hold on for dear life.

"I am so proud of you," he says loudly, making my friends grin like lovesick goobers. "Congratulations, Nix."

I stand on my toes to press a kiss to his cheek, then turn back to Mayor Jansen.

"Thank you so much, sir," I say breathlessly.

"Can I get a picture or two, Mayor Jansen? With the whole group?" Kevin asks from behind us, waving his ever-present camera.

Mayor Jansen nods politely. "Certainly. Let's go, everyone."

He motions me to his side, and Andrew steps in next to me. Hillary comes forward to arrange the Rebels and my friends until she's happy with where everyone is. Of course, Dan has also inserted himself into the group. As we pose in the wings, we're facing out to the stage, and I have a good view of the huge crowd that's out there. People are still filing into the seating area. Music is playing over the speakers, uniformed firefighters are walking around with those cute plastic firefighter hats for kids, and everyone looks like they're having such a great time.

Kevin snaps several pictures, then thanks us all and steps back. The group breaks up, and Kevin moves over to take some shots of the audience from the wings, capturing the spirit of the day in his unique style. Mayor Jansen ushers Andrew and me over to the side.

"I just wanted to say how much I appreciate what you're doing," he says. "From what I gather, this started small, but it's now snowballed into something much bigger. It may not be what you intended, but the positive vibe it's spreading through our city is palpable. Thank you both."

Well, now I've heard everything. This day is insane. Andrew and I thank the mayor and watch as Hillary escorts him down to the VIP seating I didn't even know we had. She's literally taken care of everything. I wave at him as he disappears from the wings, and turn back to my friends.

"Okay, so how are we doing this?" I ask Zach, the most chill person I've ever met.

He gestures at Dan, who still lurks nearby.

"We can have Dan start the festivities and introduce the Howdies," Zach begins. Dan steps over to us when he hears his name, of course. "After they play, I think that's a great time to bring you and Andrew on stage if Dan agrees, yeah?"

Dan nods and points double-finger guns at Zach. Ugh.

"That's the Dan plan, you bet," he drawls. "We'll have the Phoenix and the Fireman out on stage, and you can tell them how much we raised. That'll—"

"Wait a minute," I interrupt. All heads turn to me. "I'd like to bring everyone from Engine 14 up on the stage. They're the real heroes. They deserve some attention. Andrew, do you know who's here?"

He nods. "Jake, for sure. I think Leonard, Todd, and Amy are here. The others are either working or I'm not sure."

"That's a great idea, Phoenix," Dan says. "We'll get them up on stage for a good round of applause."

I nod my thanks at Dan, trying to give him credit for agreeing with me.

"After we do all of that, then I'll introduce The Royal Rebels, and then we can sit back and enjoy the rest of the concert," he continues.

Zach and the guys give a thumbs up, then head back to chat with the Howdies.

Someone taps me on the shoulder, and I turn to find Hillary smiling at me. I laugh and grab her for a quick hug.

"I swear you're like some kind of magical creature," I tell her. "You pop in at just the right moment."

Hillary laughs and taps her watch.

"Well, right now is the moment where I take you guys down to your seats so we can get ready to start the show," she says.

She gives each of us bright red VIP wristband to put on in case we have to leave the seating area and need to get back in.

I smile at Hillary. "I'm thankful you're in control. We're in the best hands."

She grins, then looks at our group. "Marina, Ashley, and Merry are with us as well. Shall we?"

My friends all file in behind Andrew and me as we follow Hillary out of the wings and down a set of stairs that leads from the stage to the area behind the barrier. Security officers and San Francisco police are dotted along the front of the barrier, and I do a double take when we walk close to one of them. He is so familiar.

A security officer opens the barrier for us to step through, and Hillary leads us to a roped-off row of seats in the front row. Jake, Leonard, and Todd are seated on one side of Mayor Jansen, who's with the fire chief. Jake looks a little nervous, but his face breaks into a full smile as soon as he sees me.

I hurry over to him, giving him a huge hug and then hugging Leonard and Todd as well. It's so great to see them. I've missed them so much. I get teased a little by Todd, who tells me he's already made some excellent grilled cheeses on the new stove and promises one for lunch tomorrow.

Tomorrow!

I actually get to go back to work, which just adds icing to the amazing cake of today.

I'm introduced to the fire chief, who's sitting next to the mayor, and then I head back to my seat between the mayor and Andrew. I lean into Andrew's side, and he wraps his arm around me. It's incredible to be in the front row for this concert, sitting next to the mayor and the fire chief with all my friends and waiting to watch more friends perform on stage. I let my brain skip right over the fact that I'll soon be performing on that stage myself and just try to relax and enjoy this time.

It's a beautiful day today. The sun is out in full force, and the sky is a vivid blue with big, puffy white clouds dotted around. The scents of so many delicious foods hang in the air. Andrew checks his watch, then starts looking all around us.

"Whatcha lookin' for, Superman?" I tease.

He smiles at me and leans in for a slow kiss, which I'm more than happy to give him. He presses his forehead to mine for a moment.

"Be right back, Nix," he says. "Save my seat, baby."

I laugh as I watch him head off on his mission, whatever it is. I look over at Marina and give her shoulder a nudge.

"Hey," I call out. "Your husband is awesome."

Her whole face lights up. She and Zach are newlyweds, only married a few months, and I love how happy he makes her. Especially considering the fact that she tried her best to stay away from him when they met. He really is the sweetest guy, always giving back, as are all The Royal Rebels. I was kind of a fan before we all met, but I'm a die-hard fan now.

"I love him so much," Marina sighs. "And I love watching him play. I'm looking forward to this."

Ashley leans back so I can see her on the other side of Marina. She points at Marina and mouths *you're next*. I erupt into a mass of giggles. Merry wiggles her eyebrows and winks at me, and I'm done. Can't. Stop. Laughing.

"You know what's really funny? I don't even care," I tell them. "I am crazy about him. I'm here for all of it, girls. Gone are the days of me not wanting a relationship or saying marriage is for much, much later. You'll have to find something else to tease me about, ladies. I am crazy for him."

Marina reaches over and grabs my hand, squeezing it and giving me the most ridiculous schmoopy face. I laugh under my breath and shake my head. The police officer catches my attention again and I nudge Marina.

"Does that cop look familiar to you?'

Marina looks in the direction I'm pointing and purses her lips, shaking her head.

"I don't think so."

"It's been a while, but you know who he reminds me of?"

Marina shakes her head.

"The cop on the bridge, remember? He told us we could stretch our legs and we ended up causing all that ruckus singing The Wellerman—"

Marina laughs under her breath. "If it is, the poor guy can't get away from us, can he?"

"Miss Jackson?"

I turn towards Mayor Jensen. "Call me Scarlet, please."

The mayor points to himself. "Dirk."

I nod graciously. "Dirk. How can I help?"

"I was wondering if I'm allowed any inside scoops on the design scheme," he asks. "I mean, I'm the one who pushed your background check through, after all."

I crack a smile at that one. "Actually, now that I'm allowed to go back to work, I was wondering if I can send you an invite to the big reveal party? You and the Fire Chief, of course."

Dirk's expression lights up with excitement. "Absolutely I would," he says. "Can I get you to make it after 5 PM? My days are pretty busy, but I can usually bump my evenings around."

"You bet I can," I answer. "That's helpful."

"You can send the invite through Dave if you like," he says. "Now that he's retired, he has all the time in the world to nag me about things I might forget."

"Absolutely, sir," I reply. "Would you like to see some photos of what's done so far? Kevin hasn't published any of these because of the design contest I'm in, so no one has seen these."

He nods excitedly, and I pull my phone out of my pocket. I find the pictures of Nick's engraved panels and hand him my phone to let him scroll. The fire chief leans over to see as well, and I answer questions as they ooh and aah over the beautiful panels. Next is the selfie I took of us in the kitchen together with the new appliances, and both men break into laughter when they see it. Dirk hands me my phone back.

"Those are great, thank you," he says. "I'm not sure I've ever been that happy over an appliance."

"Oh, well, let me know show you what they had before, sir," I flip through my photos and, bring up the pics I took on day one, and hand the phone back.

Mayor Jansen scowls. "Those are pretty gross."

I nod. "Apparently, they'd been overdue for replacements for a few years."

Dirk gives me a sobering glance. "And yet Mr. Mercer decided to shut you down for...you know what? Never mind. What time do you plan to be at the fire station tomorrow?"

"Uh...about 9 am, sir."

He nods. "Good. If I can't be there to welcome you myself, I'll make sure someone from the city is."

"Oh, no, sir, that's not necessary. I'm just grateful to go back to work."

He winks at me. "Done deal."

Andrew comes back in time to distract me, holding a cardboard box loaded with food.

"What on earth?"

He shrugs. "I was hungry. I thought you might be too."

Andrew pulls an ice-cold bottle of water out of his pocket and hands it to me, then makes a show of pulling another one out of the other pocket for himself. Then he shows me the box of food. Wow. He has a huge order of fries and a giant smoked turkey leg in there. Yikes. Oh, but the turkey leg smells incredible. My mouth waters, and I steal a few fries.

He flashes the dimples. "I know my girl so well."

I steal more fries, and he offers me the turkey leg. I just laugh.

"I can't get my mouth around that thing. It's huge!"

Wordlessly, he pulls a little package with a plastic knife and fork inside out of his back pocket and hands it to me. I grab them without hesitation, open them up, and tuck into that turkey leg like a contestant who just got kicked off the Survivor TV show. Andrew grabs a packet of ketchup for the fries and wiggles it at me.

"Do you like ketchup?"

I scrunch my face up and shake my head, making him laugh out loud. He opens the packet and squirts the ketchup out inside the cardboard box, but not directly on the fries. I take a few fries, and Andrew points to the turkey leg.

"Do you mind if I just bite it?"

I smother a giggle and shake my head. "Go for it, babe."

Andrew takes a huge bite just as the audience erupts into applause when Dan walks out on the stage, waving and offering up his cheesiest grin. He holds a mic up to his mouth.

"Hello, San Francisco!" he yells, making the crowd go wild. "Welcome to our little pop-up concert starring The Royal Rebels!"

The crowd cheers like crazy as Dan gets them all warmed up. He introduces the Howdies, who come out with such spirit. Their lead singer makes some very moving comments about our first responders before they launch into a really fun set of three songs. I've never heard of them before, but I make a mental note to add more of their music to my playlists because they're really good. As their third song begins, Hillary comes out to get me, Andrew, and the girls.

As soon as we hit the backstage area, I'm a ball of nerves...but there's no turning back now. Time for a different kind of bravery. The Howdies end their third song, and we cheer for them from backstage. As they exit, we all give them high-fives and tell them how much we enjoyed their performance. They're super nice, and they head over to talk to Zach and the Rebels as Dan takes the stage. Here we go.

"Ladies and gentlemen, before we bring The Royal Rebels out here, I wanted to introduce a few of the reasons we're here today."

Marina comes over to stand by me as I try not to chew my nails.

"I'm kind of excited that we're doing this," she says. "We haven't sung together since we quit our little side hustle. This'll be fun."

I force a smile. "Just as long as I don't look at the fifty thousand people out there. Honestly, Marina, I don't know how you ever had the courage to get on stage with Zach that first time."

She nods in understanding. "Pro tip: you don't have to look at all fifty thousand. You only have to look at one."

I shake my head at her, unsure of what she means.

"Find Andrew," she explains. "Look at him. No one else matters."

I'm pondering her advice when Dan's voice breaks through my thoughts.

"Ladies and gentlemen, please give it up for our very own Phoenix and the Fireman...Scarlet Jackson and Andrew MacLachlan!"

Andrew plants a quick kiss on my cheek and wraps his hand around mine, walking us out of the wings and onto the stage like he does this every day. The man constantly surprises me. A stagehand passes us each a microphone as we walk out.

I keep a death grip on his hand and manage to smile at the crowd and wave as they cheer for us.

Dan nods at me to take over, and I'm instantly fueled by my fear of looking ridiculous in front of a giant throng of people. I cling to Andrew's hand and raise the mic to my mouth, hoping that I'm giving off the air of a person who's used to this kind of attention.

"First and foremost, I'd just like to thank everyone for coming today," I say as I look out into the crowd. "In purchasing your ticket, you did something amazing. You donated to the city's retirement fund for the brave men and women of our fire department."

A wave of applause comes through the crowd, encouraging me.

"I know we've shared this in all our communications about this event, but a very small portion of the funds will be used to purchase new furniture for the firefighters stationed at Engine 14," I say. "New chairs and a couch, a new dining room set, new end tables, lamps, you get the picture. I expect it to be between five and ten thousand dollars if that's okay."

The crowd cheers, and Andrew pumps an arm in the air, making me laugh.

"The reason for that is simply because city funds are tight, and I wanted to be able to give them furniture that'll be comfortable and hold up well. So thank you from the bottom of my heart for your generosity."

More applause.

"And Scarlet's not the only one who's grateful," Dan pipes in. "We have several members of Engine 14 in the audience today. Can we get you to stand up, please?"

Jake, Leonard, Todd, and Amy all stand up in the front row. Hillary comes down to usher them to the stage, and the crowd goes absolutely crazy as they join us. I step over closer to Dan, slipping the mic between my arm and my body so I can applaud as well. They join Andrew and wave at the crowd, taking the occasional bow and nodding to show how much they appreciate the love they're being given. My eyes fill with tears as I watch them, feeling my gratitude anew for the fact that my life was literally saved by these heroes.

Andrew steps forward and raises a hand to quiet the crowd, then raises the mic to his lips.

"Thank you, everyone," he says in a voice thick with emotion. "I'm sure I speak for all of us at Engine 14 when I say we all love our jobs, and we're all very grateful for your support. And while none of us does what we do for attention or applause, I'd like all firefighters and first responders in the crowd, whether you're here to see the concert or you're working the event, to stand up right now and wave a hand so we can thank you."

The crowd goes wild as men and women stand and wave from all different spots in the concert space. Dan lets them do their thing for quite a bit before he steps in again.

"Scarlet, if you'd like to tell us all how much this concert has raised for the firefighter's retirement fund?"

I nod and step back to Andrew's side. "I'm very proud to share that we've raised just over five million dollars today."

More cheers and applause, and the fire chief and mayor both stand up. It starts a standing ovation that brings my firefighter friends to tears. Miracle accomplished.

"I guess there's nothing left for me to say," I say into the mic, "except thank you again, so much, for helping me support these amazing humans. When the rest of us run from danger, they're running to our rescue. I'm so proud to be part of something like this that supports them."

Hillary gets Jake's attention and leads them off stage, including Andrew, who runs over to me and kisses me soundly before running off stage. The screams and cheers coming from the crowd are hysterical. Dan waits until they're back down in the front row, seated and ready to enjoy the show.

"So before I bring The Royal Rebels out here, I have a bit of gossip to share with you," Dan says, giving the audience his best evil eye. "Do you want to hear it?"

More cheers.

"Of course, you'll all remember a certain viral video a few years back...when there was a mermaid in a traffic jam on the Golden Gate Bridge?"

Everyone cheers.

"Everyone remembers the mermaid, but who remembers that there were also three women dressed as sailors? Hmm? Did you know one of those sailors is on this very stage?"

There's a mixture of laughter and cheers from the audience, and then when I raise my hand and plaster a guilty expression on my face, they go absolutely nuts.

"That's right, folks! Our Phoenix was one of those sailors...and I've convinced her, Marina, and the other sailors to do an encore for us right now."

I laugh nervously as the crowd turns absolutely feral. Wow. They're really going crazy. Thankfully, Marina, Ashley, and Merry step out of the wings and join me on stage, each of them with their own handheld mic.

We line up together and take a bow as Dan scoots back into the wings to watch us. I look over at Marina and nod, then Merry, Ashley, and I all take two steps back so she's in front.

"Hey, can I get a beat from you guys?" Marina asks the crowd as she smacks her hand on the side of her leg to the beat of The Wellerman.

The crowd cheers and begins rhythmically, clapping to the beat. Perfect.

Marina begins to sing the lyrics about the fabled ship that fought a whale. I look over to Merry in a panic.

"Are we doing the choreography too?" I whisper.

"Oh heck yeah," she answers just in time for us to begin the chorus.

We all yell, "HUH!" and begin dancing around Marina, singing the chorus just like we used to. I can't believe we remember the dance moves, but we do.

Remembering Marina's advice, I find Andrew in the crowd and make eye contact. He's watching me with such love in his eyes I lose track of what I'm doing twice. I just want to climb down from the stage and kiss him for the rest of the day.

Before I know it, we're done, and I'm grateful it's over. The crowd applauds, and we all take a bow. Then the girls exit the stage while I step forward one more time.

"Thank you all for being so kind. We haven't done that routine since the mermaid video," I say with a quick laugh. "I just wanted to add my thanks to the Howdies for volunteering to play for you today without pay so that our firefighters could get the most from this concert."

More applause, as certainly expected.

"And I also want to give a very huge, very humble thanks to my friends Zach, Rick, Sam, and Jimmy...The Royal Rebels."

I have to pause because of the cheers that erupt at the mention of the band.

"They're also performing for you without compensation today so we can raise as much money for our firefighters as possible. All I had to do was ask, and the answer was 'Yes. Tell us when and where.' That kind of generosity should never go unnoticed."

We all applaud, and I wave at the crowd as I walk off stage with the mic.

"Thank you, everyone, enjoy the show!"

I step into the wings and get a huge hug from Zach, Rick, Sam, and Jimmy. My eyes are full of tears as I thank them again, and they run out onto the stage. The cheers are deafening, and I hug my friends as we watch for a few minutes before going back to the audience to sit in our seats.

"Well, hello, San Francisco," Zach growls into the mic. "It's lovely to be back with you again in the city by the bay!"

They immediately begin to play one of their biggest hits, and everyone in the audience is on their feet.

I walk up the front row and step straight into Andrew's arms, wrapping my arms around his neck. His large hand comes up to the back of my head as he holds me, and I melt against him.

"That was epic and unforgettable," he murmurs against my hair. "Just like you."

I wrap my arms tighter around him, the love in my heart overflowing and overwhelming. I don't hear the crowd or the music or anything else around us. I only feel Andrew's heart beating steadily against my cheek as he holds me, and I hope I never have to live a day on this earth without feeling like this.

Chapter 22

Scarlet

I pull Ashley's car into the driveway at Engine 14 the very next morning at 9 AM on the dot. This is going to be a great week. I'm back at work, and last night I got an email from the Home Network telling me when the judges are coming.

I spotted Kevin and Nick's vehicles parked on the street. There is a very nice Mercedes parked in the driveway. I can't believe it, but it looks like the mayor actually made good on his promise to be here this morning.

Andrew comes out the front door to greet me. He's not working, so he's in regular clothes, and he looks incredibly handsome in blue jeans, a fitted blue t-shirt, and that same black leather jacket. I step into his arms as I get out of the car, kissing him soundly.

"I take it the Mercedes means the mayor is here?"

He grins. "Not just the mayor. I can't wait to see your face."

I feel like my eyes are going to bulge out of their sockets. "Who else?"

Andrew shakes his head. "Nope. Just leave your stuff for now and come with me."

I grab his hand, and we head inside, my heart beating wildly against my ribs. Once inside, I see all the familiar faces gathered around a box of donuts on the kitchen island. The mayor is laughing at something Jake has said as we come into view.

"There she is," Jake says, walking over to give me a hug.

"Good morning, everyone," I say breathlessly, and then Leonard steps aside to reveal Mr. Mercer standing there. "Um…eew."

Todd doesn't bother stifling his laughter. I glance up at the mayor. "Sorry."

Dirk extends his hand, and I shake it. "Good morning, Scarlet. It's great to see you again."

I nod. "And you as well, sir."

He steps over to Mercer and smacks a large hand onto his shoulder. "I brought a friend who'd like to welcome you back personally."

Mercer steps forward and offers a quivering smile as if it causes him physical pain to even attempt such a thing. I force myself to remain stern as I tilt my head and wait for him to speak.

"Miss Jackson," he begins, clearing his throat. "It's my pleasure to welcome you back to work at Engine 14, and I'd like to extend my humble apologies for any misunderstandings."

I have no freaking idea how I'm able to refrain from jumping onto the counter and dancing a jig around this horrible man but manage to plaster a pleasant *I told you so* smile on my face.

"Thank you very much, Mr. Mercer," I say smoothly. "It's very nice to be back."

Mercer looks up at Dirk, who nods in satisfaction. "Back to work, Monty."

Without another word, Mercer dips his head and skitters out the door as we all watch in absolute shock. The door snicks shut, and the guys all cheer louder than anyone at the concert. I laugh out loud as they take turns giving me hugs and offering congratulations, the mayor looking on.

"Well, I had to blow off a meeting to pull that off, but it was worth it," Dirk says. "I'm going to let you get back to work, Scarlet, but I'll be watching for that invitation."

I shake his hand again. "Will this Thursday work for you? 6 PM?"

He nods. "I'll check with my assistant, but I think so. I'll see you soon."

With that, he walks out the door, and I'm left alone with my friends.

"How did he even know to make that horrible man apologize?"

Kevin steps forward. "Uh…I told him yesterday. We were talking at the concert, and I gave him an earful about what an arrogant jerk Mercer was…and how you put him in his place when you left."

Andrew high-fives him. "Well done."

"So now what, Scarlet?" Jake asks. "What's next?"

I clap my hands together excitedly.

"The judges from the Home Network will be here this Friday, so our private big reveal party has to be Thursday. That means I have about three and a half days to pull this whole project together. Thankfully, Nancy will be here with the art today. And I'll call the furniture store and place my order as soon as they open. I'd already picked out all the pieces while I was away."

I jolt out of my skin as the station's alarm sounds, sending Jake and Todd into action. Andrew and Leonard aren't on shift today. A tremor shudders through my body, followed by another, as my mouth goes instantly dry. In a flash, Andrew is by my side, pulling me into his arms.

"It's all right, Nix," he murmurs into my ear as his warm embrace engulfs my senses.

I still can't stop shaking as my brain frantically struggles to make sense of things. Alarms. The lights begin flashing on the fire truck as Bruce starts it up. The disembodied voice on the speaker blares something about a fire. Andrew is going to another fire.

"I've got you," he whispers. "I'm here, baby."

No, Andrew is here. He's not going to the fire. But Jake is. Bruce and Todd are. Andrew is here.

"I'm here," he says gently. "You're safe, Nix."

I'm ushered over to the living room, where I'm carefully pulled into his lap and held tightly while the others disappear from my line of sight. I burrow my face into Andrew's neck and draw in a shaky breath.

"You're here."

Andrew nods. "Right here, baby. Right here."

I nod. "Okay…okay."

I remember my meditation techniques. I try to focus on my breathing, but I'm so shaky it takes a few attempts. Finally, I take a breath in. Then out. I repeat it. A deeper breath in. A deeper breath out. I'm not sure how much time goes by before I feel my heart rate return to normal, but when I sit up to look at Andrew, his expression borders on tortured.

"What is it?" I ask in alarm. "I'm okay. I'm sorry."

He shakes his head as if to tell me that's not it and that he's fine, but he's anything but fine. He pulls me against his chest and holds me tight, and I clench my fists in his shirt. I'm okay. I'm safe. He's here. We're both here.

***

Andrew

Scarlet is not okay. She says she is, but her reaction to the alarm was so hard to see. She was absolutely petrified, and it killed me to watch it. Thankfully, she's back to normal for now. The guys came back after the call, safe and sound, and then Nancy showed up with her artwork shortly after. They're in the living room hanging them now, but there's a heaviness in my spirit that I can't seem to get rid of.

I turn back to my phone, willing myself to concentrate. I'm reading Kevin's latest article about us. It's a recap of the concert and how much the community helped in making it a success. In addition to the backstage photo with the mayor that we all posed for, there are quite a few candid shots that I plan to have printed and framed. My favorites are the one of us backstage, huddled together. There's no mistaking the fact that I'm in love with her in the first picture. It's all over my face. And the second is when I dipped her, and she's clinging to me. The absolute joy and love in her expression makes my heart pound even harder.

I finish reading the article and step back into the living room to watch Scarlet work her magic. Nancy's paintings look incredible in this room. While the buttery yellow walls and copper engraved panels lighten everything up, Nancy's art provides balance. The dominating colors are navy and dark gray, with sprinkles of red and orange peppered in. They almost look abstract when viewed from far away, but when you get closer, you can see that there are actually scenes on these canvases. Firefighters working. Putting out a fire. A close-up of water pouring over flames in the distance. Nancy is incredibly talented, and her art compliments Scarlet's vibe perfectly.

"Hey," Kevin says as he sits on the couch. He motions for me to join him.

"Hey, Kev," I say as I sit across from him.

"Are you okay? You seem a little bummed out about something."

I purse my lips and shake my head. "No, I'm good."

I'm definitely not good.

Kevin nods. "I was going to get some coffee down the street while these two tinker with the paintings. Want to come?"

I consider his offer, watching Scarlet in her element as she chatters excitedly with Nancy about the art and where to hang which piece.

I'm only in the way here, and in my current mood, I'll just brood more over things I can't control.

I nod but can't take my eyes off Scarlet. Her expression is electric as she talks with Nancy about the different art pieces. So beautiful. So talented. So mine, even if that feels incredibly selfish right now. My mind keeps drifting back to her anxiety attack when the alarm sounded. I don't know why I'm dwelling on this, but it's really bothering me. I can't shake it. I make a mental note to head to the gym today for a swim. It'll help me burn off nervous energy, and my race is this weekend. I could use the extra training.

I smile at Kevin. "Yeah, let's go."

"Hey, Nix," I say as we head to the door. "We're going to the coffee house...you want your usual?"

She nods and blows me a kiss, making me grin like a lovesick teenager.

"Nancy, would you like anything?"

She thinks about it for a moment. "A cafe mocha would be awesome."

"Done!" Kevin replies, and we head out the door.

Kev and I fall into step with each other on the sidewalk.

"I love the new article, Kev," I say as we walk. "You covered so many things I didn't get to see. It was great."

And it was. He got photos of the Howdies laughing with the Rebels backstage and the mayor engaging with others in the audience. There were some great photos of kids and firefighters. The story itself was awesome. No one tells a story like he does.

"Thanks, man," Kevin replies. "That concert was incredible. This story is writing itself."

I nod, a smile playing at my mouth.

"Scarlet just seems to create amazingness wherever she goes."

Kevin laughs. "That's true. And you guys are a great couple. You're so cute together. It's a little disgusting."

Guilty. And I don't care one bit. I just laugh at the joke and think about my girl. It really killed me to see her go from joyous to devastated in two seconds this morning. She just looked so lost.

"Dude, c'mon," Kevin says as we stop for the light. "What is going on with you? You're weird."

We stop for the light, and I shove my hands in my pockets, tilting my head back and heaving a great sigh. I should get it out, but part of me doesn't want to speak it into existence.

"I, um...I'm worried."

Kevin nods. "About?"

I shake my head and step into the crosswalk with him when the light changes.

"I feel like my job is killing her," I confess. "I mean, not literally, of course. But any time there's an alarm, she has an anxiety attack, which is so understandable, but it kills me to see it happening."

Kevin listens intently, then considers.

"She does seem to be getting better when they happen, though."

True. She does. If only I decided to be a construction worker or a scientist or...anything but a fireman, she'd be getting better even faster.

"I just can't deal with the idea that I'm causing her pain," I tell him.

"You're not," Kevin insists. "Have you seen the pics I got of you two at the concert? She's nuts about you."

We step inside the coffee house, as I smile to myself. Those pictures are amazing.

We place our orders and take a seat at Scarlet's table. I run my hand over the surface and grin at Kevin.

"This is her table," I tell him, the memory of the first time I saw her so vivid in my mind. "Before we met, I was sitting over there, and she walked in and sat here...and I couldn't catch my breath."

Kevin grins. "Instantly hooked?"

I nod. "Pretty much. She had her sketchpad and was so focused I kept wondering what was in it. She was so pretty it was hard not to stare. And then I kept seeing her here. I've never looked forward to grabbing my morning tea so much in my whole life."

Kevin laughs under his breath. "Yeah, she's pretty special."

"She's the best," I agree. "I just don't want to be something else she has to survive."

Kevin tilts his head at me as if he can't imagine anything like that happening, but I can. And I hope I'm wrong.

***

Scarlet

"Okay, wait 'til I get it all set up," Merry instructs us excitedly.

Ashley, Marina, and I are all seated in a booth at Nonno's, watching her set two small dishes of hot sauce at the center of the table. One is labeled A, and the other is B. She opens a bag of tortilla chips and fills a bowl for us.

"Now?" Ashley asks, positively drooling from hunger.

"Make sure you take a taste of both, and let me know if you can tell the difference," Merry says with a nod. "Go ahead."

I grab a chip and dip it into dish A, then pop it in my mouth. It's delicious. Smoky and a good amount of heat. I let it sit in my mouth for several seconds, committing the taste to memory. I pop a plain chip into my mouth and take a huge sip of water, then I go for dish B.

"Wow," I say as I crunch through the dish B chip. "I cannot tell the difference at all."

Marina grins. "Me neither."

Ashley nods. "Same, girl. I think you did it."

I nod with a big, stupid grin. "I know you did it. Oh my gosh, he's going to be so blown over by the fact that you figured out his dad's hot sauce recipe. Merry, you're amazing."

Marina nudges me across the table.

"This is the sweetest idea, Scarlet. If he's not in love with you already, he will be after this."

I fall back against the booth cushion.

"I am so over the moon crazy about this man. He is amazing."

"So, how will you give him the hot sauce? What's the plan?"

"At the big reveal party tomorrow night," I share. "I didn't realize it until Jake gave us the bottle of hot sauce, but Andrew's dad actually had a name for it and everything. He called it Mac14 hot sauce... because his nickname was Mac, and he was stationed at Engine 14. So I designed a logo for it, and Nick's going to create some art for the kitchen."

Merry grabs a chip and dips it in dish B, crunching and nodding like she's so proud. And she should be. The girl's tastebuds should be insured.

"Can you make me some labels for bottles?" she asks. "I picked up a dozen hot sauce bottles from the restaurant supply store we use. Wouldn't it be cool if we could label them?"

"Oh, that would be cool! I'll bet the print shop down on Jones Street could do a rush order for me. I'll go straight there when we're done."

Ashley wraps an arm around me and gives me a squeeze. "I'm so proud of you. I can't wait to see it for myself."

Marina nods.

"Me too! When do the judges come to see it?"

"The very next day," I reply. "When I completed the check-in paperwork, I had to give pictures, so they've seen all of that, but they also come in person. I scheduled it this way so we could do our reveal party first."

"Nonno is catering it," Merry chimes in.

I squeeze Merry's hand across the table.

"And I am so grateful for that. He'll be there, too. I told him he couldn't cater if he couldn't come and celebrate with us."

"So do you find out if you won the contest when the visit, or do you have to wait?" Marina asks excitedly.

I hold up a hand in warning.

"I'm not going to win, guys," I say calmly. "And that's okay, I'm cool with it. I told Andrew as well it's just not going to happen, and I'm fine. I've changed since the fire. I'm not so obsessed with winning this thing."

Ashley purses her lips.

"You deserve this."

I give her a nudge, loving how much my friends fight my corner with me.

"I'm not saying I don't," I explain. "I'm just saying that the other contestants have been working longer on their projects without fires and hospital stays and rude city clerks getting in their way. If I'd been able to stick with my original project, I'd feel like I had this bagged. But it didn't work out that way. I'm proud of what I've done at Engine 14, but it's not going to blow any of my competition out of the water."

I fight back a smile as my friends all look confused at my outlook.

"I'm not trying to say my work isn't good," I explain further. "I'm just being real about it, like I always am. I have a lot of experience entering this thing. I know the caliber of work that the other contestants are going to have. Mine doesn't measure up, and I am still proud of it. I love what I've done, and I love that I got to do it for the people who saved my life. In the end, that's really what matters."

Ashley takes a deep breath.

"Well, we're proud of you, regardless. And when you're done with this, what's that look like? How are things with Andrew?"

I grin like a lovesick fool.

"He's great. He's been such a cheerleader for me, and his race is coming up, so I'll get to be his cheerleader soon."

"I can't believe he swims in that crazy thing," Marina says with a laugh.

"He loves it, so I'll be there to cheer him on," I tell her. "It'll do him good to get out there. I think he's a little sad that I'm almost done and we won't see each other so much every day, but it'll be okay. I adore him."

***

A few days later, I'm pulling Andrew to the other side of the kitchen island with brute force.

"Stop fussing, Andrew," I warn him with a mischievous grin. "You are not going in the kitchen, and that's final."

I laugh as he gives me his best pouty expression, but I'm not swayed. Not one bit. I assigned Merry to guard the kitchen with her life. Nick arrived thirty minutes ago, and we hung his artwork over the stove in the kitchen. I upgraded the frame that holds the photo of Andrew's dad, and Merry is putting the bottles of hot sauce on display on the stovetop. The labels turned out great, and I think both Andrew and Jake are going to be bowled over by the surprise. To be extra safe, I picked up a black curtain at Swap House yesterday, and we secured it over the stove area in case anyone gets through Merry's barricade. No one is seeing this surprise until I'm ready. Now I just have to pray the city remains relatively peaceful and Engine 14 doesn't get an emergency call in the middle of the celebration.

Andrew wraps an arm around me as I look at the living and dining areas, which are teeming with guests. Marina, Ashley, Zach, and Rick are here, of course. My mom and Nonno. Ashley's dad is here as well. We're waiting on the fire chief and the mayor, but Kevin is here, as well as Mrs. Davis, who made the quilt for Andrew. Nancy is also here, as well as the owner of Handy's Hardware. I haven't had time to walk around and thank them all yet, but I will. Right now, I'm a ball of nerves.

"Hey," Andrew says as he turns to face me. He puts his hands on either side of my face and draws me in for a gentle kiss. "Have I told you lately how proud of you I am?"

I grin up at him and wrap my arms around his waist. "Only every three minutes, and I'm here for it."

A fleeting sadness flickers behind Andrew's eyes, and I shake him gently.

"Hey, you...are you okay?"

He smiles at me, but it doesn't feel genuine.

"Always with you in my arms."

I study him for a moment.

"It's okay if you're not. If you need to talk about something."

He rubs a hand up and down my back. "I'm fine, baby."

I'm not convinced. "It goes both ways, you know," I tell him gently. "I know I've been going through a lot lately, but I want to be there for you too. If you're having a hard time with something, I want you to feel that you can talk to me. You can tell me anything."

That look is still on his face as he pulls me fully against him and holds me. I hold him right back, hoping he finds a way to confide in me if something is bothering him. I hope he realizes he doesn't always have to be the strong one. The protector.

Excitement stirs near the front door, and I look over to see that the mayor has arrived, with the fire chief right behind him. I squeeze Andrew to get his attention.

"Show time," I say lightly. "You with me?"

Andrew presses a kiss to the top of my head.

"Always, Nix."

I take his hand, and we make our way over to the mayor, who surprises me by giving me a big hug as soon as he sees me.

Wow. Hi, I'm Scarlet Jackson. I'm on hugging status with the mayor of San Francisco.

I know they're not here for long, so I decide to get right to the point.

"Okay, baby," I say to Andrew under my breath. "You stay right here while I reveal this last surprise, and I hope you love it."

Andrew kisses me on the cheek and stays put, and I grab Jake and have him stand right next to Andrew. The room quiets as I step into the kitchen and stand next to the black curtain, with Merry smiling like a Cheshire cat on the other side of it. Our guests gather around the kitchen island and in the dining area, allowing them a view of the final reveal.

"I just want to thank everyone for coming tonight," I say in a voice much calmer than how I feel right now. "This project has been the most important one of my life for many reasons. Most of those have nothing to do with paint colors or appliances and everything to do with the amazing friendships I've forged during these past few weeks."

It's hard not to get completely choked up as I look out at the smiling faces of Engine 14's firefighters standing with my friends and family. This is special in a thousand different ways. I point to the curtain behind me.

"I have one final reveal, and this is dedicated to Andrew and Jake," I begin, my voice wobbling. "When Jake showed me the kitchen for the first time, I had a lot of questions about a framed photo they kept right here above the stove. The photo was of James MacLachlan, Andrew's father and Jake's best friend, who died in the line of service many years ago."

Andrew's jaw muscle ticks, and his mouth quivers into a smile as he listens. I raise my eyebrows in silent question. Are you okay? He gives me a little nod, and Jake wipes a tear away from his own cheek.

"His nickname was Mac, and the more I learned about him, the more I knew I wanted to do something special to honor him," I continue.

I look around for Nick and motion for him to join me.

"Mac loved to cook, and that's how he's remembered in this fire station," I explain. "As it turns out, he used to make his own hot sauce, which was pretty legendary, and Jake still had a bottle of it in the back of his freezer that Andrew loved to tease him about."

Laughter ripples through the group as our guests listen to my presentation.

"He even named his hot sauce. That's how proud he was of it. It was called Mac14, so I asked Nick to make a piece of art to give Mac a proper memorial in the kitchen where he loved to cook. So without further delay, here we go."

Nick takes one side of the curtain, and I take the other, and when I nod, we pull it down to reveal the beautiful piece Nick made. Nick forged the Mac14 logo in copper, which is now mounted on the backsplash over the stove.

Our guests gasp and applaud, cheering loudly as Andrew and Jake take it all in. I watch them both as a thousand emotions play over their faces. Andrew shakes his head like he can't believe it, and Jake looks like he'll be speechless for the rest of the night. Andrew's eyes meet mine, and he's in my space in two seconds. He pulls me into his arms and spins me around slowly, much to everyone's delight. When he sets me down, his eyes are full of tears.

"You okay, Fireman?" I murmur.

He presses a kiss to my forehead.

"Perfectly. Thank you so much for this."

I pull away for a moment. "Well, good. Because I'm not done."

I reach behind me and pick up a bottle of hot sauce, holding it up for all to see.

"Now it's my turn to brag on my girl Merry over here," I tell our guests. "She has bionic tastebuds and can figure out any recipe. She took Jake's bottle and was able to replicate Mac's formula. So we're excited to give these bottles of Mac14 to our friends tonight."

Jake has completely lost his cool. Leonard grabs a paper towel and hands it to him to dab at his tears. Nonno takes over, encouraging people to get plates and start dishing up his catered appetizers. Merry helps him as people begin asking her questions about those amazing tastebuds.

I take the bottle of hot sauce in my hand and give it to Andrew, who takes it from me with complete reverence as he blinks back tears.

"Nix, I don't have words," he croaks as he turns the bottle around in his hand.

I press a kiss to his cheek.

"You don't need any. Not with me."

He shakes his head, eyes still glued to the hot sauce bottle. "This is the most thoughtful thing anyone's ever given me."

I nuzzle our noses together. "You deserve it. I can't take credit for all of it, of course, but we all did it for you."

Andrew's eyes search my face as he rubs a thumb across my cheek. His heart is definitely full right now, and he looks like he's fighting back words he doesn't want to say in front of everyone else.

"I…" he stammers. He kisses me softly. "I'm so grateful for you, Nix."

I wrap my arms around Andrew's neck and pull him in tight. We stand in the kitchen holding each other indefinitely. I'm vaguely aware of Jake moving over to pick up a bottle of hot sauce. Todd is with him. I hear something about adding hot sauce to his grilled cheese, but I'm focused on the amazing, wonderful, sweet man in my arms and how absolutely crazy I am about him.

"Oh! Wow, yes, she's in the kitchen," I hear Merry say. "Come right in. This is so exciting. Welcome!"

Andrew and I pull away from each other just as Merry leads three strangers in to meet us. I don't recognize any of them, but judging from the looks on their faces, they know me and Andrew. Merry looks at me from behind them and gives me an excited thumbs-up.

"Miss Jackson, I'm Kelly Hennings," the woman says with a smile. The two men with her are grinning and looking around the fire station excitedly. "I'm the Vice President of Programming at the Home Network."

Chapter 23

Scarlet

What?

What?

Andrew's arm tightens around my waist, no doubt in case I faint. They weren't supposed to be here until tomorrow. And even then, I don't think the vice president was supposed to show up. I was expecting judges, not executives.

"Um, I wasn't expecting you until tomorrow," I say breathlessly.

I feel the panic setting in. Nothing is ready for their eyes right now. There's wall-to-wall food and people here. These rooms should look pristine. I feel Andrew's hand rubbing up my back, trying to steady me.

"Please don't worry about that," she says gently. "This is Louis Earnwright, Director of Programming, and David Wheeler, one of our series directors."

Andrew and I shake their hands, and I'm still fairly speechless.

"I realize we crashed your party," Kelly continues, "but can we step outside to chat for a few minutes?"

I nod wordlessly, and we all step outside into the chilly San

Francisco night air. The cold air is a jolt that helps bring me out of my stupor.

"We have bad news and good news," Louis blurts out, only to be immediately scolded by David.

So it's official. I've lost my final bid at the contest. Not that it's a surprise, because I've been trying to prepare my friends for this inevitable outcome for days. It still stings to know for sure.

"You've entered the Decorator's Showcase competition for quite a few years," Kelly begins. "So you're very aware of how highly competitive it is."

I plaster a polite smile on my face, taking a glance over my shoulder through the windows at our party guests as they mingle. I nod.

"Yes, of course," I reply. "I do realize that this project can't really compete with—"

Kelly holds a hand up to stop me. "You've done a lovely job here, Miss Jackson. Truly."

I shake my head. "Please call me Scarlet."

"Scarlet, what you've accomplished here is incredible. We've been watching the story unfold for some time."

Andrew squeezes my hand. "You have?"

Louis nods. "Indeed. One of the other competitors reached out to withdraw his entry due to a fire. I believe he's your friend. Brad? He also made us aware of the unique circumstances of your arrangement here. When he told us the beginnings of your story, we were enthralled."

Now, it's David's turn to nudge Louis.

"We were not enthralled that you survived a horrific fire. What my colleague is trying to say is that we found the San Francisco Times articles, and *that* had us enthralled."

Louis rolls his eyes at David, and I have to suppress a nervous laugh.

"The way you inspired an entire community is incredible," Kelly continues. "The hardware store donating paint, the local artists coming together to help, the neighborhood grannies bringing quilts and cookies. The concert in the park? This story unfolded like a Hallmark movie."

My head is spinning. I have no idea where this is going, but I feel like there's something big here. What is she leading up to? Why are they actually here? Surely, this is more than just breaking the news that I didn't win.

David leans forward. "We went to the concert."

I jump. "You did? Oh boy…um, I'm sorry about the whole performance thing."

Why on earth did they have to see that? The mental image of me running around that stage and singing a sea shanty fills my gut with dread.

Andrew squeezes my hand.

"Hey, you were amazing up there, Nix."

Kelly laughs and nods. "You really were. We sat in the audience, absolutely mesmerized by how natural you were on that stage."

"You were? *I was?*"

Louis grins at me. "You were charming. Not reading from a speech on paper. You spoke from your heart in front of a crowd of thousands. It sealed the deal for us."

I swear I'm going to have a heart attack. My heart is pounding so wildly.

"Deal?"

"David?" Kelly says, stepping back.

David reaches forward and takes both my hands in his.

"Scarlet, I'm gonna get real for a moment. Can you stay with me?" he says excitedly.

Something about it makes me feel like he's about to make my whole day. I nod silently.

"I think we both know you couldn't have won the Decorator's Showcase, even though your work here is wonderful," he begins. I nod again. "But I am about to launch a new series on the Home Network. It's centered around taking ugly, unloved spaces in communities across the nation and turning them into places people can truly enjoy."

My mouth goes completely dry, and I feel like I might be squeezing David's hands too hard, but I can't stop.

"Okay…" I murmur, not sure what to say.

"We were going to open a frightfully long audition process, trying to find just the right hungry, young interior designer to star in the show. But we're not going to audition anyone now."

"You're not?" I ask in a voice trembling with emotion.

Does this mean what I think it means?

He shakes his head. "No, we're not. Because we found her. Right here in San Francisco."

Tears fall from my eyes as I take in his words. My eyes dart to Kelly.

"We would love for you to take the job, Scarlet," she says with a bright grin. "You're absolutely perfect for this."

I'm nodding, but I can't find the words. I open my mouth a few times, and nothing comes out. David and Louis are both laughing softly at my reaction, and Andrew wraps his arms around me and picks me up.

"Oh my gosh…I can't believe it…" I say against his cheek as he spins me around.

He puts me down, and my hand flutters up to my throat as I try to catch my breath.

"So this is a job? Really?"

Kelly nods. "And it's a lot of work. We can send you the contract to review, but we plan to shoot in communities all over the place. We'll be doing a lot of traveling while we're filming. There will also be quite a bit of press. Talk shows and the like. There's a lot for you to think over."

I nod, feeling like I'm going to jump right out of my skin.

"I understand. I understand, and I'm so grateful. I definitely want the job."

David pumps a fist in the air. "Yesssss!"

I laugh out loud and shake all their hands again. "Thank you so much."

"I'll have my assistant send you the contract first thing in the morning," Kelly explains. "Will two weeks be long enough to review it with your attorney? You might also want to find an agent to negotiate for you."

I nod and wipe another tear off my cheek. "Two weeks is more than enough, thank you."

"Now, this is up to you," Kelly says. "I can have the judges keep their appointment and come tomorrow afternoon, or we can tell them we've stolen you away. Your choice."

I laugh under my breath and nod. "You can tell them you've stolen me away."

Andrew sweeps me back into his arms and spins me around until I squeal so loud a dog barks in the distance. I squeal again, and he puts me down. Merry opens the door of the fire station and peeks outside at us.

"You okay out here?" she asks cautiously.

"Merry, I just got a job!" I yell, bursting into grateful tears.

Our party guests begin spilling out into the driveway, plates, and drinks still in hand, to see what the commotion is about. I turn back to Kelly, David, and Louis.

"Will you stay for the celebration?" I ask. "I want you to meet my mom. And my friends. This is incredible."

My three new bosses nod eagerly, and as people continue to pour into the driveway, the news spreads quickly. I make sure to call my family over immediately and tell them myself. Then, I introduce them to Kelly, Louis, and David. I step back and cry the happiest tears as Mom, Nonno, Dave, the girls, Zach, and Rick talk to them about how proud they are of me. And Andrew? Andrew doesn't leave my side, and I don't let go of him.

"Should I start calling you Sugar Momma now, Nix?" Andrew teases. "You're about to make a whole lot more money than me."

I laugh, and it reverberates through my whole body. I have never been happier than I am at this moment, surrounded by the people I love the most, handed an amazing job opportunity that I'm sure I can't even fathom yet. This is the best day ever.

"You can call me anything you want," I tell him quietly. "As long as I can call you mine."

"Done," he murmurs, showering me with delicate little kisses across my nose, my cheeks, and my forehead. His gaze flicks over my shoulder, then back to me. "Jake is coming to steal you away from me, so let's enjoy the party, and then I'll take you out for ice cream when it's done."

I gasp and nod just as Jake gets to me and pulls me right out of Andrew's arms.

"Sorry, kid, you've monopolized her long enough," he teases as he pulls me in for a hug.

"Scarlet, I'm supposed to deliver you to the mayor," he tells me. "He'd like to talk to you about the window treatments you made out of braided fire hoses. There's a whole conversation going on in there about how you came up with that."

I laugh out loud and nod. "I'm not sure if I can explain how my crazy brain works, but I can try!"

"First, I need to say thank you. For what you did for Mac's memory. I couldn't imagine anything better."

I loop my arm through Jake's as he takes me over to the mayor. "My pleasure, Jake. And also…my honor."

The rest of the evening passes as a beautiful, perfect blur. I am congratulated more times than I can count. I am surrounded by the love of my family and friends. Most importantly, the firefighters of Engine 14 have a beautiful, comfortable place to call their second home. They will no longer sit on chairs with duct tape over tears in the upholstery. They won't have to notice scuffed-up paint or put their feet up on a coffee table that is barely holding up anymore. I am leaving them with sturdy, comfortable furniture that will hold up to the beating they're about to give it. And no coasters will be required. I made sure to make everything low maintenance. The nod to Andrew's dad is the special touch I'm most proud of.

As guests trickled out at the end of the evening, Andrew and I made sure to thank every single one of them. I'm pretty sure Kevin got enough photos for a thousand stories, including Nonno hugging Kelly and pinching her cheeks. I'm not sure I'll sleep tonight or ever again, and I can't wait to get a look at the contract from the network.

But for now? For now, I am more than content to lean against the warm, safe, incredibly muscled body of my sweet boyfriend while we eat ice cream sundaes at Ghirardelli Square. I take another bite of my chocolate on chocolate with more chocolate on top sundae and groan around the spoon. This is amazing. This whole day has been like nothing I've ever experienced, and I don't want to forget a single minute of it.

"Have I told you in the last five minutes how proud I am of you?" Andrew asks.

I shake my head. "In the last five minutes? No, but we've talked about my stuff all day and all night. Can we please talk about you? Your race is coming up so soon. How do you feel about it?"

He smooths a hand over my hair as he wraps an arm around my shoulders.

"Pretty good," he replies. "Like you tried to tell me about your contest, I know I'm not going to win it. I like to race against my own time from last year. I'm pretty confident that I shaved a good thirty seconds off last year's time."

I close my eyes and shake my head for a moment.

"I can't believe I'm going to watch you dive into the bay and swim two miles in that choppy, cold, shark-infested water."

Andrew laughs loudly, squeezing around the shoulders. "It's not shark-infested, Nix, cut it out."

I shudder beside him. "I'll be so happy when you're back on land and safely in my arms."

His expression sobers, and it feels like there are a thousand questions hanging in the air that he wants to ask. I take the last decadent bite of my sundae and give him time to say what he needs to say.

"I'm sorry that it bothers you," he says quietly.

I shake my head. "No, baby, it doesn't bother me. I'm only teasing. I want you to do the things that make you happy."

My gut dips as his eyes empty of all contentment, and sadness seems to take over.

"But those things make you unhappy."

I sit back and look at him soberly. "What? Andrew, what are you talking about?"

He shakes his head. "I just feel like my job causes you so much anxiety and stress."

I frown, unsure of how to respond. He's not wrong, really, but I would never ask him to change jobs or do something he's not passionate about. Sure, I'm still having anxiety attacks, but I feel like I know how to handle them when they happen. I've been feeling pretty good about how I'm handling them, but now I worry about how they're affecting Andrew.

I'm about to open my mouth to ask about that when the sound of screeching tires sounds just outside. People at tables against the windows gasp and jump up just as the unmistakable sound of metal crashing against metal makes everyone look. Whatever the car, or cars, impacted was close. I see smoke rising from below the windows, and several people rush outside to see what's going on.

I look at Andrew, and he's on high alert, eyes darting around to see what he can see. He makes a move to stand up and then thinks better of it. His eyes meet mine.

"Do you want to go see what happened?" I ask, understanding the fact that his first responder instincts are probably screaming right now.

He just looks at me, not answering, and his gaze flicks back to the windows. I decide for him and reach for my bag.

"Andrew, go," I say gently. "I'll be right behind you. Go see if you can help."

He nods, kisses me quickly on top of my head, and he's gone in a flash. We already paid the check, so I don't worry about that as I scoot out of the booth and take a minute to make sure I have everything. Someone screams outside, and a cold wave of fear runs straight through me to my core.

What's that about...

My feet start moving before I even know what's happening. I'm suddenly overcome with a primal need to lay my eyes on Andrew and make sure he's all right. I burst through the door and tear down the steps to the sidewalk, turning the corner just in time to see Andrew rushing from his car toward the wreck with a large wrench in his hand as onlookers stand by and scream for help.

Two cars are wrapped around a street light pole, leaking fluids everywhere, and one of the engines is engulfed in flames. They shoot higher and higher, fueled by who knows what right now, but I know that's gasoline running down the incline from the back of one of the cars. Just as the smell of it hits my nose, my throat closes up, and I feel panic setting in.

"Andrew…" I try to scream, but only a whisper comes out.

I manage to take two steps out into the street before everything locks up. I try to breathe, but I can't think. I know they should be deep breaths, but I can't manage it. Andrew's standing right up against the burning car, pulling bystanders away and yelling at people to get back. No one is helping him.

He bangs a fist against the closed window of the vehicle on fire, trying to wake up the driver to no avail. Then he takes the wrench and swings hard at the window, shattering it in one blow. I jump from the sound of breaking glass and watch as Andrew reaches in to unlock the door. He swings it open and unbuckles the occupant's seatbelt, then hauls a heavy-set man out of the driver's seat.

Another man finally rushes over to help Andrew, picking up the man's feet so they can carry him to safety. Other onlookers block traffic while half a dozen people are on their phones, hopefully calling 9-1-1. Sirens wail in the distance, muddling my thoughts even more.

Sirens.

Fire.

Andrew…

I feel tears falling as I shake my head, trying to think. My ears are buzzing so loud that I can't hear anything else. Andrew's leaning over the man lying in the street. His mouth is moving, but I can't hear him. I can't hear any of them. Andrew looks up at me and yells something, but I can't make it out. He waves frantically. I don't understand.

I can't get any air. The edges of my vision are darkening, and I stumble backward, my fall broken by a car parked behind me. I land on the hood, trying to stay upright as the buzzing gets louder and louder. Lights are flashing now. I can only see them in the very center of my field of vision, but they're so bright. Tingles rush up my spine as I feel my control slipping and the street tilts.

"Scarlet!" Andrew cries just as he stops me from falling over onto the hood of the car. "Baby, come here. Come here."

I shake my head, staring ahead at the flames that have now fully engulfed both cars. I can't move. Can't think. Suddenly, I'm lifted off the car hood, and I realize I'm in Andrew's arms. He rushes away from the fire with me, setting me down just around the corner on a bench. His face fills my vision just before things begin to get dark.

"Baby, here…lay down…"

Strong hands gently guide me into a lying position on the bench. I close my eyes and begin to cry again. His hands are on my face, calming. Stroking.

"It's okay…I'm here…"

One of his hands wraps around mine, squeezing.

"Scarlet, I'm so sorry…please…"

I manage to open my eyes, and Andrew is there. I still feel dizzy from the panic attack, but I finally remember what I need to do. Keeping my eyes on him, I take a deep breath and slowly let it out. He watches me, frantically nodding.

"Good girl…another one…"

I take another deep breath. And another until I feel strong enough to sit up. He helps me, and as soon as I'm sitting up, I pull him straight into my arms and wrap him up tight. I shudder against him as a wave of relief hits me. He's okay. I'm okay. His strong hands rub up and down my back, as he murmurs into my ear.

"I'm so sorry, Nix…I should never have done that…"

Eventually, I calm enough to let go a little. I pull away enough to see him and nearly start crying again at how beaten down he looks…like he lost a battle.

"Did he die? Are you okay?"

Andrew shakes his head and reaches up to hold my face in his hands. "He'll be all right. EMTs are with him now."

I nod, feeling grateful that no one lost their life. I manage half a smile at Andrew.

"Thank goodness."

Andrew sits beside me on the bench and pulls me against him.

"I am so sorry, Scarlet," he croaks against the emotion in his throat. "I should never have put you through that."

I look up at him and frown. "You didn't put me through anything…I told you to go."

I sink into his side, willing him to understand that this isn't his fault. He kisses the side of my head, and I lace our fingers together, welcoming the calm that Andrew always brings.

***

Andrew

I hate myself. How could I be so callous? So insensitive. At least when I got called out at the station, she had someone there with her. Merry or Kevin. But not this time. No, this time, I left the woman I love all alone to go racing off to a dangerous situation…not even thinking about what it would do to her.

The look of absolute terror on her face plays over and over again in my mind. I did that to her. I caused her that pain just by being who I am. Because I can no more ignore people who need help, than she can stop her creativity from happening. I did that to her, and it kills me. I can't keep letting this happen to her. Not when I can do something to ease her pain.

I can't believe I'm about to say what I'm going to say. It feels like time has slowed almost to a halt, my body at war with itself. My heart is fighting a losing battle, and the knowledge of what I must do hits me like a physical pain ringing through every cell of my body. I don't want to say these words, but I'm helpless to stop them. It's the right thing to do.

"Scarlet," I murmur against her hair one last time. "I'm sorry."

She pulls out of my arms and looks up at me in confusion.

"What's going on with you, Andrew?" she asks in bewilderment. "This wasn't your fault. Stop blaming yourself."

I shake my head. "I think I have to let you go."

"What?" she gasps, eyes growing wider by the second. "What are you talking about?"

I close my eyes and take a deep breath, trying to find my center in a world that will never be the same for me. Not without her. It's useless to try to calm myself as I do this, so I open my eyes and look her squarely in her beautiful face.

"I am a constant trigger to you," I explain. "I can't put you through this for one more second. That peace you seek would come so easily without me. I have to let you go."

She shakes her head at me.

"Andrew, no. That's crazy. This is crazy."

Conflict rages in my heart, and I swallow it down. I focus on the tracks of her tears, still stained on her cheeks. The tracks that I caused by rushing off and putting her through another fire.

"I can't be the reason for your tears, Scarlet. Or your panic. Every time I'm called away, I worry about what it's doing to you."

She furrows her brow and shakes her head.

"I'm working on that," she says quickly. "You know I am."

"You are, and you're doing such a great job, but you can't heal like this, baby," I plead. "I'm constantly reopening the wound."

Scarlet looks at me as if she doesn't know who I am, and my heart begins to protest by pounding against my ribs.

"You're not at fault for this," she sputters. "This isn't about you or your job, Andrew. If you want to blame something for my panic attacks, blame the fire. Or that stupid, rickety ironing board of Brad's that fell over and caused it. I don't blame you. Is that what you think?"

I shake my head.

"Not now," I admit. "But you will if this keeps up. You need peace, Scarlet. And space to heal."

"I need *you*."

I close my eyes against the wave of emotions that has me ready to take it all back. I fight the urge to pull her back into my arms and never let her go, but the damage that would cause over time is something I can't live with. I shake my head firmly.

"I need you too," I choke out. "So much. But I can't live with the damage I'm causing you, Scarlet."

"This is crazy, Andrew. Stop it."

She's right. Stop. Stop this right now.

"You know I'm right about this," I argue, barreling straight ahead.

She shakes her head furiously.

"No, I don't. I know you're about three seconds from breaking my heart. What is this really about?"

"This is me giving you what you need despite how much it hurts us both in this moment."

I watch her lower lip tremble as she struggles for words.

"It's not up to you to do that."

I work the muscle in my jaw as I mull over her words. She's right, it's not. But how can I just stand by as my existence keeps throwing hers into such turmoil? I couldn't have stopped myself from helping that driver any more than she could stop herself from making beautiful things. It breaks my heart that I have to do this, but it'll give her the space she needs.

"I can't quit my job, but I can—"

"But you can quit me," she says coldly, a stillness coming over her.

"You can just cut me out. Walk away from us."

I shake my head and open my mouth to answer back, but she scoffs. She stands and looks down at me.

"What am I talking about…there is no us. There never really was if you can just walk away so easily."

I shake my head again. "This isn't easy. Not by a long shot. But I can't keep causing you pain."

She lets out an exasperated sigh.

"What do you think *this* is? What do you think you're doing right now if you're not causing me pain by walking away from…"

She pauses as she searches for words, then lets out a bitter laugh.

"You know what? I was going to say you're walking away from one of the best things that's ever happened to me: our relationship. But it's not, clearly. Because how can it be if it means so little to you?"

"Scarlet, it means everything to me. You know it does. But you deserve someone who doesn't cause these horrible triggers."

My gut wrenches as she lets out a heartbroken sob, and I stand up and try to reach out to her. A tear falls down her cheek, and she wipes it away furiously.

"How dare you. How dare you presume to tell me what I need or what I deserve. Who do you think you are, Andrew?"

"Nix, I—"

She thrusts a finger at me.

"No! You don't get to call me that."

I stand silent, unable to form a single sentence in my defense. There is no defense. I am the worst person in her world right now, and I will be for a very long time. Every cell of my body throbs in misery over the knowledge of that fact.

I keep my focus on Scarlet, drinking in everything about her and knowing I'll never see her again after this. I hate myself for it. I memorize her beautiful hair, her flawless skin. Those gorgeous blue eyes are full of fury right now, raging against me.

"How can you be so brave and still be such a coward?" she asks, taking a step away from me.

"Scarlet..."

She shakes her head at me and takes two more steps backward

"You're a coward," she says in a voice thick with emotion. "This isn't about me. It's about you. You're hard-wired to jump in and help. You fix things. You save people. But I don't need to be fixed, Andrew, and you can't stand it."

I flinch at her words as they hit home. The truth of them wriggles under my skin and won't let go. I do always jump in to help. To save.

"I don't need your misguided attempt at saving me," she says coldly. "I needed you. I needed your love, Andrew. That was enough for me. It was all I needed."

Needed. Past tense. I feel a fissure the size of the Grand Canyon tear through the center of my heart. Panic begins to swirl in my gut.

"You know what? You've managed to do exactly everything I didn't want," she croaks out. "I opened my heart to you, and I get it handed back to me in a million pieces. I'm trying to put my life back together, and now I get to put my heart back together too."

She takes another step away from me, and I take a step forward. She puts a hand up.

"Don't you take one more step towards me," she orders. "You don't want to be part of my life? Fine. Don't be. But don't think for one minute that you're doing some kind of chivalrous thing by making a sacrifice for me and my healing process. You *hurt* me."

I force myself to stay silent and take the verbal lashing that I so clearly deserve. She points at the restaurant behind us.

"I'll go inside and call a ride share. You can go ahead and walk away, Andrew. That's what you want."

My breaking heart keeps me pinned to my spot, and I'm unable to tear my eyes away from her. I want to take it all back now, and I don't know what to say. I'm torn between my head and my heart like never before. Scarlet looks at me with utter heartbreak in her eyes, shaking her head.

"You're not Superman after all," she says. "You're just some guy I used to know."

And with that, she turns on her heel and heads back into the restaurant as I stand on the sidewalk with the remnants of my heart.

Chapter 24

Scarlet

I jolt awake at the sound of Merry's animated voice down the hall, followed by a lot of hushing that my muddled brain guesses is coming from Ashley or Marina. Or both. Because in the time it takes me to sit up and rub the sleep out of my eyes, the three of them are standing in my bedroom and looking at me like they're ready to go to war for me. Or with me.

Jury's still out on that.

"What's going on?" I ask in a croaky voice.

"Emergency conclave," Ashley says calmly, tossing a box of donuts into my lap.

I shove them aside. "Why? What's up?"

Merry huffs. "I don't know, what's new with you? Break up with anyone last night?"

I blink up at my friends.

"How did you know about that?"

Marina stalks forward and sits on the edge of my bed next to me. "How could you not tell us?" she counters. "Are you okay?"

I look to Merry. "He told you?"

Merry nods solemnly. "He texted me this morning because you've gone quiet. He's pretty devastated, dude."

I let out a bitter laugh. "*He's* devastated? *He* broke up with *me*."

My heart hurts as memories from last night flood back. I love Andrew. I'm sure of it. I don't even know how I go forward from here. As furious as I was, and still am, I miss him so much. I love him so much. How could he—

"Have you checked your phone lately?" Merry asks, interrupting my thoughts.

I look at my nightstand, and my phone isn't plugged in where it usually is.

"Where is it?" I muse.

I think back to last night after Andrew broke up with me. I called a ride-share service and had the driver bring me straight home. I went right to bed. I point at the evening bag I was carrying last night, now lying on the chair where I threw it. Merry grabs it immediately and tosses it to me. I pull my phone out, and it's dead.

"Well?" Marina says impatiently.

I grab my charger cord and plug the phone in.

"It's out of juice," I say as I hit the start button impatiently.

I fight against the tiny spark of hope in my heart. If Andrew is devastated, that sounds like regret. But does he regret the whole break-up or just the way I took it? My phone comes back to life and starts vibrating like it's been hit by lightning. My friends watch with bated breath as I swipe the screen to read my notifications.

I gasp quietly. "Eighteen missed calls," I say breathlessly.

I swipe over to my text messages.

"He texted me..."

Marina puts a reassuring hand on my shoulder, and I look up at my friends with tears in my eyes.

"I'm sorry I didn't text you guys last night," I say quietly. "It was just late, and there was nothing any of us could do about it. I just wanted to cry and go to sleep."

Ashley offers me a sad smile.

"We were just worried. Sometimes you need quiet, and that's okay too."

I nod, and turn back to my phone. I have six texts from Andrew.

Andrew: Scarlet, please answer...I need to talk to you.

About what? The fact that you broke my heart in a million pieces and left them all over Hyde Street?

Andrew: If you're not going to answer, I have no choice but to say what I want in a text and that feels wrong...

Oh, does it? More wrong than breaking my heart. Ugh. This man.

Andrew: Okay, fine. Scarlet, I'm so sorry. I'm an idiot. You were absolutely right when you said you don't need to be fixed. And I did make this about me when it isn't. If you're happy in our relationship that's all that matters. Please talk to me.

I gasp out loud. My eyes fill with happy tears, and relief floods in so quickly I feel like falling back against the pillows. I look up at my friends as a tear falls down my cheek.

"He's sorry..."

Marina wraps an arm around my shoulder as I look back at the screen.

Andrew: Scarlet, please...

Andrew: Okay, you and I are fighters...I'm not giving up. I'm going to do my swim this morning and then I'm coming for you. I was an idiot, so if you don't want me back all you have to do is say so...but you'll have to say it to my face, Nix.

Andrew: ...or you can come for me if you forgive me. I'll be in San Francisco Bay, baby.

I let out a little sob and clutch my phone to my chest.

"He's coming—oh, my gosh, what time is it?"

My eyes dart to the clock on my wall.

"It's 9:15," Merry says with a grin. "Going somewhere?"

I bolt out of bed and run into my bathroom to start the shower, then run back to my friends.

"I'm going to a race," I reply with a big, stupid, lovesick smile on my face.

All three of my friends let out a whoop.

Ashley jingles her keys. "I'll drive."

I start doing the math in my head. The race starts in forty-five minutes. In the morning, with a big event like that down at the wharf, traffic will be terrible. It's not likely I'll get down there before it starts, but I have to find a way to get to Andrew. I look at my friends.

"Okay, I'm gonna take the fastest shower ever, and then we're going to the wharf to try to find Jake."

Marina frowns. "Jake? Andrew's captain?"

I run to my bathroom, yelling back at her, "Yep. I'm gonna need a boat."

***

After the fastest shower of my life, I jump in the car with the girls, and we head to Fisherman's Wharf. On any normal day, traffic would be congested in this part of the city…but today? Today, it's a nightmare. The police have blocked most of the streets leading into the wharf area, and the limited parking lots are all full. The race started ten minutes ago, and I need to get out of this car.

I look around us for any sign that traffic is going to get better, and there are cars everywhere. The only people moving are the ones walking on the sidewalks.

"Guys, I'm gonna make a run for it," I say as we stop at a light.

I slip the strap of my crossbody bag across my neck and shoulder so it won't slip off.

"I promise to call you after I kiss my boyfriend."

I throw open the car door and get out, making a mad dash up the sidewalk, yelling, "I love you guys!"

I hear my girlfriends cheering me from Ashley's open convertible. Pure adrenaline takes over as I weave my way in and out of tourists and locals, getting closer to the water as quickly as possible. The swimmers take off from Alcatraz Island, but that's not where I need to be. Andrew is swimming in the cold waters of San Francisco Bay, making his way toward the finish line near Bay Breeze Yacht Club. Jake and a few of the guys from Engine 14 are going to be on the fireboat in the bay, cheering on Andrew, and I need to find them. I've never actually watched this race before. I have no idea what I'm doing.

When I get down to the wharf, the situation is even more insane. People are everywhere. Food vendors with little carts blocking the sidewalk. It's anarchy everywhere. I have no idea how I'm going to get through this, but I start running anyway. Over the next several minutes, that's my pattern: run, stop, recalculate route...like some kind of GPS out of sync.

I feel like my heart's going to beat right out of my chest as my feet finally hit the pavement near Pier 39. I stop to catch my breath, straining my eyes to try to find the fireboat in the swarm of boats floating in the bay to watch the race. I pull my phone out of my bag and hit Jake's contact info.

Please pick up. Please, please, please...

"Scarlet?" Jake's voice sounds over the phone, much to my relief.

"Jake! I'm at the wharf...are you on the boat?"

Jake's husky laugh sounds on the other end of the line.

"Have you come to get your man, Phoenix? He was in a horrible mood when I saw him this morning."

I laugh into the phone. "I'm at the boat slips by Pier 39. Can I get a ride?"

"We're on the way, Scarlet!"

I squeal and hang up, running down the steps to the boat slips and weaving my way in and out of the many rows of boats. I know I have to get to the farthest slip out, where there is a small dock that juts out into the bay. Hopefully, there isn't a sea lion on it. They've taken over a huge part of the docks here, but I'm running to the opposite side and silently pray there's a way for Jake to get me.

I hit the last row of boat slips and look down to the end. No sea lions on this side, thankfully. I stand and wait, trying to catch my breath, looking down into the blue water of the bay. The water is no more choppy than usual, but I can't fathom why anyone would try to swim in this.

He's crazy. But he's mine.

The fireboat appears, and I wave at it as I run to the far end of the slips. The boat slows considerably, and I silently marvel at the skills of the person guiding the vessel. Jake comes around the side of the boat as it inches closer to me. He shakes his head skeptically as he gauges the situation.

"I can jump, Jake," I declare boldly. "Just tell him to hold it steady."

Jake shakes his head again. "Let him get closer first."

I wait, shifting my weight from foot to foot impatiently as I watch Jake rummage through a storage hold on the boat. He holds up a life vest and tosses it to me. He's so close I could have almost grabbed it from him. I make quick work about putting on the life jacket, and then Jake steps away to give me ample room for landing. I take a running jump and land squarely on deck, grabbing onto Jake's outstretched arm as a safeguard.

The boat takes off again, cutting through the bay towards the sectioned-off portion where boats are allowed. I stand at the bow with Jake, taking a few seconds to hug Amy and Leonard hello. The race rules dictate that the swimmers start from Alcatraz Island and make one lap around it before heading farther into the bay and ending at the yacht club close to the Golden Gate Bridge. As I look across the water, the swimmers are still on the back side of the island. I reach out and grab Jake's arm excitedly.

"I can't believe it. Thank you so much for coming to get me."

Jake grins down at me.

"Are you kidding? If I had to deal with one more minute of that mopey, sad face of his, I was going to come get you and lock you both in a room together."

I laugh out loud.

"Well, I'm glad it won't come to that," I reply. "I know he won't see me on the boat, but I wanted to cheer him on, and then I'll figure out how to get to the finish line."

Jake smirks. "Oh, he'll see you. Who do you think is doing the water cannon over the route the swimmers take?"

My eyes nearly bulge from their sockets. "Water cannon?"

He nods. "He made me promise not to hit him with it, as if I would. We're just shooting a high arch over the route, but he'll look for us, I'm sure. Not like you can miss the only fireboat on the water."

"Will he even look? He'll be focused on speed, won't he?"

"He only competes against himself," Jake replies. "Which is incredible enough when you think about how tough this race is, but he won't be in the lead group."

I nod and stand with Jake and Leonard as the boat bobs up and down on the water. I look at the bay and marvel at how Andrew can swim in this for such a distance. Alcatraz is not small, so swimming around it is crazy, not to mention the distance from the island to the yacht club where the finish line is.

The sound of a boat horn gets our attention just as I glimpse the first group of swimmers coming around the island. There are about six swimmers in the group, followed by a cluster of another ten. Jake slaps Leonard on the shoulder.

"Fire it up!"

Leonard goes to work, and soon, there's a huge spout of water shooting up from the boat. He adjusts it so the water forms a high arch over the bay, and several observers from the other boats begin to cheer. The swimmers in the front group get closer to the boat, then their route turns as they head straight toward the Golden Gate Bridge.

I watch in awe at their powerful muscles as their bodies cut through the water, their eyes laser-focused on technique and speed. The second group comes through soon after, and again, their determination floors me. It's incredible to see. Then again, they'd be in awe if they got a look at me bargain shopping at Swap House. I'm pretty amazing in that environment.

I smirk to myself just as the main group of swimmers round the corner. Jake squints his eyes against the sun, then he grins widely.

"There he is!"

I laugh. "How can you tell?"

Jake smiles softly and nudges me. "See the orange on that guy's head?"

I put my hand over my eyes like a visor against the sun, searching until I find him.

"Yeah…"

"That's him," Jake says. "He's wearing a swim cap with a phoenix on it. It was going to be a surprise for you."

I feel my lower lip tremble as raw emotion rolls through me. I shake my head, waiting for the lump to clear from my throat.

"He is so incredibly…"

"Stupid? For trying to let you go?"

I laugh. "Well, yeah, but I'm going to forgive him."

Jake grins at me, then smacks the side of the boat.

"Get ready, Sam!"

I assume Sam is the guy driving the boat when he gives Jake a thumbs-up through the windshield. I look around at the others on the boat. They're all firefighters from various stations in the city. All wearing t-shirts with their station insignia displayed. I realize this is probably one of the coolest things I've ever done in this city, and I couldn't find better people to be with as I cheer Andrew on.

I watch the orange blob on his swim cap get closer and closer until it does, indeed, become a phoenix when he's near enough. Jake gives the signal, and Sam sounds the horn as we erupt into cheers, jumping up and down and yelling Andrew's name.

My heart is absolutely swelling with pride as I watch a smile appear on his face when he hears his friends. We don't stop cheering. We keep it up as he gets just a bit closer. And then the unthinkable happens. He stops.

Jake laughs. "Oh boy…"

"What is he doing?" I gasp, grabbing Jake by the arm.

"Pretty sure he spotted you, Scarlet."

Even at twenty yards away, I can see those dimples flash as Andrew smiles.

"Nix!"

Laughter bubbles up out of me, and I shake my head.

"What are you doing?! Keep going!"

Andrew dives beneath the rope line that defines the route and comes up on our side of it, but I hold my hands up.

"No, no, no, Andrew! Get back there! Go finish your race!"

He shakes his head, still panting from the exertion of the race, but not heading back into the lane. He swims closer, now only about ten yards out from the boat.

"Why would I care about a race when I won something so much better?" he asks.

I smirk at him. "And what's that?"

He swims another few yards closer.

"You, baby. Another chance with you."

I can feel everyone's eyes on us on this boat, even amongst all the craziness around us. The water cannon streaming overhead, all the other boats lined up along either side of us, and the race observers cheering. And Andrew…smiling at me after abandoning the race he's worked for a year to swim.

"You're so crazy," I say breathlessly.

He bobs closer in the water.

"Nix, I have to tell you something," Andrew says, clear mischief in his eyes. "I don't know if you're ready to hear it, but it has to be said."

I shake my head. "Gee, I don't know, Andrew…I didn't really like the last big revelation you gave me."

He smirks. "This one's better."

I nod nervously. "Okay, sure. What is it?"

I watch Andrew bob in the water, his breathing slowly returning to normal. He grins up at me.

"I'm in love with you," he replies, absolutely beaming. "I love you so much it hurts. You don't have to say it back, but I had—"

I've heard enough. I throw myself off the boat with all the energy in my body, losing the last part of his sentence when my head goes underwater just briefly. His strong hands are on me so fast, pulling me up and against him. His lips immediately find mine.

I think I found a new favorite thing. Wet, salty, San Francisco Bay kisses. Andrew's arms around me. Heaven. Although it's pretty freaking cold here. Maybe not my absolute favorite.

"I love you, too, Andrew," I say from behind my chattering teeth.

He kisses me again, and I just float in the water like a lovesick lump, letting him have complete control of it all. I'm done. I've got my man. I don't need anything else. Andrew breaks off our kiss and presses our foreheads together.

"C'mon, Shark Bait," he teases, "let's get you out of this cold water."

His joke is a slap back into reality as I realize I actually jumped in this water on purpose.

"Jake!" I scream as Andrew turns me around to face the boat.

Oh. I was going to scream for a ladder, but there's already one there. Jake stands on deck, laughing and shaking his head at us as we swim over to the boat. Andrew makes sure I have a good foothold, and then I start climbing my way up. I turn to look behind me, making sure he's there, and he is. Right behind me.

"I'm here, baby," he says sweetly.

I'm here. You're safe.

I climb up to a point where Jake can grab me, and I'm hauled over the edge of the boat. He makes sure my feet are firmly planted on the deck, then he shakes me a little and looks directly into my eyes.

"That was a little dumb, my friend."

I laugh out loud and hug him, soaking the front of his shirt. Leonard comes over to me with a blanket and wraps it around my shoulders.

"Thank you," I say behind my still-chattering teeth.

I hear Andrew behind me, and I turn right into his arms as our mouths come together. I open my arms with the blanket and wrap him in it with me. I feel like I'll never be warm again in my life, but I have what really matters. I have the other half of my heart. I pull away enough to look up into his eyes.

"R-r-r-repeat af-f-f-ter m-me," I say, trying to sound tougher than I am at this moment.

Andrew nods with a mockingly solemn expression.

"I will n-never do that ag-gain, Nix."

A beautiful smile blooms on his face. "I get to call you Nix again?"

I raise my eyebrows and wait for him to repeat. He laughs softly and steals a kiss.

"I will never do that again, Nix," he says huskily. "And I'm so sorry I hurt you. I love you more than anything in this world."

I feel my lower lip tremble as all my feelings well up. This week has really been nuts. I relax in Andrew's arms and let my hands fall to his chest—

Oh.

I look down and notice for the first time that my boyfriend isn't wearing a shirt, and my boyfriend is hot. His pectorals are incredibly sculpted, and I'm pretty sure there's at least a four-pack down there. Probably a six-pack. I can't count reliably right now.

"See something you like, Nix?" he murmurs, smirking at me.

I smirk back at him. "You better have a shirt on this boat somewhere. I don't want all this eye candy walking around on the wharf, tempting all the other girls."

He laughs and shakes his head. "I don't care about them. I only have eyes for you."

A violent shiver runs through me as a cold breeze hits the boat, and Andrew's arms tighten around me. He moves us over to a low bench, and he sits, pulling me into his lap.

"Did you come out here alone, or are the girls with you?"

"I— oh, no," I reach down and pull my crossbody bag up to eye level. Water is still dripping out of it. "My new cell phone is toast."

Andrew adjusts the blanket, so it's completely over my shoulders. "I guess you love me a lot then, huh? You dove right into shark-infested waters, not even thinking about your phone. Lucky me."

I laugh and give him a shove.

"It's fine. I've got my own TV show, you know. I can afford it."

He pulls me close and sighs against my hair. "I love you, Nix."

"That's all I need to hear," I say softly, burrowing against his chest.

"The rest we can figure out."

"Mmm. Starting with getting you warm and dry," he says with a laugh. "I can't believe you jumped in after me."

I pull back and smile at Andrew. "It was worth it."

Three hours later, I blow on my hot cocoa as Andrew adjusts the blanket covering us. I burrow closer into his side, sighing happily as he kisses the top of my head. After we left the boat, Andrew drove us to my house, where he took a hot shower in our guest bathroom and changed into the clothes he'd brought with him for after the race. I also took a hot shower in my bathroom and threw on my favorite flannel pajama bottoms and a sweatshirt with The Royal Rebels logo on it. Andrew brushes his foot against mine under the blanket.

"I like your fuzzy socks," he says quietly.

I smile back at him. "Thanks. You want a pair? They're really warm."

He shakes his head. "If my feet get cold, I'll just rub them on your fuzzy socks. Problem solved."

I take a sip from my mug. "Thanks for making the cocoa."

"It's kind of our thing," he says sweetly. "I drink awesome green tea lattes, and you drink gross black coffee, but we both agree that hot cocoa is the best."

I laugh and take another sip.

We sit in relative silence, watching the fire Andrew built in the fireplace after asking me about ten times if I was sure I was okay with it. There was a point when the boat was speeding back to the dock when I thought I'd never be warm again, so being cuddled under a blanket with the love of my life and feeling that wonderful heat from the fireplace is a huge treat. And I've got my fireman here if anything goes wrong.

"Thanks for building the fire," I tell Andrew, nestling my head on his shoulder.

I feel him kiss the top of my head and smile against my hair. "Thanks for running to my rescue, Nix."

EPILOGUE

Three Months Later

Scarlet

I maneuver my new SUV up the long driveway at Hathaway House, a long-forgotten architectural gem in the heart of Sacramento. It's a beautiful building with a gorgeous wrap-around porch, but it has fallen into a sad state of disrepair. Of all the potential projects I was given to choose from, this one spoke to me the most. The building has great bones, and there's a local charitable organization that would love to use it for their headquarters...but they don't have the budget to renovate it. Now, it's the very first project I'll be taking on for the first episode of my new TV show.

"Oh, wow, baby girl," Mom croons from the passenger seat. "I can already see the potential."

"It's amazing," Merry says from the back seat as Marina and Ashley try to get a better view from either side of her.

"Wait 'til you get the whole tour," I tease excitedly. "It's incredible inside."

I put the car in park, and we all pile out. I look around for Andrew, who was supposed to step outside once we pulled up, but I don't see him anywhere. Merry groans loudly behind me.

"I've gotta stretch," she bellows. "I hate road trips."

Marina scoffs. "It was an hour and a half."

Merry shrugs, then launches into four consecutive cartwheels across the grass.

Ashley giggles and shakes her head in disbelief.

I look over at Marina.

"Sometimes I wish I had her energy," I say with a laugh.

"It's the extra-ness that fuels her," Marina says. "Pure unicorn power."

"It's very brown," Mom says beside me. "I'm sure that's the first thing you'll change."

I grin at her. "You're not wrong. And get ready. It looks like 1975 threw up all over the inside."

"Ew!" Merry yells, launching four more cartwheels in the other direction.

"Okay, let's get inside before Merry breaks a bone," I tease.

Merry comes running over and takes a bow.

"Yes, get me inside," she mocks in her best old lady voice. "Hurry up, youngster, or the spinster DeLuca will break a hip."

"Oh, Merry, stop," Ashley cries out.

This is the latest trend coming from Merry, unfortunately, and I am desperately trying to find a way to make her snap out of it. She keeps making spinster jokes about herself since Marina, Ashley, and I are all in relationships. I want her not just to know but to feel in her heart that the best is yet to come for her...and it is coming soon.

"Please tell me there's a working bathroom in there?" Merry blurts.

"Second door on the left down the hall."

She nods quickly and takes off to the house while the rest of us walk at a regular pace.

"Has Andrew started the new job yet?" Mom asks as she loops an arm through mine.

We mount the porch steps together, and I hear Ashley let out a huge sigh.

"I love this porch," she says, spinning around in a circle.

I look over at Mom. "Next week. His last day at Engine 14 was Wednesday, and he wanted a little time off before he goes to the office."

A few weeks after our twenty-four-hour break-up, a position opened in the Fire Investigations Division, and Andrew applied. Jake and the fire chief wrote letters of recommendation for him, which meant so much to Andrew. He got the job, and although I know he'll miss his family at Engine 14, he is excited to start this new chapter.

We step inside the house into a grand foyer that I know must have been something to see back in the house's prime. It's dark and dingy now, but when this place is transformed, it's going to be a tranquil, serene, and welcoming space where people suffering from addiction can come to heal. I can't wait to bring this house back to life and give it back to the community.

"Andrew?" I call out.

He's nowhere to be found. At least he laid out the snacks and drinks that I asked him to.

"Ladies, Andrew put out some refreshments if you'd like anything," I explain.

I grab one of the metal bar stools I brought with me on my first trip here and sit at the bar top table where I plan to meet with my team. Once Mom went over the contract with a fine-toothed comb, I called Hella Bella and asked her how I find an agent. As it turns out, Bella was happy to add me to her list of clients, and she negotiated my contract with the network for me.

Among the clauses she insisted be added, I'm allowed to choose my own collaborators to work with on the show. David has been a dream to work with as the director of the show. He wanted two to three people to help me on the show, so I went straight to Brad, Kayla, and Sarah and asked them if they wanted a job. Sarah passed, as she's decided that designing isn't really her jam. Brad and Kayla were thrilled, so they're joining the show just as soon as they get their contracts signed. Once we start working on the project, I fully intend on throwing some work to Nick and Nancy to spotlight their art in a big way. And who knows who else we'll meet along the way?

Merry comes back from the bathroom and pulls up another bar stool.

"Did you see Andrew back there at all?"

She looks at me like a deer caught in the headlights for two seconds, then shakes her head and mutters, "Uh uh."

Okay. Weird. I open my laptop and bring up the design plans for this space, then call everyone over to have a look. I show them the renderings for each room on the ground floor, but I haven't finished the bedrooms yet.

I slide off the bar stool and look in the next room. No Andrew. I start to head down the hall since he's been hanging out in the study a lot, but Merry jumps in front of me.

"Hey, where ya going?" she asks with so much energy. Even for her.

"I'm looking for Andrew. Are you sure you haven't seen him?"

She shrugs. "Try the backyard."

I scoff. "There's nothing out there but grass and a few trees."

"Hmm. Thought I saw him."

I do a double-take at Merry. First she doesn't see him, now she thinks she saw him.

"I think we need to check you for a fever," I joke, then I step back into the kitchen to look out the window that overlooks the backyard.

What on earth…

I step closer to the window and gasp. Andrew is outside in a suit, standing in front of a long path marked by fiery orange flower petals, waiting for me.

Ashley wraps an arm around my shoulders and squeezes.

"I think you should go out there," she says lightly. "That boy looks like he has a question."

My hand flutters up to my lips as I hold back tears and head out the back door and onto the porch.

Andrew grins up at me, looking so incredibly handsome. He spreads his arms wide and yells, "Nix!"

Tears threaten my eyes as I take the steps down into the backyard. As I walk up the path of flower petals, he slowly sinks down to one knee and extends his hand. A tear falls as he smiles up at me.

"Baby…"

Andrew shakes his head. "I have a very specific question I need to ask you, Nix."

I wipe a tear away. "Yes."

He laughs softly, as do I. "You don't know what the question is yet."

I shrug, and my lower lip quivers. "The answer is still yes."

There's so much love in his eyes, but he still smirks. It's our thing.

"What if I want to shave my head?"

"Andrew, don't make me get surly."

He reaches for me, and I give him my hand.

"Scarlet Marie Jackson," he begins. "From the moment I saw you walk into that coffee house in your sassy orange pantsuit, I knew you were going to make a difference in my life. And the more I got to know you, the more I knew you were the only one for me. You are my phoenix. I love you more than anything in this world. Please do me the honor of becoming my wife."

Completely crying, I get down on my knees in front of Andrew.

"Yes, baby," I say as a hiccup escapes my throat. "I can't wait to be your wife."

Andrew pulls a ring box out of his pocket and opens it for me, and I gasp. A fiery orange gemstone sits in the middle, surrounded by rubies and diamonds. It's gorgeous. He slips it onto my finger, and I bring our lips together in a soft, slow kiss.

"I hope you don't mind, but I invited some people to celebrate with us, Nix," Andrew says with those devastating dimples on full display.

He stands and helps me up, then turns me around in time to see not just my mom and girlfriends but his mom, Jake, Brad, Kayla, Nick, Nancy, and Kevin, all filing out of the house and into the backyard. I turn back to Andrew and wrap him in my arms.

"You are the best man in the universe," I say as I kiss him again.

His strong arms wrap around me, holding me tight. I take a deep breath against him, and a little shudder rolls through me as I think about how incredibly lucky I am. I'm standing in the backyard of my first major project, for my very own TV show, in the arms of the man I love…who I'm going to marry someday. Someday soon, if I have anything to do with it. Andrew is about to start a new role in his career. Everything feels new. Everything feels right. I look up into those beautiful brown eyes of his.

"I know we've got a lot going on right now, but how do you feel about house hunting?"

He raises his eyebrows in surprise. "Yeah?"

I shrug. "Yeah. If we're going to get married, why don't we tackle that first? Then we have a place to get married."

He frowns down at me in confusion. "You don't want a big wedding in a church with hundreds of people watching?"

I laugh under my breath. "Nope. I want a small wedding with the people who mean the most to us. That's all I want."

Andrew flashes me those devastating dimples.

"Then that's what we'll have, Nix."

I give him one more kiss before stepping out of his arms.

"Let's go see our people, baby."

He laces our fingers together and nods.

"Let's go start our life together."

I swing our hands between us as we close the distance between us and our loved ones.

"That's officially my favorite thing on my to-do list."

We walk together into the arms of our loved ones, and I can't imagine a more perfect day.

BONUS SCENE

Kindle Readers, click here to sign up for the newsletter and claim your bonus scene! (Paperback readers...flip the page!)

You're Invited...

to Scarlet and Andrew's wedding!
Paperback readers can scan here to subscribe to my newsletter and get some extra swoons.

SNEAK PEEK: Happily Ever After in the Hollow

Author's note: *this novella will be a fun, fall-themed romp that stars all the friends and their significant others. The chapters will be slightly longer than the ones in my full-length novels, and each chapter will be from one of the friends' POVs: Marina, Ashley, Scarlet, or Merry. The opening chapter is from Marina's POV. This is just a sneak peek (which includes a tiny spoiler if you haven't downloaded your bonus scene yet). This is not the whole chapter...but I hope you enjoy!*

Marina

I stand at the kitchen sink, watching the love of my life fussing over a pumpkin vine in the backyard garden and laugh under my breath. This is all my fault. My husband. My sweet, gorgeous, sexy, rockstar husband is looking for squash bugs and it's all my fault.

There are times when I think of all that's transpired over the past few years and I marvel at how this is my life. Whatever the reason, I'm grateful for all of it - including the fact that I'm a born and bred city girl who has no idea how to garden and should definitely not be trusted to care for anything that doesn't have a face. Now poor Zach has to deal with the result of my ignorance. He's handling it like a champ.

It's actually *his* fault, anyway. The backyard at our Sleepy Hollow, New York estate is massive, and Zach thought it might be fun for us to start a garden together. On the surface, that seemed like a great idea. Until I realized that there are lots of bugs in gardens. That's a big no for me. But my folly doesn't end there. Nope. Zach left me in charge of planting the pumpkins, and I thought it would be great to have three pumpkins amongst the fall decorations on our big wrap-around porch. So I planted three pumpkin seeds, not connecting with the fact that pumpkins grow on vines. Multiple pumpkins per vine. So now my sweet husband is knee deep in a field of pumpkin vines doing what he can because I checked out the first time I saw a squash bug. At last count, there were seventeen pumpkins growing. *Oops*.

The muffled sound of footsteps upstairs brings a warm smile to my face. Merry. She flew in from San Francisco last night, arriving early to help me prep for the biggest party Zach and I have thrown since we've been married. Almost all of our loved ones will be here for it, many of them staying either in the house or in the two guest houses on the far side of the backyard.

As the resident newlyweds of our group, I've assigned Scarlet and Andrew to one of the guest houses. Rick and Ashley have the other. Everyone else is in the main house with us and, with twelve bedrooms, we're still packed to the gills. Both Zach and I have been looking forward to this weekend for months, for quite a few reasons, but my biggest goal is to try and pry Merry out of the emotional funk she's flirting with.

Merry is the unicorn energy of our group. Fantastically extra in all the best ways, she can make any of us see the light in the darkest of circumstances. She is a beautiful ball of bold energy and kindness, and we're all a little worried about the fact that there's a little less rainbow in our unicorn lately.

"Hey, girl," Merry says cheerfully as she breezes into the kitchen. She immediately hones in on the pink box on the counter. "What's in the box?"

I turn away from the window and pull two coffee mugs from the cabinet. The coffee maker is gurgling away, filling the kitchen with the most wonderful aroma.

"Pumpkin spice donuts, and they're fabulous. Help yourself. I've got bacon cooking in the air fryer. Did you sleep well?"

"So well I feel like accusing you of putting melatonin powder in my pillow."

I giggle and shake my head, then grab a few napkins from the pantry and put them next to the box of donuts.

Merry flew in from San Francisco last night, arriving a full day before the rest of our friends in order to help me with the baking for our weekend Halloween celebration. Because, hey, when you own an estate in the legendary town of Sleepy Hollow, New York, you celebrate Halloween.

Merry sighs dramatically as she plops herself into a barstool on the other side of our massive kitchen island. She flips the box open and inhales.

"Wow," she groans. "That smells so good I felt it in my ovaries, dude."

I laugh out loud, then immediately hear the screech of a sneaker against the tile. Zach is frozen in the doorway.

"Are you ladies having girl talk? I can come back."

"It's safe, baby, get in here."

Zach grins at me and steps over to give me another good morning kiss. I'm not sure how many we're up to this morning. Fourteen maybe? After kissing me, he heads straight to Merry, who gets a hug and a very loud, smoochy kiss on the cheek because it always makes her laugh. He grabs a seat at the island as well, and I grab the creamer jug and sugar bowl and set them in the middle of it.

Merry and Zach chatter to themselves while I head into the dining room and look through the china cabinet for the gift I picked up for Zach earlier this week. I carefully pull out the tea cup and saucer and make my way back to the kitchen. He's busy with Merry, so I hit the power button on his electric kettle to flash boil the water. I grab the carafe of coffee and set it on a trivet on the island for Merry and me. When the water boils, I prepare Zach's favorite breakfast tea in the new tea cup and gently place it in front of him as I wait for him to notice.

"I thought it was working out with Jeremy?" Zach says, sounding sincerely disappointed for Merry.

"Nope," she shrugs. "I can't be with a guy who hates sugar. What would we ever talk about?"

Normally I would argue, but she has a point. Merry is a wonderful baker, and her dream is to open her own bakery. Poor Jeremy would never survive it.

"It was that bad?" Zach probes.

Merry smirks. "After I spent six hours baking and frosting a cake order for an anniversary party, he picked me up for our date and told me I stunk."

I purse my lips and pour some coffee into my mug while Zach chuffs, offended on Merry's behalf. He reaches over to pick up the creamer jug and finally notices his tea cup.

"What's this?" he gasps as he lifts the tea cup for a closer look.

I beam as I watch him admire the black tea cup with an intricately painted headless horseman galloping around the edge. The saucer is also black, with the words "the horseman comes" painted in gothic white letters. It's the perfect gift for Zach, who has loved the story of Sleepy Hollow and the headless horseman since he was just a boy. Zach carefully sets the tea cup back on its saucer and stands, coming around the island and pulling me into his arms.

"I love it so much, Siren," he tells me in his sexy British accent that I never tire of hearing. "Wherever did you find it?"

I rub my hand across his back. "In town, if you can believe it. I've never seen it in that shop before, but I guess now that Halloween is here they're stocking new things for all the tourists."

"I love it," he says sweetly, brushing his lips to mine briefly. "And I love you."

"Mmm…same," I sigh as I watch him sit back down. He grabs the one and only plain donut I made sure was in the box.

He puts it on a napkin for himself, then plucks out a pumpkin spice donut and puts it on a napkin for me. I finish doctoring my coffee and then take a seat between Zach and Merry, taking a bite of my donut and letting out a satisfied groan.

"So good."

Zach's husky laugh sounds throughout the kitchen. "You Americans and your pumpkin spice."

Merry snorts. "If you don't like pumpkin spice, you're not gonna like about forty percent of what I bake today."

Zach winks at Merry. "But I'll be sure to enjoy the sixty percent that isn't. And I one hundred percent appreciate you helping my darling Siren, love."

Merry wags her head with a silly grin. The combination of Zach's accent and calling any female "love" usually creates a blush, or a giggle, or…in Merry's case…the head wag. It's adorable.

"Do we not know any single, worthy gentlemen that we can set Merry up with, darling?" Zach asks over his tea.

Merry waves her hands in the air. "Nope! No outside interference, thank you. I appreciate the thought, but no."

Zach tilts his head at her. "You don't like to be set up on dates?"

She shakes her head. "Nope. I think if someone is meant for me, they're going to show up. And they're not going to tell me I stink just because I smell like sugar. And they certainly won't tell me I'd look better as a blond."

Zach gasps. "Who said that to you?"

Merry laughs out loud and waves him off. "That was like…three hundred dates ago. I can't even remember his face, but the comment was so ridiculous I remember it."

"What a creep," Zach says. "You're beautiful just as you are. I'm sorry he was unworthy."

Merry grins. "Are you sure you don't have a twin?"

Zach laughs. "Sorry, love."

"Well, whatever his name was, I excused myself to go to the ladies room and never went back to the table."

Zach holds up his tea cup to her. "Cheers, Merry. Well done."

She carefully clinks her mug against his tea cup and sips her coffee. The air fryer dings and I open the door, pulling out several strips of delicious bacon and dropping them on a paper towel. I blot all the grease off before putting the slices on a plate and placing it next to the box of donuts.

Merry takes two pieces and I offer the plate to Zach, who winks at me.

"That's not bacon, Siren."

I smirk at him. "We are on the west side of the Pond, baby. This is bacon."

Zach shoots me his best fake scowl and I giggle, then turn to Merry. "So what does my favorite baker require today? I can be an extra set of hands."

Merry turns her lips inward as she tries to come up with a reply that isn't a thousand percent honest, so I get ready for a real zinger.

"I've seen what your hands can do in the kitchen," she says with a barely suppressed grin. "Keep those mitts away from me, madam."

I feign shock, holding up my hands and wiggling my fingers. Not like jazz hands…more like look what these bad boys can do.

"I'll have you know that these babies can open the finest cans and frozen food boxes the world has to offer."

She shakes her head. "None of those are allowed on my watch. You can go decorate or do other pre-party shenanigans and leave me alone with the flour, sugar, and all the baking goodness."

I smirk at my friend. "Okay, well, all the ingredients you requested are in the pantry and I guess I'll waffle around between watching my genius baker friend and doing party stuff."

Merry takes a bite of her donut and nods. "Deal."

"So what delicacies will you be baking, Merry?" Zach asks as he adds a little milk to his tea. "Will there be unicorn cookies from our unicorn friend?"

"Those were not on Marina's request list, sorry," she replies. "But you can enjoy salted caramel cupcakes, freshly made apple pies baked in cute little jars, or maple creme sandwich cookies. I won't mention all the pumpkin spice lovelies I'm baking."

Zach grins at her. "Sounds like I'll be in a proper sugar coma by Sunday. Looking forward to it."

"Just part of the excellent service I provide," Merry beams proudly. "So what else is planned for the weekend?"

I grin excitedly. "I can't wait for you to see how this town celebrates Halloween. We'll go for a walk tomorrow night around sunset. There's an actor who rides a horse dressed as the headless horseman, and the main street that runs through town looks incredible."

Merry looks incredulous. "Headless? How does he see?"

I laugh and give her a shrug. "I have no idea how it works, but it looks freaking cool."

Merry grins and takes another bite of her donut.

"Tonight is cocktails and dinner," I explain. "Everyone should be here by six. Scarlet, Andrew, and Max will get here just in time."

"She's so busy lately. I'm glad she's able to be here this weekend. I miss her so much."

"She had to work right up till the last minute," Zach chimes in. "There weren't any commercial flights that worked with her schedule, so I'm bringing them over in the Rebels jet."

Merry laughs. "What did we ever do before you fell in love with Marina, dude?"

Zach bolts off of his seat and grabs me, burying his face in my neck and growling dramatically. The combination of his warm breath against my skin and the very sexy growl sets me on fire. I hold on for dear life. He kisses me soundly and sits back down with a wicked grin.

"I don't know what I ever did without my Siren, Merry," he says sweetly. "And all of you welcomed me into your lives like it was no big deal, in spite of the media mess and all that. There isn't anything I wouldn't do for any of you."

Merry gestures at him with the remnants of her donut. "You're good people, Zach. I wish we could clone you so I could just marry Clone Zach."

We both laugh, but I'm a little worried about Merry. She changed her anti-dating policy around the time Scarlet got married, but she's been kissing a lot of frogs and still hasn't met anyone resembling a prince. I want to help her. Hillary's brother is a nice guy, and I'd love to set them up, but she's already told Zach no. I don't want to push it. Still, something's got to give. Merry is the best…and I just know there's someone out there for her.

About the Author

Dianne Oren writes sweet rom coms and lives in Texas with her husband, crazy doggos Duke & Daisy, Finn the cat, and an 8 pound murder muffin named Rebel. She loves embroidery, travel, and is completely addicted to iced coffee.

You can connect with me on:

https://dianneoren.com

https://www.facebook.com/DianneOrenOfficial

Subscribe to my newsletter:

https://dianneoren.com/subscribe

Also by Dianne Oren

How to Date a Mermaid

After a rough start in life, Marina's worked hard to make sure there are calm seas ahead. She has three ride-or-die girlfriends, a job at the most prestigious law firm in the city, and big, big plans. She just has to stay focused. So it figures the one time she does something spontaneous it lands her in a viral video with a world-famous rock star…while she's dressed as a mermaid.With the media on the hunt for the infamous mermaid, she'd love nothing more than to get away from this handsome, muscley complication as soon as possible. But Zach has other plans. He can't get enough of her. And there's something about his dark good looks and that gravelly, oh-so-sexy British accent that keeps her anchored even when she wants to run.Now she faces the challenge of whether to trust her heart or stick to her plans and ignore the magnetic pull she feels toward the only man who's ever truly shown up for her.

How to Date a Mermaid is book one of five in the San Francisco Hearts series.

Fake It Till You Make It

Ashley

My ex-fiancé jilted me twice, proof that I don't make the best decisions when it comes to relationships, so I'm done. Just call me the Dragon Lady, because I guard my heart like a dragon guards treasure. But now the jerk is back, and I need to prove I've moved on. I have no choice but to turn to Rick, who is six-feet-two inches of Viking god come to life...and the sole-surviving resident of my friend zone. A fake date with him on Valentine's Day is my only real choice, as long as I don't catch feelings.

Rick

Ashley's too afraid to risk our friendship for something more, even if the chemistry between us crackles like a live wire. Now she needs me to be her fake date and this is my chance to show her what we could have together. The lines we've drawn begin to blur, and I'm left wondering: can Ashley finally take the leap and trust me with her heart? Or will I be stuck in the friend zone forever?

Fake It Till You Make It is book two of five in the San Francisco Hearts series.

Happily Ever After in the Hollow
Coming in Fall 2025

Travel to Zach's estate in Sleepy Hollow, New York for the gang's Halloween party in this charming novella.

Even though it's just a novella, this is book four of five in the San Francisco Hearts series.

Merry & Bright

Coming November 2025.

Merry was born looking at the bright side. Her outlook is all rainbows and unicorns, until a runaway car puts an unflappable police officer in her path with his less than rosy view of the world. But Merry likes a challenge, and there's something about his grumpy demeanor that makes her want to push all his buttons.

Officer Nicholas Bright is all kinds of awkward when he's not hiding behind dark sunglasses and a badge. He has absolutely no idea what to do with a woman who constantly exudes unicorn energy and bakes the most over the top cookies he's ever seen. When there's a break-in at her grandfather's restaurant, he becomes a frequent visitor to make sure she's safe. But once he gets a glimpse of life in her sunshiney world, he realizes the future looks awfully dark without her.

Merry & Bright is a grumpy sunshine feel-good Christmas romance that'll have you swooning on the couch with your hot cocoa in hand. It's the final book in the "San Francisco Hearts" series.

Made in the USA
Columbia, SC
21 June 2025